ALSO BY LAUREN LANDISH

CHAPTER 1

WILLOW

"Quit staring at me!" I snarl, emphasizing my point with a huff that sends my bangs up then right back down into my field of vision again.

The recipient of my bark, which like the popular saying is worse than my bite, stares back, unmoved by the order. Fine, so it's a mountain, not likely to sprout legs and move out of my way, nor is it going to quit looming over me like a judge.

Stupid mountain.

For most people, that's probably the exact view they come here for, a quaint escape from their daily life to small town, rural America.

Too bad I'm not here for a quick trip from the city. No, Great Falls is my new hometown. And the fancy mountainside resort I can now see is most definitely *not* my destination.

"Ugh," I growl, though there's no one to hear me since I made the trip alone, driving for hours over the last three days with nightly stops at motels. I've been living on the cheap—scratchy sheets, sketchy neighborhoods, and greasy takeout. If I see one more slice of pizza I'm going to scream.

The road is straight and empty, giving me time to glance up again. Broad strokes of nature's grandeur, striped with green and brown and even . . . I lean forward to glance out the top of my windshield . . . yep, white at the very tippy-top of the peak. It's beautiful, I'll admit that at least.

But still it feels . . . judgy. The weight of the horizon presses in on me, even heavier than my conscience. But not even that mountain could withstand my Mom's earnest gaze begging for help.

Fine. I'll go to Podunk, Nowheresville, Mom. Just quit looking at me like that.

I come to a blinking red light and take a right, thankful to put the mountain behind me. But now, I'm almost there . . . and that might be even worse.

"Destination is on the left. You have arrived." My phone tells me the dreaded news.

I park in the packed dirt lot, my ten-year-old Subaru one of only two cars versus nine—no, ten—trucks. They come in two varieties, old and dented or jacked-up and pristine other than the layer of fine red dust on the lower half. "Toto, I'm not in Kansas anymore."

I shut off the engine but make no move to get out. I'm not the type to get nervous, but this is an extraordinary circumstance, so I'm basically shivering inside my skin with jitters. Hence, the grumpiness with the inanimate mountain. It's not every day you waltz into a place uninvited and announce yourself. Especially when I'm not sure the welcome is going to be all that friendly. It's entirely possible that I might get hustled out of town faster than I got here.

Despite my hesitation, the heat gathering in the car forces me out. *Crunch-crunch-crunch.* My flips flops are nothing against the small pebbles mixed into the dirt, and I'm nearly dancing before I'm halfway across the parking lot. I pause at the door, my hand on the brass handle, and look up, praying for strength.

The only thing I see is the neon sign proclaiming this place as *Hank's.*

Resigned to my fate, at least for the foreseeable future, I open the door and step inside. Part of me expects it to be like one of those low-budget, B-grade action flicks where the city girl walks in, a record scratches—even though no one plays those anymore —and a dozen sets of narrowed eyes turn to me in suspicion. Two heartbeats later, there'll be a redneck slurring out that my kind's not welcome here.

Despite years of late-night movies telling me so, none of that happens.

No one even looks my way, which gives me a chance to take everything in with a quick scan. Wood floors, wood walls, wood tables, all gleaming in the overhead lights, which are bright considering it's mid-afternoon. There are a few booths with pleather that, even from here, I can see is patched with red duct tape like someone was doing the best they could to hold it all together and keep the stuffing inside. Country music plays faintly, with the chatter of the patrons mixing in easily.

Automatically, I reach for my back pocket to grab my phone. Its camera isn't the best by any stretch, but it's the least intrusive. Still, I can't exactly start snapping shots in the middle of the bar so my hand falls back to my side, though my fingers itch to press the shutter. My brain does it anyway, framing each take mentally.

An old guy, wrinkles lining his eyes and mouth, the edge of a bottle of beer paused at his lip as he stares at the television over the bar. *Snap.*

A group of five guys wearing neon vests, work boots, and dirty jeans crowded around a table, looking like their day has already been enough to make them weary. *Snap.*

A bell rings out, drawing my attention to a cutout in the wall framing a middle-aged, heavyset woman who's setting a plate in the window. "Order up!" she calls out. *Snap.*

I intentionally ignore the man behind the bar and make my way to a corner table, hiding in the slight shadow offered by a couple having a leisurely lunch, judging by the number of empty beer glasses that decorate their tabletop. To further disguise myself, I pick up a menu from the holder by the wall and duck into my shoulders.

"What can I getcha?" a voice asks from right beside me, the sentence all run together like it's one multi-syllable word.

I startle at the direct question, but the waitress is looking at her notepad, not me. "Oh, uh . . ." I stammer, so caught up in my own mental games that I haven't really looked at the menu. I hate being unprepared, but I make the quick decision to play it safe. "A cheeseburger."

"Howd'ya want it cooked?" Her blonde ponytail swishes impatiently, her lashes dark against her cheeks. She's young, at least a few years younger than me. Twenty-one or two, I'd guess, to my twenty-five.

Was I ever that young, though? Even as a child, I was an old soul. Not sure what that says about me now.

"Medium."

"Ell-tee-oh-pee and fries?" Olivia asks. Olivia. That's her name, according to her nametag. I have no idea what she's asking, other than fries, and the confusion must show on my face. "Lettuce, tomato, onion, pickles, fries?"

"Sure." She scribbles on her notepad before hustling away. I realize a moment later that I forgot to order a drink. But as I watch the goings-on around me, Olivia saves me by bringing a glass of water with a lemon wedge.

"Let me know if you want a beer or soda or anything."

A shot of whiskey, I think but don't say out loud. Instead, I smile politely and nod.

I take my time squeezing the lemon and unwrapping the straw just for something to do. But once that's done, I can't put off the inevitable any longer.

I look at the bar. More specifically, I finally look at the man behind the far end of the bar . . . Hank Davis. He's over seventy now, but the leathery skin peeking out of his short-sleeved T-shirt is covering lean muscles and etched with old tattoos. The scowl on his face is familiar, gut-punchingly so, but I swallow the bile that tries to rise, helping it down with a sip of water. His eyes are blue and bright, clear as a summer sky, and full of sharp intelligence even from here. If he's anything like I remember, I'll have to be careful or he'll figure me out in an instant.

He's talking with the old guy watching the television, but I can't tell what they're saying, only that they seem friendly. Hank is mindlessly drying a beer glass with a white towel, which he sets on a shelf beneath the bar before grabbing another glass. I imagine the two men are giving each other shit over the ball game playing. Maybe they have a bet on who's going to win. I do that a lot, create entire scenarios for the people around me, giving them personalities and backstories. I like the real stories too, but when I don't know, I fill in the blanks for myself.

The lady in the window calls out for another order and Olivia grabs the plate. Not needing to check her ticket, she brings it directly to me. "Anything else?"

Having decided against the whiskey for real, I answer, "No, thank you." I bite into the burger, moaning at the unexpected deliciousness. It's fresh, hot, and stacked with the crispness of fresh veggies. A pickle falls out, and I snag it, crunching it alone. I think it's home-canned. Oh, my God, I could eat this for breakfast, lunch, and dinner every day. I want to go peek in the cook's window and tell her that I appreciate the life-changing flavor of her food as an accompaniment to my day.

Because today is the day my life changes.

But there are some things that will never change. I promised myself that when I agreed to this fool's errand.

I set the burger back on the heavy white plate and pull my phone out. I snap a quick shot of the burger and fries, make a few adjustments for the lighting, and add a caption that says *TDF good*, a skull emoji, a halo emoji, then hit *Post*. I stare at it for a moment, counting the seconds until the first heart appears. Twenty-two seconds. I smile. More hearts and comments start appearing, but after reading a couple, I shut it off and set the phone facedown on the table.

I eat. And watch.

I have a unique ability to disappear, be invisible and forgotten. When I was younger, it used to eat me up inside, making me feel unimportant. As I got older, I learned how to put it to good use as a photographer. People don't notice me, which gives me a sneak peek into their world, their experience in a way I couldn't get if I were bolder. It took time, but I've turned my weakness into a strength.

Once I've stuffed as much burger into my belly as I can—okay, maybe more than I should've—I gather my courage, stuffing it into every nook and cranny of my soul not filled with ground beef. I lay a ten on the table for Olivia and put my phone in my pocket, wishing I could capture the look on Hank's face when he sees me.

But I already know I'll memorize it with my eyes. In that look, I'll know if this is going to work. My heart races with hope that it will.

I walk up to the bar, between two stools, and wait for his eyes to drag away from the television. "What can I getcha?" he asks in the same run together, one-word way Olivia did. It's something they both must do dozens of times every day.

I smile even though my lips are shaking and my knees are knocking. "Hi, Uncle Hank." As I say it, the words sound foreign. I always called him 'Unc', but I'm not sure if he'd welcome that familiarity after all these years.

Those blue eyes narrow dangerously before they pop wide open and he grins. "Willow? Well, I'll be damned!"

I return his smile, that hope blooming quickly and spreading warmth through my body.

"Get over here and give me a hug, girl." The order is accompanied by a wave of his arm toward the opening in the bar. He comes around quicker than I would've thought he could, wrapping me up in a squeezing embrace that lifts me clean off the floor to spin me around.

Hell, he's unexpectedly spry for an old guy.

"You are a sight for sore eyes, honey. What are you doing here?" He sets me down, petting my hair and scanning my face like he thinks it's entirely possible that I'm a mirage.

"Needed a change, I guess you could say. And I thought of you . . . and Great Falls."

That part's not a lie, at least. I did think of him in a bent old photograph kind of way. The way you remember someone from years ago, when they seemed larger than life because you were just a kid.

Unc, because that's who he is to me, chuckles, the sound rougher than sandpaper. Smoke. I remember he used to smell like clove cigarettes that brought to mind the Christmas crafts with oranges we did at school as gifts for our mom. I wonder if he still smokes now? I didn't smell it on his hug, though.

"Well, I reckon Great Falls is a might bit different for a city girl. Have a seat and tell me everything."

That sounds ominous to my ears. I swallow, knowing I can't tell him everything, but I can tell him a lot. And I want him to tell me things too, like his version of why I never saw him after I turned fourteen. I've heard Mom's version, and I heard Grandpa's curse-laden one a time or two, but never Unc's. Then again, does it even matter now?

He gestures to the end of the bar, following me over. I sit, my legs dangling until I rest my feet on the crossbar. Unc more perches than sits on his stool, but he bends a knee and places his boot on the crossbar too, taking pressure off his leg. Oh, I remember that now. He always had a hip-rolling gait that made me think of a cowboy swagger, but Mom told me it was because he had an old injury that flared up sometimes. I'd preferred my story to hers back then, and I want to believe it even now, though the signs of arthritis are in his bony hands too.

His eyes narrow ever so slightly, and my reprieve is over. I've practiced this. I know what to say, so I launch into my prepared speech.

"It really is so good to see you, Unc." I test out the affectionate nickname and he doesn't so much as flinch. "I don't know how much you've kept up, but my mom and dad are good, driving each other crazy, but they wouldn't have it any other way. Oakley is as all right as a pain in the ass older brother can be. He's an accountant, got married last year, and probably has a five-year plan for home ownership, two-point-five babies, and a Labradoodle named Daisy."

I smile even as I'm smack talking my brother. He's the sore thumb in our family, rebelling against Mom and Dad's creative, hippie hearts and souls by going full suit and tie. He even carries a briefcase. Shudder.

"And what about you? Last time I saw you, you were in middle school, wearing paint splattered overalls with your head buried in a sketch book. You still drawing?" Unc seems genuinely interested, but the nostalgia of the image he paints isn't the warm fuzzy of a happy memory. Those were hard days where my awkwardness made me a weird outsider, Mom hadn't understood why that was a bad thing, and I struggled to become 'normal', whatever that meant. News flash, I failed on that mission spectacularly.

I shake my head. "No, not much anymore. I moved on to photography in high school for the yearbook and never looked back. It's everything now."

He asked for me to tell him *everything*, and photography is my most important truth. I can at least give him that.

"Whatcha take pictures of?" he asks.

Safe territory, thank goodness.

I pull out my phone and show him the picture I snapped of the burger I ate. He grabs my wrist, pushing the phone further away like he should be wearing glasses but refuses to on principle. When he focuses on the screen image, his mouth moves a little as he reads the caption.

"What's tee-dee-eff? And the little pictures?"

I can't help but grin. "It means 'to die for', because it was so good. The skull is shorthand for dead, the angel for heaven. Just saying it was really delicious, basically."

He quirks a bushy white brow. "Then why not just put delicious? You kids are taking the nuances of the English language and turning it back into hieroglyphics for no good goddamn reason."

I shrug, amused at the drawl of his accent. High-ROW-gli-fix. That second syllable lasted at least a full two seconds. "Just how we communicate to keep the old fogies from understanding," I tease back.

"I'll show you old fogie," he scowls before winking, and it feels so easy and right, as if no time has passed. "So, what brings you to Great Falls?"

"Wanted something different than the city, I suppose." *Just keep repeating that as your mantra, Willow.*

"City life not treating you kindly?" He sounds irked at the very idea.

"It was. I make money off my pictures, but like to stay busy. Just realized that I've never been more than an hour from home and thought this sounded like as good a place as anywhere. At least I have family here." His jaw tightens, and I rush to fill the moment with chatter before we get off on the wrong foot. "I considered a beach in Mexico too, but you won out, so feel special," I tell him with a smirk, hoping to ease those questions in his gaze.

"You picked this shithole over a beach? You are stupid, ain't you?" There's no heat in the insult, more that he's laughing with me at the joke.

And it's okay. We're okay for the moment. Too bad it's time to pick at the sloppy stitches of family that are barely holding us together.

"Stupid enough to pick up with no notice and drive across the state to a town I've never been to with only a few hundred bucks to my name and approximately no plan past this moment right here." I cringe. "Actually, I thought I'd see if you need any help around here." I look around the bar before focusing back on Unc. "I bartend in the city too."

That bushy brow lifts incrementally and his arms cross over his chest, not believing a bit of my bullshit.

I roll my eyes and push at my bangs, which are stuck in the top of my glasses because this trip happened so quickly, I didn't even get a haircut before setting out. "I'm good, can keep up with a busy weekend night pulling beers, mixing drinks, and making sure people have a good time—but not *too good* of a time," I assure him. I'm not usually one for tooting my own horn, but I need to right now because this is the make-it or break-it moment. I need Unc to say yes to me working in his bar. It's the pivot point to Mom's whole plan.

One gnarled hand reaches up to stroke his chin as he thinks and my fate hangs in the beer and fried food-scented air between us. "Can ya waitress too? You a switch hitter?"

I blink, having zero plans to tell my old Uncle Hank that switch hitter does not mean someone who can waitress and bartend. "Yes sir, I can." I've never waitressed a day in my life, but if that's what it takes to get a foot in the door here, I'll do it.

"You cook?"

"Uhm . . ." I can probably fake waitressing having worked in bars, and now I know what LTOP means, but actually cook the food? That's not something you can fake.

Unc laughs. "Just pulling your leg, girl. Ilene won't let a soul in her kitchen unless she's training them herself. Not sure how she chooses 'em, but she's definitely pickier than I am, luckily for you. When can you start?"

A relieved breath gushes out, along with all my excitement. "Really? Oh, that's great! Thank you!" I grab around his shoulders for a hug, a habit that Mom instilled in Oakley and me from a young age.

Everyone needs hugs. Every day needs hugs.

Thankfully, he hugs me back, and for the first time in a long time, I feel a twinge of hurt over losing my grandfather. He wasn't an easy man to love, but I did, and he loved me back the only way he knew how. But having Unc's arms wrapped around me for this tiny space of time feels like family, even if all we share is a blood-line at this point since we barely know each other anymore.

I talk into his shoulder. "I can start right now."

He leans back, humor dancing in his eyes. "At least take the day and get settled, though I wouldn't say no to you hanging around and watching the comings and goings if you'd like a little education about what you're getting into. Tonight's two-dollar drafts, so it'll be a busy one."

As he says it, I can see a flash of weariness in the depths of his eyes, though he hides it quickly behind a blink. Even as he straightens his back, looking strong and formidable, I know what I saw. He's tired after doing this on his own for so long. But I'm here to help now.

"I'm your girl."

CHAPTER 2

WILLOW

J set my bag down in the living room of the short-term rental my mom is paying for since she's the one who sent me off on this *adventure*. It's an end unit in a small row of houses that look like small summer camp cabins, with white siding and green trim. From here, I can see everything but the single bedroom. The living room has a small fake leather couch in bright red, the kitchen's wood cabinets are painted a sunny pale yellow, and the Formica table and vinyl chairs remind me of a 1950s diner. It's nice, bright, and cheery.

Who am I kidding? It's better than my studio apartment in the city that's more of a walk-in closet than living space. But that's home. This . . . isn't.

I walk down the hall, not surprised to see a small but cute bedroom. The full-size bed is a bit tight for two people, not that I'll be sharing it with anyone, and decorated with more pillows than I can possibly ever use in the few months I'll be staying here. I toss my duffel bag of clothes onto the closet floor, though I promise myself to hang stuff up later, and carefully set my camera bag on the chest of drawers.

Home, sweet home.

I take a shower, letting the hot water wash the stress of the drive and the nerves of seeing Uncle Hank for the first time in years down the drain with the sudsy water. After, I use the hand towel to swipe the fog off the mirror and stare into my own eyes, gray just like Mom's and Grandma's. I never gave them much thought. They're just what looks back at me from my reflection. Now, I wonder if they mean something more . . . to Unc. Does it hurt him to look at me? Hurting him is the last thing I want to do. I want to help him.

All right Willow, get it together. Tonight is no big deal. Go in there, watch Unc, and maybe serve some beers. That's it, easy-peasy, lemon-squeezy.

The pep talk doesn't work. I don't believe me, either.

* * *

HANK'S IS A MADHOUSE. I have worked bars that would kill for this kind of crowd on a weekend night, much less a Thursday. But two-dollar drafts are apparently the magic ticket that brings people in. There's a line of people waiting to play pool in some self-organized version of a tournament, Ilene's bell is going off almost non-stop, though her smile never falters, and Unc is pacing back and forth behind the bar to keep up.

I can't sit back and watch anymore.

I get up from the spot where he put me to 'watch and learn' and walk behind the bar to wash my hands in the sink.

"What're ya doing?" Unc snaps. I'd be worried he would shoo me out of his area if his hands weren't full of drinks and Olivia wasn't tapping her empty and waiting tray on the bar in time to the country music playing.

"Helping. You do the beers, keeping them rolling. I'll do the mixed drinks."

Under normal circumstances, it'd be the opposite. You'd put your newbie on the beers because is a drunk guy really going to notice the difference in a draft Miller Light and a Coors Light? The answer's no. Mixed drinks are a fickle creature, though, and people want that one thing they had that one time in some random bar, but they don't remember what was in it, only that it was red, and they're pissed at me when I don't know exactly what they're talking about. Or they read some snobby article online about top ten mixed drinks you need to try before you die and decide to order one, even though they don't even know what's in it. Newsflash, if you order something with bitters or sour mix, you're going to get something with bite.

But this isn't that crowd. The beers are the busiest station and will let Unc stand in one place and quit running himself ragged. And I can sure as hell mix Jack and Cokes all night.

I don't give him a chance to argue, hip-bumping him toward the beer and taking my new place by the bottles and glasses. I get started, filling orders as fast as Olivia brings them in. I know Unc is watching me out of the corner of his eye, seeing if I can put my money where my mouth is. I'm not worried. I can. I even make a tray full of Long Island Iced Teas—gag—for a table of women who don't want to drink cheap beer for their buzz.

We stay steady until about midnight, when it slows down considerably as if all these people are Cinderellas who need to get home before they turn into pumpkins.

I load the big industrial dishwasher again, the third time in an hour, and wipe down my station.

"You done pretty good."

Unc's praise is kind but delivered a bit begrudgingly, so I compliment him right back. "You do this by yourself all the time, six days a week? You must be a machine!"

His lips purse as he fights a smile.

"C'mon, you can tell me. You're a robot, right?"

He lifts his elbow, his arm dangling down and wiggling right and left. I realize it's his really crappy attempt at the robot dance. "Oh, my God, please don't do that again. Rule number four, no bar dancing." Really, I wish I had my camera so I could've captured that, especially the boyish grin on his wrinkled face.

"What's one through three?" Those bushy brows rise, looking like snowy caterpillars, and he takes a small sip of the beer he poured for himself. Not the cheap draft stuff but a craft ale I was surprised to see on his beer list.

What a man drinks says something about him, and Unc's got layers and depth.

"Uhm . . ." I was just kidding, but I'm not going to lose this

13

battle of wits. No way, no how. It's a matter of honor among bartenders now.

"Rule one, no free drinks. I don't care who you are. Pay or go thirsty." Unc tilts his head, and I wonder how many of his friends drink for free.

"Rule two, heavy till ten, we'll see you again. Light after midnight because they're too drunk to give a fuck." Crass maybe, and not language I typically use, but it's one of the staples of tending bar I learned working in college bars. Those early drinkers are the ones you want to come back again and again, so you pour just a little extra drop in their glass, toss them a wink like they're getting special privileges, and they'll be your best customers. The folks who come in late at night are already half-tipsy, can't tell if a drink is strong or weak, and skinny pours are a way to keep costs down. Unc gives me a nod this time, which I take as agreement.

"Rule three, drinks first. I'm friendly, sociable, and I'll be your free therapist on a slow night and listen to all the ways your day sucked and your wife did you wrong. But if it's busy, I'm slinging drinks first and chatting second."

That one was the hardest for me to learn. I'm a reluctant people person by nature. I don't want to talk to them, I'm too quiet for that, but I love to hear stories. I'm the random stranger people open up to in the grocery line, at the bank, and yep, at the bar. I enjoy hearing about people's days, their lives. Even if I can't take a picture, it's like a snapshot into who they are. But a bit too long at one end of the bar with one customer means you're neglecting others, and that affects the bottom dollar, for me and the bar. Sad but true.

"Which leads to rule four, I guess." He's smiling, and I know he's well aware that I just made those rules up on the fly. I'm decently quick on my feet, though, so I think they're pretty on point.

"Right. No bar dancing. This ain't *Coyote Ugly*. It's Hank's, the best honkytonk in town." I add in the slogan I read on the paper placemats as an extra sparkle of *so there*.

"I think you're gonna fit in just fine, Miss Willow. Welcome to the team, officially." He sticks his hand out, and I shake it, but then he pulls me in for a hug and I wonder if he remembers Mom's saying too.

* * *

TWO WEEKS PASS by in a blur.

I get to know Olivia and Ilene better, and yes, they both tell me their life stories, which are full of obligatory small-town drama.

Ilene's been married to her high school boyfriend for thirty-eight years, she proclaimed proudly, and they have five kids who are all grown and on their own.

We weren't sure our middle boy was gonna make it. Cops brought that punk home more times than I could count, and he worked his butt off to make reparations for that tractor he messed up on his field trip.

She'd had to explain that she literally meant he drove his truck through a field, hence 'field trip', and he'd crashed it into a rusty tractor, causing thousands of dollars in damages.

But he went into the Army and they took him down a peg or two. He's got a wife of his own now and two little boys who are the apple of their momma's eyes and are gonna give their daddy a helluva ride when they're teenagers.

She seems a bit too gleeful at that prospect.

Olivia surprises me even more. I was right about her age. She's twenty-one, but she's not still 'finding herself' like so many are at that age, or at least like I was. She knows exactly who she is and who she isn't and doesn't have time or patience for anyone who doesn't agree. I like her a lot.

Moved here a couple of years ago with my girlfriend. We live down-town above her boutique. She sells Western clothes, boots, and hats, mostly to tourists who want a 'look' for their vacation but to locals too.

She'd emphasized the word 'girlfriend', then waited and watched for my reaction to her verbal bomb which had been nothing more than a promise to visit if I needed some Western gear. Olivia smiled, and I knew I'd passed a test.

Unc has been another matter altogether. We chat as we work side by side behind the bar, which is huge progress, but I don't feel like I've gotten to know anything more than the front he puts on for the customers. Gruff, hardass, hard-working old man whose life is inside these four walls.

I keep trying, though.

"You've got something special here. What made you open Hank's?" I ask on Saturday afternoon while we're prepping for what he promises will be our busiest night yet. I'm not sure I believe him because we've been dead since the lunch rush ended two hours ago.

He looks around as though he's seeing his own bar for the first time. "A man needs a place to go have a beer, in good times and in bad. So I made one of my own so I'd always have a place to go."

That onion layer peels back a little bit, letting me peek underneath.

"I think a lot of people are glad to have Hank's and you," I say honestly. I've seen the people who come in here every day, from workers who want a quick and delicious lunch to the regulars who perch at the bar every night to chat with Hank instead of going home to an empty house. "I know I am."

This is a temporary visit for me, a few months at most, but it's not as bad as I thought it'd be. I've found a coffee shop down the street that makes deliciously frothy, foamy lattes I crave on the daily. The grocery store is staffed with friendly people who smile easily and is stocked with most of my favorites, from my indulgent bark-thin chocolates to my I'm-not-cooking-tonight cauliflower crust frozen pizzas, so the kitchen in my little house is well-supplied. The mountain even feels less harsh now, magnificent and grand rather than judgy and looming.

My biggest fear, that my online photography work would crash, hasn't come true, either. My photo blog, *A Day in the Life of a Tree*, is maintaining a steady following, losing a few here and there but gaining some to make up most of the difference.

I started the blog years ago, thinking the cutesy name had been a catchy reference to my name. I never dreamed it'd blow up like it has. I have 'Tree-ers' who comment on every photo, sharing their days with me the way I share mine with them. I stay anonymous, posting pictures of the things around me and bits of myself, but never anything that would make me identifiable. They like it that way. I like it that way.

Nothing has changed since my move to Great Falls. I spend most of my free time taking photos, usually on walks around town. I've posted pictures of gorgeous sunsets turning fields into sparkles of gold, a floppy-eared, tail-wagging dog I saw running through town chasing a school bus, and the rusted orange and blue of an old truck fender. I long ago gave up trying to figure out what people want to see and simply photograph what speaks to me—in lines, shapes, colors, and emotions—but so far, everyone seems to be along for my journey from city life to country life photography.

And now Unc looks pleased at my confession, so I take advantage. "Freeze, just like that." I pull my phone out of my pocket, my eyebrow asking permission, which he gives with a blink.

Click. I capture him with a genuine smile and affection on his face. This is how I want to remember him.

"Get in here, girl. If I gotta get my picture taken, so do you." He grabs at my shoulder, pulling me close, and I sink into him. Holding the phone up, I take a burst of shots—us looking at the camera with cheesy smiles, me looking at him, then him looking at me too. These pictures are for me, not for my blog.

I drop the phone to my side, feeling like . . . I found my family.

Mom and Dad, and fine, even Oakley, are great and I love them dearly. But I missed out on a life with Unc because of other people's stupidity, and I'm not going to let that continue.

His smile is soft, his eyes sad, but he hugs me tight. "Glad to have you here too, Willow."

Olivia interrupts. "Sorry to break up the love fest, but you know we've got a lot of shit to do and not enough time to do it. Those lemons aren't gonna cut themselves."

I look over to find her leaning against the bar, likely realizing something major had just happened between me and Unc. As much as she's opened up to me, I haven't told anyone why I'm really here. It's not their business, not yet, hopefully not ever. But she knows Hank is my grandfather's brother and I hadn't seen him in years before walking in that door and ordering a life-changing burger.

I grin. "You volunteering to help?" I tease.

She shakes her head, ponytail swishing behind her. "Hell, no. I've got silverware to wrap, but I'll keep you company while you slice."

She sets her basket of cutlery and stack of napkins on the bar in front of me. "Skedaddle, Boss Man. We've got girl talk to discuss, so it'd be best for you to check on Ilene in the kitchen."

He grumbles something about bossy girls but heads off to the kitchen, probably legit scared that we're going to talk about breasts or periods, though looking at Olivia, I hope that's not what's on her mind. Some people just tell me some extremely personal and TMI things.

Olivia grins as she watches him go, whispering out of the side of her mouth, "Ilene's in a great mood tonight, mouth running and ass swinging to the radio she's got back there. She'll have Hank laughing and singing some old Keith Whitley in no time."

I chuckle, slicing away at my fifteenth lemon. "You sure we'll need all these? I've got a bin full, another in the fridge, but Unc said to do one more too."

"Tonight? You'll be lucky if you don't run out. It's show night." Olivia fans herself dramatically with a paper napkin, but at my confused look, she straightens. "You don't know, do you? Oh, shit, girl. We're gonna show you how it goes down in the country tonight! Bobby Tannen is taking that stage, singing his growly little heart out and lighting panties on fire across the whole county."

I have no idea what she's talking about. Unc said that tonight was one of the live music nights, but Olivia makes it sound like there's a celebrity coming. "Even yours?" I joke.

She nods, ponytail bobbing. "Hell, yeah! Me and my girl have a deal—if that man so much as crooks a finger at either of us, we'll follow him like the Pied Piper of Great Falls . . . *doo-doo-doo-doo-doo*." She mimics some sort of flute with a fork held sideways at her mouth.

I can't help but laugh at her outrageousness.

"That man is everyone's free pass, eighteen to eighty, not that it matters a bit. He don't give anyone a lick of attention, and not for their lack of trying, neither." Her eyes go big and round, her mouth following a second later. "Ooh, or maybe he just hasn't been interested in the local fare and what he needs is some fresh meat. Some city girl to sweep him off his feet."

She points at me with both index fingers, proud of what she obviously thinks is a brilliant idea. It's not, at all.

"Oh, no, slow that crazy runaway train down right now. I'm not here looking for some country boy, and I'm not exactly what panty-fire-starting guys want anyway. I want to work and take pictures and that's it."

She believes me because her face falls. "What the hell you talking about? You're adorable. Bobby Tannen would be lucky if you looked his way." I think her vision of me sashaying up to this cowboy-lebrity was going to be her entertainment for the night, but I have never sashayed a day in my life.

"*Adorable*, just what every woman wants to be," I say sarcastically, planting my hands under my chin and batting my lashes angelically. "That's right up there with *funny* and *nice*. All one-way tickets to the friend zone."

Olivia pokes my arm with her fork, having not wrapped a single set of silverware. "Shut up. Some of us are hot, some of us are adorable, and some of us are plain Janes, but it's what you do with it that matters. Everyone's got someone out there. Just gotta find them."

"Why, Olivia, I do believe you're a romantic at heart!" I exclaim in my best *Pride and Prejudice* accent.

She holds up that same fork threateningly, though she's trying not to laugh. "Don't you tell a soul, or there'll be hell to pay."

We both dissolve into giggles right as Unc walks back in from the kitchen, a smile on his face. He sees us and makes a right-hand turn, muttering about checking the bathrooms, which only makes us laugh harder.

Hours later, much to my astonishment, I'm out of lemons—three whole bins of them—but the sweet tea orders keep coming, right alongside the beers and cocktails. Unc is stationed at the beer taps again and I'm running back and forth, up and down the bar, trying to keep up. As it turns out, he was right—two-dollar draft Thursday has nothing on live music night.

The pool tables are stacked, every seat has a butt, and the

dance floor is full of people who are swaying more than two-stepping because there's simply no room to move around the space.

And the infamous Bobby Tannen hasn't even taken the stage yet.

CHAPTER 3

BOBBY

"Thanks for coming out tonight. I'm Bobby Tannen."

That's the extent of my welcome speech because nobody wants to hear me talk, anyway. They're here to listen to me sing, and I'm here to feed the monster inside me that needs this outlet.

Some folks have told me my voice is a gift from God, and maybe that's true, but most days, it feels like slicing open my chest on stage and inviting every Tom, Dick, and Harry into my thoughts and emotions. It's painful to do but worse on my own well-being if I don't. Songwriting and singing are my sanity.

Maybe that's true for the crowd too? Maybe the music gives people who can't put their feelings into words a way to say what they can't? I'd like to think so.

Unconsciously, my fingers work the frets of my guitar. Betty is both an extension of me and my best friend. The mahogany is warm beneath my touch, the strings dig into the calluses I've earned with hours of play, and the resonant twang is the sound-track of my life.

I start my set list for the night, opening slow and strong with *Strawberry Wine*, tweaked slightly so it doesn't sound like I'm losing my virginity to some dude in the backseat of his car. The crowd sways and sings along with the 90s classic, and I'm home.

I never would've thought I'd say that about being on stage. Once upon a time, I was shy and uncertain to the point of not telling my family when I was performing. I didn't want them to see me. I needed a nameless, faceless, anonymous crowd that I could walk away from without any real care whether they liked the show . . . or me. But a few years ago, that changed.

Dad died.

Everything changed then. We lost the farm, literally. We sold it to the Bennetts, our neighbors, which should have been an utter and complete clusterfuck because we'd had a feud going on for years. As it turns out, that was Dad's doing more than anything, and with him in the ground and not spewing his bullshit, we realized that the Bennetts are good people. So good that they kept me, my brothers, and sister on as workers when they bought our land, and over the last year, we've created a sort of adoptive, one big happy family situation with them and us. It's weird as fuck but better than I ever thought it would be.

It's good enough that the whole pack of them often comes hear me perform now, taking up a whole corner of Hank's, being obnoxious with their hooting and hollering for more and generally giving me shit for being a soft-hearted pussy.

I love those fuckers, even if I don't tell them. They know, same as I know they love me, or else they wouldn't take the time to piss me off.

But they couldn't come this evening, leaving me solo for tonight's show.

After a couple of cover songs, I play a little shuffle riff and talk into the microphone.

"I was hoping you'd let me play a few of my own songs tonight too. Ones I've been working on, tweaking a little here and there. Y'all okay with being my guinea pigs and letting me know what you think?"

The crowd cheers back, and I hear a female voice call out, "I'll be your guinea pig, Bobby!"

I'm not exactly sure what the hell that means, but I think she intends for it to be sexy. I smirk, my head tilted under the straw cowboy hat that keeps the spotlight out of my eyes. "That's a mighty fine offer, ma'am. Maybe just the music for now." I add a wink to soften the rejection. It's not my first rodeo putting someone off because I'm not here for that.

A sad 'awww' works its way through the women and I can't help but chuckle. These people will damn near cross the street to get away from my brothers, Brody and Brutal, but they think because I play guitar and sing a little that I'm not as much of an asshole as they are. They're wrong. I'm probably worse than my brothers because where they let their asshole-ism out, I bury mine deep inside and let it out in a different form.

In music.

I sing one of my originals that the locals know.

Whatever you want,
Whatever you need,
I'll get it for you,
You can count on me.

I see a guy singing along with me, his mouth close to his woman's ear as they rock together. That's my favorite, when a song can resonate with people for a multitude of reasons. To that couple, it's about them, him making a promise to her. To me, it's about Mom and my pledge to take care of her when she was sick. This song took away her pain for a little bit, and that was enough for me, but the smile on the woman in the audience means a lot too.

I play another few songs, then it's time to ramp up the crowd. "Olivia?" I scan until I see her hand sticking up, a thumbs-up shooting my way because she knows the routine and is grabbing me a drink already. "Everyone, get a drink and raise it up high."

I give Olivia and Hank a chance to refill everyone's glasses and serve up another round, telling a story to fill the time.

"There are two true testaments of a song. One, it hits something deep inside and makes the audience relate with exactly what the singer is feeling. It's a powerful connection." I play a few chords, thinking of the songs that have done that for me over the years, then a cocky smirk stretches my lips. "Two, it's a damn good song that no matter if it's the first time you've heard it or the hundredth time, it instantly makes you smile. A few of you probably remember when this song was released, but I wasn't even born then . . ."

I pause because Hank always gives me shit at this point. He likes me too, despite his protests to the contrary. At least, I'm reasonably sure he likes me and not just the positive impact I have on his bottom line on live music nights.

"Damn young'uns wouldn't know good music if it smacked you upside the head!" Hank's rough voice sounds out across the room.

The crowd chuckles at his insult, looking toward the bar at the back of the room and then to the stage. I shrug, not offended in the least since this is our usual schtick. I hold up the glass of Jack Daniel's Olivia delivered to the stage, waiting for everyone to hold up their various drinks. I see beer bottles, wine glasses, sweet tea, and mixed drinks appear over their heads. "Here's to cheating, stealing, fighting, and drinking. If you cheat, may you cheat death. If you steal, may you steal your beloved's heart. If you fight, may you fight for a brother. And if you drink, may you drink with me." I swallow a sip of the whiskey, and everyone follows suit.

"Let's see if this one qualifies as good music for our host, Hank." I roll into an acoustic version of *Friends in Low Places*, the entire room filled with voices singing off-key—the audience, not me. The rowdy song merges us into one, all equal for the moment as strangers toast and wrap their arms around each other like long-lost buddies.

"Great job, everyone. Don't forget to tip your waitress." I find Olivia's ponytail working back and forth across the room and point her way.

Answering back, she calls out, "And your bartenders!"

Bartenders? There's only one, Hank. He's the only one allowed behind the stretch of shiny wood that's seen beers, cheers, and barfights its whole existence. Unless the old man finally hired someone to help?

If so, it'd be about time. He does almost everything around here as a one-man show. I try to help when I'm here, hauling heavy boxes from the stockroom to behind the bar, but he's a stubborn old coot who likes to refuse any assistance out of misplaced pride.

I scan the room, trying to catch sight of who else is working behind the bar. I'm protective of Hank, even if I would never dare tell him so. He'd beat the shit out of me for thinking he can't protect himself. I've seen him use the Louisville Slugger he keeps beneath the bar, and he can pack a wallop of a swing. Still, he's getting up there in years, and I've noticed it's been a little easier to talk him into letting me do a bit of the heavy lifting around here. I want to be certain that whoever he's hired is worthy of Hank's bar top.

It takes me a few seconds, but finally, the mass of people moves enough that I can see. And my heart fucking stutters in my chest before going dead still.

There's a woman with light blonde hair, short with side-swept bangs, and round black glasses behind the bar. She's got on a black tank top, a hint of cleavage peeking out at the neckline. She's talking to a regular, Richard, as she sets a fresh beer in front of him, her pixie nose crinkling as she flashes him a soft smile. She never stops moving, efficiently setting drinks up and down the bar, to Olivia and to customers, never missing a beat.

Unlike me.

I've been playing the opening chords to another original and missed my own entry. I blink, forcing my attention back to my guitar, play the start again, and sing.

But my attention never leaves the mystery woman.

I need to know her name.

I need to know who she is.

I need to know what the fuck she's doing behind Hank's bar.

I need to know where she's been my whole life.

Okay, that might be dramatic, but there's something about that sweet smile and the way she brushes her bangs back with delicate hands that makes me want to cut the set short and walk across the room to her. And I never do that. Hell, I've never even thought about doing that.

Until right now.

Thought I could see, but never saw a thing until I laid my eyes on you. Then the world exploded into view.

* * *

Usually, when I finish a set, I head to the back for a while to cool off. The lights are hot, making me a bit sweaty, and the crowd still feels entitled to a piece of me. Tonight, I can't handle the delay and won't risk that she might slip out the door. I wrap up my set, put Betty into her case, safe and sound behind the burlap stage curtain, and hop directly off the stage.

A few people surge forward as if we're friends, but I bark out, "Move." They recoil, somehow surprised that I'm not eager to high-five and fist bump them. But I've got more important shit to do.

As I'm coming up to the bar, I overhear Olivia, who's not trying to be quiet at all. In fact, she's speaking . . . loudly.

"Ooh, look out, girl. He's on his way over. Remember, he's everyone's free pass." She's talking about me. Not to be arrogant, but I've heard that from women before. Honestly, I find it to be grossly disrespectful to their relationship with their partner, but that's on them, not me. I'm not interested in shit like that.

What I am interested in is *her*.

She's laughing at Olivia's comments, and it's a bright, bubbly sound. I have a twinge of jealousy that I wasn't the one to make her laugh. Not that I'm a funny, laughs-a-minute sort anyway, but I want to capture that sound and listen to it late at night when the dark feels a little too endless and the bed a little too empty.

So I stick my hand out. "I'm Bobby Tannen."

She wipes her hand on the towel stuck through her belt loop and shakes my hand. I feel a shock of electricity shoot up my arm the instant I touch her, but she seems more confused by my direct attention than anything.

"Willow Parker, the new bartender. You seem rather popular."

An insult or a compliment? I'm not sure.

I shrug, not sure what to say. Olivia is looking between us like the ping pong match of the century has just started. I raise one brow expectantly, silently telling her to get lost. Olivia taps her tray against the bar. "Oops! Let me check on table thirteen really quick. I'll be back for those drinks, Willow." She scoots off but must throw a glance back because Willow glares off to my left. I'm instantly hungry to have her eyes back on me.

Willow sets a large glass of ice water on the bar in front of me, which I drink gratefully. "Thanks." I want to ask about a hundred questions at once, but what comes out is, "How in the hell did you get Hank to let you behind his bar?" My voice is deep and rough, nothing I can do about that, but the growl makes it sound accusatory. Maybe unconsciously, I mean for it to be because curiosity about her sudden appearance is eating me up inside.

She flinches, dark lashes fluttering a little too fast behind those owl-like lenses.

What the hell, man? Fix it.

I flash the smile that's gotten me out of trouble for most of my life and am rewarded with a hesitant, slow-motion version of one of her soft smiles.

"Right place, right time, I guess," she answers without giving anything away.

A voice calls out 'bartender', and she moves away without another word but gives me the first view of her lower half. She's wearing denim shorts that sit low on her hips, exposing a small sliver of her midriff I'd like to trace with my tongue. Her legs are shapely and tan, ending in black and white Nikes that have seen better days.

I'm lost in every curve, tracing the line of the nape of her neck with my eyes, and flexing my fingers with the urge to reach out and drag her back to me. I want more of her—her words, her smiles—and maybe I can get one of those laughs of my very own.

Richard slides over next to me, lids half-lowered, but I'm not sure if it's because he's tipsy or if he's checking me out. "What're your intentions with our Willow?"

"Our Willow?" I snap. For someone I've never seen before, she seems to have crawled under everyone's skin pretty damn fast—mine, Olivia's, Richard's, and Hank's. My Spidey senses start tingling in warning. Or maybe it's jealousy.

His lips quirk in amusement and he drawls out, "That's what I thought. You wanna know what I know?"

I blink slowly, not sure I like where this conversation is going. I mean, yeah, of course I want to know, but there's a part of me that wants her to tell me. But given how she walked off without a care, maybe a little intel would do me good.

I tell myself that I'm looking out for Hank, because maybe he's been taken in by her sweet, innocent looks too. Deep down, I know it's for my own personal satisfaction. Nobody else needs to know that, though, so I shrug casually, feigning indifference.

"All right, I'll bite. Whatcha got?"

Richard takes a long, leisurely sip of his beer, delighting in the fact that I'm on his hook. Desperately twisting and turning in anticipation on it, in fact. "Willow Parker, Hank's niece, city girl. Showed up a couple of weeks ago as a surprise. Said she needed, and I quote, 'a change.' She's a photographer of some sort, always snapping away on her phone, though I saw her with one of them big, fancy digital ones once. Thing was nearly as big as she is. And she's a damn good bartender." He winks as if he told me all her deep, dark secrets. "Be good to her or Hank'll have your hide, and I'll be backing him up." He moves back to his own barstool several seats away.

Actually, there is some good information in what he shared, answering at least the first of my questions—why the hell Hank had let her behind the bar. If she's a relative, it makes sense that he'd trust her. Why didn't she just say so?

Which leaves me to my second question . . . what's she doing later tonight? Because I'd like to get to know her better.

Maybe I can do something with Richard's information. I give him a nod of appreciation and sip at my water, watching and waiting impatiently for her to come my way. The tension in my body rises with every customer she talks to, every lift of her lips for someone else, making it difficult to keep my ass on this stool. I want to stride right behind the bar and demand her attention again.

Back and forth she goes, and after a few trips up and down the bar, I realize she's intentionally avoiding me. She's not even looking my way, skipping over my barstool as she scans customers.

Fuck that. But I've got enough respect for Hank to not pass into the no-man zone of his behind-bar space. If I did, I would definitely get his Slugger to my knees because this bar is the only thing keeping me from backing Willow up against the long stretch of wood and learning everything about her. So I make the safe choice, something I'm not always known for.

Waving her down, I see her throat work as she swallows, but she heads my way.

"Another J.D.?"

She thinks we're keeping this all business. We're most definitely not.

"Yes, please." I'm an asshole, but I've got manners, especially when I need them, and something tells me I'm going to need every trick I've got with Willow.

While she pours, I try to engage her. "Richard says you're Hank's niece? That why he let you into the sacred space known as 'behind the bar'?"

"Yeah, though my years of experience as a bartender probably didn't hurt." Her eyes sparkle behind her glasses as she pricks back at my unflattering assumption. Well, if my sister, Shayanne, said that, it'd be a sarcastic snapback. Willow seems to just be stating facts.

"Must be why he also said you're a good bartender. Actually, his words were 'damn good'. Which is high praise from him."

I swear there's the slightest hint of pink on her cheeks, but it might be the neon lights. She looks down the bar and scolds with a single word. "Richard." He grins and shrugs like 'whatcha gonna do?' and she rolls her eyes, any tiny bit of ire already evaporating as she laughs along with him like they're old friends.

I lean in. "Don't be mad at him. He's just trying to help me out."

She leans in too, elbows on the bar and head tilted my way. "You usually need help? Seems like you've got your pick of women to take home tonight."

That was most definitely an insult, the slight crinkle in her pixie nose clearly showing her distaste as she looks past me. I can imagine what she sees. Bar bunnies, mostly local girls, who see me as some sort of mythical unicorn-level creature, a dirt-roughened cowboy who sings about love and forever. The truth? I've seen love and I know it's real, but I've never been in love myself. I figure I'll know it when I feel it, though.

"Not my style. I'm a pickier sort, and right now, I need all the help Richard can give me because I think I'm in real danger of striking out." My eyes tick down to her pink lips, which tilt up ever so slightly, letting me know I'm not that close to the danger line.

"What's your type?" she says, barely louder than a whisper so that the conversation is just between us. "Maybe I can help you out too."

I scan her slowly. "A blonde with glasses, a nose I want to rub with mine, lips I want to taste, sweet smiles she hands out to everyone she sees, she heavy pours Jack Daniels for me, a new to town city girl I'd love to show around so she can take pictures of anything her heart desires." Tension builds in the inches between us with my every word.

I'm coming on hard, and I know it. I pray it's not too much because this is me holding tight restraint over every caveman urge I have, gentling them for her as best I can.

She ducks her chin for a second before lifting it again. Completely unaffected by my charm, she asks, "Does that usually work?"

She doesn't believe me, thinks I'm feeding her bullshit like some bar schmuck looking for a hookup. The worst part is that I'm telling the God's honest truth.

"Not a line. Mean every word." I move my hand to my chest, feeling the racing thump against my palm. "Cross my heart."

She nods. "Uh-huh." But she looks a little less sure that I'm being slick.

Olivia reappears at the end of the bar. "You have no idea how much I *hate* to interrupt this, but three margaritas or table two is gonna riot."

The moment pops like a bubble and Willow stands upright. "Oh, sorry. I've got them." She moves down to the other end of the bar, and I feel the loss of her, though she's only a few feet away, her eyes focused on the mixers in front of her.

"Not used to seeing you like this," Olivia says, a question laced in the comment.

"Okay." Words aren't my strong suit unless I'm singing them, and those take me weeks, or sometimes even months, to get just right.

"Take it slow and don't hurt her. She's got something going on, something she's not sharing." Olivia follows my eyes down the bar, looking at Willow and seeming more like a big sister than the barely-adult she appears to be.

"What makes you say that?"

Olivia looks at me like I'm stupider than the goat on our farm that keeps getting stuck in the fence when she tries to escape.

"A girl doesn't up and leave her life for no good reason. So be easy with her. She's not them." She looks pointedly at table two, the margarita girls who are dressed up in miniskirts, fancy boots with fringe, and plunging necklines.

"That's why I'm sitting here and not there."

Olivia backhands my shoulder, pleased. "Good answer, Bobby."

Willow reappears, setting down three margaritas for Olivia, but before I can say a word, she's off again. Back to ignoring me and doing her work.

I get it, she's busy. And I can wait. I've got nowhere better to be than right where she is, gleaning every tidbit of intel I can about this woman who has captured my attention more than anyone else ever has. And she's barely said a word to me. There's just something about her that is drawing me in.

Magical threads pull me into you, and I swirl into your orbit, lost to anyone but you.

CHAPTER 4

WILLOW

*H*is eyes, dark as night and heavy with intention, follow me. I can feel them, the heat singeing me as I work.

A couple of women have approached Bobby while he's sitting at my bar, but both walked away after a few minutes of ignored conversation. My insides buzz a little because not only did he not talk to the women, he didn't even look at them. Oh, no, those eyes stayed locked on me the whole time.

At first, I'd discreetly checked to make sure I hadn't had a nip slip or raccoon eyes, something that would explain the stare treatment, but the thumbs-up Olivia shot me told me loud and clear that Bobby's attention wasn't to gawk at the outsider. But rather that he's interested . . . in me.

That seems ridiculously unlikely, though.

He's a star, having held the entire room in his hand as he created a world of his own, inviting us into it in incremental bits with each song.

I've never heard anything like him before, that deep and sultry voice making every emotion ring through my whole body, especially down low in my belly.

I've never seen anything like him before, either, like he was supposed to be a pretty Hollywood boy but was born too rough and dark for anything prissy like that. He's walking, talking, singing . . . sin.

Currently, he's also the last fifteen pictures on the camera gallery in my phone, not that I'll show them to anyone or post them anywhere. Nope, those Bobby Tannen stage shots are all for me.

As much as I hate to admit it, I can't help but look at him too, though I try to keep it to quick side glances. He's broad-shouldered in the denim shirt he's wearing with the sleeves rolled up to show his ropey forearms. I can honestly say I have never noticed a guy's forearms until right this moment, but apparently, forearm porn is a very real thing. Who knew? Not me, for sure. He's taken his cowboy hat off, setting it on the bar beside him, and his dark hair flips up at the ends in the back. His full lips are surrounded by a five o'clock shadow, and every once in a while, his fingers dance on the bar as though he's playing a song. I wonder if it's a habit and what song he's hearing in his mind right now.

He stays there for over an hour, watching and waiting like a hunter, which must make me his prey. Somewhere around the beginning of the second hour, I decide this isn't a prank and eventually stop feeling like I'm going to trip over my own feet or drop a glass and make a fool of myself. Instead, his intense silence turns into some weird form of foreplay. He nurses the single glass of whiskey, shoots me a cocky half-smirk that promises filthy things when he catches me looking back at him, and basically manages to make it seem like we're the only two people in the room.

I swear I can feel his gaze along my skin, drinking me in and driving me wild. And that's from several seats away as I do my best to keep up with the incoming orders since Unc disappeared to the back. He swore he was fine, just needed to catch up with some liquor orders, and promised to return for closing duties. I didn't believe him, but I let him take the break he was unwilling to confess he needed.

As things start to slow down and customers go home, some alone and some partnered off, I finally make my way back toward Bobby feeling like an out-of-her-league moth drawn not just to a single flame but to a huge bonfire.

He'll burn me. I know it as surely as I know the sun's going to rise in a few hours. Hell, he'd probably destroy me, leaving ash in his wake as he sauntered on to the next groupie.

So it's a good thing I'm not here for him. I'm here for Unc, and I don't need any distractions.

Not even Bobby Tannen.

"Couldn't avoid me anymore?" His voice is gravel and grit, like he gargled sand for breakfast, followed it with a diet of black coffee and whiskey, and then screamed his throat raw. It sounds more animal than man, but I know that when he sings, honey coats that gruffness, making his words melt into your heart.

"I wasn't . . ." The words taper off at the sharp rise of his brow. I'm busted. I know it. He knows it too, so there's no point in pretending. "Sorry."

"Apology accepted." He blinks and it's like it never happened. "You think about my offer?"

My mind whirls, not sure what he's asking because his eyes have been offering me all sorts of things. As if he knows exactly the thoughts going through my head, he leans closer and whispers, "For me to show you around town. I can take you to all the best spots for pictures."

How does he make 'pictures' sound like 'sex'? Or is that just my mind dipping deep down into the gutter?

I push my bangs to the side, slipping them behind my ear so that I can focus and see him better. Seeing inside people, past their fronts and defenses, is what makes me good at what I do . . . both behind the bar and behind the lens.

On stage, he somehow seemed softer. Or vulnerable, maybe?

But now, at the bar, it's like he's closed off part of himself, going hard, dark, and aggressively flirtatious. I can't decide if I like it or if it scares the shit out of me.

Instead of answering his question, I ask one of my own, going well beyond the standard superficiality of bar room flirtation and straight into date-seven territory, which is usually more than enough to scare off the typical beer drinker looking for a hookup. "What's your happiest memory?"

"Hmm, deep question. Is this a test?" He spreads his hands out wide on the bar, and I notice just how large they are. They'd seemed almost delicate when he played his guitar, but now I can see the scars and torn cuticles. Working man hands. "So we're clear, I like it either way." He waits a beat then clarifies, "Test or not."

He knows what I'm doing, trying to run him off, but he isn't swayed in the least. If anything, he seems more intrigued by the too-personal question. Why does that smile of his feel like the sun is shining on me?

"Maybe it's what I ask everyone who sits at my bar? Something to focus on the good times," I say coyly, both of us knowing I don't ask people that. But I asked *him*.

And not because I'm trying to run him off but because I'm flirting with him.

Me, Willow Parker, a quiet and invisible mouse, flirting with Bobby Tannen, the big, growly lion. *Maybe he'll let you check out his thorn?*

My mind is so weird sometimes.

One of his dark eyebrows raises as if he's reading my mind and agreeing with my assessment of my own oddity. But he answers my original question. "My eighteenth birthday, I was an asshole kid who thought he knew everything. Only one thing in my life kept me from the really stupid shit. Music." He glances over his shoulder toward the stage and points to his guitar case, sounding a bit wistful as he continues. "My family saved to get me a new guitar. It wasn't so much the guitar, though. When I opened that wrapping paper and saw Betty, I could feel their support. I still do every time I play."

"Your parents must be proud of you."

He shrugs heavily. "They're both passed now. But I like to think so. Mom's probably two-stepping around a cloud, pissing off the angels with her loud clapping and whistling." He smiles like that image speaks to him, but there's a tinge of sadness to it. He doesn't mention his father, so neither do I. People are open books about some things and not others, and I learned long ago to be okay with that.

"She sounds like fun," I tell him.

He lays his hand back on the bar, his pinky finger a bare inch from mine. I'm acutely aware of the small space, wondering if the heat I feel is radiating from him or my insides melting to mush and racing out to my extremities. "What about you? Happiest memory?"

Tit for tat seems fair, I guess, especially since I started this round.

"My first paycheck from photography. Not because I needed the money, though I did splurge on a fancy dinner. No ramen noodles that night. No, this girl got a whole rotisserie chicken," I joke, remembering how I'd eaten the whole thing with my hands while sitting on the floor because I didn't have a couch yet. More seriously, I say, "But like you, it was that it symbolized something greater. That my art was worth something, that I was worth something."

"What was it a picture of?"

I shake my head, feeling ridiculous for getting choked up over something so trivial. "Something stupid. It wasn't that. It was what it meant to me."

His eyes narrow, his voice going impossibly deeper. "What was it?" he demands.

I sigh, already knowing I'm going to tell him. "Promise not to make fun of it?" He doesn't agree, but I say it anyway. "A doughnut. A close-up of a big pink doughnut with multi-colored sprinkles."

He laughs, a deep, rusty chuckling sound that forces a smile to my face.

"Don't laugh at me. It was a big deal. That doughnut got me a whole chicken!" And now I can't help but laugh too. "It had the doughnut shop owner's wife smiling in the background too, so proud of her doughnut baby."

"Doughnut. Baby." He repeats my words, and we both laugh harder, our heads getting closer as we share in the private joke.

The moment freezes, and I suddenly become very aware that he's moved his pinky finger over mine and our mouths are inches apart. He licks his lips, and I know with every fiber of my being that he's going to kiss me. I'm waiting, ready, damn near holding my breath in anticipation of tasting him, of being under him if only for a kiss across a sticky bar.

Bar.

Oh! The bar.

And the world outside the bubble I was in with Bobby comes roaring back into focus. I pull back, my hands feeling the instant cold at the loss of contact with him. "Work. I have to . . . work."

His lips part ever so slightly on an exhale, and I know he was just as primed for that kiss as I was. But he lets me go.

Just in time, too, because Unc comes around the corner calling out, "Last call. You don't have to go home, but you can't stay here."

"Do you even know that song?" My words are too fast, but not as fast as my heart is racing.

"What song?" he grunts, passing me to get back into his sacred space behind the bar. "Would you help Olivia out and do a round of bussing glasses so we can get out of here tonight?"

That's the first time Unc has asked for my help nicely instead of bossing me around as though my very presence is somehow both welcome and unwelcome at the same time. I'm calling it progress.

"Sure thing."

I grab a dish tub and start my way around the room, grabbing empties as I go and letting my mind race away.

What was that? What just happened? Oh, my God, I almost kissed Bobby Tannen. It is a well-known fact that hot musicians do not kiss girls like me. Nope, never happens. But it did. Well, almost.

Distracted, I lean over table nine, trying not to interrupt the guys' conversation. But the blond closest to me runs the back of his hand up my arm and a creepy shiver runs down my spine.

"Hi there." He's not drunk, or at least he's not slurring and his eyes are focused. But he's clearly lost his ever-loving mind.

"Hello," I answer coldly, shifting away from him.

I hate to say it, but I've been in enough bars that I'm well aware that friendliness can be mistaken for flirting for the lonely-hearted. And the last thing I need to do is overreact in the middle of Unc's bar and cause a scene, even if I'm gritting my teeth to keep from telling this guy to keep his hands to himself.

"Chill out, Joe," one of the other guys says, shaking his head and giving me a look that says *Sorry, my friend is an asshole.* "Here, thanks." The guy holds up his empty glass and I reach for it.

As soon as my hands grab the offered glass, Joe grabs my ass and yanks me into his lap, bouncing me with his hips and laughing like he's having a grand old time. I can feel his dick hardening beneath my thigh.

Scene be damned. The glass shatters on the wood floor as I push against Joe's chest, yelling loudly, "What the hell?"

Joe starts to say something, his breath smelling like stale beer, but I'm suddenly flying through the air and whirled around. Before I'm even seeing straight, I'm planted almost gently on my feet, a wide, denim-clad back in front of me.

Bobby.

He ripped me out of Joe's lap and now has Joe's T-shirt fisted in one hand, his other holding Joe's arm behind his back. Joe is stone-cold sober now and pissed as hell. His toes are barely touching the ground as Bobby holds him up, but he's yelling at Bobby as he struggles. "What the fuck, man? Put me down!"

A loud bang comes from the bar, and I glance over to see Unc with a baseball bat slammed on the bar top. My uncle might be old, but right now, I have no doubt that he could take someone's head off with that thing.

"Bobby," Unc says in warning, though I don't know why. Bobby is protecting me and not the bad guy here.

"Don't. Touch." That's all Bobby says to Joe, but it has the power of an order. He slowly lowers Joe's feet to the floor, keeping a careful watch on him. Bobby's eyes narrow a split second before Joe bellows.

"Motherfucker!"

Joe rears back and punches Bobby clean in the jaw. I gasp in horrified shock, but Bobby grins, his tongue peeking out to test the lip I was so close to kissing just minutes ago. "Hank, you saw that? He threw the first punch."

All at once, hell breaks loose.

Unc curses and tries to rush around the bar as Bobby hammers Joe's gut and makes him fold in half before uppercutting Joe's nose. I hear a crunch, and Joe falls to his knees, holding his nose.

"You broke it." Joe sounds whiny and stuffy, probably from the blood leaking from between his fingers.

Joe's friends all push back from the table, and Bobby looks up, glee in his eyes that tells them all to bring it, but they're not getting up to jump to their friend's defense. They're getting out of Bobby's way, same as I'm doing, backing away slowly like sudden movements will make them a target too because his hands are still loosely coiled, ready for round two.

"Get out, and don't come back!" Unc tells Joe and his crew.

The guy who tried to apologize for Joe's earlier behavior helps him to his feet. Joe splutters out, "Get out? Fuck that! Call the cops! I'm pressing charges!"

Joe glares at Bobby, and my heart races even faster, though it's pounding away like a hamster's from the adrenalin of the fight right in front of me. He's going to get in so much trouble. For me. Over nothing. What Joe did was wrong, obviously, but it's not the first time a customer has gotten a little handsy, and I've always handled it just fine and without bloodletting.

Unc grins at that. "Cops? Okay, man, your funeral. Hey, Patrick, this guy wants a police report filled out on this little incident."

A rotund guy in a plaid snap-front shirt gets up and saunters over, pausing to take in the scene with his hands on his hips. Unc and Bobby seem to know something Joe, his buddies, and I don't know, because they don't seem concerned in the least.

"Patrick Gibson, Chief of Police for Great Falls. I hear you want a police report. All right, let's start with you, Willow."

It hits me all at once, and I can't help but feel a little vindicated. There really is a police officer in the right place at the right time for the good guy.

I tell Patrick what happened precisely, and then Bobby does the same. Joe tries to interrupt, but then Patrick asks Unc, who also confirms it. Finally, Patrick asks Joe, whose bluster is fading. His version is more that Bobby is a hothead who came out of nowhere for no reason and beat the shit out of him.

Unc offers, "If you have any doubts, I can pull the video." I turn to him in surprise because there are no cameras that I know of. Unc winks at me, his straight face giving nothing away.

Patrick summarizes, "Well, it does sound like an open and shut case of sexual assault against Ms. Parker and battery against Mr. Tannen. Bobby, I mean, Mr. Tannen, had every right to defend himself. Willow, you wanna press charges too? I can take our friend down to the station, but it'll probably be Monday afternoon before he gets arraigned because the judge teaches up at the university in the morning."

Joe, though, wants to argue. "No, I'm pressing charges."

Patrick stares him down. "For what, exactly?"

Joe's buddies seem to have caught on to just how much trouble their friend is in and are trying to herd him out with promises of 'no problem, Officer' and 'so sorry, ma'am'. I shake my head, telling Patrick, "No, I think we're good."

Patrick nods, putting his cowboy hat back on. He sticks a hand out, which Bobby shakes. "Good show, son. Like that new one you're doing." To Unc, he says, "Damn tourists, think they can do whatever they want." Unc flashes a lopsided grin and walks back behind the bar, swinging his bat with every step.

I look to Bobby in shock. "What just happened?"

He steps in close to me, the knuckles of his left hand brushing over my cheekbone. I'm surprised at the gentle touch, lighter than a butterfly's wings. "Are you okay?" His eyes flash . . . worry, fury, fear, and tenderness.

He's an exciting blend of intensities.

"I think so. That was just . . . crazy."

Olivia walks by, serving beers as though nothing happened. "I told you live music nights are the best."

I blink at her no-big-deal tone and then laugh, though it's probably a little manic. Bobby's lips quirk up too, as though my laughter reassures him that I'm okay.

Unc calls out, "Hey, Willow, take an ice pack to my office and get the first aid kit. Bobby's gonna need some ointment for those knuckles. No telling what that prick had up his nose." He taps his nostril like Joe was some coke-head druggie rather than a handsy drunk.

Both Bobby and I look at his right hand, where the joints are a little puffy and red. "Oh, my God, let's get you taken care of."

He smiles and jokes, "It's fine. Been there, done that, even got the scars from the other guys' teeth a time or two."

Wait, that didn't sound like a joke.

Bobby heads back to Unc's office like he knows where he's

going, so I grab a Ziploc bag and fill it with ice. Unc watches me but stops me as I pass him. "You really okay?"

I nod. "Yeah. Just not used to being up close and personal with UFC fights, you know?"

Unc smiles, though the joke isn't the least bit funny and my nerves are still shot. "Looks like you might oughta get used to it if Bobby Tannen is taking a liking to you. You sweet on him too?" His eyes narrow, like he wants to read my answer from my face, not just hear the words. I think Unc would go meet Bobby with that bat if I said no.

"I just met him."

"That don't mean a thing, girl. Take the rest of the night off. I can handle closing." I start to argue, but he cuts me off. "Been doing it myself for damn near thirty years. Once more won't kill me." And with that, he turns back to Richard and continues chatting about the ballgame as though nothing else of interest happened tonight.

Olivia stops me too. "Ooh, girl. I'm so excited I could spit. You have to tell me everything, okay? I want to live vicariously through it *all.*"

My cheeks heat. "I'm going to put ice and ointment on his knuckles. That's it."

She pats my shoulder. "You keep thinking that. I'm already hearing wedding bells. Can I be your maid of honor?"

"What?" My eyebrows climb up my forehead and my jaw drops open. "We're not—"

"At least you got the nice brother. The other ones are monsters."

"Olivia, he just beat the shit out of that guy. Broke his nose!" I whisper-scream, not wanting to drag it out if everyone else is acting like it's no big deal. Which they are, having returned to their beers and their conversations, though there's a fresh round of female glares coming my way from the margarita girls.

Olivia looks at me in confusion. "Willow, his brother's name . . . his *actual* name . . . is Brutal. Bobby is just a little wild, a bad boy who needs some sweet, sweet loving from a nice girl." She pats my cheek a little too hard and walks off, her tennis shoes squeaking on the wet floor where she's already cleaned and mopped up the broken glass.

I think I must've bumped my head or something because tonight has been crazy, but it seems like I'm the only one who thinks so.

CHAPTER 5

BOBBY

*I*n Hank's office, I take a few deep breaths that smell like stale cigarette smoke, reassuring myself that Willow is okay. When I turned around and saw her in that guy's lap with a look of horror on her face, fear had shot through me, dropping my gut to my boots. It'd climbed right back up paired with fury. How dare he lay hands on her? I'd reacted instantly. Once upon a time, I would've punched first and dealt with the fallout later, but a conversation or two from Chief Gibson in my younger days taught me a solid lesson—let the other guy throw the first punch and have a witness.

Willow comes in, her voice gentle. "You okay?"

I flex my hand, clenching and flattening it slowly. "Yeah, no big deal. As long as you're okay?"

She sits down next to me on the retired booth bench that acts as both seating and storage, judging by the stack of papers that have fallen off the far end. "I don't know if *okay* is how I would describe how I'm feeling right now. That was . . ."

Her words taper off like she can't find a suitable label for the last fifteen minutes. "Sexy?" I suggest, deadpan.

Her pink lips part as her jaw drops in offense. "What? No!"

I break, letting my infamous grin do its work, and she realizes

I'm fucking with her. She bumps my shoulder with hers, looking slightly less shell-shocked. "That was insane. *You* are insane."

I shrug, intentionally drawling out extra slowly, "Aw, thanks."

"Seriously?" She sighs, shaking her head. "You didn't have to . . . why did you . . . do that?"

I sober up, looking at her evenly. "Look, I'm not some hothead asshole who goes around beating people up." Her brows jump, arguing my assessment, and I correct myself. "Not anymore. But you shouldn't have to put up with shit like that. That guy had it coming because I guarantee you that wasn't the first time he's pulled a stunt like that, but hopefully next time, he'll have some second thoughts and make a better decision before laying hands on a woman without an explicit invitation." I manage to bite my tongue and not add 'and never touch you', though that's what's rolling through my mind. That asshole thought he was worthy to touch her? No fucking way. I'm not either, but damned if I don't want to. But I'll wait for her signal, even if it guts me to delay a single moment.

She's quiet for a long heartbeat as her eyes search mine. Now that we're in better lighting, I can see that they're an unusual gray color and currently filled with confusion.

"That's unexpectedly . . . nice. I think?"

I can feel my insides twisting and turning as she tries to put the jagged and worn puzzle pieces together to solve me.

Good luck, sweetheart. I gave up on that a long time ago.

Wanting to wade back to safer territory, I drop my eyes to her lips, remembering the almost-kiss we shared earlier. Attraction, I understand. Lust, I recognize.

There it is, the green light I'm looking for. Her breath hitches, her lips parting a millimeter I want to measure with my tongue.

I lift my hand to cup her cheek and flinch as I bend my fingers a bit too fast. She sees it and grabs my wrist.

"Let me get you doctored up."

Kiss, foiled again.

She wipes an alcohol pad over my knuckles then smooths on ointment with a delicate touch. Her teeth bite into her bottom lip as she concentrates, doing some magic trick with a regular band-aid that makes it cover the one knuckle I split open.

"Thank you," I whisper. Our thighs are pressed together, and she's cradling my hand in her lap, staring at it instead of looking at me. If I weren't currently feeling my heartbeat in my knuckles, I might consider sliding that hand up her thigh. Her very bare, toned, tanned thigh that's so temptingly close.

Slow down. You've been warned twice about her. Don't scare her off.

"You ready to go, or do you need to close up first?" I say lightly, easing her into this but well aware that I'm not giving her a choice. It's a trick I learned from watching my sister-in-law, Allyson, with her son. Don't give options you don't want them to pick. Never say 'you want broccoli or fries' because everyone will pick the fries. Instead, offer 'broccoli with butter or cheese' so that it's broccoli no matter what.

Willow's only option is now or later, not never.

"Go where?"

Thank you, Allyson! The psychology tricks she plays on Cooper, and fine, me and my brothers too, worked for me this time because Willow didn't even try to say no.

"Welcome Wagon tour of Great Falls. I'll show you everything —the best places to eat, *where to take pictures*, the best shopping area, *where to take pictures*, downtown Great Falls, *where to take pictures*." I'm not stupid, and I know the key to getting her excited. If photography is her thing, I'll exploit the hell out of it to get her to say yes right now.

"It's the middle of the night. I'm not going anywhere but home."

"Or we could check out all those places, and I'll tell you everything you could ever want to know about Great Falls. Then we can eat fresh doughnuts, pink with sprinkles, of course," I say, letting her know I haven't forgotten her earlier confession, "and watch the sun rise. That'd make great pictures."

Her light touch traces along the calluses on my fingertips, swirling and teasing as though she's learning my skin. But I can sense the turmoil inside her, the desire to say yes warring with a need to say no.

"Are you usually this friendly and welcoming with newcomers?" she says behind a shy smile, melting for me by degrees.

Chuckling, I confess, "Not at all. I'm more a 'silent but deadly' type, but you're special."

Her jaw goes rigid and her eyes narrow. "You can stop whatever game you're playing."

She hasn't moved an inch, but there's an instant, yawning void between us and I don't know how I fucked up. She closes the first aid kit and stands, trying to put it back in Hank's desk.

Elbows on my knees and hands clasped between them, I silently watch her fumbling with the contents of the overstuffed drawer.

She gets the kit situated and shuts the drawer with a slam that feels like an alarm bell going off. Leaning a hip against the desk, her arms crossed over her chest defensively, she locks her eyes on me. They swirl like a mood ring, tortured and thoughtful.

I get the feeling she has no idea how gorgeous she is and has no defense against someone like me other than being enticingly skittish. But I don't want to make her uncomfortable. I won't be like Joe, thinking that I'm entitled to her just because I want her.

But fuck, I want her.

I haven't been this instantly attracted to someone in . . . maybe ever. I don't know what it is about her. She's more cute than hot, more sweet than sassy, and it's entirely possible that a rough cowboy like me might not be what she wants at all. But I'm willing to try, again and again, because something in that soft smile tells me she'll be worth it.

I dig deep, searching for words on demand, which is not something I'm good at by any measure. Studied, practiced, written and rewritten phrases I can do, but turning the jumble of images and thoughts in my head into something that expresses them to someone else in the moment is unfathomably difficult. And it's why I usually just keep my mouth shut.

"What just happened? I'm not playing games." I copy her words, keeping my voice steady and low, "but if I said something wrong, I'm sorry."

I honestly can't remember the last time I apologized. For anything.

"It's fine. I need to go help Unc with closing. I'm sure you know your way out."

Every word is crisp and clipped, and she doesn't seem to suffer from the same affliction as I do. She is saying exactly what she means, dismissing me as she walks out the door with her head held high.

Total crash and burn.

* * *

I'M three cups of coffee in and it's barely past sunrise. The sunrise I should've spent watching Willow snap away on her camera. It was a damn gorgeous one too, with pinks and oranges lighting up the purple sky like blooming fire I wish she'd seen. But I feel like I'm the one who missed out, not her. Because she's probably at home, warm and snuggled in her bed, and I'm out here in the fields.

"What crawled up your ass?" Brutal asks.

Oh, yeah, and I'm not alone to wallow in my failure, either. I've got my older brother trying to figure out what pissed in my cereal this morning and I don't even eat cereal.

"Nothing," I snap, focusing on the plums from the handful of trees we're harvesting today.

"Hey, think fast!" That's all the warning I get before one of the fruits is hurtling straight toward my head.

Reflexively, I catch it, pain shooting through my knuckle. I toss the plum to the bucket that's already half-full. My sister, Shayanne, is going to have enough to make a fair amount of jam. She sells it at the local farmer's market, to the restaurant at the tourist-filled resort in town, and to folks all over Great Falls and Morristown.

"What'd you do to your hand?"

"I didn't know it was twenty-questions day. My hand's fine."

I yanked the Band-Aid off as I got dressed this morning, not wanting to invite questions. But Brutal's got eagle eyes and probably noticed some small detail, like the speed of the middle finger I flip him or the tightness in my fist as I pluck plums, and that was enough to clue him in that something's wrong.

He hums his disagreement and is quiet for a moment, seeing if I'll fill in the blanks. When I don't, he theorizes for me.

"You played at Hank's last night. Fan's jealous husband?"

I told Willow that I'm not a hothead who throws hands all the time, but it probably says something about my family that it's an often-enough occurrence that we don't so much as blink when it happens. Another day, another tussle, sometimes with each other, sometimes with someone else.

I cut my eyes his way, throwing daggers that should shut him up. Instead, he takes my glare as an answer about the imaginary jealous husband.

"Or not. Well, you didn't get arrested, so it must not have been too bad. And you don't have a scratch on you, other than the swollen knuckles, so the other guy must've been a pussy."

He's trying to throw me off. It won't work.

"Unless you started it and took him out with one sucker punch?"

"I know better. I let him throw the first punch—weak, like the guy." Fine, it worked. And now I'm amped up again, growling, "Asshole had the new bartender bouncing in his lap like a fucking Tilt-a-Whirl."

Brutal grins, knowing he got me. To anyone else, his smile looks like a promise of death and dismemberment, but I'm not scared of him, even if he is a huge motherfucker who looks like he eats steel for breakfast and shits out bolts. The men in our family aren't known for being tall, dark, and handsome. It's more like tall, dark, and scary, each of us damn near replicas of our dad's black hair, dark eyes, tanned skin, and broad build. Brutal's the scariest of us all until you get to know him, then you see that he's the mushiest guy ever, wrapped around his wife and son's fingers.

"I saw one of those carnival rides when I took Allyson and Cooper to the fair. They wouldn't let me on, said I 'exceeded the weight limit' or some shit." He throws up dirt- and sap-covered fingers in air quotes, rolling his eyes. When he sees the set of my jaw, he laughs. "Not the point, got it. New bartender, asshole, Tilt-a-Whirl. I vote we talk about the new bartender because I didn't think Hank would ever hire help."

Delight dances in his eyes. I'm the 'last man standing' in our motley crew of blended family. All three Bennett brothers are married now, one of them to my younger sister Shayanne, and both of my older brothers are in relationships, Brutal married and Brody doing the no-marriage-but-committed thing with his woman, Rix. All of which inconveniently leaves me as the only single. My sisters-in-law have tried to remedy that, repeatedly attempting and failing to play matchmaker.

But my focus has only been on music.

At least until last night.

I'm not getting out of this. Brutal has his ways, one is easy and the other is hard, so I can spill my guts now or after he tackles me to the dirt and forces it out of me. Sounds barbaric, but it's our way and done in brotherly love. Mostly.

Still, I try to keep to the bare bones. "Bartender's name is Willow, and she's Hank's niece."

"*And*?" he prompts threateningly.

"And nothing."

He takes one giant step closer, and I'm on the edge of doing this the hard way. I consider it for a moment. Getting out some of this liquid uncertainty in my veins would be nice, but I'm already down my right hand and we've got shit to do. Words it is, I guess.

Hey, Universe! I notice a running theme of my last twenty-four hours. Try these words on for size . . . fuck off.

I sag, sighing heavily. "And *nothing*. She shot me down."

Brutal freezes with his brows comically high on his forehead. "She . . . shot . . . you . . . down?" His smile blooms as slowly as the heirloom tomatoes we grew last spring, then he damn near busts a gut laughing. "Holy shit! Never thought I'd see the day that Pretty Boy Bobby would get turned down by anyone. I like her already." He's bent in half, hands on his knees, eyes watering from laughing so hard that he's speaking in short bursts of phrases before the next hee-haw of laughter.

I shove him and he stumbles, but only because he's so off-kilter from laughing at me. The stutter in his steps and the angry scowl on my face only make him howl again.

More pissed than ever, I grab another plum from a low branch and toss it in the bucket, being too rough with the fragile fruit.

"Hey! Don't damage the merchandise with your pissy attitude," Brutal scolds, as if I'm a stupid kid or a newbie laborer he's training. I throw him a middle finger, making sure it pops up good and strong despite the twinge in my knuckle. His shit-eating grin of victory is audible in his tone. "I'll let Mama Louise know you won't be at dinner tonight, seeing as you'll be eating at Hank's for round two, loverboy."

And with that, he gets back to work too.

It's his version of advice, basically telling me to quit moping, get my shit together, and try again. I grunt, the unofficial Tannen family language, saying thanks and that I appreciate it.

He's right. I just need to figure out what I said wrong, figure out how to say it right, and try again. Just like a song.

Last night was just a first rough draft of our meeting. I hope.

CHAPTER 6

WILLOW

*S*unday evenings are slower than molasses. The lunch rush after church is busy but light on bar work, so I spent most of that time helping Oliva. I'm nowhere near the waitress she is, but I can run food when Ilene dings her bell.

Now, as the clock on the wall approaches six, I'm beyond bored and desperate for something, anything to do because I can see my own reflection in the bar after the number of times I've wiped it down. "Unc, what can I prep for this week? Or need me to deep clean anything? Sort the paperwork into the file cabinet?"

He looks over from the table where he, Richard, and a guy who introduced himself as Doc are sitting and drinking a beer. As I suspected, neither of the guys paid, but Unc doesn't seem to mind the loss of revenue to friends. Richard is nursing his first Miller draft, Doc's on his second Budweiser can, and Unc has another bottle of that craft beer he prefers.

"Willow, you've been buzzing around like a hopped-up bee on crack. Sit down and relax, for God's sake. You're making me jumpy." He pushes out the fourth chair at their table in invitation.

I perch on the edge of the chair, still wanting to work, but as soon as I stop moving, the tiredness washes through me and I feel just how heavy my feet have become.

"I just want to help, earn my keep, you know?" I tell Unc. "It's one thing for the owner to sit around on his ass, another for an employee to do it when she's on the clock."

Richard smiles, flashing his slightly yellowed teeth. "Hey, Olivia, whatcha doing?" he calls over to where she's sitting in a booth with her feet up and crossed at the ankles. She can see the front door, but we haven't had a real customer in almost an hour and she's already done all her side work, stuffing sugar packets into the bins on the table, filling salt and pepper containers, and deep cleaning the coffee machine.

She lifts her eyes from her phone to answer, "Talking to Hannah. You need something?" She makes zero move to get up.

Richard shakes his head. "Nope, you just proved my point. Thanks." To me, he says, "See, Olivia's on the clock and she's chitter-chattering away with her girl. She look anxious about that?"

I glance over and see that Olivia is smiling at her glowing screen at something Hannah said, not a care or concern in the world with doing that while she's supposed to be working.

Unc lowers his voice, leaning in to me, "Ain't her fault we aren't busy. She's guaranteed forty hours and she works 'em, whether I need her or not. Sure as shit, someone comes in, she'll hop up and take care of 'em like she's s'posed to."

I know he's right. I'm just used to buzzing around, being busy. Being in the city, there's always something going on. This slower pace of life is . . . different.

I like it, I think. It's just going to take me some time to get used to.

Doc drops his beer can to the table with a thud. "I got a question. Hank tells me you take pictures and sell them on the interwebs, but not portraits and such. I ain't never heard such a thing. People pay for pictures that aren't their kids or their dogs?"

I laugh. It's a generational thing. "It's a bit more complicated than that. I do photography—portraits and commercial stuff when I get a client. But mostly, I get paid from my social media account, which is monetized because of the number of followers I have. For that, I take random shots of my day, usually close-ups with short captions, and post them. People check in and see what I'm up to."

Three sets of scrunched brows meet my explanation so I try again.

I pull out my phone, click into my social media app, and show them. "See, here's today . . . my morning cup of coffee, a stoplight over Main Street, the parking lot out front, and a shot of the neon reflecting off the spotless bar."

I click into each picture, pointing out the number of hearts and comments. "The more people who look at the pictures, like them, and comment, the more money I get."

Doc moves his glasses down his nose and leans in closer to focus on my phone. "That's a job? Those pictures are real nice, I guess, but you can't even see you in them. Or anyone. It's . . . a cup of coffee." He shrugs, and I can't help but giggle a little.

"I know, it's different. People are curious creatures by nature. We like to see what other people's lives are like, so I show them mine. It lets me do photography, stay anonymous, and make a living. Well, that plus 'working' behind the bar." I do air quotes around the 'working' as I look at Unc because I'm still sitting on my butt, talking instead of helping.

The sound of gravel crunching out front breaks up my TED talk on creative ways to turn hobbies into careers. I hop up, pointing at the three guys, asking if they want another round, but they all decline. "Nah, we've got a game to get to. Sunday night poker. Hank's turn to host."

"Don't go too hard on him, fellas. Payday's coming and I've got my eye on a new lens filter for my camera." I smile and swoop behind the bar as Olivia pockets her phone and goes to greet the next round of customers.

The dinner rush is more of a trickle, but it gives me something to focus on as I make drinks for Olivia. I add a couple of cherries and a dash of grenadine to some Sprites for a family with two little girls, delivering their Princess Punch to delighted giggles. A few beers here and there, but mostly, I pull soft drinks and sweet tea to accompany the food the few tables order from Ilene.

Unc leaves with Richard and Doc, heading to their weekly game. I'm glad he's got friends, and now that I'm here as bar backup, they can play earlier because I can close up. It's the least I can do, but I'm willing to do so much more. Anything I can to help him.

The door opens, and I automatically look over to see who our latest customer is. I find . . . Bobby Tannen filling the doorway.

Whew, boy, he looks good! Good and . . . determined.

He's got on a black T-shirt that hugs his chest and biceps, dark-wash jeans slung low on his hips with a black belt laced through the loops, and black cowboy boots that look like they've seen a lot of dance floors and very few pastures. I realize something . . . he's dressed up, like for a date. This is fancy Bobby.

A stone settles in my stomach, knowing I'll have to watch him have dinner with whoever he's going out with tonight. Maybe she's still outside? Or he's meeting her here?

But I'm not surprised. A guy like that must go on dates every night of the week, probably with a different woman each time, judging by how many were throwing him come-hither looks. And fine, also by the fact that even I almost fell for it, wanting to meet his kiss when he moved in closer. Luckily, sanity reigned supreme because that whole 'you're special' thing was straight out of '*How to Hit on Chicks at Bars 101*'. In other words, no thanks, Bucko. Any interest I'd harbored had floated away like smoke.

Until I see him standing in the door and that sour taste climbs the back of my throat. Jealousy? Of his potential date?

Yeah, that's what that feeling is. On the bright side, maybe I can get an up-close look at what a guy like him goes for. I'm thinking a pretty, blonde, cheerleader type. I don't say that to be bitchy, more like my observations of life have led me to believe that's how it always works.

And that's what I expect . . . right up until the moment he walks over to the bar and sits down. Right in front of me.

Oh, I might be in trouble here.

Olivia is dancing around behind Bobby, eyes huge and mouth silently screaming 'yessss!' and 'get him, girl!' while she does some version of a pelvic thrust I think is supposed to be sexy but mostly just looks like she's humping empty air.

I drag my eyes back to Bobby, who's smirking like he can guess exactly what I'm looking at behind him and gives zero fucks. "Hey, Willow."

Grit and gravel, no honey to smooth the roughness of his voice. I swear it vibrates through my skin and muscles and straight to my core.

"Hey, Bobby." See? Playing it cool here. No big deal. Just another customer, like any other. "What can I get ya? Jack? Or is it a beer night?"

"Sweet tea, please."

Hmm, unexpected and interesting.

I set a glass in front of him, watching as he fishes out the lemon wedge and squeezes it into the drink. "Dinner?" I ask, holding a menu between us like a shield. "Or are you waiting on someone?"

I lick my lips, wishing I could chase those words back and swallow them down. Why did I ask that? It makes me sound needy, like one of his groupies. Which I'm not. Nope, not a bit.

"Yep. What time's your dinner break?" he drawls out slowly. But it's not casual. If anything, the speed makes his intention clearer.

Me? Me. He really is here for me. He's dressed up like walking sex for me. The very idea is almost laughable.

"Oh, I don't really get one. I'll grab something later." That's the truth, but also, I'm trying to put some distance between us. I'm not sure what to do with him, with this intensity, with this directness.

I wipe down the spotless bar aimlessly, quiet and waiting. He came here for a reason and will spill eventually. I can be patient.

He watches me again, eyes tracking me closely. After a solid five minutes of silence, which feels like an eternity, he looks over his shoulder. "Hey, Olivia?"

She's been watching from a booth with some folks she must know because she's sitting down with them, all four sets of their eyes on Bobby and me too. "Yeah?"

"Can I get two of whatever Ilene thinks Willow would like to eat for dinner, please?" He talks to Olivia but is looking at me again, daring me to disagree. When I'm quiet, he smiles ever so slightly, the smallest lift of the corners of his mouth. Victory. I can see it in his eyes. But he balances it with his words. "If you want to take it to-go for later, that's fine. But I thought it'd be nice to have dinner together and didn't figure you'd go out with me after I crashed and burned last night."

Bold self-deprecation? I hadn't expected that from the cocky cowboy either.

"So you thought a captive audience while I'm at work was the better option?" He cringes, despite the decided lack of heat in the accusation.

He sighs heavily. "Look, I'm really bad at this, but I'm trying. I'm trying to get to know you. I'm just not that great with words."

I scan his face, his jaw set tight as though those were the hardest words he's ever said. I believe him. I heard him express himself beautifully and confidently on stage last night, but he seems more real, more vulnerable now than the larger than life version he was then.

Olivia sets down two blue-plate specials, Ilene's brown butter seasoned chicken breast, homemade mashed potatoes, and fried okra. She disappears as quickly, and the aroma wafts up, making my stomach growl. Bobby smiles hopefully. And I give in, knowing it's an unwise decision, but it's only dinner across the bar. How bad could it be?

I unwrap the silverware, watching as he mirrors my movements. First up? A bite of mashed potatoes, full of peppery goodness and covered in brown gravy. "Mmm," I moan reflexively. Ilene can really cook, and if I keep eating every dinner here, I'm going to be the size of a house because she has never met a stick of butter she didn't turn into something delicious.

Bobby freezes, his bite of mashed potatoes halfway to his mouth, and mutters under his breath. I swear he says, "Is she trying to kill me?"

I have no idea what he's talking about, but I dig in. Now that I've got food in front of me, I'm starving. I'm several bites in when I remember that I didn't take a picture. Food pics are one my most popular posts and an easy capture with a variety of texture, colors, and shapes. But I'll have to do something different tonight. I'll see what strikes me on the way home—maybe a moon shot or my freshly painted toes in the tub because I promised myself a long, hot soak days ago.

Bobby's taken a few healthy bites too, shoveling it in as fast as

I am as though he hasn't eaten all day. I swallow, lifting my chin toward his plate. "Hungry after a hard day?"

He pauses, setting his fork aside. "Same as usual. Picked plums all day."

"I expected you to say you'd be riding horses all day or rustling cattle. Something like that," I tease, faking a country accent.

He flashes white teeth so fast it might've been a smile or might've been a threat. "That what you think a cowboy does all day?"

I shrug. "Isn't it?"

He mirrors my shrug. "That's mostly what my brother, Brody, does with Mark. They handle the cattle. My brother Brutal and I do the farming. My sister, Shay, does whatever shit she comes up with—soaps, jams, cakes, and such."

I blink, trying to filter all the info he shared into something resembling a family tree. "So, you have three brothers and a sister? Brody, Mark, Brutal, Shay, and you?" I swear Olivia said there were two brothers, but the name Brutal is all that really stuck in my mind. Well, that and the image of Bobby throwing a hell of a punch, because that was definitely memorable.

"Nah," he says, shaking his head. "Two brothers, one sister . . . officially. But the Bennetts, that's who bought our ranch, took us on, and we're thick as thieves now. There are three Bennett brothers too, Mark, Luke, and James. And they're all married, Mark to Katelyn, Luke to my sister, and James to Sophie. Plus, Brody's got Rix, and Brutal's got Allyson and a boy, Cooper. And on her throne sits Mama Louise, riding herd over all of us." He doesn't sound like he minds that at all, which is surprising. He seems like a rogue, lone wolf somehow who doesn't let anyone or anything tell him what to do.

But maybe I'm wrong about that? It doesn't happen often, but sometimes, people are more complicated than they first appear.

Like Unc.

Almost reading my mind, Bobby asks, "What about your family? Big? Small? Normal? Crazy?" He goes back to eating while I think about how to answer that.

"Small and somewhere between normal and crazy, I'd say.

Mom and Dad are both hippies who somehow managed to raise two kids. Mom owns an art gallery, Dad is a freelance environmental scientist, and my brother, Oakley, is the black sheep of the family." I lower my voice as though I'm sharing a secret. "He's an *accountant*. And his wife, Madison, is a *forensic accountant*. They literally discuss math and spreadsheets over dinner." I shudder, my eyes wide in fake horror.

He chuckles, sipping at his tea. "What about Hank? What's the thread from you to him?"

Isn't that a knotted tangle of a snag? But I answer anyway, hearing the pain in my voice but not trying to hide it. "He's my mom's dad's brother. I hadn't seen him for a while because there was some drama I was too young to really understand a few years back. But when my grandfather died and I got older, it just seemed like it was time. I didn't want to miss out on something— on Unc—because of things that didn't have anything to do with me."

Bobby places his hand over mine comfortingly. His skin is warm, soft, but I can feel the rough calluses along his fingertip where it dances over my knuckles. "I know Hank is glad you're here. I haven't seen him smile this much in years."

I smile, having guessed that Unc isn't really the smiling sort, but I have seen a softer side coming out the last few days. He's been less grumpy about letting me help, and he even thanked me for doing so much. And he did leave early for poker, something Doc said was a first. Unc might have been surprised at my unexpected visit, but I think he's glad I'm here now, which means I'm doing exactly what I'm supposed to do.

"I'm glad you're here too."

Blunt and bold, and suddenly, his touch is full of heat, not comfort. His finger traces down the length of mine, then back up and down the next. It's as though he's memorizing my hand, inch by inch, and for such a relatively casual touch, it feels immensely intimate.

His eyes follow his finger, devouring my skin, and I watch as his jaw tightens. He is a monster in cowboy clothing, a Wrangler-wearing good old boy who is so far out of my league, it's not even funny.

I should move my hand away. I know I should. But I'm frozen in place, stuck in his magnetic pull that feels so good, sending tingles from my fingertips to places much more needy.

He threads his fingers through mine, effectively holding my hand like we're kids on a date across the bar. Slowly, his eyes trace higher, eventually meeting mine directly. I know my gray eyes are probably as wide and bright as his are hooded and dark.

His voice is low and rough. "How about that tour tonight, Willow? I know a great overlook to watch the sunrise. You'd be able to get some beautiful shots there."

God, every single cell in my body is humming in tune . . . *Yes*.

Luckily, I have one single, solitary, lonely brain cell that hasn't been completely lost in the waves of Bobby Tannen pheromones the rest of me is swimming in. That one cell is screaming that I know better than this. Sure, maybe I'm interesting in an out-of-towner-fresh-meat challenge sort of way. But let's be real. While I'm only here for a few months at most, it's going to be awkward as hell when I fall under Bobby's sway only to be left in the dust when I'm not shiny and new anymore. And there will still be the shows, where I'll have to watch him sing in that no-big-deal, casually sexy way and feign nonchalance as women throw themselves at him. I'll have to pretend I'm the sort that's cool with a fling when I'm not. I'm *so* not.

And that's my answer right there.

I untangle my fingers from his, pulling back. "Bobby, thank you. Truly. But I'm not here for . . ." My tongue ties at the heat radiating off him in waves. Anger? Disappointment? Shock? Something heavier, maybe? "I'm here for Unc, that's it. I'm sorry."

What the hell am I apologizing for? I don't know, but it seems like the thing to say.

He nods, reaches into his back pocket for his wallet, and sets down a twenty. All in complete silence. It takes maybe three seconds, but it feels like three lifetimes.

"See ya soon, Willow. Sweet dreams."

* * *

59

HANK'S IS CLOSED on Monday. Even Unc can't go seven days a week. But Tuesday night, it's burgers and fries across the bar.

"What made you want to be a photographer?" Bobby asks before taking a monstrous bite of his burger. He's got on a blue shirt with a yellow logo that's so faded I don't know what it once said. Before he sat down, I saw worn blue jeans and dirt-kicker boots. He's not dressed up tonight, but he still looks good. If I nuzzled into his neck, I think he'd smell like sunshine, sweat, and sex. Even though I'm across the bar, I take a deep breath, wondering if I can catch a whiff and confirm that hopeful dream.

I take out my phone, snapping a shot of my lemon wedge-topped tea reflecting in the shine on the bar and highlighted by the neon-lit beer sign on the wall. A quick caption, *Sweet tea is the new coffee,* and the *yum* emoji, and then I post. I don't even wait for the first heart or comment, putting my phone into my back pocket without a thought.

"I think I always was to some degree. Mom taught me to see the world through different lenses, literally holding up gel filters and introducing me to artists who painted from various perspectives. I drew when I was younger, was okay at it, but I couldn't get the realism I wanted. I joined yearbook as a way to participate without having to actually, you know, *participate.* And the rest is history."

I wave a French fry around like a wand that magically transported me from high school to this moment. Bobby grins wolfishly, catching my wrist in his hand. Before I know what's happening, he's snagged the fry from between my fingers with his teeth, literally eating it from my hand. His tongue snakes out to lick the salt from my fingertip, then he chews around a self-satisfied smile.

"What the?" I balk, wiping my fingers on a napkin. Secretly, I'm delighted, which is dangerous.

He doesn't react, instead focusing on our conversation like what he did was completely normal. "I looked up your blog. I started going through all the pictures, and they were cool. You're really talented, but I had to stop."

He swallows as if that's some big confession.

My brow furrows. "Why?"

His fingers dance on the bar top, and again, I wonder if he's playing a song or doing it randomly. "It felt . . . intrusive. Like if you were just this anonymous person, it's a peek into your day to day life. I get that, it's what you're intentionally doing. But since I know you and want to know more about you, it felt creepy. I want you to share those stories with me willingly, not learn about you from whatever you put online. Does that make sense?"

He shakes his head like he uttered complete nonsense.

I feel like it was pretty profound. Both that he gets why I do what I do and that he wants more than the snippets of me I share publicly. He wants more than *more*. I get the feeling he wants it all. All of me. The question is . . . why?

"It does," I tell him. "It makes sense."

His shoulders drop two inches I hadn't realized they'd climbed up, almost like he was nervous. But he's Bobby Tannen, star of Great Falls.

"Tour tonight?" he asks, setting another twenty down.

"I can't. The tour or the money. That's too much by at least twice." I push the twenty back his way. "You got the last one, so let me pay tonight. I'll let you in on a secret . . . I get an employee discount."

He chuckles lightly but shakes his head, not touching the money. "No worries, I'll see you tomorrow. Sweet dreams."

* * *

THURSDAY NIGHT TWO-DOLLAR drafts are in full effect. Along with the early evening crowd, everyone is clamoring for a bowl of Ilene's chili, which is apparently blue-ribbon award-winning at the town's annual chili cookoff six years in a row.

Ding. Ding-ding-ding.

Her bell hasn't quit ringing all night as she serves up bowl after bowl. I peeked through the window earlier and saw four huge pots simmering on the stove top, which had seemed like a lot, but given how many Olivia has served, I bet we're running low by now.

There's only one thing missing . . . Bobby.

He's been by every night this week. He sits, and we talk about everything and nothing, our days, our lives. I've heard stories about his family and family by extension, I've told him about adjusting to Great Falls and how he was right about the doughnut shop on Main Street, which really does have the best doughnuts I've ever tasted. He's talked about farming and animals, music and songs, both others and his own. I've shown him pictures of my favorite places back in the city and made him one of my favorite mixed drinks, which he dutifully drank, even though it was pink and came with a lemon slice and a name like Girly Beer.

That was just last night.

"What the hell is this?" Bobby asks, his full lips screwed up in a scowl as he glares at the glass like it personally offended him.

"Just try it. I'm trying to get Unc to do a drink special, especially on the weekends. This is one I used to make at a bar I worked at. It's cheap and sells like crazy, so the overhead is good."

He sniffs it once and then again. "Lemonade? Beer?"

I tap my nose, pleased. "Good job. It's light beer, for the ladies, you know, pink lemonade concentrate, and vodka. Over rocks is good, but tossed in a blender with some ice makes it into an alcoholic slushie."

"You first," he orders, offering the glass back my way.

"Despite the fact that I'm lazing around, eating dinner with you, I am still on the clock and can't drink. Just try it." I push it back his way, not missing the way his hand clenches the glass a little harder when I touch him.

His sip is tentative, like he's fully expecting to hate it and have to gag it down to be polite. But his brows shoot skyward. "Fuck, that's good." He takes another drink, this time a big gulping one. "Aw, hell, you're gonna have everybody in here drinking frilly pink drinks, aren't you?"

The lift of his lips and the teasing glimpse of his tongue as it swipes out to catch every drop of alcohol says that's not a bad thing.

"May-be." My shrug is casual, though I'm delighted he likes it. If I can get Bobby on board, I know I can get Unc on board too. "If it helps Unc's bottom line, it'll be worth it."

He eyeballs the glass again, teasing, "Can you drop some food coloring in it or something?" But he doesn't seem to mind as he takes another drink. "Shit, that stuff is dangerous. You don't feel it at all, like Kool-Aid sneaking up on ya."

He sets it down, returning to the second garlic-crusted pork chop he's been working on.

But it's past seven now, and Bobby is nowhere to be found. I wonder if turning him down on that tour for the fourth time was the final straw, and I feel a thread of disappointment weave through me. I didn't realize how much I counted on seeing him every night until right this second.

The door opens, and I look over hopefully, even though I hate that I'm doing it every single time the door makes its trademark creak. But it's not him, just another two guys coming in for their weekly cheap beers. They hold two fingers up to Unc, and he nods back, already pulling their drafts.

Unc's staying on his stool tonight, which I'm taking as a win, and he did agree to let me do a trial of the Girly Beer on Saturday, another win.

"Hey, Willow?" Unc says from his perch.

"Yeah?" I answer, instantly at his side.

"Could you sneak in the back and get me a bowl of Ilene's chili before she runs out? I don't want to miss out this time." As soon as I nod, he goes back to talking to Richard and simultaneously pulling beers for Olivia.

Work and talk, he's a pro at the multi-tasking. And now that he's sitting more, I have noticed that his limp isn't quite as severe.

"Knock, knock," I call out as I enter the kitchen. Ilene is protective of her domain and I know she'll be in the groove with the dinner rush, so I don't want to disturb her.

As expected, Ilene is working away at the stove top, which is still covered with four steaming pots of chili, but now there are three empty ones on the floor by the dishwashing station. She's definitely going through it.

"Hey, Ilene, Unc asked for a bowl when you get a second. Said he didn't want to miss out this time."

She hums, acknowledging me even though she doesn't look my way. "Daniel . . . get me a bowl and a big Tupperware so I can pack Hank up a bit of chili for tomorrow too."

A guy I've never seen before pops around the corner. "Sure thing, here ya go," he tells Ilene, holding out two bowls, one heavy ceramic and one plastic, but then his eyes land on me.

"Hey, I'm Daniel, Ilene's sometimes kitchen help. The few, the proud, the chosen," he offers, holding out his hand after setting the bowls down. He looks to be a few years younger than me, with dark skin and dancing bright eyes. His smile is kind and friendly.

I shake his hand. "Nice to meet you, Daniel. I'm Willow, Hank's niece and bar help."

His face changes instantly, eyes going wide and brows going high, and he pulls his hand back like the mere touch of my skin burned him. He's still smiling, but it's less friendly now and more guarded. "You forgot the most important part . . . Bobby Tannen's girl. Sorry, didn't mean anything by anything, just introducing myself to a fellow co-worker, you know?"

My hand falls to my side as my brows knit together, "What? I'm not Bobby's girl. We're friends. He just stops by for dinner and a beer."

Okay, I know it's more than that. Those dinners have become the best part of my days, seeing the curl of his lip when he smiles, the hungry way he watches me eat, and how it feels like he's barely holding himself back from jumping over the bar to get at me. And I like it, I'll admit that, but I'm not *his girl* or anything.

Daniel nods, though it's clear he doesn't believe me, and holds his palms toward me. "Sure, whatever you say. But no offense, I'm gonna take his word for it because he's a bit bigger and meaner than you seem to be. And you know, the whole town has seen him marking his spot at the bar every night. It's quite the news bulletin."

And with that, he hustles back around the corner. I turn to Ilene, who's finishing up Unc's dinner. "Ignore Daniel. He's a great help and a hard worker, but hoo boy, that man flaps at both ends. You don't worry about a thing, Willow. You and Bobby are doing just fine taking things slow."

And with that, she dings the bell, effectively dismissing me.

What. The. Hell?

Mindlessly, I set the bowl of chili and plate of cornbread by Unc, telling him that I set another bowl to-go on his desk. He nods appreciatively. At least I think he does, but I'm not really sure because my mind is spinning.

I see that a couple of drink orders have come in while I was in the kitchen and get started on those. Olivia comes up. "Those table four's?"

I don't answer that question, instead telling her what just happened in the kitchen. "Daniel said I'm 'Bobby's girl.' I'm not his girl. What does that even mean?"

"Aw, that's sweet," she replies, grinning like she actually means that. But how could she? That's crazy talk.

"No, it's not. I'm not some territory he can piss on to claim."

Her nose wrinkles. "Not when you say it like that. But it's romantic, don'tcha think? He's all in, claiming you far and wide when you haven't even realized what's looking you right in the face."

"What's looking me in the face?" I say, not willing to concede that it might be the tiniest bit sweet. In a Neanderthal, caveman sorta way. That I do not like. Not a bit.

Liar.

"He's here," Olivia whispers, but it's somehow a squeal all the same.

I turn toward the door, mad but still excited to finally see him. The door is closed, not even creaking a bit.

Olivia's finger is suddenly in my face. "That. You want to see him. You like him coming here to see you too. Hell, when was the last time someone made this much of an effort to get you to go out with them? I can tell you, for me . . . that was right about *never*. Just do the tour, go on a date with the man."

"You mean sleep with him?" I bite out, not having forgotten about her earlier warnings about Bobby, no matter how kind and sexy and intriguing he seems to be.

"Tomato, to-mah-to. Or maybe he's just asking you out and it's you who thinks *tour* is synonymous with *sex*. Just go out with him and see. What could it hurt?"

"Me!" I say a little too loudly.

Olivia looks taken aback. She looks over her shoulder toward the door then back at me. "I think maybe I gave you the wrong idea about Bobby. Or hell, maybe I had the wrong idea, along with everyone else in this town."

"What do you mean?" I ask leerily.

She shrugs, sighing a bit. "Look, Bobby Tannen is a monster of a man, and sexy as fuck to boot. Get it? To boot," she teases with a smile I don't return. "Right, too soon. Let's just say that he has a reputation, but it's not exactly for being a player. More like that everyone wishes he was so they could get their piece of him. Honestly, I don't remember the last girl he went out with. So either he's hella quiet about it, and to be clear, this is a town where everyone knows everyone else's business, or he hasn't dated. But damned if he's not trying his hardest to date you. Lucky bitch." There's no heat in the last bit, more of 'open your eyes, girl' than anything laced through the words.

She looks at me carefully, curiously.

I look through my brain and my heart just as carefully, realizing something I knew days ago but smushed down deep inside. "Oh, God. I do want to go out with him, but I'm scared because . . ." I swallow. "Have you seen him?"

Olivia grins hungrily. "Oh, yes, I have. Don't get me wrong, I'm not on that team, but even I can appreciate that God knew exactly what he was doing when he put that man together."

I swat at her shoulder, getting her attention, then gesture to myself. I've got on my usual work gear, which is also my usual everyday clothes—jean shorts, tennis shoes, and a three-dollar discount store T-shirt. My bangs are swept over to the side, my glasses are halfway down my nose, and my face is bare. In short, I'm just . . . me. Which I'm totally cool with, except when Bobby looks at me and makes me feel naked on the inside.

"What? You look great," she says, not getting the point.

"He's not a player?" I clarify.

Olivia shakes her head, eyes getting brighter by the second.

"This isn't some 'haze the new girl' prank?"

"What kind of people do you know back in the city who'd do shit like that? That's awful, and no." She shakes her head again, but this time it's in disbelief that people would be that cruel.

Right as my heart starts climbing into my throat, I realize something important. "It doesn't matter. Looks like I blew it, anyway, because he's not here tonight."

"Yes, he is."

The door creaks, and when I look over this time, it is him.

Finally.

The air charges between us, across the bar, across the room. I know something has changed. I have changed. But though he doesn't know what twister of emotions I went through in the last fifteen minutes, he seems to feel that something is different too.

He tilts his head toward the door behind him, not even taking a step closer.

"Hey, Unc?" I say out of the side of my mouth.

"It's about damn time, girl. Get out of here. I can handle tonight. Been doing it for years by myself. I can damn sure do it just fine." I can hear the grin underneath the gruffness, and I choose to not argue, even though helping Unc is what I'm here to do. I reach to my belt loop, unhooking the bar towel I keep there and setting it on the bar.

As I pass by Unc, he catches my arm and crooks a finger my way. I bend down and he lays a soft, dry kiss to my cheek before whispering in my ear, "Give 'im hell, Willow-girl. You're worth it." He smells like hops and chemicals, with a faint hint of after-shave he probably slapped on hours ago.

I smile, feeling a burn in the corner of my eyes. "Thanks, Unc. I'll see you tomorrow."

He winks. "Now git."

I don't delay any longer because that's exactly what I've been doing. Delaying the inevitable. I hope this doesn't go sideways, but as I cross the room to Bobby, his eyes watching me approach with possessive heat and unguarded hunger, I know something important. After three not-date dinners, four conversations, and not even a single kiss . . .

I am Bobby Tannen's girl.

CHAPTER 7

BOBBY

*T*oday sucked ass. And not in the sexy, fun, kiss that little pucker way. But in the muddy, messy, sweat dripping into your eyes, and back so sore you can barely stand up straight kind of way.

Welcome to farming, fucker. Same shit, different day.

Actually, it was literally shit today. We had to fertilize the new plot of land Brutal and I tilled up to expand Shay's planting operation. She's got some big plan for a bumper crop of lettuce that grows in thirty days and hopes to make jarred summer salads. It sounded like a fine idea until I'd realized it meant prepping for planting again. But we'd gotten it done before the sun went down, which is what mattered.

Right up until I walked in the house and Brody had started fanning his nose and squealing like a pig about how rank I was. I thought he was fucking with me until Allyson ran from Brutal's hello hug too. She never does that.

So my quick shower had turned into a scrub down because I sure as shit wasn't going to grab dinner with Willow smelling like actual shit. And now, I'm late.

Not that we have a set time for me to show up. Or that she's even given me a hint of encouragement to keep coming by to see her.

But she hasn't told me to stop, either. And that's an important distinction. So I keep on coming back.

For her.

I'm already an addict to the way she talks, her stories twining this way and that, the pink hue her cheeks take on when she's excited about something, and the quiet way she can make me feel ten feet tall and bulletproof with just a look. And I need my daily dose of her or I'll likely go mad with curiosity about what she's doing, thinking, feeling, and saying. I want it all, like little treasures of her day she doles out for me to gather up.

When the door creaks open, I find her easily. Standing behind the bar, her cheeks flush and her eyes widen when she looks over and sees me.

Is that happiness in those swirling gray mood-ring eyes? Or more?

My feet root to the floor, in awe of her the same way I am every time I see her. She reigns over this bar like a queen, though she might not know that. Hank has taken to sitting his ass on a stool more and more, letting Willow handle customers and do inventory. I never thought I'd see the day, but I'm damn glad. For him, for Willow, and for me.

I feel the tension in the air, and though my instincts are telling me to look for a threat, I can't take my eyes off her. Something's different, something has changed, and I absolutely hate not knowing what.

Did someone say something about me to her? I know my reputation's not the best, but I'll kill whoever told her some story about my reckless, youthful redneck days. Or has she decided to tell me to fuck off and leave her alone tonight? I've been so careful to not come on too strong, even though my heart has been demanding that I scoop her into my arms and get to know her from the inside out. Okay, maybe that part was my dick too.

Willow's bottom lip disappears behind her teeth for a split second as though she's nervous or thinking. I see it. She's mine and she finally knows it, the way I have for five long fucking days that feel like an eternity despite whatever the calendar says.

I nod toward the door, silently asking if she's ready for that tour, and to my shock and joy, she starts walking my way. She pauses when Hank grabs at her arm, and I swallow down the growl that threatens to escape. He's not stopping her, just telling her something and then she's walking to me again.

Mine. Mine. Mine.

My heart beats out a too-fast rhythm, and when her toes are nearly touching my boots, I ask quietly, "You ready for this?"

She looks up at me, sparks dancing in her eyes as her lips lift ever so slightly, like she's not sure how she got here. "I don't think so, but . . . yeah."

Slow as molasses, giving her time to stop me if she needs to, I cup her cheeks in my palms, finally feeling her skin beneath mine again, and bend down, letting my intentions be quite clear to her. Her tongue darts out to wet her lips and I know she's more ready than she thinks she is.

Soft as I can be, I take her lips, tasting and sipping at her breath, wanting to steal it into my lungs so that I have a part of her inside me. My tongue swipes along the seam of her mouth, requesting entry, and when she sighs, I fight my way in, devouring and claiming her right here in the middle of a Hank's Thursday two-dollar draft night. By the time I come up for breath, the whole town will know that she's mine and I'm hers. There's no doubt about that.

A flash blinds me even through my closed lids, and regretfully, I pull back to see who the fuck is interrupting my first kiss with Willow.

Olivia is grinning like a loon, fanning her flushed face with her phone held up. I shoot her a glare and turn back to Willow, but the moment is fading. She looks shell-shocked and blissed out from just a kiss and my pride swells up at that.

Oh, darling, if you thought that was something, just wait until I'm kissing you all over. "Let's go," I say, taking her hand in mine. My fingers wrap gently around hers, caressing her and making sure that this is real and not another figment of my imagination, which has been getting quite the workout after our dinners. Hell, I barely made it home one night and almost had to jack off on the side of the road in my truck. But I'd managed to wait . . . just barely. Mostly out of fear that Chief Gibson would catch me and never let me live that shit down.

I open the door for her, that same creak the door's always had meaning something else entirely now. It almost sounds like a song, like the start of something new.

Olivia calls out, "I'll text you that picture, Willow, though I don't think it'll be going on your blog." One glance back tells me that she's still looking at the picture on her phone. I'd like to see it too. Me and Willow, our first kiss.

Our last first kiss, if things go the way I'm thinking.

I lead her to my truck, opening the door and helping her climb inside. It's not too jacked up, not like Brody's truck, but it's high enough that it needs side rails to climb inside comfortably. I shut the door behind her with a finality, a signal to my overworked heart that it has what it's wanted for so long.

Her. Willow.

I damn near jog around the hood and climb into the driver's seat. The engine growls to life, and Willow flinches ever so slightly. I glance over to find her looking as jumpy as a cat on a hot tin roof.

"Hi," I say soothingly.

She pushes her hair behind her cute little ear and softly replies, "Hi."

"You good?"

Rookie mistake to give her an out, but I don't want her to regret this later. I get the feeling that if Willow backslides, there will be no two steps forward afterward. She'll go back into her shell, the one I've carefully chiseled away over the past few days, to make a little hidey-hole for myself inside her walls.

She licks her lips again, but this time, it's not an invitation. She's preparing herself, and I give her time to do so. "I just . . . I'm not sure . . . what you expect." She sighs like that was the hardest thing she's ever said.

Everything.

But that's not what I tell her. "Anything, Willow. I want to know you, spend time with you." Dropping my voice a little lower and quieter, I admit, "Kiss you again."

Even in the fading light in the cab of my truck, I can sense her blush. "Oh. Okay."

"Okay," I agree, my voice heavy with intention as I lean across the center console. I reach out to cup her cheek again as she leans forward. It feels like a victory, like she's giving in to this inferno between us . . . the one I've been trying to withstand without her. But now that she's in it with me, it feels like a warm caress that's gently melting the frost from my bones.

Our lips meet, tender as we explore each other. I breathe into her, and this time it's *her* sweet tongue demanding more. Growling, I take the kiss deeper, hotter, wilder, and to my surprise, she's right there with me. No holding back, no reserve . . . just free and passionate.

"Mmm." She moans as her hand works its way into the too-long hair at the nape of my neck.

"Fuck," I groan when I feel her give my hair a little tug. My dick lurches in my jeans, trying to get to her.

But it's way too soon for that.

No, it's not.

My dick tries to argue, but my brain wins. Actually, I think it's my heart that wins, because it's yelling at me, *don't fuck this up, asshole*!

Too soon, I pull back. She chases me for one more kiss, and I'm *this close* to giving in, but I stay still. "I promised you a tour. I keep my promises, Willow."

She sits back in her seat, another one of those blissed out smiles on her face that I want to keep there always. "Okay then, show me what you . . . I mean, Great Falls . . . has to offer."

Challenge accepted, woman. Challenge fucking accepted.

* * *

I LET Willow give me the directions to her place, even though I already know where she lives. The whole town knows where Hank's niece lives because she's the biggest news to happen to Great Falls in ages. Tapping on the steering wheel to practice a riff I've been playing with, I watch as she runs inside to grab her 'good camera', as she called it. She reappears a few minutes later, camera bag slung across her chest, wearing a fresh shirt and a new slick of lip gloss on her pale pink lips.

I see you getting gussied up for this. She wants this as much as I do. Well, maybe not that much . . . yet. But we're getting there.

Slow and steady, Tannen.

For all her sweetness and open-hearted conversation with the bar folks, Willow is skittish with her real self. She'd give you the shirt off her back, help you on the side of the road, or listen to you wax poetic about your problems, but share her truth? Not likely, and not easily.

But that's exactly why I want it. I want to earn it, straight from her lips, when she lets me inside her heart.

She climbs back in the truck, and I catch a whiff of something floral and light. She perfumed for me too. The parallel makes me smile. I showered so I didn't smell like manure for her, and she's spritzing on girly stuff so she doesn't smell like beer for me.

I drive us through town, giving the tour I promised. "In the middle of the town square is the courthouse. Judge Myson's been on that bench for longer than you and me together have been alive. He's old-school, believes in working off your debt to society and paying back your neighbors."

She catches something in my tone that clues her in. "Speaking from experience?"

I lift one shoulder casually, amused but not hiding anything. "Nothing serious. Me and Chief Gibson might've had a little chat with Myson in my younger days. Nothing that couldn't be solved with painting a fence or plowing a few fields, though. You?"

She laughs. "No. Probably the worst thing I've ever done was protest environmental toxins at a corporate headquarters or something."

"That sounds serious," I tell her honestly. "The environment a passion of yours? From your dad?"

She shrugs, sort of a yes-no all at once. "I was a kid. I was just along for the ride because holding a sign and marching around with Dad all day sounded like fun."

I can see that. Little Willow, blonde hair streaming wild behind her as she marches around yelling words too big for her little girl brain, but I have no doubt she was able to define each and every one of them better than Merriam-Webster.

"Hopefully, we can manage to find a little more fun than that,"

I say, pulling into the drive-through of a burger joint. "This won't be nearly as good as Ilene's cooking, but I figure you didn't get dinner yet. We can take it with us where we're going."

"Where's that?" she asks curiously.

"It's a surprise," I tease, expecting her to argue and demand to know where I'm taking her. But she just settles into the seat a little deeper, looking cozy and relaxed as can be.

I like that. A lot.

People always have expectations and assumptions about me. That I'm scary because of my last name, that I'm soft because of my music, that I'm down to fuck because of my face. None of that is totally true. Yeah, I can scrap, had to in order to survive with my brothers and our old issues with the Bennetts. Don't mean I look to start fights. Yeah, I have a soft side, but it's not all I am. And yes, I like to fuck, but I'm not a manwhore. I ain't a monk, either. I'm more complex than all of that shit.

But Willow seems to be taking me as I come, the same way she does everything—people at the bar, every day, and whatever brought her to Great Falls. I'm definitely curious about that, but she hasn't said a word so I'm leaving that question alone for now.

I order us a two-pack of burgers, fries, and chocolate milk-shakes, then glance over for her approval. We're good. I pay at the window, noting that Esme is gawking into the truck as she hands over the food. The grapevine will be lit up like a Christmas tree before we get halfway through town as Esme makes sure that everyone knows she's the one who spotted Bobby Tannen and Willow Parker grabbing a bite of dinner on their way to 'only God knows where' to do 'only God knows what'.

Too bad she's too late since everyone at Hank's already knows.

Willow takes the food from me, and I set the shakes in the cup holders before setting off for our tour.

"Best barbecue in town," I say, pointing at a half-fallen down shack on the side of the road. "Doctor's office, dentist, hair salon," I add, pointing at each in the strip center of offices.

"Just one of each in the whole town?" Willow asks, craning her neck to look back.

"Pretty much. I mean, we have more doctors, I guess, at the hospital. Or Doc Jones for animals. There's a barber shop for the guys too, and a few ladies who make house calls for hair, but they're more the 'set and curl' type." Willow smooths the short hair at the nape of her neck. "And there's stuff like that at the resort. It's probably different from what you're used to, but we've got everything we need out here."

She has the good grace to cringe. "Sorry, I didn't mean to seem critical. It's just different. But I think I like it. It's simple and easy. The whole town feels like that. Like a warm hug from a friend you never knew you needed."

"Pretty imagery. Mind if I write that down?" I ask. When she smiles, I pull my phone out and hit *Record* on my voice notes, which is my version of 'writing it.' I hold it out to Willow and she leans in to repeat herself.

"Like a warm hug from a friend you never knew you needed." She laughs a little at the awkwardness of talking into my phone, and I make sure to get that too. I toss the phone into the console and we roar to the outskirts of town.

"You'd be able to get some great shots downtown during the day of the hustle and bustle of folks visiting and shopping on the square. There's a park on the east side where ducks and geese congregate. But if you want animal shots, I've got a whole zoo's worth at home you're welcome to photograph. Horses, cows, pigs, goats, dogs, a barn cat, and a bunch of asshole guys who'd probably smile pretty for you. Well, except for Mark. He don't smile much."

"That's the oldest Bennett brother, right? The one in charge of everything and married to Katelyn?" she says. We've talked through a lot of this already, but I like that she remembers the details.

I nod. "Yeah. If you wanted some nature shots, we've got fields and trees and crops that'd be pretty too." I'm trying to give her as many things as I can, hoping she'll want to photograph them all and that it'll take a long, long time to do so. Time she can spend at my side and I can spend soaking her in.

"We'll see. I usually take pictures of whatever I'm doing that day, nothing special, nothing particularly planned out, but I like to take the opportunity to explore and see what I can experience and share."

I can feel her eyes on me, tracing over my profile as I keep my eyes on the road. "You can take a picture of me if you want to." I'm half-joking and half-serious, but I'm still surprised when she dives for the floorboard and comes back up with her good camera. Richard was right, it's nearly as big as she is, especially with the lens that she's got on it. She does a quick change, carefully setting the lens back into the bag and coming out with another, smaller one, which she attaches easily.

"Tell me about you," she orders gently, already snapping away.

I chuckle, self-conscious. "I don't know what to say. I'm just me—a farmer, a singer. Not much to tell."

Click. Click.

"That's a bold-faced lie, and you know it, Bobby. Don't go getting shy on me. I like when people talk as I'm taking pictures because then I catch every expression. Tell me . . . about when you were a kid. What was little Bobby's big dream?"

She never goes for the obvious question, that's for sure.

"That's easy. To be a famous country musician one day. I thought I was going to get out of this small town, never have to shovel shit a day of my life, and would fill stadiums with people chanting my name." I smile at the ease with which that dream comes roaring back to life. "Younger me thought this town was basically a prison. I guess all small-town kids think that to some degree, drawn to the excitement of the flashing lights of the big city. Probably the same way city kids think life out in the country is slow and easy." I throw her a knowing sideways glance.

Click.

"And now?" she says.

I can't see her face, not really. She's hidden behind the camera, and I'm trying hard to keep my eyes on the road so I can get us safely to Lookout Point. But there's a deeper meaning to what should be a light question. Surprisingly, with my attention half on driving and half on her, the words spill out.

"Now, I see why people stay here. It's not because they're trapped. It's because it's . . . home. Shay is always leaving—she and Luke travel a lot for his work with horses, and she's so excited to go every time. No matter where they're headed." I shake my head a little, chuckling. "She'd be excited about the armpit of New Jersey during a heat wave. That's just how she is, wants to see it all, do it all. But when they get back, I can tell they're exhausted. A few days at home, working their asses off in the sunshine and fresh air, and they're back to being right again. It's different, but it's good. And I've made my peace with it. I'll work the land I grew up on as long as Mark'll let me, sing at Hank's as long as he'll let me, and make my life right where God stuck me twenty-eight years ago." I shrug, a little embarrassed at how unambitious I sound. I might be in a rut, but it's a good one, with a long, steady, straight line that gets me where I'm going—to a life well-lived and hard-worked day by day.

"And a bar full of folks chanting your name is enough, even though it's not a stadium and you smell like shit at the end of every day?" she prompts, clicking again.

A cold sliver of ice slices through my heart, knowing that's not entirely true. But sometimes, what you get has to be enough. Not every singer gets the big deal. Not every farmer owns his land. But I take the opportunity she's giving me and laugh. "I don't smell like shit every day. Just on fertilizer days, and I showered." I sniff my pit obnoxiously, but really, I'm making sure that long shower did its job.

She laughs, and the seriousness is left at mile marker ninety-one.

A moment later, I turn off the main road onto a dirt road that starts climbing quickly. "Is this the part where you take me out to the middle of nowhere to kill me and bury my body? If so, tell my mom I love her for me, 'kay?" she says dramatically, ending with a smile.

"If I were taking you to the middle of nowhere to kill you, I wouldn't have done it in front of a whole bar full of people. Plus, I own pigs. I'd just feed you to them. They can pick a body clean in a few days. Don't ask me why I know that," I deadpan.

She looks over at me, grinning and not scared in the least. At least she gets my humor. That's a major point in the win column. "Did you know that there was a guy who almost got away with murder because he killed a dog?"

I hiss. "What the fuck?"

She pats my arm. "Wait, it's bad but surprisingly smart. And bad." I lose track of what she was saying after feeling her palm on my skin. She continues, "So, this guy killed someone . . . I don't remember the circumstances, though. Accident? On purpose?" She waves her hand. "Doesn't matter. But he buried the body way down deep, then halfway back up to the surface, he buried a dead dog. The police dog sniffed around and they dug up the grave. So the police found the dog and thought the police dog had gotten confused. Killer almost got away with it too, except the police dog kept whining then jumped in the grave, pawing at the ground, so they dug a little deeper. And boom . . . dead body. Or well, another one, I guess."

"Jesus, that's awful. Why do you know that?" I ask.

"True crime shows on late-night TV. Sad story, but I liked that the police dog outsmarted the criminal." She seems equally horrified and vindicated.

"I'm surprised you watch that shit," I say honestly. She seems like she'd watch Hallmark movies or romantic comedies, something light and fluffy like cute kitten shows.

"I work late hours and there's nothing on but *Unsolved Mysteries* and infomercials at three in the morning. Netflix is a lifesaver, but when I was saving up for my last lens, I canceled it to save money."

Frugal. Willing to sacrifice.

I store the informational tidbits away in my mental Rolodex of Willow Parker facts.

We break through the last few overhanging branches and into a clearing. "We're here."

There's the complete blackness of the night surrounding us, broken only by a curved slice of moon too high in the sky to offer any real light. "Where's here?" Willow asks, looking through the front window and then her side window.

"Lookout Point. Hang on," I tell her. I pull a U-turn, backing up carefully. In the glow of the reverse camera, I can see the questioning look on Willow's face. "Trust me. Close your eyes. It'll be worth it."

To my surprise and delight, she does, though she warns, "Just a reminder . . . a whole bar full of people, including Unc, saw you take me out of Hank's. You'll be the first suspect."

I chuckle and turn off the engine. "Stay there, keep 'em closed." I get out and run around to her side, opening her door. I help her down, careful to not get too close . . . yet. Slowly, I walk her toward the back of the truck. "Stand right where you are for a second. Lemme lower the tailgate."

Down it goes with a slight thud, and I steer Willow in front of it. "Okay, I'm gonna pick you up and set you on the tailgate. Still got your eyes closed?"

They are. I can see how she's pinching them shut against the desire to open them and see what's around her.

I circle my hands around her waist and lift. She naturally jumps a tiny bit and I set her on the tailgate. She leans left a little and I steady her with strong hands. "Ohh!" she exclaims, then laughs at her overcorrection.

"Okay, one last thing . . . don't move and don't peek." I run back to her side of the truck and grab her camera. I'm no pro, not even an amateur, but I can press a button. Hopefully, that's enough. Standing beside her again, I aim the lens at her.

"On the count of three, I want you to open your eyes and see Great Falls. One, two, three . . ."

Click. Click. Click. Click.

I have no idea what I'm doing, so as she opens her eyes, gasps, and covers her open mouth with her hands, I just keep pushing the button. She looks from the view before us, inky blackness dotted with white lights and the surrounding mountains, to me. She's looking through the lens into my eyes, I swear it.

Click. Click.

"It's beautiful," Willow whispers, even though it's just the two of us.

"Gorgeous," I answer, not talking about the city view but about her.

Her eyes meet mine, and I lower the camera. The yawning space between us disappears, though I stay rooted where I am, and the invisible thread between us pulls tight, humming with possibility.

"Do you feel this? Am I crazy?" One quick, audible swallow,

and she adds, "This is crazy. Never mind. Pretend I didn't say that."

I have zero intention of doing so.

I carefully set the camera down, knowing it's her baby as much as my guitar is mine. The mere fact that she let me hold it and didn't freak out is more than I could say about Betty. Nobody touches her. Nobody but me.

I step between Willow's knees, lightly laying my palms on her bare thighs. Looking her directly in the eye, I say with no reservation, "I saw you across the room a week ago and wanted to know, one, who the hell was behind Hank's bar, and two, why the hell you weren't already in my arms. I've been going crazy inside thinking it was just me. So no, I don't think you're crazy. Or if you are, I am too. Yeah, I feel it, Willow."

I take her hand in mine and lay her palm on my chest, letting her feel the way my heart is racing. Slow and steady has left the building. Well, we're outside, so there is no building, but the point's the same. I'm going whole-hog, full-steam ahead, and praying she doesn't slam shut the door she cracked open.

"Oh." Her eyes are locked on our layered hands on my chest, but the edge of a smile lifts her lips.

I press a kiss to her forehead, not wanting to push too far, too fast. "Take a few shots of the city lights while I get our picnic set up, 'kay?"

She nods silently, and I give her a little space to get comfortable with where we are now. I had a little hidey-hole carved out, but now I'm hauling in one of those big, fluffy La-Z-Boy recliners and making myself right at home in her heart.

In the cab of the truck, I send a quick text to Brody.

Don't wait up.

He wouldn't, but it's only polite to let your roomie know when you're not coming home. Besides, I know Brody and Rix would love to have the house to themselves for the night. It's awkward when we both still live in our family home, though Brody did finally move into the main bedroom.

Then I shoot one to Brutal.

You're on your own in the morning.

Brody replies first with his usual response . . . a middle finger emoji which translates to everything from 'okay' to 'fuck you' to 'I love you, bro'. Brutal texts back too.

About damn time. Can't wait to meet her. She like chicken?

The seemingly nonsensical question is anything but. It's a sort of code in the Bennett family and now ours. If you pass the family litmus test, Mama Louise gives her approval by showing you how to make her famous fried chicken. If you fail, no chicken cooking lessons for you.

I send Brutal a thumbs-up because I think Willow is the most chicken-frying worthy woman I've ever met, then grab the bag of food and the shakes. Juggling them, I drop them onto the tailgate beside Willow and climb up.

"Shakes are melted enough to be drinkable now, but we need to dig in or the fries are gonna be cold and gross."

She sets her camera down to take the cardboard sleeve of fries I'm holding out. She munches on a few, and I do the same, comfortably silent for a moment as we stuff our faces.

"What about you? What was Willow Parker's big dream when she was a little girl?" I ask, returning to our earlier conversation.

She disappears inside herself for a moment, her head tilted as she thinks. "I don't know that I ever really had a dream, per se. Do you believe in destiny?"

I chew thoughtfully and nod. "Yeah, I guess. I mean, I think we've all got free will to do right or fuck up, but I'd like to think there's some bigger plan somehow. You?"

"Growing up, Mom and Dad were all about experiences. That's what they encouraged Oakley and me to chase. It was never 'make the winning goal'. It was more about 'being a part of a team' or 'learning something new' and 'how can I help this cause or solve that problem?' So I never really thought that one day, I want to be an astronaut or a teacher or a photographer like most kids. My dreams were to learn a language, visit the country, and be fluent enough to get around on my own. Things like that."

"Damn. That makes my bright lights big city dream sound shallow as hell," I say with a laugh. "And boring as fuck."

Willow bumps me with her shoulder. "No, it doesn't. A dream can't be wrong or right. It just is."

Still not convinced, I ask, "Did you get to use whatever language you learned?"

"*Comme ci, comme ca,*" she says, which sounds like gibberish to me, but she seems pleased with herself as she explains. "So-so in French. I have the absolute basics of greetings, food, and asking for the bathroom in French, Spanish, and Italian because I went on a work trip with Mom one summer to visit an artist friend of hers. I knew more back then and thought I was so fancy, but I lost it because I never had a reason to use it after that."

Suddenly self-conscious, I confess, "Shit, I barely speak English."

"Whatever," she says with a slight eye roll. "You sing it in a way that resonates with people, makes them feel something deep and powerful, and that's a universal language."

"Thank you," I whisper huskily. Her single compliment means more than the truckloads of ones I've gotten in the past. Granted, those so-called fans were half-drunk and-or trying to get in my pants, but that's beside the point. It's because these kind words are from Willow that they mean so much.

"Did I see your guitar in the backseat?"

She's being generous in calling the tiny bench a backseat. The only person who can fit back there is Cooper, Brutal's stepson, and with another of his summer growth spurts, even he won't be able to fit. But Betty does.

"Yeah."

"Will you play while I take some pictures? Not for the blog but just for me."

"Of course. Anytime." I absolutely mean it. For her, I'd play concerts twenty-four, seven until my fingers bled and still keep going if she wanted me to.

I get Betty and climb back up on the tailgate, letting the curved wood rest against my thigh the way I have so many times before. I pluck at the strings mindlessly, watching Willow move around with her camera. She's doing something to the settings, turning a dial and checking, then turning it again.

Click. Click. Click.

I start to softly sing an old favorite, *The Man in Love with You* by George Strait. It's not one of his biggest hits and doesn't even suit my deeper, grittier voice, but Mom used to play it and she and Dad would dance around the kitchen to its slow beat so it seems like sharing that is a good omen with Willow too.

I get lost in the music but never lose track of Willow. She's a woman on a mission, and though I'm not sure what she's capturing through that lens of hers, she seems pleased with whatever she sees. One song turns into two, then I don't even know how many. But I play on, singing to her but also somehow becoming a part of what she's doing every time she glances over and gives me one of those soft smiles.

A knot in my belly is loosening by the minute, and I want to stay here in this moment, just like this, forever. A melancholy melody plays through my mind, and I play it on a loop, forgetting all the covers I know in favor of teasing out what this new tune might be. One of hope lost but found in the most unexpected of ways, when it'd seemed least possible.

"That's pretty," Willow says. The first time we've spoken in probably an hour, but it hasn't been uncomfortable at all. To the contrary, it's been perfect, the two of us lost in our passions but together the whole time. It's like a beautiful weaving of interests, of attraction, of perspectives merging through two vastly different mediums. "What is it?"

"I don't know yet. It just came to me, so I'm still playing around with it." I pluck out the melody again and Willow hums along with the notes.

"How about one of those strummed, vibrato notes after that to lead in to the next bit?"

I stare at her in surprise. "You know music?"

She laughs. "Obviously not, or I'd know what that kind of note is actually called, but I can hear what you're doing and I like it. It's pulling me in, right on the edge of falling, and a bigger, longer note will feel like crashing through the surface to the rest of the song."

She's fucking stunning—her mind, her heart, and that smile— as she uncertainly asks if I get what she's saying.

Instead of answering in words, I play the melody over and add in a long vibrato note, letting the deep tone resonate before diving back into the tune again as I start to hum. She nods and turns back to her camera.

The repetitive click becomes my inspiration as the song takes shape. Notes, feelings, phrases stacking together into something greater than the sum of its parts.

> "It gets drowned in a rainstorm,
> Buried in the mud,
> Lost in my daily hustle,
> And slowly stripped from my blood.
> But your kiss sparked something, baby,
> The burning in your eyes,
> My hopes and dreams reignite,
> Don't tell me it's all lies.

I FUMBLE my way through a rough chord progression, only coming up to breathe, and find Willow sitting next to me, watching closely and swaying slightly to the tune. "Oh, shit, sorry. I sorta got lost . . ."

She smiles. "I'm glad. It's beautiful, and I bet I'll hear it on the radio one day when you're a big star." From most folks, I'd think they were giving me a hard time, but when Willow says it, it's like she's putting it on the wind to send it to the Sisters of Fate, putting the wish into the very fabric of my future. It's never going to happen, but her faith that it could, that I'm good enough, is a blessing I'll take gladly and thankfully.

"Thank you. Sun'll be up in a few minutes," I say, lifting my head toward the horizon that's fading from indigo to lavender. "You want to photograph it?"

Those mood-ring eyes swirl, and I wonder what's going through that brilliant mind of hers. A second later, she stops my guessing and tells me flat out. "No, I think I'd rather sit here with you and just experience it fully. I think I'll remember this sunrise without the photograph."

It's important. I can feel it in my bones. She's choosing presence in the now over an opportunity to look back in the future.

I put Betty back in her case and set it aside in the truck bed. Turning to Willow, I open my arm in invitation and she scoots closer to me, her head going to my chest as I lean back against the cab of the truck. Silent as can be, we watch the sun come up together, starting a new day with pinks and oranges that set the sky on fire.

Below us, the quiet lights of overnight Great Falls turn to activity as trucks start to appear on the roads and people walk along the sidewalks to get to work.

"You were right, you know . . ." Willow says, her voice trailing off.

"I usually am, but what was I right about this time?" I tease.

I feel her cheek puff up against my chest from her smile at my cocky joke. "You're a great tour guide."

Still teasing, I squeeze her a little tighter. "Don't you wish you'd said yes sooner then?"

She shakes her head. "No, I think I'm glad you kept coming back for dinner and we got to talk first. It made this more . . . *more*."

I know exactly what she means. I won't say I've never been to Lookout Point, which is more commonly called Make-out Point by the local teenagers, but with the time to get to know Willow and see beneath the pretty exterior and beyond the magnetism I feel, tonight has been something truly different.

Even if it was just greasy burgers, cold fries, and another sunrise, because it was with her, it felt like the first time. She made it special.

CHAPTER 8

WILLOW

"*T*ell me everything. And don't you leave one single thing out or so help me, I will pull the truth out of you with interrogation techniques only Chief Gibson is allowed to use," Olivia threatens me the next day.

I should be tired. I only slept for a few hours before coming in for the Friday lunch rush, but I'm buzzing with pent-up energy. Because I know Bobby's coming in for dinner again tonight.

"I told you. He was a perfect gentleman. We had dinner—"

"At Lookout Point," Olivia says, interrupting me. She's already heard this story three times, but I think she's hoping that, in repetition, I'll let her in on some new secret. Maybe she's been paying attention to Chief Gibson? Or bingeing late-night crime documentaries like me?

"And watched the sunrise. He played his guitar and sang, and I took pictures. You want to see those again too?"

I took hundreds of pictures last night, playing with my settings to get the lighting just right to capture the stars, the town, the beauty. And Olivia has seen all those pictures, along with the select ones I posted to my blog last night and this morning.

I didn't show her the ones I took of Bobby when he started really getting into his songwriting, though. It'd been like seeing a private side of him, and I'd felt like a voyeur but hadn't been able to turn away from the gut-wrenching process he went through to get the song to come to life. He played the same few chords at least a hundred times, humming under his breath and finally getting louder as he felt it improve bit by bit. Eventually, the hums had become words, his every thought and emotion laid bare right in front of me with no filter or façade. It'd been beautiful to witness, a true gift, and those pictures are private. They're not inappropriate, there's no skin showing or anything like that, but Bobby's heart is blatantly and vulnerably wide open in each and every shot.

Olivia sighs, disappointment written in the roll of her eyes. "No, unless there's some naughty pictures mixed in there that you forgot to show me?" she asks hopefully, batting her lashes at me with her hands clasped below her chin.

I glare at her. "No naked pictures. But after Lookout Point, he drove me home, walked me to my door, and kissed me good night. Or well, good morning because it was after sunrise?" I shake my head, unworried. "He kissed me goodbye, how about that? And he said he'd see me tonight for dinner, like usual."

"You lucky bitch!" Olivia exclaims. I shush her when a family of four glares over at her language, but she's on a roll. "I am so excited for you. And for me."

"You?" I ask, my brow furrowing.

"Girl, I got a front-row seat to the one and only Bobby Tannen falling head over heels for you and your getting swept off your feet so fast you didn't know what hit you. Hell yeah, for me. This is exciting stuff!" The mom at that table lifts her hand and Olivia waves back to let her know she's coming. "I want to hear the kiss part again after I get this lady another glass of tea." Lowering her voice, she whispers, "Can you say die-ah-beet-us? I mean, I could've given her a straw and pitcher if I'd known she was gonna go through five glasses before her burger is even ready."

Quick as can be, Olivia is off, getting the lady a glass of tea with a smile that belies the smack she was just talking before checking on her other tables too. Truthfully, I'm not in a hurry for her to get back and needle me into repeating the kiss story again.

I kept it short and sweet and honest. Bobby walked me up to the porch of my little cabin and pushed my hair behind my ear.

He'd gotten in close, pressing me against the front door. Sandwiched between him and the door, I'd felt just how much he wanted me. Let's just say it was . . . a lot. Like more than I've ever had in so many ways type of a lot. Then he'd cupped my face like he had at the bar and bent down to kiss me as I lifted up to my toes.

That was what I told Olivia, but the real truth was that Bobby had knocked my socks off with that kiss. It'd been sweet and sensual, passionate and powerful. He took his time, his kiss a drawled-out, unhurried expression of need and desire. And if I'd been a different sort of girl, I probably would've done something slick like open the door behind me and pull him in with me. But I hadn't. If I'd done that, I probably would've fallen inside and busted my ass on the wood floor, and Bobby would've laughed before helping me up.

He would kiss my boo-boos better, I bet.

I groan at the errant thought. I'm not innocent by any stretch, but I get the feeling that what I consider sex and what Bobby Tannen considers sex are two completely different things. And like my Mom always told me, I need to *experience* things with reckless abandon. I think Bobby Tannen is one of those things for sure.

I only have time to cut one lemon before Olivia is back. She hops up on a stool in front of me and muses, "Okay, where were we?" Her palms slam on the bar. "Duh, the kiss. Spill it, girl. Every dirty, filthy, detail."

I can feel my cheeks warm and renew my efforts at cutting lemons and not my fingers. "I told you already. He was a perfect gentleman . . ." —Olivia's eyebrows lift high in disbelief— "who kissed the hell out of me."

"I knew it," she snaps gleefully. "Are you sure he wasn't leaving this morning after a night of wild sex and you're just making up the Lookout Point all-nighter?"

My face blanches, which is way worse than the pink of embarrassment. "No! And hush!" I really don't need that getting out because according to Bobby, the grapevine of Great Falls is thick and wide and moves faster than the speed of light.

Olivia laughs at my reaction. "Chill. I'm just kidding. Trust me, everyone knows he didn't spend the night because they all heard his truck rumbling down the street and were peering through their blinds like Gladys Kravitz so they'd be the one in the know. Fair to say, that kiss had an audience. Forewarned is forearmed, so know that when you do have a certain male companion overnight, everyone will know in approximately point-oh-two seconds and will be judging how you're walking the next day."

I pray she's exaggerating and at the same time fear that she's not. At all.

The door creaks, and Olivia is up and at 'em again, seating the newcomers and leaving me to my lemons and swirling thoughts.

Why is this such a big deal to everyone?

Which leads into something even more important, *why is this such a big deal to Bobby?*

And most important of all, *why does this feel so deep to me?*

Last night, in the black blanket of the night that made it feel as though it was only the two of us, this thing between Bobby and me felt so big and powerful, which made it seem perfectly reasonable and full of possibilities. By the light of day, alone with my thoughts, I have to think I was imagining that or overreacting or something. People don't fall that hard, that fast. Do they?

Maybe . . . sometimes, they do, a voice whispers hopefully in my head. Or maybe in my heart. I'm not sure since they sound pretty similar to me.

For now, I choose to ignore the questions playing on a loop in my mind and also choose to pretend that no one is looking at me and whispering. Instead, I help the folks at the bar, pull beers and drinks for Olivia, and get set up for tonight's weekend rush.

"This seat taken?" a voice asks a bit later, and I look up to see Unc's friend, Doc Jones, smiling at me.

"It is now," I reply, pushing a menu his way. "What's your pleasure, Doc?"

He waves off the menu. "Whatever Ilene's cooking today is fine by me. And a Coke, please."

I place his order and set an already sweating glass in front of him. He takes a healthy drink and sighs gratefully. "Needed that sugar. Been up since before dawn helping a bobcat that got stuck in a trap. Damn things shouldn't be out like that, anyway . . . the traps, not the bobcats, obviously. We're in their world, you know? But we can't have 'em eating up the livestock either. Rock, hard place." He shrugs one bony shoulder.

I nod, not sure what to say because wildlife rescue is woefully out of my area of expertise. "You help the bobcat?"

"Of course I did!" he says with a touch of pride. "His leg's a bit messed up, but it'll heal. Took him to a rescue a few towns over. Just getting back, and figured I had time to eat before anyone else started looking for me."

He holds one gnarled finger to his lips, telling me *shh* as though I never saw him here. I smile agreeably and he nods his appreciation.

He's halfway through his pan-fried pork chop when he says, "I'm glad you came. He needs you, even if he's too much of an ass to admit it."

He's talking about Unc, no doubt.

"Glad to be here and helping." It's the truth. Great Falls now seems like a step in the right direction, and the morning view of the mountain is one of my favorites as I sip at my coffee. Okay, so it's not 'morning' exactly, since it's usually creeping up on noon, but it's my morning with the hours I keep.

"You got plans on how long you're staying? I hear that might be changing." One of his eyebrows climbs questioningly.

I ignore his dig for intel on Bobby and me and focus on Unc. "However long Unc will let me stay, I'm here."

Doc's eyes narrow. "He's going to try to run you off, you know that, right? And that'll be when he needs you the most. Don't let him, 'kay?"

I consider that carefully, weighing my words. "What makes you say he'll need me more than I need him?"

Everyone who's asked has gotten the same answer out of me —that I wanted to get away from the city, needed a change. There's no reason anyone should think or suspect that I'm here for any other reason, but Doc Jones sounds like he's thinking something else entirely. Like he knows I didn't show up here in Great Falls randomly looking for a change of scenery but that I was sent here by Mom. For Unc.

"He's needed someone for a long time, Willow. Well before

now, but he's old and grumpy like me. Old fellas like us don't much like figuring out that we can't do what we once could. Hurts our fragile egos." He smirks as he talks about his ego, like the word alone is funny.

"Your ego is probably the only thing fragile about you. And Unc's the same. Tough as shoe leather down to the core," I tell him, hoping the compliment eases over the truth of Unc's fragility. Especially given that he's not here.

He's usually the first one in and the last one out, but he called at noon and asked if I'd be okay on my own, saying he had some 'shit to do'. He'd been sketchy when I asked what he was doing, and I suspect it includes a whole lot of nothing. But I keep that quiet, not telling Doc because I would never throw Unc under the bus, even with his friends. I'll cover for him, always.

Doc nods, adding sagely, "We'd like to think so. We'd like for everyone else to think so even more." He finishes up his pork chop and sips at the last of his drink before flagging me down again between rounds of helping Olivia. "Will you see if Ilene will make me a plate of scrambled eggs and toast to go? Or something bland like that? Think I'll run by the house and see if I can get that stubborn mule to eat something."

He's not talking about a donkey and we both know it.

He's going to check on Unc, which means he knows something's up. Actually, looking at the 'nothing to see here, move along' blank stare on Doc's face, I can see why he's good at poker. He's got a great bluff. But I read him loud and clear, as he intends for me to.

He doesn't suspect, he *knows* something is up, especially with Unc not being here, and he's following up with his friend. Hopefully, Unc will take the support from Doc better than from me, though he's leaving his baby in my capable hands today and I doubt he'll be in tonight. So we're essentially babysitting for a weekend night too, a major trust move on Unc's part. Or desperation. One of those. But I'm choosing the positive . . . that he trusts me, Olivia, Ilene, and Daniel to take good care of the bar.

"I'm sure Ilene won't mind a bit," I answer, leaving the rest for later examination. "I probably won't have a chance to check on that mule until tomorrow morning, so thank you for going by."

Doc nods, and dismissed, I go back to get him a full box of goodies for Unc, hoping he'll eat something.

* * *

"THREE JDs AND COKE, two Girly Beers, and one draft Miller Lite. Got it," I tell Olivia, and though she looks like she's not listening, her nose buried in the tickets she's flipping through, she nods affirmatively.

"Lemme run this to table twenty, and I'll be back for them," she says, and she's off. I have no idea how she can work this whole floor alone, but she does. I've worked at bars half this size that would have three waitstaff running around like chickens with their heads cut off. But Olivia is cool as a cucumber and everybody's happy. Maybe it's the slower pace and the friendlier vibe in town, or maybe she's that good, or some combination of the two, but it makes working the bar with her a pleasure.

I pull her drinks, setting them on the end of the wooden top for her to grab, and turn back to check my own spaces at the bar. Everyone's drinks are full and they're talking among themselves. Not even Richard is here tonight, and I wonder if he's at Unc's too. Maybe Doc pulled the lunch shift and Richard took the dinner one? Since I'm not sure, I'll go by early in the morning, maybe take Unc some of those doughnuts Bobby told me about and see if some sugary, greasy goodness tempts him to eat.

I'm unloading my third run of the dishwasher when I sense him. My smile is already spreading on my face when I look up to find Bobby leaning over the bar. I have less than a heartbeat to react before he grabs me around the back of my neck and pulls me toward him for a proper hello.

His kiss is a mint-flavored claiming of my mouth that leaves no corner unexplored or possessed. I feel more than hear him hum, "Mmm." With two quick smacks that promise much more, he pulls back, and I fall back to my heels, only now realizing that I'd lifted to my toes to reach him too. "Missed you today."

His tone is heavy, but even so, I think he's kidding. I mean, I know what he said last night and this morning, but it's seriously been maybe ten hours and he's been working, same as me. I've thought of nothing else all day, but he probably hasn't given me a thought until he was on his way here. But that's okay, he's here now and quite obviously happy to see me. His eyes scan me from head to toe, seemingly in awe of what he sees. I don't understand why—I'm just me—but the intensity in the depths of his eyes, the relief at merely seeing me again, is near palpable.

From behind him, a deep voice barks out a laugh. "That's putting it mildly. Dumb fuck wouldn't shut up all day. Willow-this and Willow-that. If he hadn't been talking about you all damn week, I would've thought he'd taken up with a tree."

Bobby takes the teasing good-naturedly, to my surprise, throwing up a middle finger behind him to whoever spoke but grinning as he does so. He explains, "I've been holding 'em back with promises of introducing you when you were ready. Well, ready or not, here they come."

He steps to the side, and I realize that the group of folks behind him aren't the latest rush for the bar to grab a round of beers but Bobby's *entire* family. The extended one. I can tell who is whom from listening to his stories.

His oldest brother, Brody, dark and broody, and Rix, short and savage and currently picking what looks to be grease from beneath her nails. I hand her a napkin, which she takes with a dip of her chin.

Brutal, the teaser who is, to put it nicely, scary as hell and as tall as a tree. Not just any old tree, either, but one of those Christmas trees you think looks grand until you get it in the house and the top bends sideways because it's smooshed up against the ceiling. That's Brutal. Even with several feet between him and the ceiling, he just feels . . . big. Next to him is a blonde wearing white frayed-hem shorts, a blingy tank top, and a kind smile. That'd be his wife, Allyson.

Another lighter version of Brody, grumpy and seemingly put out at being out, so that'd be . . . Mark Bennett. He's got his arm locked around Katelyn, a curvy blonde whose eyes haven't left his. They seem to be having some sort of silent conversation that even from here feels private.

A blonde guy wearing a big belt buckle and holding hands with a pretty brunette, who's eyeing me curiously. That'd be

James and Sophie Bennett. She works for Doc Jones, and he speaks highly of her intelligence and work ethic.

And last but not least, a younger-looking woman with honey brown hair, who is currently bouncing on her boot-covered toes and being held back by another blonde guy. Luke and Shayanne Bennett, A.K.A. Bobby's sister.

"Let me at her. I'm a hugger, it's who I am!"

"Shay, she's working. And she doesn't even know you. Hugging could be construed as assault," Bobby warns.

"Pshaw," she argues, as if that's an actual argument. I get the feeling that in her eyes, it is. And that it usually works and she gets her way. But I already like that she's a hugger, even if she's on the other side of the bar.

"Hi," I say, waving awkwardly. "I'm Willow."

Smiling faces greet me, and almost in tune, they answer, "We know." Brutal adds, "Fuck, do I. Nonstop, I tell you. Non-fucking-stop."

Allyson lays a hand on his forearm, and he looks to her and shrugs. "What? It's the truth."

Bobby isn't as nice and backhands his brother's arm with a smack. "Shut up, man. Did I go around telling Allyson when you were all boohooing over her and whining about how you couldn't live without her? No, I did not. So don't fuck this up for me or I'll never babysit Cooper again and you'll be forced to sneak in quickies while he's watching a twenty-minute cartoon. God knows I love the kid, but he's got the attention span of a gnat, so twenty is pushing it. Maybe . . . eight at most."

Brutal glowers. "One, low blow, man. Not cool. Twenty minutes is not enough time, ever. Two, you didn't tell Allyson all that crap because you were pissed at her and pulling out the silent treatment like a pouting toddler throwing tantrums, so payback's a bitch."

I'm watching the exchange like a live-action play right in front of my face. I don't know what Brutal's talking about, not having heard that story, but Bobby shrugs. "Fair enough. But leave Willow out of it like I left Allyson out. You can give me all the shit you want, though."

Seeming to have reached some agreement, they shake hands, though I have zero idea what just happened.

Bobby turns back to me. "I promised them I'd buy the first round, but I didn't promise they'd get to pick. Did I see you making Girly Beer when I came in?" He gives me that cocky smirk that says we're in on this together.

I return the grin, leaning on the bar and casually wiping at a nonexistent spot. "You did see some Girly Beer. You thinking on the rocks or frozen?"

"Oh, frozen. The only thing better than seeing these assholes drinking pink drinks is knowing they can't chug them without getting a brain freeze."

"Pink?" a deep voice says. I'm not sure who because I'm caught in Bobby's dark eyes, loving the way he's lighter and sillier with his family around him. Silly is not a word I thought I'd ever use to describe Bobby Tannen, but there you go.

"Ooh, I'm in," Allyson says.

"Table," Mark says and moves off toward a freshly empty booth. Everyone follows him, though he didn't order, or even ask, them to.

Bobby hangs back with me, draped on the bar like he couldn't be more comfortable if he were in his own living room.

"We're a lot, I know. But it's fine. They just wanted to meet you. I promise we'll drink and eat and dance, and it'll all be fine. See you when it slows down. I'll be the guy over there" —he points the direction his family went then to his eyes with two fingers— "watching you like a creeper." He winks after he says it, but I think his eyes will be on me all night. Pretty sure mine are going to be drifting his way too, then to the clock, counting down until two o'clock when I can be with him again.

I don't realize until he's walking off that maybe he was telling me that it'll be fine that his family is all here, given their rather wild reputations and all. Or maybe that it's fine that they're all here . . . for me.

CHAPTER 9

BOBBY

I mosey over to sit with my family, taking one of the chairs they've crowded around the empty edge of the largest booth in the place. We're a big bunch, both in number and in size, so we take up the whole corner, but there's plenty of space because people tend to give us a wide berth.

Except for one dumbass woman who comes by and coyly asks if I'm going to play tonight while twirling her hair around her index finger. It's a proposition if ever I've heard one.

"No." I answer both her question and her *question*, and the whole crew backs me up with mean glares that communicate clearly 'get the fuck outta dodge . . . pronto.'

Shot down, she slinks away to look for another horse to ride tonight. It's not me, it's never been me, and it certainly isn't now that I'm with Willow.

I look over to see Willow's brow lift questioningly and give her a heated look that says 'you've got nothing to worry about, woman.'

"Damn, man, turn the smolder down or you're gonna get the whole place pregnant," Rix deadpans. Brody snorts out a laugh, and as I turn around, I can see the whole table is fighting back grins or some version of a chuckle.

"Not me," Mark decrees, and they lose the battle, the laughs bursting out.

"Fair enough," Rix agrees. "But every vagina in here just went slicker than snot from Nashville's Flynn Rider look." Rix is not exactly a subtle woman. As a mechanic, she spends all day with the guys in her shop and all evening with us assholes, and she has zero smooth edges. She's as rough as the rest of us, maybe more so.

Brody growls, "Quit talking about your vagina and my brother in the same sentence."

Rix smirks. "Or what?"

Brody doesn't answer, but Rix suddenly goes quiet and sits up straight. My guess is he's doing some talking under the table given the smug satisfaction on his usually stoic face.

Olivia appears with a tray of frosty mugs filled to the brim with pink slush and starts to pass them out. "What the hell's this?" Luke asks.

"Round of Girly Beers, as ordered," she answers, tipping me a wink. "Don't worry, boys. It takes more than a little light beer to void your man cards."

There's one of us who's always willing to try anything, literally anything . . . as in we dare him to do shit all the time just to see if he will, and he always does. So to no one's surprise, James grabs his and starts sucking at the straw. After a few draws, he holds it up, surprised. "That's delicious. What's in it?"

I proudly tell them all about Willow's recipe and how Hank agreed to sell it as the whole table slurps theirs down happily. With it being light beer and sweet, it doesn't even give me a buzz, but I feel bubbly inside anyway as I watch Willow work.

Bubbly? A rough motherfucker like you can't be bubbly. It's downright physically impossible unless you're talking gas.

Yep, even I can do bubbly, so suck it.

I argue with myself, knowing that it's the truth. It's that feeling so many songs have been written about. Hell, I've written some myself, thinking I knew what I was talking about. But I didn't until right now.

Champagne rushing through my veins, but it's not the liquor. It's you.

Conversation turns to work stuff, as usual, and we discuss the latest cattle prices, herd health, crop yields, and Shay talks about the planned fall offerings for her homemade goat soap and food goodies business. "Pumpkin spice soaps again, because of course, those are my best sellers. *Pumpkin spice everything!*" she says, feigning a basic Starbucks bitch voice and garnering a few smiles. In her own voice again, she continues, "But I think I want to try a new apple scent. Something brighter and lighter, like a honey crisp and floral combo. I'm not sure, though, because the apple cinnamon set with the soap, apple butter, and candle is such a seasonal favorite."

Sophie raises her hand. "If you do the new one, you'll still make the apple butter, right? It's Cindy Lou's favorite." James gets real interested in Shay's plans at that and parrots, "Yeah, it's *Cindy Lou's* favorite." Sophie's brow raises sharply at his emphasis on their baby girl, and I think maybe James is helping his little daughter make the apple butter disappear. *One for you, one for me. One for you, two for me.*

"Of course, I'll still make it. For Cindy Lou." Shay knows good and well who's eating it too. "But before all that, we still have next week's deliveries to discuss."

We all groan. Shayanne has become quite the entrepreneur, which we support wholeheartedly as her staff. There are deliveries every week of every season, which we tackle on a rotating schedule. But for a whole bunch of grumpy assholes, making deliveries to people all over town is basically signing up for a day of hell.

"I need to check with Willow first. I'm not sure what days she's off, and I want to be sure I can spend those hours with her," I tell Shay, looking to Brutal for confirmation. We work together most days, handling the planting and harvesting as a two-man team, though we occasionally have to hire a day worker to help. He nods that he'll cover for me whenever I need to step away for the day.

"*Whoopsh,*" Luke says in his version of a whip sound. With a grin, he adds, "She's already got you whipped."

I chuckle at that, shoving his shoulder. "Fucker, have you looked in a mirror lately? My sister has your balls in a jar in the deep freeze with the roasts. You're the most whipped of us all."

He shrugs, unconcerned. "Hey, if my woman wants to play with my balls and smack my ass a little, I'm game."

"Enough," Brody barks out.

We all like Luke. Hell, I'd fight alongside him any day. But he's still fucking my sister, which makes our friendship a bit tenuous, no matter what. I'm not one to share sexual escapade stories, and I definitely don't need the details of his sex life, especially if Shay is smacking his ass like a damn pony ride. Ugh.

Shay can sense the tension, and used to it, she intervenes easily, changing the subject to the reason they're all here tonight. "I like her. She seems nice and didn't shrink when we all swarmed, so she's got that going for her."

"You just met her," Katelyn tells Shayanne, finally joining the conversation instead of making fuck-me eyes at Mark.

"Yeah, but I have a good feeling about her. Like I had with Sophie when I met her." Shay grins and Sophie cringes.

"Oh, my God, girl. You nearly had me running for the hills. You were like, 'hi, nice to meet you . . . now, we're BFFs . . . wanna come over and see my goats?'"

Shay balks. "But you did! And look how it turned out!" She gestures around the table at our whole motley crew.

Sophie smiles back and offers an apologetic high-five to Shay, which she returns begrudgingly.

I want my family to like Willow. More importantly, I want Willow to like my family. These people are my everything. Well, them and music, and now, Willow.

After a while, everyone's taken a turn on the dance floor, some have had a second drink, Katelyn and Allyson even go for another Girly Beer, and we play a team game of pool.

The whole time, I'm watching Willow work. She's at ease behind the bar, handling the whole thing without pause, almost dancing her way from the beer taps to the liquor bottles. Every once in a while, her eyes will find mine and I'm rewarded with one of those soft smiles that I'm starting to feel possessive of.

Starting? Who am I kidding? I want to gather each one of them and keep them in my pocket so I can have one any time I want.

It's been hours since I've touched her, and that kiss was only a friendly greeting, not what I really need from her. I'm getting itchy, ready to go visit her at the bar, when I see her heading my way. Maybe she's feeling the same way, like she wants to be closer to me the way I need to be closer to her.

She stops by my chair, and I wrap my arm around her waist, pulling her in tight. Her arm goes to my shoulders and I welcome its light weight. I squeeze her side, finally settling now that she's with me.

Home, that's what she feels like.

And fuck, do I want to go right on in, get cozy and comfortable, and never leave. Just live buried inside her. At this rate, I might go crazy before I find out what she looks like under these tank tops and cut-off shorts and what she feels like coming on my cock. But I'm enjoying the journey to finding out, slowly but surely.

A week ago, she wouldn't do more than have a friendly dinner with me across the bar. Now, she's damn near claiming me, letting me claim her in her uncle's bar and hanging with my family.

With a knowing smile, she asks the table, "How were the Girly Beers?"

Allyson and Katelyn hold up their second empty glasses in answer. The rest give her some version of 'delicious' or 'good'. Brutal dryly says, "Better than I expected, that's for sure."

I kick his boot under the table. "Told you so."

Katelyn smiles at Willow. "If I promise not to tell the bartenders at the resort the recipe, can you tell me how to make that? I think it'd be perfect for our next girl's night in." Katelyn runs events at the local resort, and the bar there is known for being our small-town version of swanky, but she'll keep her promise and stay mum on Willow's recipe.

Willow automatically and easily offers, "Sure. For a batch, it's a six-pack of light beer—"

"Better yet, why don't you come and you can make it!" Katelyn's gear switch is smooth as silk, just like she is.

Surprised, Willow looks at me with raised brows. Her eyes swirl like she's trying to figure something out. Me? My family? Is this a set-up? I squeeze her hip encouragingly, praying she says yes. After a second that seems like an eternity, she turns back to Katelyn. "That sounds great. Let me know when, though I work every day but Monday."

That answers Shay's earlier question. I'm busy with Willow all day on Monday, so someone else will have to handle deliveries.

"Six days a week till two a.m.? Nobody's gonna accuse you of being lazy," Shayanne teases, then starts singing, "She works hard for that money . . ." She's horribly off-key and not even following the famous tune, making up her own notes and not even hitting those and getting the lyrics wrong too. To say that I got the lion's share of the musical talent in my family is a gross exaggeration. I got it all, every last drop of musical DNA.

Willow laughs. "Yeah, bartenders' hours are pretty much the opposite of farmers' hours, I guess. I usually crash around four, sleep until ten, then back behind the bar by noon if I'm pulling a lunch shift. But I don't mind. I'm happy to help Unc." A shadow passes through her eyes, and I sense a slight tension in her when she says that. I hope she's not overdoing it.

The girls chatter away, talking about this and that, and we guys stay as quiet as church mice. I'm well aware that they're testing Willow, checking her out and seeing if she slides into our group easily. Dynamic is important—like music, it has to flow naturally, and so far, Willow seems to fit right in.

I'm not surprised. Who wouldn't like a sweetheart like her?

After a bit, she says she needs to get back behind the bar, and I feel the loss of her at my side. Back at her station, she hollers out, "Last call!" and there's a sudden influx of orders that has her scrambling up and down the bar. But she handles it all with grace and a smile.

Not soon enough, it's time to close and Willow does the 'don't have to go home but you can't stay here' spiel. Olivia clears tables left and right, thanking people for their tips and promising to see them tomorrow night.

A drunk guy loudly asks why she's not kicking our table out, and Olivia laughs as she follows his pointed finger to our group. She dares him, "You want to be the one to tell them?" Toward us, she calls out, "Hey, Brutal, think this guy has something to discuss with you."

The guy looks over, and Brutal glowers back, squaring up and clenching his jaw. He doesn't even need to say anything as Drunk Dude pales, gets up unsteadily, and heads for the door with the help of what I assume is his designated driver.

Brutal relaxes with a smirk. "Must've been something I said." We chuckle because Brutal is the biggest teddy bear of us all, probably the least likely to get in a tussle, but he knows how to work his size and mean mug to his advantage.

"We'd better get going, anyway. Mama Louise is keeping Cindy Lou tonight," Sophie says, standing up.

Next to her, James confides, "She's hoping for another grandbaby."

Allyson laughs. "She's got Cooper tonight too. Told me that he helps her with Cindy Lou. Hope she's not dreaming of another one from us. This shop is closed." She waves her hand around her middle section.

But Brutal growls, "It'd better not be closed."

Allyson rolls her eyes. "Not for you, but for babies . . . closed indefinitely."

They all head for the door, leaving me alone at the table. I gather up our trash and glasses, stacking them the way Olivia does and taking them to the back. Ilene doesn't blink at my being in the kitchen, and Daniel simply takes the glasses with a sound of appreciation and gets back to work.

I help clean up the front of the bar, pushing the broom and mop around after flipping the chairs up on the tabletops, and before long, everything's done.

Daniel walks behind the bar and says something quietly to Willow. She looks at me, leaning on the far end of the bar, and I know my eyes are dark as night and promising sin. Dirty thoughts assail me . . . what I could do to her on the bar, behind the bar, over any table in this place? I don't hide a single filthy idea from her.

Slowly, she pries her eyes from mine and turns to Daniel. With a nod, he waves at me and escorts Ilene and Olivia toward the door. On her way past, Olivia says quietly, "Fuck this up and you'll only live long enough to regret it. Between Hank and me, we'll put the meat grinder to good use and no one will be the wiser."

What is it with women and true crime shit? Do they have lessons on how to get away with murder?

Wait, that's got the potential to be a good song lyric. Oh, shit, no . . . the Dixie Chicks already did that with *Goodbye Earl*, Carrie Underwood killed her dad in *Blown Away* and her husband in *Two Black Cadillacs*, and Garth Brooks did *Papa Loved Mama* too. Maybe I'll skip the murder music for now.

Once Willow and I are finally alone, murder is the last thing on my mind. Unless it's *little deaths* . . . fuck, I could make her come all night. Make her sing with pleasure for me. That's the music I'd love to hear. It'd be my new favorite song for sure.

Needing to hold her, I walk to the jukebox and hit *J14*. Hank keeps this thing pretty updated, keeping classics but adding new tunes regularly. Chris Jansen's *Done* pours through the speakers, saying what I can't to Willow.

She's it for me.

I'm done for, no doubt about it.

I hold out my hand, and from across the bar, she takes it. I walk her down to the end and around, finally holding her in my arms again. We don't do any fancy footwork. This isn't the time for that. For now, I just sway her back and forth, feeling her body pressed to mine. She feels so right, so mine, and I want to soak her up, slide into her soul, and fuse us into one.

"Fuck, I've wanted to hold you all night," I confess quietly. I'm acutely aware of her weight shifting from side to side, her skin which is now covered in fine goosebumps, and the hitch in her breathing at my throaty admission.

She gives me one of those smiles that drives me wild and lays her head against my chest. Her arms go around my waist and mine drop over her shoulders in the tightest, sexiest hug I've ever had. She even squeezes me a bit.

"I like this," she whispers against my T-shirt.

"I like you," I tell her. Weak words for the thunder raging through my veins, but my racing heart is doing its best to get blood to flow north to my brain.

We sway quietly and I breathe her in. She smells like she's

been working, lemons and beer and bleach, but underneath is her own unique scent, and I take it into my lungs. I sing softly, a grittier, rougher version of the sweet song, and the jukebox plays on, serenading us.

After a few songs, Willow pulls back and looks up at me. Her eyes are begging for something she won't say. "Bobby—"

I don't make her ask. I've waited long enough already.

My mouth is instantly on hers, exploring and possessing. I trace her sides, brushing along the sides of her breasts before reaching back to firmly grab her ass. She whimpers in response to my tight grip, and I hungrily swallow the sweet sound. I pull her toward me, grinding against her, and a groan of pure bliss vibrates through my chest. I lower my hands to the backs of her thighs, encouraging her up, and lift her to straddle my waist, needing more, wanting to give her more.

Walking backward without breaking our kiss, I find the bar and set her on it. She pulls back long enough to warn, "I am not having sex on my uncle's bar."

Devilishly, I grin. "Not *tonight*, you're not."

Her mouth drops open in surprise, and I can't help but laugh a little. But when she pushes at my chest in protest, I don't move an inch. "Tonight, I'm going to kiss you, get you drunk on me, and make you so needy that you want me deep inside you. Then we're going to go home . . . alone."

Her face falls a bit, which gives me a twisted bit of reassured joy. She does want me.

"Don't pout. Know that I'm going to be fucking my hand and wishing it were your sweet little pussy taking my cum." Behind those big, black frames, she blinks at my words, and I wonder if anyone has ever talked dirty to her before. Softening a bit, I tell her, "I'm not going to rush this, Willow. We only get to do this buildup for the first time once, and when I get inside you, I'm going to want to stay there forever, so I'm going to enjoy this part and drive us both crazy until we can't stand it anymore. Make me earn it, make me work for you. Don't give in to me too fast because as soon as you do, I won't be able to stop."

Her smile returns in increments. "How do you make it sweet

that you don't want to have sex with me? Most guys would take the easy lay."

"I'm not most guys," I tell her. "And you're not an easy lay. You're . . . everything."

Shit. Cat's out of the bag now.

I watch her carefully, hoping she doesn't bolt. To my delight, her smile grows to the point where her eyes crinkle at the edges in true happiness.

Relief washes through me, and before she can think on it too much more, I dive back into her for another kiss, returning us to the crazy beauty of this madness.

Her tongue thrashes against mine, and I moan at the power of her hunger. Weaving my fingers into her hair, I tilt her head to the side and trace down the line of her neck, nipping and kissing my way to her collarbone, which I lave with my tongue. She tastes like salt and sweetness, and I lap at her skin for more.

Her hands grip at my shirt, fisting the cotton before splaying wide to roam over my abs. I flex beneath her touch, wanting to rip my shirt off and feel her palms against my skin. But I don't. If I start taking off clothes, I'll have my jeans around my thighs and her shorts around her knees in an instant.

But shirts don't have to come off to get at what I want. I slide the strap of her tank top off her shoulder, giving myself room to work, and push the neckline lower. With one finger, I follow the edge of the black cotton bra I find. I can see her nipple through the thin material and groan. "Mmm, sweetheart." She arches beneath my touch, giving me silent permission to go further, and I swipe my thumb over the nub through the fabric, feeling it harden even more.

Needing to see her, I pull the cotton down to expose her small tit. I knead at the skin roughly, making tight circles around her dusky pink nipples. "So pretty," I growl before I suck as much of her skin into my mouth as I can. I form a tight seal around her nipple, sucking and teasing at her with my tongue at the same time.

"Oh!" she cries out, leaning back with one hand supporting her on the bar as the other rests on my shoulder. I feel the bite of her nails into my skin and take it as a sign that I'm getting to her, especially as I feel her hips buck on the bar, searching for my cock.

Shoving the other triangle of her thin bra down, I give that mound some love and attention too. I lay worshipping kisses all over her exposed body, breasts, chest, neck, shoulders, then work my way back up to her mouth.

My hands go to her thighs as we kiss, squeezing and kneading the warm satin skin I find there. Getting higher and higher, my thumbs are on the edge of her pussy beneath her shorts. Her ankles wrap around my legs, holding me in place as if I have anywhere else I'd rather be right now. I can feel the heat of her core, am right on the edge of testing her wetness beneath her panties—going slow be damned—when a loud bang on the door interrupts us.

"Willow? You good?" a voice booms.

"What the fuck?" I mutter, instantly on alert.

Willow jumps off the bar, yanking her bra and shirt back in place as she strides to the door. I beat her there, covering the distance in furious strides. I throw an arm out, keeping her behind me with a forceful look. It's two in the morning and no one should be bothering her. The very idea makes my blood run ice-cold. Great Falls is safe, but Willow is precious. She looks at me wryly, likely thinking my protectiveness is unnecessary, but I couldn't tone it down if I wanted to.

"Who is it?" she calls out.

"Chief Gibson. Doing a drive by and saw the lights still on and your car outside. Open the door." His voice changes from congenial to authoritative.

"Oh, okay," Willow says, looking at me in amusement as I step back to give her the space I couldn't a second ago.

She twists the lock that Ilene closed when she left and cracks the door open. "Hi, Chief. I'm good, just . . . working late."

She can't lie to save her ass and Chief Gibson hears it. He pushes in, taking a few steps inside, but freezes when he sees me.

"Bobby."

"Chief Gibson."

He looks from me to Willow and back, seeming to fight a smile in favor of his blank 'cop face'. Well, this particular cat's out of the bag. By sunrise, the whole town will think the chief busted us having wild sex in the middle of Hank's, no doubt.

"So, I guess you're all good then, Willow?" he says, not bothering to hide his grin now that any fears he had have been allayed.

She nods. "Yeah. Uh, all good. We were just leaving."

Doing his job, the chief turns back to me once more. "You been drinking tonight, son?"

I'm not his son, but I'm not going to piss him off by correcting him. "Yep, had a Girly Beer around eight and a draft around nine. Nothing since but dinner and Sprite. Ilene's chicken fried steak sandwich was delicious."

He takes my measure, looking me up and down. I've never been a heavy drinker, saw too much of that with Dad for it to have any appeal, but it'd take a whole lot more than a couple of drinks several hours ago to affect me in the slightest, especially at my size. "Damn, wish I'd gotten one of those sandwiches. I'll have to swing by tomorrow and see if I can snag one myself."

He touches the brim of his hat and dips his chin. "You kids have a good night, y'hear?"

"Yes sir," Willow says.

I grunt an agreement, still a bit put out that he interrupted us. But it is good to know that he's keeping an eye on the place and my girl.

Closing the door, Willow spins in place and puts her back against it. She's breathing hard like we got busted doing something wrong, but what we were up to was so, so right.

"Oh, my God. That was terrifying." She does look a bit mortified, but the way her eyes are dancing, she doesn't seem too upset about it. She actually looks . . . invigorated.

I crowd in, pressing her against the door. "Yeah, terrifying," I agree dryly.

She laughs. "Okay, Mr. Bad Boy, maybe not for you. But I'm a good girl, and usually invisible. Certainly not used to having the cops bang down my door when I'm in the middle of . . ."

Her voice trails off like she's not sure how to describe what we were doing, and I'm now certain that no one has ever dirty talked to my sweet Willow. And I'm even more certain that she hasn't dirty talked either.

"Foreplay?" I suggest.

Her cheeks pinken adorably.

"If Gibson had been a few seconds later, I would've been finger fucking you and at least then, I'd know what you feel like, how you smell, how you taste." My voice has gone low and husky, and even just the thought of slipping a finger inside her has me adjusting my cock in my jeans, which are suddenly way too tight.

She blinks, owl-like behind those frames, and inhales sharply. "Bobby . . ." That breathy sound almost has me saying 'fuck it' and giving in to what we both want and know is coming, but delaying the inevitable has its reward too.

I rub a thumb along her cheekbone. "Time, Willow. We have plenty, but if you remember nothing else from tonight, I want you to know that you are never invisible to me. You're all I see—your eyes swirling as you think, that smile that goes a little higher when you're extra happy, how comfortable you are in your own skin and because of that, you make everyone else want to be around you, the way you double-tap the whiskey to the counter but single-tap the vodka and tequila, though I don't know why you do either, how you take pictures of simple things that bring you joy and share them because it's your way of brightening other people's day too, and most of all, how your breath gets a little shallow when I get too close and you get nervous. Like now."

She takes a deep breath, forcing air down into her lungs, but it's too late. I already saw those little pants she was making. I'm not too close to her physically, but I'm too close to her truth, and that's an itchy-irritable feeling to let someone that close, this fast.

Even though it's not the real issue, I'm willing to give her an inch for now, so I step back. Her hands stay pressed to my chest, though at her own doing, and I hope that she doesn't want to lose contact fully.

"You're intense. You know that, right?" she whispers, as if that's supposed to be a newsflash to me.

"Been told that a time or two. Never mattered till now. Too much?" I dare to ask.

Her bottom lip disappears behind her teeth for a second, and she stares at her tanned hands against the black cotton covering my chest as she thinks. Finally, her eyes lift and meet mine. She shakes her head, gifting me one of her soft smiles. "Not too much. Just right."

"Come on, let's get out of here," I tell her, and she brightens. Laughing, I scold her, "Not yet, woman. I meant for you to go home and me to go home and jack off. Fuck, you're gonna kill me, but I do want to wait. It matters, Willow. You matter. We don't have to rush."

Her cheeks pinken again, and her innocence washes over me like a balm, telling me that waiting is the right thing to do, but damn, her eagerness makes it so hard. "Okay, but I'll see you tomorrow?"

"Wild horses couldn't keep me away."

In the lot, I make sure she gets in her car safely and watch as she pulls out to head home. I have a split second where I consider turning right and following her home to finish what we started, but in the end, though it's agonizing to do so, I turn left and go home as I promised.

* * *

THE KNOCKING on my truck window comes way too early, with the sun barely past the horizon.

"What?" I groan.

Knock. Knock. Knock.

I peek one eye open to see Brody standing at my driver's window, holding up a cup of coffee. The aroma's enough to motivate me to wake up. I sit up straight, stretching out the new kinks in my back from sleeping slouched down in the cab of my truck.

Opening the door, Brody hands me the coffee. I grunt my appreciation, speaking his first language. Hell, it's damn near his only language. I have trouble expressing myself at times. Brody just gave up on even trying years ago. He's more the point and grunt type, but somehow, we can all decode what he says, even when he doesn't really say it.

He waits for me to get a few good swallows down, letting the caffeine do its job, before he asks, "How long ago did you get in?"

Knowing the sun rises at six, I estimate, "Couple of hours ago. Didn't want to wake you and Rix up because I knew you had an early day."

He grunts back, showing his appreciation in return. Today is the monthly farmer's market day, and Brody and Shay spent several minutes last night talking about what to take. Well, Shay talked and Brody listened. They work together at the market, selling off the crops we grow and Shay's products.

"I'd love to tell you to sleep in or skip out and leave Brutal to it today, but he's gonna need you. I can't fill in because I've gotta go to town. Shay needs me."

That's not exactly true, but also not exactly a lie. It's more complicated than that.

Brody is the oldest of us all, and when Dad went off the deep end after Mom died, Brody took responsibility for us all, becoming a de facto dad in a lot of ways. He and Shay were the right and left hands of the family, leaving Brutal and me to our own devices, but somehow, we all worked together toward a common goal—keeping the family farm.

A goal we failed at meeting spectacularly, thanks to dear old Dad fucking us over, even from the grave. That's how we got hooked up with the Bennetts. It's been a while now, and we've all adjusted for the most part, though Brody has big dreams of saving up enough money to buy our land back. He says Mama Louise is just 'holding' it for us, but I think that's wishful thinking.

Still, the bit of money Shay makes at the farmers market is split three ways—a bit to the Bennetts to buy supplies, like the plums from the trees, a bit to Shay as a salary for all her hard work, and a bit to the Tannen family account. We all donate to that, giving as much as we can, as often as we can, hoping that Brody will find a way to get that deed back. I think it'd be different now that we're so dependent on the Bennetts and they're so dependent on us, but it'd be nice to have the iron *Tannen Farms* sign above our gate mean something again.

But basically, we all need each other to play the roles we're assigned, and mine is as a farmhand.

"I know. I wouldn't ditch Brutal. We've got crops to check," I tell Brody, having had zero illusions of taking the day off. That's not what farming is about. There are no days off, only days you pay someone else to do what you were supposed to be doing in the first place.

I take another sip of coffee, praying that increasing the amount coursing through my bloodstream will also increase its effects. "So, what'd you think?"

He doesn't need me to spell out the subject change. He knows I'm asking if he liked Willow. Another piece of his being the father figure for so long is that we don't like to disappoint him. Shay and me, in particular, are sensitive to making Brody proud. Brutal does his own thing, and I don't think he gives two rat shits about what Brody thinks, but luckily, they stand on the same side of the fence most of the time anyway.

He looks at me through narrowed eyes, though the sun's barely up and he's got on his camo cow hat, like always. He hums thoughtfully. "You don't need to know what I think. You already picked her."

I nod. "I know, but I trust your opinion. Always have."

He's silent for a long moment, and I think he's not going to answer, but he finally says, "I like her."

That's it. Brody Tannen's official stamp of approval.

"Thanks."

He clears his throat and turns to head back into the house, leaving me alone with the early morning light. A few more sips of coffee and I'll get going on the day. Brutal and I have two pastures to check for pests and problems, and walking their long rows sounds like a good way to think. It usually becomes slightly meditative, sometimes resulting in a song melody or lyrics and sometimes just letting me clear my head a bit.

I already know what I'll be thinking about today . . . Willow.

CHAPTER 10

WILLOW

"*D*o not eat the doughnuts. Do not eat the doughnuts," I tell myself aloud as I drive to Unc's. "Not yet, at least."

I stopped by the Main Street doughnut shop, where they greeted me by name, which surprised me, considering it's only my second time being there, but I guess word spreads fast. At least the kind lady with the big smile behind the counter had called me 'Hank's niece' and not 'Bobby Tannen's girl'. I might be both, but one feels like family. The other feels a bit like jealousy, at least from the women in town, though Doughnut Darla, as she told me she's known, didn't seem like the type to fawn over Bobby at sixty-plus and white-haired beneath her hair net.

Regardless, the sweet smell of doughnuts is calling my name from the big white box on my passenger seat. But I manage to hold strong, pulling into Unc's driveway without so much as a crumb on my fingers or face.

Unc's house is a cute ranch-style home, with blue-painted brick and white shutters. The flower beds are a bit overgrown, long shoots popping up through the line of shrubs, and the scalloped concrete barriers are a bit askew, even cracked here and there. I add yardwork to my list of things to help Unc with. It's not urgent, but I'm sure he'd appreciate it being taken care of since he's obviously not able.

Getting out, I balance the box of goodies in one hand so I can ring the bell.

No answer.

Maybe he's still asleep? He probably keeps bartenders' hours too, and it is early, but I wanted to stop by before opening for the lunch crowd.

I ring the bell again and hear muffled noise from inside. I open the storm door, holding it back with my butt, and call through the door, "Unc? It's Willow. I brought doughnuts."

The knob rattles as it's unlocked, and I'm not sure if Unc is opening the door because it's me on the other side or because of the doughnuts. Either way, I'm calling it a victory.

"Willow? Girl, I wasn't expecting you this morning," Unc says. His voice sounds scratchy, like he hasn't used it for a couple of days. I wave the doughnuts around enticingly, and he steps back with a sigh. That answers that, I guess . . . the doughnuts are my ticket inside. As long as I get one too, I can handle that.

Inside, my eyes adjust to the dim lighting and I get a good look at Unc. He looks like he took a trip to hell, walked through fire, and came back through the grease pits. His hair is slick with oil, but not smoothed back like usual. Rather, it looks like he fixed it a couple of days ago and has slept on it against every flat surface since. His face looks more heavily lined, even from just the short time since I've seen him, and I realize it's because he's gaunt and probably dehydrated. His eyes are glassy blue and staring at me harshly. Or what should be harshly but looks tired and weak.

Every nurturing cell in my body wants to force him to bed, tuck the blankets up under his chin, and feed him soup. If I so much as attempt to suggest that, he'll kick me out onto my butt before I finish getting the words out. Alternate strategy time.

"Okay, lead me to a table where I can set these down because they've been calling my name the whole way here." I hold the box to my ear and sing-song, "Willow. Eat me, Willow."

Hank's answering smile is tentative. "All right, girl. Come on in here. Fair warning, the maid ain't cleaned in a while."

"You have a maid?" I ask, surprised.

One of his bushy brows lifts sardonically. "You're looking at him."

That makes more sense. Unc is a do-it-yourselfer if ever I've met one.

I follow him into the den, then the small kitchen, where he waves a hand at the four-seater round table pressed up to the wall. I guess he only needs three chairs for poker nights. "Have a seat. I'll grab us coffee and plates."

"Oh," I say with a start toward the cabinets myself, intending to help. But at his glare, which is gaining strength by the second by the sheer force of his will, I do as ordered and sit down to let him keep his pride.

He pours two mismatched mugs of steaming coffee and sets them on the table, then gets plates. I manage to pull two napkins from the holder on the center of the table and hand him one.

Quietly, he opens the box and takes the first pick, putting a bear claw on his plate. Licking the glaze off his fingers, he moans, "Mmmhmm, Darla makes a damn fine doughnut."

I select the pink one with sprinkles that I bought hoping I could have it. I take a ginormous bite without even setting it down, open-mouth chewing as it dissolves into sugar in my mouth.

Unc chuckles. "Guess you agree." He makes no move to eat his bear claw, though, seemingly satisfied with a sip of coffee instead. "What brings you by so early? Everything go okay last night?"

I swallow thickly, getting the doughnut down. "Did you hear otherwise?"

Oh, no. Chief Gibson probably already told Unc about my late-night guest at the bar and this is his way of getting me to confess.

Unc's brow lifts and he stares blank-faced at me, straight as can be, with no hint of what he's thinking.

I finally set the doughnut down and wipe the frosting and sprinkles off on the napkin. "Chief Gibson stopped by, though I guess you already know that." His lips quirk, confirming my suspicions. "We weren't doing anything, just talking. And we left right after the chief."

Unc takes another sip of coffee. "And by 'we', you mean Bobby Tannen and you?"

My eyes widen in realization. "You had no idea, did you?"

He laughs at that, shaking his head. "Knew you two were getting friendly, but sometimes, it's best to let the other guy show their hand first."

I try to be mad, really, I do, but it's a losing battle because he's right. I sigh, give in, and spill my guts. "The whole Tannen-Bennett family came by last night, mostly to meet me, it seems. They hung out, and I made them all drink Girly Beers."

Unc's smile grows at that and he flashes me a thumbs-up. "They like it?"

I feign outrage, giving him my best 'offended' face. "Of course they did. It's delicious!"

"If you say so." He definitely does not agree. "Then what? Get to the good stuff, girl."

"Closed up shop at two, and Bobby stayed to help. He even pushed the broom and mop around. Then everyone headed home for the night, and we . . . stayed. And talked."

Unc's bony fingers bend in the air like quotation marks, "Talked. Yeah, I've done some 'talking' in my day too." He repeats the finger movement.

"No, actually talking," I insist, but he doesn't look convinced. "Okay, and some 'not talking' too, but nothing too . . ." I search for the word I'm looking for but I can't think of one that I'd feel comfortable telling a seventy-year-old relative, so I settle on, "Nothing that'd require a cleaning of the bar. I just sat on it."

He holds up a hand, palm toward me. "Say no more. And Patrick?"

Thankful to be off that part of story, I explain the rest. "Chief saw the lights on and my car in the lot, so he checked to make sure I was okay."

Unc smiles slightly. "He's a good one." He finally picks up the bear claw and takes a small nibble off one side, but it looks like swallowing it costs him dearly as he goes a little green. Sticking to coffee, he asks, "So, what's the story with you and Bobby? Seems like he's taken a mighty fine shine to you. You feeling the same way?"

Wow, direct and to the point, and staring me down with those blue eyes that dare me to lie. It'd do me no good. Unc would know it either way. "I am. It's a lot . . . and fast . . . and intense. And not what I came for, but he's . . . something else."

Unc hums like he understands my muttered answer perfectly. "He is that. Always figured he'd make it out of Great Falls. I know he wanted to in his younger days before his mom got sick. She was a sweet woman, raised those hellions up the best she could, but Paul put them through the wringer. They ended up better than I would've figured. Bobby especially. He always seemed a bit more even-keeled than his brothers. Don't know if that's true or not." He looks off to the side like he's remembering something from long ago, but he doesn't share whatever he's thinking.

"So you think he's a good one too?" I ask, using his words.

He pats my hand across the table, his dry and cold against my warmth in the moment of contact. "I think you already know the answer to that question yourself and don't need an old man's blessing to do what you want, Willow. Especially mine, given I ain't seen you in way too long."

"I know. It has been too long. I'm sorry for that—"

"Now, don't you be apologizing for things that ain't no fault of yours. Harold was a son of a bitch, too big for his britches, and hell, for that matter, so was I. We didn't appreciate what we were losing when everything blew up between us, but I sure do now."

He looks around the house and I follow his gaze. He's been alone as long as I can remember. I never had an aunt, but there are touches of softness here and there, as though someone helped him make the place cozier. Patterned pillows on the couch and a crocheted throw blanket on the back of the recliner, a flyer advertising last month's Fourth of July parade is held to the refrigerator by a pair of painted clothespins with magnets on the back, and a tray on the counter was lined with small bottles. A collection of pill bottles . . . a whole bunch of them.

I nearly choke at how many there are and I have to fight back tears. What happened between Grandpa and Unc has had far-reaching consequences I don't think any of us intended to pay.

"I'm just glad I'm here now," I tell Unc.

"Doc stopped by yesterday," he says, seeming to change the subject to something lighter. "Said you were doing a damn fine job at the bar without me and that I shouldn't worry."

I smile, knowing there's no way he wouldn't. "But of course, you worry anyway."

"Damn straight. Built that honkytonk myself, from the ground up with these two hands, and lived most of my life in those walls. Or at least the best years. So I don't need no city slicker coming in and mucking it up." He's teasing me, lights sparkling in his dull blue eyes.

"I'm not mucking up anything. We did just fine last night, and I'm ready to open for lunch and work till close tonight. We'll be fine. You stay home and nap, old man," I tease, but truthfully, he looks like he could use it.

"I'll nap when I'm dead," he retorts. "Until then, I've got shit to do. Actually, I'll probably let you handle today," he concedes, as though I'd thought he was going to hop up and go to the bar with me for the day. I had no illusions as such. "I've got some things to do around the house, but tomorrow, I'll be there, and I'll expect you to be off gallivanting around, doing whatever it is you young'uns do these days. Like 'talking' and taking pictures for your 'blogs'." He does air quotes around both words, which makes me laugh because he's using them wrong, but in his mind, he's perfectly correct.

"You sure? We're closed Monday, so that's two whole days off in a row. Wouldn't want me to get spoiled, now would you?" What I really mean is, can he handle the bar alone tomorrow?

He grins back, nodding. "Girl, if you'd let me, I'd spoil the ever-loving shit outta ya. I missed you, Willow."

What started as sweet turned deeply sentimental, and I feel the hot burn of tears in the corners of my eyes again but refuse to let them fall. Unc doesn't want me to cry over him, but it's hard to swallow down the lost time and the fear of losing even more.

"I missed you too, Unc. Anything you need, I'm your girl, okay? I don't want to let years go by again and us feel like we lost something important," I choke out.

He pats my hand again, content in that old man way. "We won't even let days go by this time. Sometimes, that's as long as you get, and you gotta take advantage of every one."

I dip my chin, half-nodding and half-hiding the tears I blink away.

"All right then, get on to the bar. You've got work to do today, girl. And I'd best not hear of Patrick having to break up any fights. Your man's or anyone else's."

I laugh lightly, hoping he's kidding. Bobby might've punched that tourist the first night, but he deserved it. Bobby's been nothing but a gentleman ever since.

I intentionally leave the whole box of doughnuts with hopes that Unc will snack on them throughout the day and let him escort me to the door. He's limping a bit more today, something that had been getting better since he's been spending most shifts sitting at the beer taps. I give him a hug, feeling the bones of his lean frame beneath his loose T-shirt.

"I love you, Unc."

"Aw, I love you too, Willow. Now I'd best not see you until Tuesday lunch, y'hear?"

I do the quick mental check on that. I'm working today and he's staying home to rest, he's doing tomorrow's shift, then we're closed on Monday, so yeah, he's right. I think I'll make sure Doc or Richard swings by tomorrow to sit at the bar with him. He won't suspect a thing if his friends come to visit and drink the day away before their poker game.

Dismissed, I get in my car and head to work knowing that I'm going to do extra prep work to make sure that Unc can do as little as possible tomorrow.

* * *

I'M waist-deep in the weeds, pulling soft drinks and beers mostly because folks don't default to the hard stuff mid-day around here very often, and helping Olivia run food to tables. It's just the three of us, Olivia and me up front and Ilene in the back. Daniel comes in at five for the dinner rush.

"What do you do when you need a day off?" I ask Olivia as I fill her tray with another round of drinks. "You're literally the only waitress who works here."

"Day off?" she sasses with a look of mock confusion. "What's that?" I wish she were kidding, but I get the feeling she's not. "Really, I work as much as I can and am happy to do it. Hannah's working too. Owning her own shop is a twenty-four, seven gig, so we'll see each other tonight after we get off work. On the rare occasion I really do need a day, Hank has customers come to the counter to order and calls them back up when their food's ready. Folks understand."

I can't help but smile. Here, in Great Falls, they do understand and are probably happy to help a fellow resident have a day off. But in the city? No way, no how. There'd be some Karen threatening a one-star Yelp review because the service was 'offensive'. But the sense of community here is something I hadn't expected, and it feels . . . right. I've been accused of being a doormat, letting people walk all over me when all I really wanted to do was lend a hand, but here, everyone's like that.

"Well, just so you're ready for it, Hank's given me tomorrow off. I'm going to do as much prep work as I can so that all he has to do is sit on his butt and pour beer, but can you keep an eye on him? Make sure he eats and doesn't overdo it?" I don't add that he looked awful this morning and was well on his way to a nap just from our visit, so I'm seriously doubting his ability to work a full shift.

Olivia's eyes narrow and she taps the bar. "Absolutely. I got the old guy covered. If he gets too cranky, I'll send him to his office to do paperwork and handle the bar myself. I can't make cocktails, but alcohol's alcohol and folks can take what they can get or go somewhere else." She snaps her fingers and grins. "Oh, right, there's nowhere else to go, so they can drink beer and damn well like it."

"Thanks," I tell her, meaning it deeply. I think she will look out for Unc. Actually, from how quickly she suggested sending him to his office, I think she's been looking out for him for a while.

By mid-afternoon, I get a lull and really get to work prepping. I've got every lemon and lime in the fridge cut, knowing I'll use some tonight but will still have enough for Unc tomorrow. I've overstocked every napkin holder, washed a whole stack of bar towels, and cleaned everything to within an inch of its life so that Unc won't even feel the need to wipe a rag around.

I move on to rearranging the most used liquors to the side of the bar closest to the beer taps. It's a huge overstep on my part.

Rearranging someone's bar is akin to pulling their socks and underwear from their dresser drawers and organizing them a different way, but I think this will be a good change for Unc in the long run.

The phone rings and I answer, "Hank's, Willow speaking. How can I help you?"

"Oh good, I was hoping it'd be you who answered," a female voice says so fast I barely catch it.

"Excuse me?"

"It's Shayanne. We're wrapping up at the famer's market and we already ate our lunch and snacks. I wanted to see if Ilene would package us up some food to go? Well, that and I wanted to talk to you too." Every word is fast, nearly on top of the last, and I have to pay attention to catch each one.

"Uh, sure. What do you want to eat and I'll go ahead and get that started?" I say, focusing on the easy part.

"Have her do a big box of fries, fried pickles, and fried mushrooms," Shayanne answers, damn near asking for a heart attack in a box. But they all work hard, so maybe they can handle eating like that?

I scribble the order on a piece of paper, making a note that it's to-go for Shayanne, and slip it to Ilene, who sticks it to her order rack before turning back to the grill.

"I was hoping to get by the market this morning too," I tell Shay. "I thought it would be a great photo op, but I didn't have time before opening. Maybe next time?"

"That'd be great! I can show you all the cute little booths and you can take pictures for your blog!" She sounds super excited about the idea, but then she screeches like a record scratch. "Oh, not that I mean you need to advertise for us. I totally didn't mean it like that, promise. I meant that it'd be fun and cute, not to take advantage, and . . . I'm going to shut up now."

I laugh, especially when she immediately starts talking again.

"I wanted to see if you'd come out to the farm sometime. I know you're off Monday—Bobby's been talking about that already. Believe me, *we know*. But being the lady of the Tannen house, well . . . kinda, considering I don't live there anymore, but

the point being, I wanted to invite you out. What do you think?"
She stops on a dime, the one run-on sentence ending abruptly.

"Oh, well . . . thank you. I'd love to, but I think it'd be better if
I wait for Bobby to invite me? I wouldn't want to intrude before
he's ready." *Or before I'm ready*, I think.

"He won't mind a bit. It could be our little secret. You'd be like
a surprise gift, and I'd be the best sister ever. Well, technically, I'm
his only sister, but the point stands that I'm the best. Obviously."
She sounds utterly convinced, and nothing or no one could sway
her otherwise. "You could take pictures of my goats. They're the
cutest critters ever, except for Baarbara. She's gotten a bit
persnickety in her old age. But I have a few babies. C'mon,
nobody can turn down fluffy, cuddly, adorable baby goats that
curl up in your lap for ear scratches."

She's wearing me down. I suspect she does that to a lot of
people. Her exuberance is . . . engaging, for sure.

"Well, I'm actually unexpectedly off tomorrow. I have plans
early in the day, but maybe in the afternoon? We could catch some
good lighting then."

"Yes!" I can almost hear her fist punch of victory at my agreement. "Okay, but here's the deal, girl. Bobby's coming in for
dinner tonight and you'd best not say a word. Got it? Don't ruin
the surprise. *Holy shit*, I can't wait to see his face when you pull
up. I'll send you the address."

"Okay," I say slowly, feeling like I might've been danced into
something I didn't intend. "Do you need my number?"

She laughs heartily at that. "Nah, I already swiped it out of
Bobby's phone. Dumb fuck's password is *Betty*. As if we don't all
know that." I can definitely hear the eye roll. "I'll be by to grab the
food, but this conversation . . . it never happened, capiche?"

"Yeah, got it," I say, feeling like I don't get it at all. But the idea
of seeing where Bobby lives and works, the land he talks and
sings about with such affection, is a damn good dangling carrot.
It's more like a dangling cupcake, drawing me near. Hopefully,
he'll be happy to see me there. I guess I'll find out tomorrow.

Fewer than fifteen minutes later, Shayanne and Brody come in.
Shay wanders up to the bar, beaming like the Cheshire Cat. "Hey,

Willow, good to talk to you again. I mean, see you again." She winks, likely thinking she's being subtle, but she's not. Not at all.

Brody looks from her to me and back, then grunts. He's on to her, I'm sure of it. But he doesn't say a word. Literally.

"Yeah, good to see you too, Shayanne," I mimic, knowing I'm a bad liar too.

I make them huge sweet iced teas in Styrofoam cups to go with their fried box of heart attack snacks and send them on their way. As they head toward the door, Shay waves her fingers at me, also not discreet at all. Brody's dark eyebrow raises, then he looks to the ceiling as though praying for the patience to get through another day with Shayanne.

* * *

THE SATURDAY NIGHT rush is decent, not too bad but not killer either. The jukebox plays song after song nonstop and most folks order beers, making my job easy. Ilene and Daniel crank out food, and Olivia doesn't even need my help to serve her tables. We're a well-oiled machine until nine o'clock, when Bobby comes in.

Every cell in my body knows the second he walks in, like they're in tune to his presence.

Bobby! they shout.

My heart stops in my chest. My hands freeze too, which means this draft is a bit overfull, but the guy at the bar doesn't seem to mind when I set it down, spilling a bit over the edge of the mug. He even offers me a smile like he thinks I did it intentionally for him.

But my eyes are all for the man crossing the room toward me. Bobby looks good, like sinful sex personified in naturally faded jeans that are molded to his thighs, a red T-shirt stretched across his chest but loose at the waist where it's lazily half-tucked behind a big buckle, brown boots, and a ball cap. He's even got the scruff of yesterday's beard on his cheeks and chin, so he must not have even taken time to shave before coming to see me.

Those dark eyes meet mine and lock me in place as he comes over to the bar, sitting down right in front of me. I love that he doesn't have a preferred barstool but rather sits down wherever will put him closest to me.

"Hey, sweetheart," he drawls out. I swear to God, it sounded like 'wanna have sex in my truck?' Or that's what my vagina heard, anyway, and the answer's a resounding yes, even though he didn't really ask.

"Hey there yourself," I reply, going for smooth and chill but sounding a bit breathless. He hears the difference, judging by the purse of his lips as he fights a cocky grin. "Beer?"

He shakes his head. "Nah, sweet tea."

I quickly pour him a tea and set it in front of him, a little off to the side because I know what's coming next. Or I hope I do.

He doesn't disappoint, leaning far across and holding around the back of my neck to guide me to meet him halfway. God, I love the way he kisses. Like there's nothing more that he needs or wants—not oxygen, not sex, nothing more important than claiming my mouth with his and that's enough.

The bar goes silent, or maybe my ears are full of the whoosh of my racing heartbeat, but it's not until he pulls back that time begins moving again. That smile of his is out in full force now. "Should've done that first," he hums. "Been wanting to all day."

"Hard day at the office?" I joke.

"No monkey suits for me, thanks. Brutal and I checked two of our biggest fields today, though. Makes for a long day in the sun, and we found some beetles so they'll have to be treated. Luckily, not on Shay's heirloom tomatoes or she'd blow a gasket. How about your day?" he asks.

"Yeah, took some of Darla's doughnuts to Unc this morning, then here by lunch."

His eyes search mine, for what I'm not sure, but carefully, he asks, "How's Hank doing? Not used to a workhorse like him skipping out." He looks around, noticing that Unc's not here again. "'Specially not two days in a row."

Not wanting to tell Unc's story since that's his place, and technically, he hasn't even told me, I shrug. "He's okay, I guess. Said he'll be in tomorrow for sure."

"I'm glad you're here to help him. Stubborn old coot needs it but is too proud to ask for any," he says, spot on with both Unc's need and unwillingness to accept help. Except he *is* letting me, and though I'd like to think it's because he's welcoming me with open arms, I think it has more to do with how bad the situation has become.

"Me too." Glancing down the bar, I see a customer flagging me. "I'll be back. Let me check on these people."

"No worries, do what you need to do. I'm gonna wander over to the pool tables for a bit until you've got a second to eat, 'kay?" He's truly asking, and if I preferred for him to sit right there and wait for me, I have no doubt he would without hesitation. Being the focus of his attention is a heady thing, but I would like to double-check that I've done everything I can for Unc for tomorrow's shift.

"Sounds good," I answer, already mentally checking whether that customer had a Bud or Coors.

"Hey," he says, drawing my attention back. "I'm glad you're here for me too, for us."

"*Wow.*"

He chuckles, and I realize I said that aloud. The couple sitting two stools down even seem in awe, watching us like their daily soap opera. I'm pretty sure I hear her whisper, "Why don't you say stuff like that to me?" He doesn't do himself any favors when he answers, "Because you don't say it to me, either."

"Us?" I parrot, still lost in his orbit.

"Us."

He turns to head to the back area where the pool tables are, and I finally close my mouth. The lady tells me, "Girl, lock that man down. Put a ring on his finger and yours, have his babies, and never let him go." To her man, she adds, "It's true." He shakes his head but looks like he agrees.

"Oh." I start, remembering that I'm supposed to be getting a beer. "Coors, right?" I ask, pointing at the guy who flagged me down. He nods kindly and even says 'thanks' when I set it in front of him.

After a couple of hours, the place slows down considerably, to my surprise. The Saturday with live music had been an absolute madhouse, but even the regular Saturdays were busier than this. I'm not complaining, though. It's given me time to watch Bobby.

I guess I expected tonight to be a continuation of where we left off. Hot and heavy, in other words, but he's been happily playing pool with a group of guys he seems vaguely familiar with. He's still shooting sexy looks my way and keeping a close watch over me and the whole bar. I have no doubt he could tell you how many people are here, who's tipsy, who's looking to get laid, and who's looking for an escape into the bottom of a glass. He also probably knows that today is wearing me out, my feet are tired, and my back is aching. I feel like he's observant of things like that, the same way I am.

Actually, I've taken several pictures of him tonight with my phone. Thank God for digital zoom. Those photos are for me, though. To my blog, I posted a tub of lemons with a caption that read, "When life gives you lemons, chop them to bits and suck their insides out." I'd thought it was funny, and it's gotten several comments agreeing with me. Now, I take a shot of my shoes on the slick floor and rubber mats add, "Feet numb. Floor slippery. Bad combo for your girl. Pray for verticality."

Having a few minutes, I make my way across the room toward the pool tables. Oh, who am I kidding? I'm going straight to Bobby like he's pulling on my strings.

The small group shifts automatically, like they know I belong at his side and make space for me to be there. "Did you eat yet?" Bobby asks with real concern, his arm going around my waist and pulling me close.

"Yeah, Ilene set me and Olivia up with some extra fries she had." They hadn't been extra at all. She'd made them for us, delivered them to the bar, then nearly ran back to the kitchen where she prefers it.

"Good."

"What about you? You want something?" I ask, knowing he usually eats with me too.

"I ate already. I was starving and grabbed a bite from Mama Louise before I came," he says with a touch of regret, like I could fault him for it. "I figured I'd snack again with you, though."

"Guess we're both good then." I laugh. Turning to the table, I ask, "Who's winning?"

"Way to back the shark's play," a guy answers me from across the table. He's got a pool stick in his hand and is looking at Bobby expectantly. I guess he's waiting on Bobby to shoot while he's talking to me instead.

"Shark?" I repeat, confused. Looking to Bobby, I ask, "You any good?"

He shrugs modestly, and I know the answer is a resounding yes.

Somehow, that challenge turns into a chance for him to show off, and a casual and friendly tournament breaks out in the group. I even play a bit, though I'm usually behind the bar too much to be any good at games. It's fun, and as we clear out, I can easily work my way back and forth from the bar to the table since I've done so much side work already, and people are slowing down on drinks now that the kitchen is closed and Ilene and Daniel are cleaning up back there.

After a bit, Olivia even plays a round, winning easily. "Take that, sucka," she hollers to the guy she beat. While she waits for her next game, she comes over to the table where I'm perched, filling salt and pepper shakers. Another guy is helping out by wrapping silverware, telling us he used to be a waiter so he's used to it and doesn't mind a bit. The camaraderie is unexpected and sweet, and we get the front of the bar ready for tomorrow too as the games rage on.

Eventually, Bobby plays against a guy named Greg, and they're both really good. Not trick shot good, but strong enough that it's a close matchup.

"Were you stripes or solids again? I forgot," Greg teases, knowing full well that Bobby is stripes and has one more ball on the table than he does.

"Keep talking, man. Fuck up your shot and give me an easy win," Bobby retorts, but there's no heat and everyone laughs.

I see Bobby in a new light, like he was on stage that first night, owning the crowd and them eating out of the palm of his hand. I like this side of him too, the charming guy everybody wants to be around. I especially like it because I know that after this game is over, they'll leave and it'll be just me and him again.

Greg doesn't miss his shot, or the next one. But after he

scratches on his third one, and Bobby takes the cue ball and lines up his shot. I watch him survey the table, planning out each one.

"You got this, Bobby," I cheer, and the fiery look he shoots my way burns through me.

He comes over to stand beside me, hands on the pool cue and eyes on me. "Kiss for luck?"

It's the first time he's asked, usually more the type to take what he wants. I like it when he's commanding, but this seems sweet and flirty. The kiss is over too fast, a quick press of his lips to mine before he returns to the table.

Quick as can be, he pockets one, then another, then another, and finally, the eight ball. Boom.

I clap, offering up a 'woohoo' that's echoed by the rest of the group.

Greg and Bobby shake hands. "Good game, man," Bobby tells him, a good sport.

"You too," Greg replies in kind.

Bobby comes right back to me, crowding in between my knees this time. "Ready for my victory kiss," he growls. There's no question this time.

"What—"

I start to ask what he means since he just kissed me, but he takes advantage of my mouth being wide open by filling it with his tongue, kissing me thoroughly and deeply. The group offers up a round of 'oohs'. I love that he doesn't shy away from showing me affection. If he wants a kiss, he just kisses the hell out of me, right then and there, no matter who's around or what's going on. It's refreshingly bold, and coupled with his bare-boned words, it leaves no doubt in my mind that he wants me.

He finishes the kiss with a sweet smack, smiling widely when he stands straight once again. When I can breathe freely again, I say, "Bar's closed. You don't have to go home, but you can't stay here."

Someone whines, "You didn't say last call."

"Yes, she did," Bobby corrects. I actually did, but it doesn't matter now. I can't serve after two, and I want these people out as soon as possible so that it can be me and Bobby alone again.

The few stragglers gather up their things, leaving with waves and handshakes and promises to come hear Bobby sing next time he plays. Olivia locks the door behind them and we do a quick clean-up of the pool table area.

Ilene and Daniel show up asking if we're ready. "Yeah," Bobby answers for Olivia and me. I'm surprised, having figured we'd stay back like last night, but Bobby walks me out with my co-workers and to my car.

He backs me against the door, sandwiching me between the metal and rock hardness of his body, and runs his thumb over my cheekbone. "You're exhausted, sweetheart. I can see it in those mood-ring eyes of yours, though you're trying hard to hide it with excitement over seeing me. It's okay, I know you want me desperately. I want you too. But I need you well-rested when we go for more. Don't want you tapping out, too weak to go on after round one."

I grin at his cocky, arrogant joke and his dry delivery. He's right, I do want him, but I would need some serious inspiration to be a good bed partner right now. I have no doubt that Bobby has that inspiration and then some, but I would like to be fully rested if he's talking multiple rounds.

Do people actually do that? Sounds like Bobby does.

He gathers me to his chest, wrapping his arms around me, and I feel him lay a sweet kiss to the top of my head. "It's all good. Go home and get some rest. I'll see you tomorrow?"

For a second, I think he knows about Shay's secret plan, but then I realize he's talking about dinner here tomorrow night. "Yeah, tomorrow," I agree, keeping the surprise.

CHAPTER 11

WILLOW

I get to Unc's a little before noon, figuring he'll be out the door to pull the opening shift at the bar. I'm maybe a bit too early, though, because his truck is still sitting in the drive, so I loop around the block, not wanting to get busted.

As I drive down the side street, I see Unc making his way from the house to his blue Chevy long-bed pickup. He's limping, but it's not as bad as yesterday, so maybe the extra day of rest did help a bit. I hope I have him set up well enough that today isn't too much for him. I cross my fingers and toes that he keeps the pockets of his baggy jeans on a stool all day long and doesn't run Olivia ragged.

Once he pulls away, I pull into his driveway spot and climb out. Stretching my arms toward the blue sky, I eye my mission of the day.

"You're going down," I tell the weeds in the flowerbeds. I'd like to think they cower in fear, but it's more likely the breeze blowing them around.

I get to work, pulling weeds first then trimming up the small but overgrown bushes. It's back-breaking work, but I'm glad to tackle it so Unc doesn't have to, or worse, pay someone to do it. Not that he would. He'd rather let the whole place fall to shambles than admit he couldn't handle things with his own two bony hands.

I even manage to pull out the couple of cracked edging pieces and flip them around so the unblemished side of the concrete is facing forward. I'll sneak back over and replace them at some point, but I wasn't sure how many I'd need so I couldn't buy them at the hardware store this morning.

By the time I'm done, my shirt is soaked through with sweat, my shoulders are a bit pink from the sun, and my heart is full of butterflies. It looks great, maintained and cared for, but not so drastically different that Unc will pull up and immediately notice that something's changed.

That had been my worry about adding any flowers or doing anything too major. Unc would probably have a fit, and this way, with it being such a minor update, maybe he won't even realize it. That's my hope, anyway—to be able to take care of him without abusing his sense of pride and independence.

I head back home, those butterflies moving into my belly. I need to shower and get dressed to head out to Bobby's for Shayanne's surprise plan. What do you wear to ambush your boyfriend?

Boyfriend?

A small laugh bubbles up at the idea of Bobby as a *boy*-anything. He's all man, from the top of his dark hair to the tips of his booted feet and everywhere in between. *Well, I assume as much from what I've felt through his jeans,* I think with a smile.

I'd like to know for real, but the way he's slowing us down physically while speeding us up emotionally is unexpected and keeping me on edge. Hunger, want, need, lust, and true enjoyment of his attention all bloom like little seeds he planted deep inside me, growing at a pace he sets.

In the shower, I take the time to shave everywhere because I know that it's only a matter of time and I want to be ready whenever Bobby is. I am ready, so ready I consider taking matters into my own hands the way Bobby said he's done. But I wait, knowing that while I'm good, I want this orgasm from him, not a weak imitation where I'm fantasizing about his fingers gracefully playing me like that guitar he loves.

After applying a bit of aloe to my shoulders and lotion to my legs, I get dressed in cutoff shorts and a fresh T-shirt, knotting it at my waist. I choose my work tennis shoes because if I'm going to be in with the goats, I'll want something more protective than my Walmart flip-flops.

I'm about to head out when my phone rings.

"Hey, Mom," I answer.

"Willow Grace Parker, I have not heard from you in two weeks. Unless you've taken up a vow of silence, there's no excuse," she replies, a smile in her voice. Funny thing is, she's not kidding. I did vow to stay quiet once, in protest for something I've forgotten about now but which had seemed hugely important at the time. The silence had lasted almost a week before I'd given up. If I remember correctly, it was to beg for a candy bar.

"No vow of silence this time, Mom. I've been working six days a week, lunch to close." She knows that already but has probably already forgotten if she's been head down in her art or someone else's.

"Oh, I didn't catch you at a bad time then, did I? I just wanted to check in and see how things are going."

"No, I'm heading out, but I have a few minutes. And things are going really well. I went over this morning and cleaned up Unc's flower beds, without telling him, of course," I say, smiling to myself. "He's actually taken the last couple of days off too and left me to take care of the bar, so that's good progress."

Mom hums agreement.

"Well, except in return, he gave me today off. Hence, the yard-work," I muse, seeing her point. "But I left him well set up to sit on his butt all day, and I set Olivia on him. I also filled in Unc's friends to do a drive-by pre-poker game check too."

"You are such a kind-hearted girl, Willow," she says proudly. "How's Hank look?"

I consider that carefully. "Lean, frail, bit pale sometimes. But he's fighting hard, which is good. Nobody here seems to know what's going on with him, so I'm keeping my mouth shut too. Seems like that's how he wants it."

"Figures. Stubborn ass is just like Dad. I wish I could come out there, but I think seeing me would just hurt him more. I'm glad

you're there, though, sweetie. He doesn't know how lucky he is."
She's getting choked up, and I know that she truly wishes she
could be here. Unc was in my life until I was a teenager, but he
was Mom's favorite (and only) uncle for her whole life until
Grandpa and him had their row.

She blows her nose in my ear and rallies. "So, a day of freedom
then? Are you off to take photos? I've seen your recent work, and
I must say, the new subject matter you're discovering there is
compelling. You're doing a phenomenal job of showcasing a
different slice of life in stunning detail."

Her compliments go straight to my heart, meaning more than
she could ever know. Mom is an amazing artist herself and knows
art when she sees it, when she feels it. So for her to appreciate my
work is a huge confidence booster.

I laugh a little, awkwardly telling her, "Yes, of goats, if you can
believe that. Bobby's sister, Shayanne, invited me out to see their
goats. And to surprise him, too."

I told Mom about Bobby after we first met, about his voice and
his punching out the handsy customer, but we haven't really
talked much since then for me to share with her the way things
have gotten more serious between Bobby and me.

"Ooh, Singing Bobby?" she squeals, as if that's his given name.
"The one with the growly, honey voice and the mean right hook?"
Mom clarifies, throwing my own words back at me.

"That'd be him. We're . . . dating?" I answer.

"That sounded like a question mark. Are you or aren't you?
You can tell me if it's nothing more than a casual hook-up situation. I'm hip like that, Willow."

The bad thing is . . . she is. She's hipper than I am, by far. I
could probably tell her that I've taken up group orgies wearing
horse reins and going full-on pony play and she wouldn't blink if
it made me happy and I was following my heart. But, for all the
creative free-spiritedness I got from my mother, I'm more of a
prude than she is and not usually a casual sex girl. In fact, I only
know about pony play because I watched a video that popped up
on my feed, and I'd been careful to clear my history after curiosity
got to me just in case the algorithm logistics decided I wanted
more of that, because I definitely do not. Not my cup of tea at all.

"It's not like that, Mom. It's more serious, but we're taking things slow-ish," I tell her, not sure how to explain the way Bobby looks at me, owning my mind and claiming my body, even if we haven't had sex yet.

"It's not slow, nor fast. It's just right and will take as long as it takes for as long as it lasts, sweetie. Remember that," she says sagely, sounding like fortune cookie advice.

"Thanks, Mom. I'd better go. It's a bit of a drive out to the farm, and I want to double-check on Unc before I head out. Love you."

"Okay, call me if you need anything. Love you, Willow."

The click is final, and I hadn't realized until just now how much I miss her. Time has flown by in the few weeks I've been in Great Falls, my new routine becoming as comfortable as yoga pants and oversized T-shirts. But I'm not just lazing about. I'm getting out there, making friends and stretching myself creatively. Like Mom said, away from the city, I'm finding a compelling new view to explore, both around me and within me.

A quick text to Olivia lets me relax that Unc is doing fine at the bar, and remarkably, he is sitting on his butt, for the most part. As expected, he grumbled about my liquor rearranging, but Olivia sent me a picture of Unc tilting the stool back on two legs to reach the bottles instead of getting up now. The balancing act makes me nervous too, but I guess it's better than laps behind the bar.

Mind and heart at ease, I feel free to focus on this surprise visit.

* * *

FOLLOWING THE GPS'S DIRECTIONS, I find myself stopped in front of a large gate that says *Tannen*. I'm so excited to see where Bobby lives because it feels like who he is, but there's a tiny bit of nerves still swirling because he didn't do the inviting.

Not leaving me any chance at backing out, I see a horse galloping toward me, a plume of dust billowing up behind it and a banner of light brown hair blowing on the rider.

"You came!" Shayanne screams before she even gets close enough for me to hear, but I can read her lips clearly.

"I did," I say softly, since there's no chance she'll hear me through the closed window. But I nod and smile, feeling slightly surer about this.

She climbs off, letting the horse nibble on grass as she opens the gate, then spastically waves a hand to guide me through. Once I'm on the other side, she closes it and hops back on the horse. I follow her down the long dirt driveway, parking in front of a two-story house.

This is Bobby's house, I think excitedly.

I want to explore every nook and cranny, study each room to see what makes him tick and what created this man who has stolen my heart. But Shayanne doesn't lead me to the house, instead flagging me over to her.

I approach the horse slowly, having never been around them before.

"C'mere, girl. He won't bite ya. Promise," she reassures me as though she's not sitting astride a one-thousand-pound animal with a mind and will of its own.

I get a bit closer, step by step, holding out my hand like you do with an unfamiliar dog to let the horse sniff me. He snorts, scaring me, and I jump a bit. "Ah!"

Shayanne laughs, patting the horse's neck. "You really are a city girl, ain't ya?"

I glare back and her grin widens. Getting a little more comfortable since the horse hasn't bitten my hand, I work up to gently rubbing his nose. Snout? Muzzle? I don't know the proper terminology, but it's soft as velvet under my fingertips.

"Can I take his picture?" I whisper, not wanting to spook the animal.

With no such worries, Shayanne says, "Hell, yeah. He'd love to be your model."

I grab my camera bag from the passenger seat of the car, throwing it easily over one shoulder and letting it hang on the opposite hip to take my baby out. Holding it up to my eye, I find the horse through the lens, framing the shot that I want.

Click.

Adjust and do it again. And then again.

As though he heard Shayanne's prediction, he holds still and lets me snap away as many shots as I want. I even switch to my phone for a few so that I can do a quick post online of the shadowed contrast leading to his beautiful eyes which stare me down.

"All right, let's get this show on the road. I can't wait to see Bobby's reaction, not George's," Shay says with another pat of the horse's neck. "Actually, I'm guessing if you've never seen a horse, you might not be ready to ride yet. Let me put him in the barn and we'll take the Gator."

I have no idea why she'd have an alligator here or how that's supposed to be better than a horse, but she's gone toward the barn before I can ask. She reappears a moment later on a big golf cart on steroids, pulling up to wave me inside. I climb in, and she takes off like a bullet, seeming to know exactly where she's going.

The rolling land gives way to a horizon of crops and trees. Getting closer, I can see two large silhouettes breaking the even spacing of the tree trunks. Bobby and Brutal.

Shayanne stops the Gator, and I get out. As soon as I'm clear of the vehicle, one of the silhouettes starts moving my way. Shayanne was excited to see me here, but Bobby is literally running toward me.

"Willow?" he shouts. "You're here!" He scoops me up in his arms, spinning me around in a circle and squeezing a laugh out of me.

Putting my feet back on the ground, he asks, "What are you doing here?"

I have that moment of doubt, but the light in his dark eyes burns it away in a flash. "Shay said it would be a good surprise and promised me pictures of the goats."

He rumbles, promising, "You can take pictures of any damn thing you want to."

He hasn't let go of me, his arms still wrapped around my waist tightly as if he's checking to make sure I'm real. I can feel his heart pounding with excitement beneath my palms as he presses his forehead to mine, breathing me in like I'm his oxygen.

Shayanne jumps in, breaking our sexy stare down to threaten, "I might have to hold you to that. But she's mine first because I had the balls to invite her out, unlike some people." Her fingers grip around my arm and pull me to her side like I'm a toy they're fighting over.

Bobby growls at Shayanne, "Fuck that."

I can't help but laugh at his reaction, teasing dryly, "Yeah, I'm totally just here for the goats. That's the *only* reason." I give him a head to toe check, taking in the sweaty hair sticking out of his ballcap, the dirty shirt and jeans that are molded to him like a second skin, and that white smile amid the scruff I want to rub against like a cat with a scratching post.

"Yeah, she likes your ugly face too, for some reason," Shay taunts with an eye roll. "But goats first, asshole brothers second." She holds up one finger for the goats, but instead of a second for Bobby, she just points at him.

"Fine, the goats are cute, I guess. But don't leave, okay?" He seems genuinely concerned that I might disappear into thin air, and I realize that my being here means something to him the same way it does to me. We've gotten so close, intimate, really, but it's mostly been within the confines of Hank's—never at my place, and never at his. How can that be for someone I'm this in tune with? I feel like I would be able to pinpoint him in a crowd, my heart drawn to him like a magnet.

"You might have to call Chief Gibson to get me out of here now that I'm past the gate," I threaten with a smile.

He shakes his head, pinning me in place with a heated look. "Never."

Shay pulls my arm again. "Okay, loverboy. Enough for now. We're going up to see the goats."

"Not Baarbara," he warns, and Shay rolls her eyes in a solid 'duh' response.

She nearly shoves me back into the Gator and pulls away, spinning the tires in the grass. "I figure we have about thirty minutes before he comes sniffing around again, so we'll have to cut short the tour of Tannen Farm and stick with just the goats." Talking to herself more than me, she adds, "He'd probably kill me if I went anywhere else, anyway." But there's an evil little glint in her eye that makes it seem like she'd like to see Bobby try.

In the pen, we're instantly surrounded by baaing goats of every color and size. They go for Shay, and she scratches behind their ears, so I follow her lead. "Keep your camera up high or they'll take it right out of your hands."

I do as she suggests but ultimately go a step further and set my bag outside the gate in favor of focusing on the adorable animals. The goats aren't nearly as scary as George was, mostly because of their smaller size.

Before long, I'm sitting in the dirt with a small, brown-spotted goat in my lap, petting its wiry hair and smiling wide. "Look, Shay. It's licking me," I whisper, delighted.

I look up to find her snapping a picture of me with her phone. I'm not used to that, never the subject of my own photography beyond a hand here or a leg there. Once or twice, I've shown a snippet of my face, basically a close-up of my eye so that I stay anonymous. But Shayanne is taking a full-frame shot of me and little Trollie. I look down shyly, but Trollie chooses that moment to lick my face.

"Ah!" I shout, laughing as I look up so that his tongue swipes along my chin rather than French kissing me.

"Got it!" she exclaims. "That's gonna be a good one, I bet. Well, not that I bet. No gambling allowed." She's mimicking a lower voice, presumably one of her brothers. At my lifted brow, she asks, "You haven't heard about our dad? Hell, girl, what rock have you been living under?"

I confess, "All I know is Unc said your dad put you through the wringer, but you all seem okay to me."

She laughs, plopping ungracefully to the dirt next to me. "We do seem okay, but most folks do on the outside. It's the inside that's all twisted up like a ball of baling wire."

That's actually really insightful, especially for something delivered so off-handedly and casually. I eye Shayanne with new appreciation. "So you're not okay?" I ask gently, not sure if I'm getting too close to dangerous territory.

She shrugs, but I see that she's picking at a ragged spot on her cuticle. "We are now, for the most part. But how you grow up, it shapes you. I reckon you mostly want to know about Bobby, so here's what I'll tell you—"

I wave a hand, not wanting to push her. "You don't have to say anything."

She ignores me. "Yes, I do. I think it's good for you to know, and fuck knows, he ain't gonna tell you shit unless he's singing it in a song." She throws another eye roll, something that seems to be a habit. "Bobby was right on the edge of greatness, has always been too good for this place. You ever heard the expression about roses needing fancy soil, but dandelions just pop right up through the concrete whether you want them to or not?"

I nod, getting what she's saying even if I haven't heard the phrase.

"Bobby's like a rose that decided concrete was good enough for him. And not just any old rose, but like one of those fancy heirloom ones that have to be cultivated from generational stock and cared for better than a newborn baby. He's like one of those that decided pit gravel was just fine. He blooms, and it's pretty as can be, but it ain't right and we all know it." She looks around, but I can tell she's seeing something other than the goats and fence around us. "But he's a hold-on-er. He lost so much—Mom, Dad, his chance at the life he wanted, the farm. So now he holds on to everything with both hands and an iron will, even if it suffocates the tar out it. He damn near killed Brutal that way one time, just hanging on so tight, trying to protect him with everything he had. He and Brutal had it out."

"Who won?" I can't imagine a battle between the two brothers. One, they seem so close, and two, their reputations as fighters definitely precedes them.

Shay's brows climb. "That you even ask tells me something about you, Willow. You think Bobby has a chance against Brutal? Hell no, but I like that you're on his side anyway."

I let that sink in.

"Tell me about you," Shay orders. "What's your damage? And don't say nothing, because we all have something, and you showed up here out of the blue, making all the tongues wag."

Those are two separate questions with very different answers. I actually grew up pretty fortunate with Mom and Dad, and even Oakley, something I didn't know to be thankful for until I saw that other people didn't have it quite so well. But as for why I came? I'm not willing to answer that. It's not my place, so I stick with my standard answer, even though it's hard to do so when

Shay is giving me so much more insight to Bobby and the Tannens. "Nothing, really. I'm just a regular girl who needed a break. A fresh start somewhere, but not too fresh, you know what I mean? I figured I knew someone here, at least."

"Hank," Shay fills in for me. "Is it true you hadn't seen him in years when you showed up?"

I nod. "Yeah, since I was fourteen. Seemed about time to lay old bones to rest."

Before she can ask me anything else, a whining noise fills the air and the goats get up to check it out.

"Damn, that was faster than I thought. Bobby's coming," she tells me right as another Gator comes over the hill. It nearly catches air on the bumpy, grassy surface before sliding to a stop.

Bobby gets out, striding straight toward me. Automatically, I rise, setting Trollie down, which he argues about loudly. *Baaaaaa!*

Bobby doesn't go for the gate. No, he hops right over the pen fencing, making the shortest distance between point A, that'd be him, and point B, that'd be me, his direct route.

"I didn't get a chance to do this," he murmurs right before his hands cup my cheeks and tilt my face up. Then his mouth covers mine, kissing me passionately. He smells like sweat and fresh dirt, and . . . man. He tastes like . . . intensity and mint, like he knew exactly what he was going to do when he saw me and prepped for it. Unnecessary—I'd kiss him even if his breath were as bad as Trollie's—but the intent is sweet.

A throat clears behind him and one of his hands leaves my face. I crack one eye open to find him flipping Brutal a middle finger, all the while giving me one of the best kisses of my life.

"Hi," I say breathlessly when he lets me go.

"Hi," he answers, smiling. "Whatcha doing?"

I blink, trying to clear my head so that I can form a complete sentence. Or even a two-syllable word would be good right now.

"Uh, goats. Pet. Soft. Pictures. Cute." It's all I've got, but it gets my message across.

His grin turns cocky, and he slings an arm around my shoulders, pulling me to his side. I fit there like the space was carved out just for me. "With your camera over there?" He points with his other hand to my camera bag outside the pen in the grass.

I realize I truly haven't taken any pictures. Shay took the ones of me, but those aren't bloggable, and I would love some cute animal pictures. One, it's a unique subject for me, which is always an exciting challenge, and two, I do think they'll be a blog favorite. Who's not going to 'heart' an adorable goat?

And that's when I have an even better idea.

I grab my camera, checking the sky and adjusting my settings. "Let me get a few shots here."

I take some close-ups of horns, eyes, hooves. *Click, click, click.*

I take some broader shots of the herd, the blending of their colors and the lines of their curved backs. *Click, click, click.*

"Bobby, can you pick that one up?" I point to the goat currently weaving its way through his legs like a house cat that wants to be pet.

"Why?" he asks cautiously.

I shoot him a soft smile, and though he grumbles a bit, he bends down and picks up the goat, its legs dangling over his arms.

"I'll do a close-up so no one can tell it's you. You don't mind being on the blog, do you?"

Let me take this picture, please.

My ovaries are literally exploding like Fourth of July fireworks right now. He looks that good. Dirty jeans with a tear by his right hip that lets the pocket show, veins popping in his muscled forearms and biceps bulging, jaw tight, eyes dark and promising me anything my heart and body desire, all topped off with the utter cuteness of the baby goat. It's easy to replace the cute animal with a baby in my mind, and the thought of Bobby's baby, of him as a dad, is sexy as hell. And not in a Daddy fetish sort of way—yes, I saw that video too—but as an actual father. He'd be good at it, protective, loving, firm, sweet.

Boom. Pop. Hiss. Yep, there go my ovaries.

"Anything you want, Willow," Bobby answers, turning a bit toward me so I can get a better angle.

Click. Click. Click.

Soon, I move to wide angle frames, getting all of Bobby and all of the goats. These are for me, I promise. *Not the blog,* I think possessively, taking a page from Bobby's book.

"Look at you, Nashville. Show us how you model. Give me a Zoolander Blue Steel look," Brutal barks out, laughing before he can even get the insult out.

I spin, capturing that too.

"Hey, I didn't agree to shit," Brutal tells me, sobering in an instant.

"Oh, sorry," I say, dropping the camera down to make eye contact.

"It's fine," Bobby interjects. "Tell her it's fine. She can take pictures of anything or anyone she wants to."

"No, really, I'm sorry. I didn't mean to—"

Shayanne whistles loudly. "Hey, Brutal, know what would probably get Allyson all hot and bothered?"

Quick as a blink, he deadpans, "Me." For a scary mother-fucker, the guy's got jokes. I think he's joking, at least. Sort of.

"Exactly. Hey, Willow, think you could send Allyson that picture? Brutal needs all the help he can get to get laid." The insult is harsh, as intended, and given Brutal's growl and Bobby's howl of laughter, it's completely untrue.

"Sure. I can do that." I laugh along with them, and any tension is broken.

Before long, I'm taking pictures of all three of them—holding goats, standing alone, standing together, sitting in the Gator, and more, and they're really getting into it, posing and pulling faces.

Mostly, I let them interact with each other, not directing them at all so I get real, candid shots. Those are the moments of true beauty. Unfiltered, unaltered moments of heartfelt connection, even if it's couched in giving each other a hard time.

When Shay decides that climbing on the roof of the Gator is a good idea, despite the loud protests of both of her brothers, I take a shot while lying on the ground so it will have the added effect of a cool perspective. Even through the lens, I can tell that Shayanne looks powerful, invincible, ready to take the world by storm, which fits what Bobby has told me about her. The second shot I take of that moment includes both guys standing at the ready to catch her and watching her closely. The affection is obvious and shines brightly.

"Oh, my phone," Shay says, jumping from the roof of the

Gator as if the five feet are no big deal. Pulling it out of her pocket, she grins that evil smile again before looking at Bobby. "Mama Louise says it's time for us all to wash up for dinner."

"Oh, I'll go then," I offer, not wanting to intrude any more than I already have. I'm sure Bobby and Brutal had chores to do today, but they've spent the last hour goofing off with me. It's been fun and I've gotten some amazing pictures, but I know their family dinners are pretty sacrosanct.

Bobby stops me with a growl and his arms around my waist. "The fuck? She said 'us all'. That means Mama Louise is expecting you at dinner too. And I wouldn't have it any other way. Now that I have you here, I might never let you go." He sounds serious, and rather than being scared at becoming his pseudo-hostage, my whole body lights up like fireworks again. He wants me here as much as I want to be here. While I'm playing through mental images of never leaving his side, he keeps talking, trying to sell me on the idea of staying. "The last person you want to disappoint is Mama Louise. You also don't refuse her food. She's the best."

"I thought Ilene was the best," I tease.

"So does she," Bobby says sadly, shaking his head like Ilene is delusional and everyone just goes along with it. I've had Ilene's food, though, and it's delicious. But if Mama Louise can top it, I'm in. Hell, I'm in if only to meet the woman he says rescued his family.

CHAPTER 12

BOBBY

I shove Shayanne toward Brutal's Gator, grabbing at the keys as she tries to hold them behind her back.

"I can drive Willow up to the house!" she argues. She knows it's a losing battle, but that doesn't stop her. It never does.

"Shayanne. Give me the keys," I sternly order. Once upon a time, that'd be enough to get her to do it, but now, she's all independent and wild, thinking she can do any old thing she wants, like invite Willow out for the day without telling me.

Shit, that could've gone so badly if Willow had freaked the fuck out. But looking at her now, wind blowing her short hair around, eyes bright behind her glasses, and a sunny smile on her face, she seems perfectly at ease. Thank fuck.

Knowing what I have to do to get the keys, I grab Shayanne around her middle, picking her up so her booted feet kick the air. Spinning her around, I tell her loudly enough for Brutal and Willow to hear, because public humiliation is key to this apology. "Thank you for inviting Willow out to the farm. I appreciate it. Now, can I have the keys . . . please?"

Sitting her back down, she laughs, her mouth open wide and grinning. "See, that wasn't so hard, now was it?" I hold my hand out, and she drops the key into my hand. "We'd best get to the house, no dilly-dallying. Mama and me made pot roast."

I groan. Pot roast is delicious, Shay and Mama Louise's even more so, but when they cook roast, it means they planned the day with ideas in mind, like ambushing me with Willow and spending the day fucking off with the goats. Shayanne is such a schemer. God, I love that girl.

At the house, we wash up on the back porch and I can feel the tension in Willow now. I throw my chin at Brutal and Shayanne, telling them to go in without us. With my hands on Willow's shoulders, I turn her to face me, quietly asking, "Hey, you okay?"

She smiles, but it doesn't reach her eyes. "Yeah, just a little nervous to meet the infamous Mama Louise. Unc talks about her too, you know? Basically makes her sound like a fictional warrior woman, battling for her family and the power of love. He talks about her pies too, says they're better than Ilene's but that I'd best take that to the grave if I know what's good for my stomach."

I laugh a little. Hank's not that far off. "Actually, that's pretty true. She's a force, but in a good way. I think you'll have that in common."

It's on the tip of her tongue to refute my assessment, but her mouth closes slowly and I can see the compliment sink into her in stages—ears, mind, heart, body. "Flattery will get you everything, Bobby. But I'm guessing you already know that," she replies, lighter than she was a moment ago.

"Not flattery if it's true," I reply. Brushing her sweep of bangs to the side, I meet her eyes. "You ready for this? You already met most of the gang, and they like you more than they like me at this point. Just the kids and Mama Louise left, and I have no doubt they'll feel the same way."

She pushes at my chest, smirking. "Pretty sure the whole town is in love with you, so quit fishing for adoration."

She thinks she's telling the truth, that the whole town loves me, but she couldn't be more wrong. They love the image they've created of me, some sappy singing cowboy who loves the limelight, when the truth is much darker and my singing onstage is one of the hardest things I've ever done.

"Don't need the town's love, just yours," I tell her, touching toward what I really want.

Her smile is the real deal this time, and feeling like she's as ready as she's gonna be, I take her hand and lead her inside.

"'Bout time," Mark grumbles, spooning more than his fair share of potatoes onto his plate.

All conversation stops and all movement freezes as eyes cut to me and Willow, who's got a death grip on my hand.

Breaking the solid block of ice in the room, I say, "Everybody remember Willow?"

There's a round of 'hey, Willow' and 'welcome' as the girls all high-five. I hear Sophie tell Shayanne, "Hell yeah, girl. Good job." Guess that's about Shay getting Willow here when I hadn't so much as asked her to come out, too fearful that she'd balk.

I lead Willow to the end of the table across from Mark. "Mama Louise, this is Willow Parker. Willow, this is Mama Louise."

Willow shakes Mama Louise's hand, "Nice to meet you, Louise."

Mama Louise shakes her head, gray-streaked blonde hair and blue eyes dancing. "None of that. I go by Mama or Mama Louise. Even your Uncle Hank calls me that, and he's a good ten years older than me, not that we're discussing age, mind you."

Willow catches the important thing. "Nice to meet you then, Mama Louise."

Mama Louise beams and nods. "Best have a seat then, or these boys won't leave you any food." She scans the table, her eyebrow rising. "Mark, I know you're not planning on eating all those potatoes yourself, are you?"

In reply, he lifts one blonde brow and forks a whole baby red into his mouth in one go, chewing open-mouthed from the over-sized bite.

Mama Louise sighs like the long-suffering mother she is to us all.

We get settled, me in my usual place and Willow between me and Cooper. Technically, he's Allyson's son and Brutal's stepson, but he's been adopted by us all.

Cooper stage-whispers to Willow, "Make sure you get enough roast and veggies so that you get dessert. Plum cobbler tonight." His face screws up. "On second thought, don't. Because then I'll get your serving of cobbler too."

"Cooper!" Allyson barks, horrified.

But he and Willow are giggling like they shared a secret. Willow reaches for the carrots and spoons a few onto her plate, then with a smirk at Cooper, she adds a couple more in a clear 'challenge accepted' sort of way. He sighs, rolling his eyes in a pretty decent imitation of Shay. Right off the bat, she's charmed Cooper too.

We get down to eating without much talking. We work hard all day, mostly outside, and need the calories, plus it's delicious. But once the voids in our bellies are satisfied, conversation starts to flow.

"How're you liking working at Hank's, dear?" Mama Louise asks Willow.

She swallows a bite of thick toast slathered in butter and dabs at her mouth before answering. It looks like manners, but I can see that she's putting off answering. She doesn't like the spotlight on her, and every pair of eyes has turned her way, interested in the newcomer to the dinner table, especially since she's by my side.

"It's good," she says safely. "I've been a bartender off and on since I was eighteen, but even I was surprised by how busy a Thursday two-dollar draft night could be. And that had nothing on live music Saturday night." She looks at me, and I can't help but place my hand on her thigh under the table. She about jumps a foot and squirms beneath my palm.

My sweet Willow is shy, I think. And maybe nervous in front of my whole crew. She has nothing to be concerned about, though. We're about as rough as they come, and Katelyn's basically doing us all a solid by sitting in her own chair and not Mark's lap. Mama Louise doesn't allow that at her dinner table, but beyond that, it's all good and no one would bat an eye at my hand being on her leg.

I shrug modestly. "We'll see how busy it is next weekend when I play again. I always figure it's going to be a show for one, just me and Hank in the place, and I'm shocked anybody else shows up to listen."

Brody coughs, muttering under his breath, "Bullshit."

Mama Louise isn't fooled by that fake cough, though. "Language."

Willow laughs, and I feel her relax now that no one's paying her direct attention. Well, no one besides me. I can't help but be focused on her every move, every nuanced flash of emotion across her face as I measure every inch of space between us.

"It's such a beautiful night. Let's take our plum cobbler out back," Mama Louise suggests.

Allyson and Cooper hop up to clear the table, and we all hand them our plates. The rest of us help put up the few bits of leftovers, wipe down the wood table until it shines, and dish up the cobbler into bowls.

Out back, the sun has fully set and the moon is rising high, bright and white against the indigo sky pricked with sprinkles of stars. We make our way to the circle of congregated wood chairs and stools that Brutal and Cooper have built over the past few months and settle in to eat.

"Mmm," Willow moans when she eats her first bite of cobbler with melted homemade vanilla ice cream. My own spoon freezes halfway to my mouth, wanting to hear that sound again . . . without everyone else around. Willow must feel my gaze on her because she blinks and looks my way sheepishly. "What? It's good," she whispers.

"It is." My agreement isn't about the plum cobbler at all.

Shayanne jumps in, "This? This ain't nothing, just a quickie cobbler. Jam plus fruit plus biscuits plus sugar butter. It cooked up while we were chopping up the veggies for the roast and was done before we were. Ain't that right, Mama?"

Mama Louise nods, spooning another bite into her mouth and watching me and Willow much more closely than Shayanne is. I see the little smile on Mama Louise's face, though, and that makes me feel like she's onboard with my thoughts about Willow. I don't need her to be, considering I'll do what I want either way, but her approval will make things a whole lot easier when Willow is here. And I'm hoping she'll be here a lot.

The evening cornhole tournament begins, and I'm immediately challenged by Cooper because we haven't played in a bit. "You're going down, Uncle Bobby! Six feet under," he taunts.

A laugh tries to burst out, but I fight it down, glaring at Cooper instead. We have a stare-off, something the pipsqueak is getting better at, much to Allyson's dismay, until Brutal says, "Let's go, boys. The rest of us want to play tonight too. Ain't got time for your trash talking, dick measuring pre-game ritual."

I snicker, fighting valiantly not to laugh, but I lose the battle when Mama Louise says with a long-suffering sigh, "Could we not talk about penises tonight, please?"

At least I'm not the only one because everyone else has a moment of shock at Mama Louise, the one who always corrects our language, popping out with 'penis talk' like it's no big deal. Technically, it's the anatomically correct term, but I can definitely say that she's not the type to use the term unless it's talking about one of the farm animals.

The laughter is enough to get the game rolling, with Mama Louise already in the lead without picking up a single beanbag. Cooper kicks my ass, as we all expected he would, me included. "Good game, kid," I tell him, ruffling his hair. He might win at cornhole, but I can still irritate him a bit in return. It's good for him, keeps him from getting too big for his britches. For now.

When I try to find Willow's eyes, I see she's behind her phone again. She lowers it slightly and smiles. She tilts her head toward Mama Louise. "She said it was okay."

I sit back down beside her and whisper in her ear, "I told you, sweetheart. You can take all the pictures you want, of anything you want. Especially me."

The games rage on, cobbler long forgotten and no one paying any attention to Willow or her phone's camera. She's turned it on silent and is capturing my family in a way I've never seen them. It's interesting to silently sit back and watch her work, to see how she frames things to give them an intimacy that evokes emotion even through the screen.

She captures Mark and Katelyn talking, their faces close together and the love readily apparent. She snaps away when Cooper loses and flops into the grass in exaggerated pained defeat. She clicks the moment when Sophie and James have a silent conversation, agreeing that they're ready to go to bed, complete with a yawning Cindy Lou in James's lap.

I move behind Willow and press the button on the screen to flip her camera. Framing both of us, I look to the screen and see her surprise at seeing us together like this. With her eyes on me, I take the picture. Then she smiles at the camera, and I turn to her, letting every bit of what I feel shine through. I might not be able to find the right words easily, but I know what I'm feeling. It's early, but it's the beginning of something deep and powerful.

I know she sees it in the resulting shot because she looks back to me, her eyes wide and unguarded. Without her walls up, I can see the doubts lurking in their swirling depths. "Willow." I start to say something, though I don't know what, but instead I see the screen flash out of the corner of my eyes as she takes another shot.

"I know," she says softly, just between us. "I want a picture of this moment right here so I always remember the moment I knew."

Fuck. She gets me. Even without words, she gets me. I wrap my arms around her, hugging her tight as though I could crawl into her skin through our clothes, right here in the heat of this summer night.

Somehow, the Earth's axis hasn't shifted for anyone else. They're playing on as though nothing significant has happened, though I know good and well that it has.

Brutal wins his game against Luke, but ultimately, it's a final match-up between Rix and Mama Louise. Any of the rest of us would let Mama Louise win. Not Rix. She's hardcore at everything she does, always fighting to be taken seriously as a female mechanic and racer, and she never takes her foot off the gas. Not even for Mama Louise.

We all celebrate Rix's win, including Brody, who gives her a big kiss. Cooper whispers, "Yuck," and we all chuckle, telling him to just wait, and if he's lucky, one day, he'll get to congratulate his girl with a kiss too. He shakes his head vehemently, deeming it 'disgusting'.

Slowly, we all start to make moves toward home. Luke and Shayanne head to their loft over the barn, where they like to be because it's close to the horses. Mark and Katelyn go to their house on the other side of the hill behind the Bennett pond. James, Sophie, and Cindy Lou already went to their house in town to get some much-needed rest. Brutal, Allyson, and Cooper go to their house on the east side of what used to be our farm. Brody and Rix head to our family home, where I sleep too. Mama Louise gives me a nod, seeing the intent in my eyes. "Will you make sure the candles are all out before you leave tonight?"

There are torches out in the yard, closer to the cornhole area to keep it bug-free while we play, and a single citronella candle on the porch giving it a warm glow. I dip my chin in agreement, simultaneously thanking her for letting Willow and me have this time and space for a bit longer.

Alone, I take Willow's hand in mine, brushing along her skin with my thumb. Even the small contact is driving me crazy. *She* is driving me crazy, gorgeously unaware of what she's doing to me with every sweet little smile, every kind word, every peek into her mind and heart.

"Today was fun," she says quietly. "I'm so glad I came, though Shayanne didn't give me much of a choice." Her laugh is muted, and I wonder how much finessing Shay had to do to get Willow to agree.

"I don't think I've ever been gladder that Shay sticks her nose in every damn thing. Seeing you across the field today was . . ." I stumble over the words, not sure how to describe that moment. The best I can do is . . . "It felt right. Like this place had been missing something, and I didn't even know it. But it was finally right."

I don't know what I expected her to say to that, but I know she surprises me again by leaning over and kissing me. She's been responsive every time, that's for sure, but I've initiated each time our lips have met. That she does it this time soothes something inside me that's been ruffled since I saw her behind the bar.

Our lips dance, and somewhere in the breath between us, she whispers, "Thank you."

I have no idea what for, and I'm far too lost in her to figure it out right now.

My tongue swipes along her lower lip and she opens for me. I tease along her tongue slowly, gently prodding her to let me in deeper. Into her mouth, into her mind, into her heart.

I want to know them all, stake a flag in them declaring them mine, and let her claim me too.

I pull her into my lap, her strong thighs going astride my hips as she straddles me. Gripping her ass, I knead the flesh there as I kiss down her neck. She's wearing a T-shirt tonight, so I can't slip tank top straps down like before, but I manage to pull at the neckline to get more access to her skin. I trace her collarbone with my tongue, sucking the tender skin above it to bring blood to the surface. I might not be in her heart fully yet, but her body I can mark as mine. Her hands grip my hair, urging me on, wanting a bruise to remember this moment the same way she wanted the picture earlier.

"Willow," I growl against her neck in warning when she rolls her hips.

"More," she pleads.

"A little," I concede hesitantly. I'm on the edge here, wanting her so badly but knowing it's too soon for what I really want.

I guide her hips, rubbing her clit against the hard ridge of my cock through the two layers of denim. "Bobby." Her moan is kerosene on a bonfire, and I move her harder, faster, letting her muffled cries direct me.

"Use me, sweetheart. Come on me, for fuck's sake. Let me see you come for me." It should be an order, but it's as much a plea as her request for more was. I need this from her, her walls down, her guard dropped, her body mine.

She bucks her hips sharply, fucking me through our clothes. I can feel the warmth at her core, hotter than the steamy night around us. Her voice breaks, a cry cut off as she buries her mouth against my shoulder and shudders on top of me.

I thrust up a few more times, prolonging her orgasm for my own pleasure. Watching her come is my new favorite thing, I decide. One I want to repeat again . . . now.

But she sags against me, breathing rapidly. "Oh, my God. I haven't . . . not since . . . phew—" She's not able to string words together, something I'm familiar with, but while mine is a failure of my brain to express my thoughts and feelings, this moment is her body completely blissed out and unable to process in the sharp way she usually does. It's beautiful and I feel fortunate to witness it, and even more lucky to have caused it.

She goes still and quiet, her pants slowing and becoming a steadier, slower pace. All the while, my hands move across her skin, touching her back, her thighs, her jawline, memorizing every inch.

"Are we going to your place tonight?" she asks when we've both recovered a bit.

"Brody and Rix are at my house," I tell her disappointedly. "Not exactly any privacy to be had when you're still in your childhood bedroom."

"You could come into town with me," she suggests.

I pull back, holding her in place. "I need to be clear here. Once I get inside you, there's no going back. Hell, I don't think there's any going back now, for that matter. At least, not for me. But there are some things we need to talk about before we . . ."

The pause is awkward, a thought I've never considered marching through my brain. I almost said 'fuck', but I don't want to just fuck Willow. I want to . . .

"Have sex?" she offers.

"Make love," I correct, knowing that's what it'll be.

Her lashes flutter behind her frames, giving her that owlish look that tells me she's thinking about something. After a moment, she lets me in on it. "Are you always so . . . committed?"

She seems genuinely curious, as though maybe I'm a serial monogamist who takes sex particularly seriously. I can't help but laugh, which bounces her on my cock, and it complains, uncomfortably arguing with my brain.

"I've never made love, Willow. I fuck. It's always been casual, scratching an itch, even when I was dating someone. But it'll be different this time. At least for me. And I think for you too."

I'm not asking for her number. I don't need or want to know what she's done in the past because it doesn't matter. What I need to know is that she feels the same way I do.

Slowly, her gray eyes clear, and she nods, whispering her agreement. "I think so too."

Immediately, she lays her head on my shoulder as though embarrassed that she said that, or maybe that she feels it. She wasn't looking for a Prince Charming—hell, she might not even want one. But I'm the one she's got and I'm not letting her go.

CHAPTER 13

WILLOW

"*Y*ou have a perfectly normal sex drive, Willow Parker," I tell my reflection, but it's obvious I don't believe the lie. Funny thing is, it's truly never been a lie before. I've never even considered that I might be a bit overactive until Bobby Tannen got me all worked up and then denied me the deep, thorough dicking I wanted.

Dicking? Seriously, Willow?

I'd be embarrassed at my train of thoughts, but I can't find it in me to blush in the slightest. Last night, I rode him through our clothes, dry humping like we were kids in high school. I'd seriously doubted my ability to come from that alone, because orgasms are mysterious things that sometimes take geometry, a psychologist, and a wish on a star, but he pulled it out of me easily with those growled words in my ear.

It was so good I'd boldly asked if we were going to his place, like some dick-starved Tinderella, which I am not, by any means.

I press my forehead to the cool mirror, eyes locked on the gray ones looking back at me. After a moment, I start laughing. What else am I going to do? This is crazy, but in the best possible way.

Today will be another first. Bobby is picking me up for our 'official first date', as he called it. I'd tried to argue that the tour had been date one and my showing up at the farm was date two, making today date three. He'd flashed that cocky smile, scrubbing at the scruff of beard on his sharp jawline as though that would hide it, then said 'fuck it' as he cupped my jaw and let that smile shine bright. Right before he kissed me, he let me in on the joke and whispered, "There's no three-date rule with us, sweetheart."

I blushed. I hadn't even meant it that way, but maybe somewhere deep inside, I had. A little bit.

But if he's coming over, I'd better finish getting ready. I don't put on makeup, knowing what I have in mind, and go for sunscreen along my nose and cheeks instead.

Right as I'm tying my tennis shoes, I hear the rumble of his truck coming down the street and pulling into my drive. I peek out the blinds, knowing my neighbors are likely doing the same thing. I let him climb out of his jacked up monster truck, walk to the door, and knock before I let the blinds close and move to let him in.

"Hey!" I greet as the door swings open.

I watch his eyes move leisurely up and down my frame, narrowing incrementally until they reach mine again. "Hey, sweetheart."

Just like that, I'm a pile of gooey, messy Jell-O for him, nearly melting into a puddle at his feet.

"Can't wait to see what you have planned today. I'll admit the girls said my ideas sucked." I'm not sure his tanned skin would show a true blush, but he looks a little sheepish, which makes me curious as hell.

"Now you have to tell me what your ideas were," I demand, crossing my arms and smiling.

He cringes, and I think the girls must've really given him a hard time if he's this reluctant to even share. But he tells me anyway, "Idea one, photo tour. They said it was lame because I'd already done that. I argued that the wildflowers over on Zion Hill are pretty and that you'd like them, but they reminded me that taking a woman to a cemetery, even a historical one, for flower pictures is weird as hell, and in Shay's words, 'is bad bow-chicka-bow-wow juju.' I told them about your watching crime shit on tv, and they said that only made it worse."

He shrugs, and I can't help but laugh a bit. "Maybe we save

the wildflowers for another day so I'm mentally prepared to pull up to a cemetery. A historical one, of course," I correct myself. "What else?"

"I asked Katelyn if she could get us in at the resort. Do some of that fancy, girly shit like gunk on your face and a massage. I thought it'd be relaxing because you work so much." I can hear that he used that argument with Katelyn too. "She said couples' massages on a first date might be a bit aggressive." He says the word as if it tastes bad on his tongue, while I have to laugh. Couple's massage is aggressive, but bad bow-chicka-bow-wow juju isn't?

I lay my hand on his chest, feeling the hard muscle there and not swooning . . . nope, not a bit. Fine, I'm like a cover model in a Harlequin romance. Giving him my most dazzling smile, I reassure him, "That would've been amazing. But I have other plans today if you're up for it." His brow lifts, and I swear his dark eyes get even darker. "Did you bring the stuff I asked you to?"

His eyes go from sexing me to curious without even blinking. "I did," he drawls out slowly, "but I'm not sure why."

"Okay then, let's go." I push him out the door and toward his truck. In turn, he lets me lead this show. I don't think he does that for many people or very often.

"Where to?" he asks, arm stretched out and hand lying over the steering wheel.

"Hank's," I answer firmly. "We've got work to do."

He blinks first, shaking his head in confusion, but without a word, he puts the truck in reverse and makes the trip to the bar as if it's a perfectly reasonable request to take me to work on the one day off I get. And, you know, our third date.

I have him park around back, not wanting Chief Gibson to interrupt again, and use my key to open the back door. "Come on. In here," I direct him. Once he's inside, I close and lock the door behind us, flipping on the light switch.

"I know I told you I wasn't fucking you on the bar before, but I'm still not," Bobby jokes.

At least I know I'm not the only one thinking sexy thoughts.

"That's not why we're here. And I'm still not having sex on the bar." At this point, I absolutely would and he damn well knows it.

I am wrapped around his little finger tighter than a spring waiting to be sprung, all this potential sexual energy bound up and begging to be released, and he's the one with his finger on the trigger.

"Then what are we doing here?" he asks, looking around Ilene's kitchen as though she might jump out from behind the stove and demand to know what the hell we're doing in her domain. Actually, that might happen, so we'd best get out of here, especially since the kitchen's not the issue.

"In here." I walk through the bar and into Unc's office, Bobby right behind me. I point at the stacks of papers—some on the desk, some on the floor, and some restacked on the booth where Bobby and I sat that first night. "These all need to be sorted and filed. The desk needs to be cleared and cleaned. And I need to bring up some inventory from the storage room."

Bobby looks at me in confusion. "Why don't you do this during one of your shifts?" I see a flash of fear on his face and he verbally retreats. "I mean, I'm happy to help with whatever Hank needs. Always am, but what's up with the sneaking around?"

My brows lift. "Have you met Hank Davis? He would as soon wrestle a greased-up pig as admit he needs me to help him organize this stuff. But he's not going to do it or he already would've. So I am. It'll be one less thing for him to worry about."

I look around the room, knowing this mess must weigh on Unc's shoulders. He's been carrying this business his whole life and done a really great job at it, but he can't do that when his paperwork is in utter chaos.

"He's gonna be pissed as hell. You know that, right?"

I shrug, using a phrase I've heard Unc say. "Then he can get glad in the same britches he got mad in. Once it's done, he can bitch and moan all he wants, but it'll still be done either way."

Bobby's smile is pure gleeful evil. "I like the way you think. Let's do it."

And with that, we get to work sorting out the piles of papers into organized stacks, then slotting them into the file cabinet in the corner. "I don't think this cabinet's been opened in at least two years," I tell Bobby, holding up a file folder as I add the latest invoices into it.

"Hank's been busy. He's a one-man show, but I know he's glad to have you here now." There's a hitch in his voice that tells me he's not just talking about Unc.

It takes us a couple of hours, but with some music from the jukebox and some easy conversation, the work goes quickly. We get the paperwork done, the desk cleared, the office cleaned, and the inventory restocked and ready behind the bar.

"Looks good. What else?" Bobby asks, ready to keep working.

"Glad you asked. This next part isn't as easy," I say slyly.

* * *

"Are you shitting me?" Bobby asks, incredulous. He looks up and down the empty street as though we're going to get busted any second.

"Nope. Completely serious," I say. "Doc took Unc fishing today. Said they'd be gone till mid-afternoon, so we can get it done if we hurry."

"Woman, you are something else." He's shaking his head, likely thinking I've lost my mind, but we get out of his truck and I walk to the back, where he's already lowering the tailgate. "This is trespassing, you know? And probably some other misdemeanor charges if we're lucky."

"And if we're not?" I joke, batting my lashes behind my glasses.

Bobby sighs, resigned. "We'll be lucky if Hank doesn't come out with a shotgun and pepper our asses."

"Then we'd better hurry."

He laughs, and I'm feeling pretty proud of myself. This is a bold move, but I think we can get away with it if we act fast.

"Tell me where I'm going with this thing," Bobby says, lifting the heavy concrete edging piece and walking through Unc's yard.

"Right here for the first one," I tell him, pointing. I turned them around when I was here yesterday, but some of them are pretty crumbled, and I figured I'd take advantage of Unc being gone and Bobby having more muscles than I do to get the new pieces in place.

He quickly moves it into position, wiggling it back and forth to plant it solidly in the dirt.

"Perfect. Four more before we get busted!"

He glares at me, that brow telling me 'I told you so' loud and clear. I know he's right, and this is risky. But it's worth it if Unc's house is well-kept. The flower bed edging is the first of two jobs and the least serious thing I'm hoping Bobby can help with.

He makes quick work of it, the new concrete in place in minutes. "Hmm. It looks too new," I decide and get down on my knees in the yard. Scooping up some dirt from around the bushes, I rub it into the new pieces to blend them in with the old ones.

Leaning up against the bed of his truck, Bobby laughs. "What are you doing now?"

"What's it look like?"

I glance over my shoulder and catch him looking at my butt, not really seeming to care at all what I'm doing other than kneeling with my ass in the air.

"Making me lose my fucking mind." It's a statement, not a question at all. Somewhere deep inside, the tiniest vixen roars to life, and I wiggle my hips a bit, teasing and seducing him. He groans and plainly reaches down to adjust himself in his jeans, keeping eye contact with me the whole time. "Now what?"

"Hammer. Nail."

He chokes on his tongue. "What?"

I'm the one grinning cockily now. "We need to fix the steps. What did you think I was talking about?" I ask innocently.

But he's way better at this game than I am. "Me hammering away at you, nailing you to the bed, fucking you hard, kissing you soft, and touching every inch of your skin with my tongue."

"Oh." The lamest comeback in the history of comebacks, but it's all I've got because my brain is busy painting mental images in vivid, photographic detail.

He presses his lips together, but I can see he's fighting a smile as he grabs the hammer from the toolbox I asked him to bring and the box of nails we bought at the hardware store when we picked up the concrete edging pieces.

"Right here." I point at the stair edge, where the nails are working their way loose, making the few steps an unsteady trip-ping hazard.

He hammers a few nails in, making the stair treads solid and safe. I grab the vinegar I brought from home and dab a bit on the nails.

"What're you doing?" Bobby's nose is crinkled at the smell.

"Vinegar makes them rust quickly. That way, they'll blend in and not look shiny and new and therefore noticeable."

Bobby seems surprised by how far I'm going to do this without Unc realizing I've done a thing, but that's key to the plan of his not feeling like I'm overstepping.

"The side's gonna need a few screws. Let me grab those and a screwdriver." He digs around in the toolbox again and comes up with a long-shanked screwdriver. "This might be a bit much, but it'll do the trick."

He's screwing in the last screw when the door opens and Unc comes out, grumpier than a bear whose hibernation has been disturbed way too early.

"What the fuck are you doing?" he demands. His eyes are bright and sharp today, no hint of glassiness or clouding. Nope, just pure fury there.

"Uh, hey, Unc. I thought you were going fishing with Doc today?" I say calmly, willing him to calm down too because we are so busted.

"Did. Got tired so I came home to take a nap and got woken up by some fool hammerin' away on my porch. What the fuck are you doing?" he repeats, getting louder.

Bobby steps forward, putting himself between me and Unc's ire, trying to ease the situation. "No big deal, Hank. No need to yell at Willow. She just asked me to fix up these steps so they don't walk away from the house."

He gestures with the screwdriver, and before I know what's happening, Unc grabs the screwdriver out of Bobby's hand by the flathead end and chunks it into the yard, where it lands blade down in the dirt, buried to the handle.

"Don't need no help," he hollers, pointing at Bobby in accusa-tion. Pointing to his own chest, he barks, "I can do it myself."

Behind me, I'm sure eyes are peeking out of every window

with how loud Unc's being. I'd expected him to be mad if he found out I was helping like this. That's why I was trying to be sneaky about it, but I hadn't expected anything close to . . . this.

I've never seen him like this.

I'm shocked and hurt at Unc's reaction, and Bobby is holding me protectively behind his back like he's scared Unc is going to charge us. I'm ashamed to admit that I shrink behind Bobby a little, letting him take the brunt of it on his broad shoulders.

"Shit," Unc hisses, holding his hand up, and blood drips down onto the porch.

"Oh!" I exclaim, my concern for him overriding everything else. I step out from my hiding spot and run up the steps to grab Unc's hand. He tries to fight me, still mad as a hornet, but I glare at him. "Let me see it."

With a pissed off sigh, he opens his fist. A gash stretches across his palm from the meat by his thumb toward his ring finger. He immediately closes his hand again, holding it over his head. "Damn screwdriver got me."

He glares at Bobby as though it's his fault when none of it is. Bobby is here because I asked him to be, doing work when I told him it would be fine, and Unc is the one who had a tantrum and grabbed the screwdriver.

All business and not allowing for any argument, I push Unc's shoulders, turning him around. "Inside. Let's get a towel, then you're going for stitches."

He relents on the towel, but when I shove him back toward the door, he refuses and plops himself down in a kitchen chair. "Don't need no stitches. It'll scab up in a couple of days."

"And in the meantime, you'll be dripping God knows what into the whole town's beer. Nope. Stitches, bandages, and sterile dressing, or I'll call Chief Gibson if you even step one cranky foot in the bar. I'll report you myself for health violations."

Unc isn't moving, not swayed by my argument in the slightest. Probably because he counts Chief Gibson as a friend and trusts that he won't shut him down. Bad thing is, I fear he's right, which leaves me stuck on how to get Unc to go for the care he needs. Bobby steps up to the plate, backing my play.

"You catch anything this morning?" he asks like they're just shooting the breeze.

Unc grunts and Bobby snorts. "How many and how big?"

Narrow blue eyes meet dark ones in a battle of wills. I'm honestly not sure which of these men will come out on top. Bobby's got youth on his side, and size for sure. But Unc has old-fashioned iron will.

"Couple each, not more than a pound or two. Catch-n-releasers."

Bobby nods. "You scrub up before you took a nap, old man? Not just rinse off at the creek, but wash up good and proper like you're eating dinner at your mama's table?"

Unc doesn't say a word, but he glares at Bobby for a long minute. "Fine. Don't want no creek funk infection. Probably lose a damn hand and it'd be your fault, Tannen."

I have no idea what happened, but Unc is walking outside and heading for his truck.

"We'll take you," I say, hurrying alongside him.

"The hell you will. I can go get somebody to sew up my hand by myself, just like I could've fixed those stairs myself." The accusation stings, but I have my doubts. If he could've, he would've already. Right?

"I was trying to help," I argue. I've already figured out that apologizing doesn't work with Unc.

"Hmph." With that, he gets in his truck and leaves me and Bobby standing in the front yard.

"What just happened?" I ask, not really expecting Bobby to answer as I nervously nibble at my bottom lip, looking down the road where Unc's blue truck disappeared around the corner. "I was trying to help," I say again, quieter this time.

Suddenly, I find myself buried against Bobby's chest, and tears are running hotly down my face, soaking into his shirt. He rubs my back soothingly. "It's okay, sweetheart. Hank's got a streak of pride a mile wide, and we rubbed up against it a little too much. That's all."

"You think he's going to be okay?" This time, I do need him to answer, to reassure me that Unc's hand is going to get stitched up and he'll be good as new.

"Of course. Hell, if we hadn't been here, he probably would've super glued it shut and kept on with business. He's tough like that."

I'd like to believe that. Except Bobby doesn't know that there's more to it. No one does.

Pulling myself together, I swipe at my eyes behind my glasses and snort very ungracefully.

"He'll be okay, and he'll get over it. At least until he shows up to work and sees what you did to his office," he deadpans. "It's all over then."

There's a beat of silence and I realize he's kidding. Sort of.

"Oh, God, he's going to kill me!" I wail, but through the last bit of tears, I'm laughing in shock, knowing it's true. He is going to be so pissed. "How in the hell can he be mad that people want to do nice things for him?"

"Some people don't get it, sweetheart. But he'll come around."

Bobby makes one last check on the stairs to be sure they're solid and stable while I text Doc to let him know we got busted and that stitches were required.

Doc: Tannen? Or you?

I laugh, amused that Doc assumes Unc did something to us.

Me: Unc. Sliced his hand on a screwdriver.

Doc: He went for stitches? Didn't glue it up?

What is it with these guys? Glue is not an appropriate treatment for gashes and never has been. A second later, another text pops up . . .

Doc: On it. You tried.

I did. I tried so hard to do something nice, and Unc yelled and stomped and cussed his way around like a drunk, wayward sailor who got off at the wrong shore for leave.

But I'm nervous about his being at the hospital alone. Maybe I should go over there too? Sit with Doc and make sure that Unc gets home okay and eats some dinner? He said he came home and took a nap. Was it because they left early to catch the prime fishing hours or because he overdid it today?

My brain whirls and swirls. It's not until Bobby puts his hands on my shoulders and bends down nose to nose with me that it stops. My brain quiets and I stare into his eyes. Deep, dark onyx unblinkingly stares back at me, steady and supportive.

"I know what you need. Get in the truck. I'm taking this date over."

"Because I messed up so royally?" I say softly.

"No, because Katelyn was wrong. You need to relax and have some fun, and while I might not be able to get us in at the resort with zero notice, I do know a spot that's perfect. Leave it to me, sweetheart."

I do, because as much as I hate to admit it, it's nice to have someone take care of me for a change. It's a relief to simply sit back in the cushioned seat of Bobby's truck and see where he takes me.

* * *

"Keep 'em closed."

I squeeze my eyes shut, fighting the desire to open them. We've been going for what seems like forever, first stopping by my place where Bobby quickly ran inside by himself to emerge with my camera bag before heading here. Wherever here is. The truck bumps along, and without knowing when to brace, my butt flies out of the seat a bit. "Whoo!" I scream, a little scared but a little . . . exhilarated?

Is that what this feeling is? And is it because of the wild ride across the field or because of the man at my side?

Both. Definitely both.

We come to a stop, and Bobby says, "Okay, you can open now."

I open my eyes and look around to find a pond sunk into a low point in the rolling green pasture. On the far side, a few cows laze about on the bank, drinking and lying down in the surprisingly not-brown water. It's not Caribbean blue or anything, but it does look fresher than I'd expect for what's likely rain runoff and collection.

"A pond?" I ask, not sure why we're here, though the scenery is pretty and my finger does itch to take a few pictures of those cows who are now mooing at the interruption of their afternoon dip.

"A spring-fed pond," Bobby corrects, emphasizing the spring-fed part. "That means it's clean enough to swim in." He smiles and reaches into the back seat, pulling up my camera bag and handing it to me carefully. "I grabbed you a suit, and yes, that means I went through your dresser drawers. If you're mad, get over it now or I'll have to start calling you Hank."

The message is loud and clear. He's doing something nice for me, offering a distraction from the disaster today has been, and I shouldn't argue about it like my stubborn uncle.

When Bobby had stopped at my little cabin and told me to stay put while he grabbed something, I'd given in easily. He'd come out with my camera bag, and I'd figured we were doing the wildflower pictures at the cemetery today.

But this might be better. It might be a lot better. Even if the worry about Unc is still sharp in my belly.

I mime zipping my lip.

"Good girl. I'll step out so you can change, and I'll meet you over there." He points to a spot on the bank by a big flat rock.

He opens his door and grabs a moving blanket out of the back, shaking it out as he goes. I'm dumbstruck as I watch him stride toward the water and spread the blanket out. He glances back at me, and though the sun glints off the windshield, I feel like he knows I'm watching him.

He reaches behind his neck, pulling his T-shirt over his head in one swoop.

"Oh, my God," I mutter to nobody.

Bobby is thick and muscled, tanned with a slight line along his arms that says he must work with his shirt off at least sometimes. A dusting of dark hair covers his chest, pulling together into a thin line that disappears into his jeans. Which is exactly where his hands are now, undoing the button and zipper. He leaves them sagging open to reach down and pull his boots and socks off. Staring directly at the truck, or at me—I'm not sure which—he pushes his jeans over his ass and down his thighs.

The man has no shame. But he has zero reason to. Standing in just black boxer briefs, he looks like hot sex and wicked sin.

And mine.

There's a hunger deep inside me that's thrilled this man wants me and wants me to want him.

There's an even bigger thrill that he doesn't want casual and throw-away but is being remarkably and unusually clear in his desire for something deeper and more meaningful.

I feel like I won the lottery with him. Not just any old lottery, either, but the Powerball. And against all my usual instincts to share and take care of others, I want to revel in him, keeping him all to myself like a stingy bitch.

He winks at me and takes off, running barefoot through the dirt toward the water. He splashes in up to his thighs then dives under the surface expertly, coming up further out with a whip of his hair that sends water droplets flying. The cows moo their displeasure, but Bobby calls out, "Come on, Willow! Get in with me!"

Oh, I'm in. I'm in deep, way over my head and treading water.

I awkwardly maneuver around in the truck to change out of my shorts and T-shirt and into the bikini Bobby tucked into my camera bag. I own two suits, and of course, he brought the smaller of the two. It's basically four triangles, one for each boob, one for my front, and one for my butt, all held together with strings that tie on my hips and at the center of my back. I make sure everything's tucked in appropriately and send a quick prayer of thanks that I had the foresight to shave my bikini area so it doesn't look like a Sasquatch bush escaping from behind the black fabric. I slip my tennis shoes back on but leave them untied so I can kick them off on the blanket, along with my glasses.

My walk to the water is nowhere near as confident as Bobby's swaggered one, but he watches me approach all the same. His eyes follow my every move, roaming and tracing my curves as I get closer. I get the sense that he's memorizing me.

Barefoot, I wade into the water. It's just this side of cool, a perfect contrast to the hot day, and goosebumps break out along my skin. Bobby swims closer and stands in front of me.

"You are stunning. I want to kiss every inch of your skin, tease at these goosebumps with my fingertips, and feel your body against mine," he says softly, grit and gravel in his voice.

"Okay," I say breathlessly.

I want that too. All of that, please.

In my brain, Ilene's bell goes off. *Ding!* I'm ready.

"Close your eyes for me again," he orders, and they slip shut of their own accord.

I feel his arms surround me, scooping me up until my legs are over one ropey forearm and his other is wrapped around my back. I try to wrap my arms around his neck to keep my balance, but before I can, I'm flying through the air.

"*Ahh*!" I squeal, my eyes flying open right before I bust through the surface, going under. Water goes up my nose, and I swallow some too, coming up sputtering and mad.

"I thought you were going to . . . what the . . ." Words aren't coming out, so I settle with slapping the water and screeching, "Bobby Tannen!"

He grins hugely, big and wide, like he's heard that more than a time or two. "Got you out of your head, didn't I? Now let's have some fun."

I blink, still getting water from my eyes because my bangs are hanging low, brushing well past my brows. I shake my head like a dog and push my hair to the side. "What?"

"Race you to the other side," he says, already swimming before he finishes the words.

I'm dumbstruck for a moment, giving him an even bigger head start, but realization kicks in and I dive after him, working hard to make up the distance.

Feet kicking and arms swinging, I cut through the water. It's not graceful by any means, but it's effective, and I reach the cows only a few seconds after he does.

"This is Maverick," he tells me, petting the cow's side.

"You can tell them all apart?" I ask, surprised. At dinner the other night, it'd sounded like they have lots of cattle, hundreds of them at least.

He shakes his head. "No, Mark and Brody can, but they go by numbers." He points to the tag on the cow's ear that says *178*. "I've made friends with a few of them, though. There are a few different places I like to sit when I'm working on a song, and some of the cows are curious. They'll come right up and sit down next to me, mooing for scratches like a dog."

"The goats did that!" I say, smiling. Slowly, I raise a hand and scratch Maverick too. The cow moos loudly, and I jump, but a second later, I realize it's the cow version of encouragement and do it again.

After a few minutes, Bobby asks, "Can you float?"

"I don't know. It's been a while since I've tried," I say, trying to think back. Maybe when I was a teenager? Since then, my water activities have been more along the lines of lying beside it than in it.

"Come on," he says, taking my hand and pulling me through the water.

We go deeper until the water reaches his chest and my chin before he picks me up again.

"No," I squeal, kicking and grabbing around his neck.

He laughs. "I won't. I'm gonna hold you so you can float. Trust me." His face is serious, and I believe him that this isn't a setup to throw me again. Slowly, I relax, and he guides me back, one hand low on my spine and one at my shoulders, and I float. Nervously, I don't let my head go too far back, not liking water in my ears, but I like the feel of his hands on me a lot.

"Relax. I've got you, Willow. Take a deep breath and look at the sky above you. Blue infinity, white puffs that look as soft as cotton. Listen. Hear the wind and the cows. Feel the water caressing you, cooling your skin. Breathe, be heavy in the water, in my hands. Let me hold you up."

I listen to his rough voice, almost meditative with calm, quiet, soothing tones, doing as he says . . . the sky, the wind, the water, and finally, him. I am in tune with everything around me, especially Bobby.

I don't know how long we stay like that, but I can feel stress and worry pouring from me, being washed away by the spring water. I feel reborn, renewed, like I breathe deeply for the first time in a long time.

I've been burning the candle at both ends for so long, I think I've forgotten that there once was a candle. I just work, work, work, slinging beer or taking pictures. And answering questions from blog readers, finding new subject matter that excites me and them, and doing what I can for everyone else. In this moment, I feel free. I feel like me.

Standing up, I find the soft bottom of the pond and look up to see Bobby watching my every move with focused attention. It warms me even more than the sun on my skin.

"Thank you," I say simply. It's not enough, but I don't know how to thank him for helping me reset, not only from Unc's anger and injury but from so much more.

"My pleasure, sweetheart." It sounds like he means it, and as he leads me back to the blanket, lifting me to sit in the sun, I consider that Bobby is a caregiver like I am. He takes care of the farm, his family, and now me. But who takes care of him?

I will.

It's who I am.

We lie in the sun, letting it dry us. I'm acutely aware of every inch where our skin touches, cradled in Bobby's arm, his fingertips dancing along my skin in that pattern I saw him playing on the bar before.

"What brought you to Great Falls, Willow?" he asks huskily.

I should give my standard answer—that I needed a change. But Bobby deserves more than that, much more. Some of it's not my story to tell, but I can share a little and keep promises that have been made.

"Unc."

He's silent, waiting for more. I sigh, knowing this will be hard to explain, especially since I don't understand it all myself. I was just a kid, after all.

"I don't know how much you know of Hank's younger days. I'm not really sure how much I know either, to be honest. But apparently, he had a girlfriend once. It was serious, like a proposal kind of serious. He enlisted to give them stability, a future, I guess? But when he came home, his brother had moved in on his girl. They fought like brothers do, arguing and punching and insulting one another. But it didn't matter, the damage had already been done. My grandfather, Harold, married the girl. She was my grandmother, really sweet. I have memories of her making Christmas cookies with me, playing dolls, and coloring on huge sheets of construction paper she'd hang up on the sliding door to let the morning light shine through."

I get lost in the memories a bit, some from when I was really young and not nearly enough from when I was older. I still saw

Grandma and Grandpa as a teenager, but the moments aren't as vivid because I was too caught up in other things to appreciate my grandparents while they were here.

Bobby lets me take my time, and eventually, I come back to him. "She got sick, breast cancer when I was thirteen. It was quick and brutal. Mom shielded me from most of it, but Grandpa didn't handle it well at all. He'd always been . . . a hard man. Strict, stoic, but I think he really loved Grandma and I think she loved him too. Or at least they loved each other, as far as I could tell as a stupid kid." I shrug, not sure but also not willing to revisit the past to analyze with an adult's heart.

"I only know this next part from later. I didn't know it at all back then, but Grandpa knew she was getting close to the end. She got confused a lot, and the meds made her lose time, I guess. But she called him Hank sometimes. I know that had to hurt. They'd had this whole life and family together, but he didn't tell Unc. They'd been distant but civil all those years. Thanksgiving and Christmas dinners, and he'd come by and see Mom and me. I just thought he was my cool uncle, you know?"

I swallow, still not able to believe what my Grandpa had done in his own selfish need. "At the end, in confusion, she cried for Hank. She thought it was a long time ago, thought he was coming home to her and they were going to get married. She didn't know who Mom was or who I was, had no idea about her whole life, any of it. And Grandpa . . . he didn't tell Unc. Didn't even call to tell him that Grandma was sick, much less that she wanted to see him. No, he let her cry every day, thinking Hank had deserted her. Grandpa stayed by her bedside to the end. He didn't give up, but he didn't give her what she needed to be at peace either, if that makes sense?"

Tears flow down my cheeks again, pooling on Bobby's chest, but he doesn't react, just lets me feel it all, even though it's not my story. "Unc found out about Grandma dying about a year too late and was understandably furious. Mom thought Grandpa had told him and he hadn't wanted to come, and it was this whole mess. I remember getting sent to my room and Grandpa and Unc yelling. They fought, two grown men punching each other over a woman who was already dead and buried, and Mom screaming at them to stop. My mom . . . she looks like Grandma, the spitting image of her, and I guess in the moment, with tensions high, they both kinda turned on her, yelling back. I don't know what they said, but in the end, we didn't see Unc anymore, Grandpa said awful things about him until he died a year later, and Mom just never mentioned either of them again."

"And now?" Bobby asks gently.

"Now, I'm not losing another day to the past, to things that have nothing to do with me. I want my cool uncle back before it's too late and will do whatever it takes to get him." I'm dancing around it, praying Bobby doesn't poke and prod too much. Though both intensely personal, sharing Unc's past is one thing and sharing his present is another.

"Are you going to stay in Great Falls for him?"

I can feel the heavy weight attached to the question and know what he's really asking, so that's the question I answer.

"He's not the only reason I'm staying, Bobby Tannen."

My words are full of interwoven layers and impact us both. I came to Great Falls for one thing, and I found it. At least I did if today didn't blow it all to pieces. But I also found something I wasn't anticipating. And like Mom always taught me, sometimes, the unexpected is what you were really meant to experience, a spontaneous growth spurt of my heart through Bobby's dark, beautiful, powerful love.

I want to believe, to experience, to enjoy him. Us.

Bobby shifts so he can search my eyes, the same gray eyes like my Grandma's that must hurt Unc to look at every day. But I've only known them when I look in the mirror and have always taken pride in looking like my beautiful grandma and mom.

Bobby seems to find something in their depths that he understands because he tilts my jaw up and kisses me tenderly, slowly sipping at me, moaning as he gives in to me and I melt for him. Not from the sun, but from his intense heat.

Somehow, in sharing someone else's past, I feel like I've created a future for myself. Here in Great Falls. With Bobby, and if Unc forgives me for a little sprucing up of his house and bar, with him too.

CHAPTER 14

BOBBY

I kiss Willow's cheek, tasting the salt of her tears. My girl, with this big, giant heart that feels for everyone and everything so acutely, is a rare specimen. Most people are out for number-one, even if they've found some shred of generosity in their soul and can balance it out so it seems like they're better than the rest of us monsters. At the end of the day, it's a kill or be killed, me or the other guy mentality that is ultimately the strongest inside most hearts.

But not for Willow.

I delicately lick her other cheek with the barest tip of my tongue, cleaning up the tears and wanting only happiness for her. She deserves it, and more.

Taste of your salt on my lips breaks my soul in two. Sweetheart, if there's anything I can do?

Willow's answer to my question is what I've needed to hear all along. This isn't some summer vacation fling to her when it's so much more to me. I didn't think she was being casual about us, but now, I truly know.

And with that echoing in my ears, I can't hold myself back from her any longer. Fuck, I should be getting a damned medal for waiting this long when I've been imagining all sorts of filthy things to do to her and with her.

"Willow, I need you. Fuck, sweetheart, I want . . ." I growl, peppering her skin with kisses, hearing the scratch of my stubble along her softness.

"Can we go to your place?" she asks, head thrown back and tits pressed up into my hands.

I swallow, willing myself to wait.

You can wait ten fucking minutes to take her in a bed like a lady, not on a rock in the dirt like an animal.

I'm not entirely sure that's true, but I'll try. For her.

I pull back in an instant, rising to my feet and offering her a hand. "Let's go," I order. I should be softer, gentler, but maintaining control over my cock is taking all the willpower I have. Luckily, she takes my hand and stands too, not at all put out at the gruff tone.

Actually, with a small laugh, she grabs her shoes and makes a barefoot run for the truck. Every instinct inside me calls out . . . chase her down. Don't let her get away!

I wad up the blanket and my clothes, not bothering to pull on a single stitch when I'm about to strip again anyway. I run after her, tossing everything in the truck bed and climbing in the cab. "Hang on," I tell her, knowing that I'm going to break the land speed record for crossing from the ranch to our farmhouse.

I push a button on the radio and the truck calls Brody.

"What?" he grunts when he answers.

"Don't come home tonight. Stay at Rix's or one of the other houses. Sleep outside. I don't give a fuck, but don't come home till morning."

Willow blushes in the seat next to me, sinking down, but I see the hint of a smile at the corners of her lips.

"What?" He pauses, clueing in to what I'm telling him. "Oh. Yeah, that's fine. I'll go to town. There're condoms in the hall bathroom. Uh, congrats?"

Click.

Maybe it's weird for him to remind me about the condoms, but that's just Brody. Grumpy asshole takes care of us in his own way. Plus, I don't bring women home. Ever. So it's entirely possible that he thinks I never noticed the stash of condoms.

I glance to the woman in my passenger seat, a sharp pain of

disbelief slicing through my gut at her beauty, both inside and out. How is someone like her sitting here with someone like me? I'm not sure, but I want to enjoy every single second with Willow.

"So the whole town's gonna know now?" Willow asks. Normally, I think she'd be shy about that, but she seems to be holding back giggles at Brody's offer of congrats and condoms.

"Nah, Brody doesn't talk much. He'll tell Rix, though, and she'll tell the girls, so the family'll know. But they already know about us."

Isn't that the God's honest truth? They all know that Willow is special to me. Hell, Brutal's been asking questions like he's got a written list, but that's his way, so I've answered what I want to and told him to quit being a nosy bitch on things I didn't want to share.

At the house, I pull up in the drive and put the truck in park.

"We don't have to go inside, Willow." I'm offering her a brake, whether it's a full stop or a slowdown, because there's no way I can do it myself. "If we go in there, I'm going to make you come until you think your body can't anymore, and I won't stop. I'm going to fill you up with my tongue, my fingers, and my cock, get to know your body from the inside. I'll pound you until I've left my mark everywhere you'll let me. I want you to know that there's no going back after this. You'll be mine. So, you decide . . . are we going back to town or are we going inside?"

My heart is racing, my breath erratic as I paint pictures in my own mind of what I want with her.

Willow's eyes get incrementally larger with my words until they look like saucers behind her glasses. She licks her lips and swallows thickly. "That, I want . . . that."

Still not one hundred percent, because she's leaving a slight margin for error, I ask for clarity. "You want what, sweetheart? Tell me, say the words." I'm on the edge, praying for my sweet-mouthed girl to say something dirty just for me.

"I want . . . I want to go inside."

I smile, encouraging her.

I can see her steeling her nerves, and with her eyes brazenly on mine, she boldly says, "I want your cock."

Holy fuck. I wasn't ready. As much as I wanted filth on her

tongue, I wasn't prepared for how it would shove me into the deep end.

"*Shit*, sweetheart. Let's go."

I'm out, around the hood, and opening her door in an instant.

In another, we're over the threshold and heading up the stairs.

One more, and she's in my bedroom. It's bare-boned, all childhood remnants long gone. Later, I'll wonder what she thinks about the worn dresser with a cracked mirror, the full-sized bed that I didn't make, and the open closet with too many threadbare T-shirts, dirty boots, and ripped jeans. Right now, all I care about is getting her out of this swimsuit that might as well be the sexiest lingerie I've ever seen.

I sit down and pull her between my thighs. Wrapping my hands around her waist, I feel her satiny skin beneath my rough palms and nearly lose it.

"I want to go slow, but I'm on edge." The confession is not a weakness I would usually show, but luckily, she doesn't take it as such, instead seeming turned on by the immediacy of my desire.

She lays her arms over my shoulders, playing in the too-long hair at my nape. "We've got all night, right? We can do slow, then fast. And then slow again. Or vice versa? Fast, then slow?"

I look up from where my eyes are memorizing the small spattering of freckles over her right hip, and she winks at me like the minx she's not. But maybe she will be, for me and only me.

I lay a sweet kiss to her hip, right over the freckles, claiming them. I nip at the curve of her waist, claiming it. I lick a line between her breasts as I cup them in my palms. Mine, all mine.

Willow reaches behind her back, undoing the tie, and the triangles fall loose from her body. Another tie at her neck has the material fluttering to my floor as she stands topless before me.

"So pretty," I murmur, teasing over both nipples with my thumbs. They pearl up instantly, proudly standing at attention to beg for more caresses. Circling the rosy tips, I fill in my fantasies with the reality of Willow, the color, shape, and weight of her tits in my palms even better than I'd imagined.

"Thank you," she whispers, her manners instinctual even at a moment like this.

Replacing my hands, I suck as much of her into my mouth as I can, using my tongue to flick at her nipple. She arches again, and I cup her back, forcing her higher, taking more of her. She cries out when I bite down a little on the tender bud.

Worried, I ask, "Too much?"

"No." She shakes her head vehemently. "More. Faster. Now."

Needy, greedy, eager girl . . . wanting me the way I want her.

I take her at her word and wrap my arms around her waist, picking her up to lay her on the bed. The sight of her blonde hair against my navy pillows is a sight I didn't know would hit me so squarely in the center of my chest, but it looks so right. Especially when she's writhing and smiling at me the way she is right now.

I straddle her right leg, my knees trapping her in place, and trace a slow line down her belly with a fingertip, all the way to the ties of her swimsuit bottom. I pull the suit from her, leaving her naked in my bed. Seeing her, my blood roars through my ears, my heart races in my chest, and any shred of control I had melts away in tatters.

I pin her arms over her head, holding her wrists to the bed with one hand so I can explore her pussy with my other. "You this wet for me, sweetheart?" I ask when I feel her slippery juices coating her outer lips.

She nods, her teeth digging into her bottom lip.

I shake my head, serious. "Nuh-uh, you can be loud with me. There's no one to hear you but me, and all I ask for is honesty. Tell me, Willow."

"I'm always this wet around you." Her admission escapes as a sigh, and I reward her bravery by petting her clit in a slow circle.

I grind her thigh, letting her feel how hard I am. "I'm always this hard for you too. So damn sexy." I scan down her body, memorizing every inch of flesh.

I don't think she believes me. She doesn't know how sexy she is, but I'll show her.

I massage her clit, dipping inside to stretch her with one finger, then two, never letting go of her hands. Her body rolls and jolts beneath me, fighting me—not to get away, but for more, as we both learn what she's capable of. I don't know what kind of lovers she's had before, but there's never been anyone who feels about her what I do, who wants to learn every nuance of her pleasure as much as me. This is an education I welcome gladly, every single lesson she'll give.

As she bucks, I fuck her with two fingers, slowly, then harder and faster. I find that ridged spot on her front wall and stroke it even as she tries to close her knees against the onslaught. I don't let her, holding her legs open with my shoulders as she cries out, almost there.

"*Yes*. Right there," she moans a second before her whole body goes tight. She shatters, hips dancing, eyes squeezed shut, and jaw sagged open. Her pussy clenches and spasms as I keep thrusting my fingers in and out of her, helping her wring every bit of pleasure from the orgasm. My cock complains, wanting to feel that tight squeeze, but I promised her more, and I keep my promises.

She's still panting when I move down, throwing her legs over my shoulders to lie between them. The first swipe of my tongue through her sweet cum has her arguing and gripping my hair in her hands.

"I can't. Let me do you instead."

I growl like a kid who won't give up his cake and go back to licking her. "I want another one. Come again, Willow. On my tongue this time, so I can drink you down as you go."

She groans, unsure but eventually settling against my mouth. A moment later, she's riding my tongue and that tight grip on my hair has her guiding me to where she wants me. My hands find her ass, kneading the muscle and holding her to me so I can get my tongue deeper. I moan at her sweet and salty taste, knowing with one drop that I'm addicted.

She's it.

She's everything.

She's mine.

I grind my cock into the mattress, willing myself not to come in my underwear. Needing her to come now, I fasten my mouth around her clit, battering it with my tongue, and slip a finger back inside her. Within seconds, she's crying out for me again.

"Oh, my God," she gasps. "Wow."

I'm already climbing her body, pushing my underwear down and off and grabbing the condom I threw on the bed when we came in. I roll it down my length, giving my base a hard squeeze to fend off my looming orgasm because I definitely don't want to be a two-pump chump, which is a very real risk right now.

No, I want to get inside her and stay there for as long as I possibly can.

Her knees fall open, and I line up with her pussy, nudging at her entrance. "Willow, look at me, sweetheart," I say. Her eyes roll in her head, but she blinks and focuses on me. "Feel me. Feel us, together for the first time."

She nods, and I push forward. Her legs quiver, gripping my hips, and in one instant, I'm inside heaven. Hot, wet home.

I slide deeper, letting her juices coat my length and enjoying the sensation of her gripping every inch of my cock. I pull back, loving the way her body doesn't want to let me go, wanting me to stay as much I want to stay. But the retreat only makes the thrust forward that much sweeter. Again and again, we become one.

I'm gentle, I swear I am, but my strokes are getting more powerful, nearly bottoming out inside her as I lose control. "Sweetheart, I need to—"

She cuts me off. "More. Harder. Bobby—"

And I'm done for.

I lie over her, the full length of our bodies touching. I slide my arms under her, holding her shoulders from behind for leverage, and she wraps her arms around my back, where her nails dig into my skin, urging me on.

I bury my mouth into her shoulder, inhaling her sweat and skin as I begin to pound her. I'm not gentle or kind. I fuck her hard and deep, fast and rough, but she's with me the whole way.

I growl into her ear, my voice low and dark. "You're mine, Willow. You know that, right? It's you and me. Tell me."

I expect her to quote my words back to me. I'm ready for them.

Instead, she says something I don't expect. Not yet, not from her.

As she comes, her pussy pulsing around my cock with each punishing stroke, she cries out, "I love you."

My brain short circuits, my body flies off into paradise, and my heart grits out the truth. "I love you too. Willow—"

That's all I have before I can't speak, too lost in her body and my own pleasure. I come hard, pumping into her as my cock jolts again and again. I murmur and realize I'm sucking on her skin, likely leaving a hickey along the curve of her shoulder. I kiss it gently, apologizing, even though I'm not sorry in the slightest. I don't regret what are likely the half-moon marks from her nails scoring my back, either. I'll wear them as badges of honor, a sign of my woman's passion.

Spent, we sag, trying to catch our breath.

When I can breathe again, I lift up and meet her eyes. Beneath the blissful pleasure, I can see worry blooming. I'm still inside her and she's already nervous. About what?

It hits me.

I brush her bangs out of her eyes, slipping the hair behind her ears. Getting in close so she doesn't misunderstand a thing, I tell her sternly, "I meant every word. You're mine." Her breath catches. Her lashes flutter. "And I love you."

She laughs, and the pressure pushes me out of her. "Oh, my God, I love you too. This is crazy."

Shrugging, I lie down beside her. "I've been called worse."

She stares up at the ceiling, occasionally looking over to me as if checking to make sure I'm real or still here. I took care of the condom several minutes ago, so I'm not going anywhere unless it's to the kitchen to get her some food. Past that, now that I have Willow here, I don't plan on leaving this bed until we have to.

* * *

THE SUN PEEKS over the horizon, my sign to rise and shine. But with Willow here, I don't want to. Not in the slightest.

She stirs and stretches, her eyes opening slowly.

"Hi," she whispers.

"Hi," I whisper back, though the quiet in the house tells me we're still alone.

"Do you have to get up for work?" she asks around a yawn. For her, it's basically the middle of the night. For me, it's the usual time to start my day.

"Soon, but not yet."

The truth is, I want her one more time to make sure last night wasn't a dream. I need her fresh on my skin and my cock to be sure. I want to mark her the same way too.

I roll to my side, letting my hand trace over her shoulder, down the curve of her hip to her center. I spread her lips, dipping deeper. She's already beginning to get wet for me. I groan at the realization.

I push her to her back, rising to my knees and climbing over her. "Condoms are too far away, but I have an idea." They're not far, literally two steps across the hall in the bathroom, which she very well knows. But she trusts me enough to not do anything stupid or dangerous. I never would, not where she's concerned.

Instead of entering her bare, I rub the head of my cock over her clit as though it's my finger. I trace circles, tap her with the head, and ultimately, we end up simulating fucking without actual penetration. It's not as hot as being inside her, but it's satisfying in a different way as I see my pre-cum glistening on her lower belly.

"Can I come on you?" I ask.

She nods her head, and I release. Jets of it spurt out to cover her mound and up to her belly. She moans happily, though I know it can't do much for her.

Maybe the sight of my cum on her gets my Willow off too?

I milk myself, getting every last drop, and she smiles, thinking we're done. I'm not remotely done. Not when she hasn't come yet.

I run my finger through the fluid, rubbing it into her skin to appease the Neanderthal monster inside me, then use it to tease her clit. I massage it into her, marking her as mine and getting her to the edge.

With a cry of my name, she joins me in bliss once again.

It's beautiful. It's stunning. It changes the entire direction of my life in an instant.

Before, she was mine. Now, I'm hers. Maybe I always have been.

* * *

COFFEE.

Still dozing, I realize what woke me up.

The smell of fresh coffee and hushed conversation.

After that last round at dawn, Willow and I cleaned up and snuggled in for 'just a few minutes.' By the light in the room, it's been a lot longer than that.

I watch her sleep for a little longer, enjoying her beauty. Even in her sleep, she must feel my eyes on her because she stirs, waking slowly.

"Mmm, that smells good."

The coffee must've gotten to her too.

"Come on. Let's get some before it's all gone," I say, already climbing out of bed. I feel fantastic, having slept better than I have in ages and later than I have in years.

I pull a T-shirt from my closet and dig in the dresser for a pair of shorts and toss them on the bed. Well, I mean to toss them on the bed, but they end up right in Willow's face and she glares.

I shoot her the smile that usually gets me out of trouble, and she sighs, but she moves to get up. She's slow rolling until she hears the voices.

"Who's here?" she whispers, her eyes wide in horror.

Holding my hands out like she's a skittish colt, I assure her, "Just Brody, probably. Maybe Brutal. They've already started the day." I glance at the clock on the nightstand. "A couple of hours ago. They're probably eating breakfast. Come on."

I'm not hiding her, not in the slightest. And I'm certainly not embarrassed about having her here. Hell, I want to strut through town with my shirt off to show what she did to my back. Maybe tattoo her name on my chest just so it's clear who my heart belongs to.

She gives me a tiny, uncertain hint of a smile, the terror abating bit by bit.

Downstairs, we walk into the kitchen to find Brody and Cooper eating oatmeal and drinking coffee. Well, Brody's drinking coffee. Cooper is drinking 'kid coffee', hot chocolate with the teensy-tiniest splash of coffee. Brutal says it'll get him adjusted to real coffee when he's older. I think it makes the kid bouncier and more talkative than he already is, but nobody asked me.

Willow freezes at my side and I squeeze her hand. "Morning,"

I offer the guys. Cooper's basically one of us these days, except he's a lot smarter than any of us were at his age.

Cooper grins widely, likely knowing too much about what Willow's presence here this morning means. Brody grunts, his version of 'good morning.'

Willow waves with two fingers.

I pull out a chair for her and move to grab two mugs, filling them nearly to the brim. She must need it because she nearly dives in when I set the mug on the table and take the chair next to her.

"What's up today?" I ask. Nonchalantly, because this is our new normal, folks.

"Work." Brody's all talk, as usual.

"I'm going into town with Mom later, but she sent me over here for breakfast with Uncle Brody so her and Dad could *talk*." Cooper wiggles his eyebrows and looks at me pointedly.

Oh, shit.

Brutal and Allyson have done that before, sent the kid over so they could have a few minutes alone. Hence, the previous tease about not watching the kid and leaving them to eight-minute quickies, twenty if they're lucky. Seems smarty pants Cooper has figured out what's up with that. I'll have to let Brutal and Allyson know because that's not a conversation I'm touching, not even with a ten-foot pole and an *After-School Special* video.

"Yeah, grown-ups do have a lot to talk about sometimes, don't they?"

Willow chokes on her coffee, sputtering. I pat her on the back, smirking. "Something you want to talk about, sweetheart?"

She swipes at her mouth with the back of her hand. "No, no. No. I was just thinking I should probably get going. I have to work today too."

I stand and she does too. To Brody, I say, "Tell Brutal I'm taking Willow home, 'kay?"

He grunts, which I take as agreement. On the way out, I ruffle Cooper's hair to remind myself that he's still just a kid, no matter how old he sometimes seems. He whines, smooshing it flat again with both palms. "Uncle Bobby, you suck cow balls!"

I can't help but laugh at that, though I wonder who taught him that particular phrase. Whoever it was will have hell to pay when Allyson hears it, but I won't sell the kid out. Not even to his mom or Brutal.

Willow is quiet the whole way back to town. I'm scared she's freaking out about us and want to address any concerns head-on, so I reach across the console and take her hand. "You okay?"

She turns those mood-ring eyes on me, swirling and stormy. "Yeah, just thinking about Unc."

Relief washes through me. Not that she's worried—I hate that —but that it's not about us. And that it's something I can help with. "Want me to go into the bar with you today? We can face the firing squad together." I would take a bullet for her. More importantly, and definitely more dangerous, I'd stand between Hank and her to take all his anger and hurt onto my back to save hers.

She shakes her head. "That means a lot. Thank you, but I've got this. You're coming in for dinner tonight, right?"

"I wouldn't miss it for the world."

CHAPTER 15

WILLOW

$\mathcal{I}$ steel my nerves, which are jangling even more than they were that first time I walked into the bar. I hold my head high and my shoulders back, making it appear that everything's fine. Just fine.

It's so not.

I know that as soon as I walk in the door. Unc is behind the bar, wiping down the already shining surface. His blue eyes, cold and hard as ice, cut to me with the creak of the door.

I crumble instantly. Bellying up to the bar opposite him, my apologies gush off my tongue in one big rush of words. "Unc, I am so sorry if I overstepped yesterday. I was trying to help, thought it'd be nice for you to drive up and see everything spic and span and safe. But I should've asked. I'm sorry. How's your hand?"

Without a word, he holds his hand up. He's wearing fingerless leather gloves, like something you'd use to work out, that block me from seeing a darned thing.

"How many stitches? What did the doctor say? Do you have an antibiotic prescription? I can pick that up for you."

Unc's eyes narrow, but he answers aloud this time. "Ten stitches. Doc said to keep it covered in ointment and bandaged." He wiggles his fingers around, and I can tell they're restricted, hopefully by the bandage beneath the glove. "Figured I'd keep the bandage covered so nothing got in it and people didn't come around asking nosy questions." One of his bushy eyebrows lifts pointedly at the questions I've been asking.

"Sure, good idea," I agree. My head bounces up and down as though I'm a bobblehead, reassuring him that everything's fine. Just fine.

Maybe if I say it enough, to myself and to him, it'll be true.

He sighs and goes to run his fingers through his hair but stops short as he remembers the injury. "Come in here a minute so we can talk. I don't need the whole town knowing my business."

There's literally no one but us in the bar right now. No customers yet, and Olivia is nowhere to be seen. But I hear clanging in the kitchen, so Ilene must be here getting prepped for the day.

Unc opens the door to his office and steps inside, indicating that I should sit on the bench. I do, watching closely as he goes around the desk and sits down. He lays his hands over one another, bad one on bottom. He's not a man who willingly shows a weakness, and an injury is definitely something he'd consider a weakness.

This feels ominous.

I think I'm about to get fired by my own uncle. I've never been fired from a job in my life, but that it's Unc doing it makes it sting that much more. Especially when I was only trying to help.

"I'm so sorry, Unc." Hopefully, another apology will soften his heart into giving me another chance?

"Willow." He pauses dramatically, and my heart climbs another inch up my throat. "I asked you this before and didn't push when you lied straight to my face, but I think it's high time you tell me the truth. What brings you to Great Falls?"

Huh? He knows I lied?

Oh, shit, he knows I lied.

I'm in deeper trouble than I thought.

He pins me in place with a glare, and I can't help but fidget, my knee bouncing rapidly. "A change. I told you." I swallow down the bile threatening to come up. It's not a lie, it's just not the whole truth.

"Tell me more. After all these years, why now?" A thread of anger weaves through the question, and while I'd like to tell myself it's a leftover emotion from Grandpa or Mom, I know it's because he can read me like a book. And he knows I'm still lying to him right now.

If the only way out of this is with the truth, then so be it.

Sorry, Mom.

"I remember you from when I was younger. You know I always thought you were my *cool* uncle. You'd take me for rides in your truck, letting me bounce around in the front seat when Mom made me sit in the back, and you'd tell stories and cuss with zero care that Oakley and I were in the room, and you . . ." I fall back into the past, into memories around the dinner table with Mom, Dad, Oakley, Unc, and me. "You talked to me like I had thoughts and opinions worth hearing. Other than Mom and Dad, you were the only adult who did that. It made me feel . . . not invisible at a time when all I felt was invisible."

He starts to say something, but I need to get this out while I have a chance. If he sends me out of here today and I go home to the city with my tail between my legs, I need him to know how much he means to me.

"But when you and Grandpa . . ." Unc flinches, and I graze around that wound. "Fought, you left. You left me like I was nothing, like maybe I wasn't so worthwhile and important, after all. And I was hurt. I was furious for a long time. But time keeps passing, and when I got older, I realized we don't always have 'later' to sort things out, so I came. For a change with you, before it's too late. Before we're out of time."

The last words are my real fear. His time is short, shorter than it was all those years ago for sure, and there's more at stake now.

He starts to speak but coughs, covering a catch in his throat. "How long have you known?"

"Since I came. It's why I came," I confess.

"I figured as much," he says dryly, leaning back in his chair. He props his feet up on the desk, crossing his hands over his belly, the bandaged one still covered by the good one. He's somehow the utter picture of relaxation, as though yesterday didn't happen and we're not discussing a cancer diagnosis.

The word alone hits me hard, which is why I've tried to avoid it, even in my own thoughts. Unc has cancer. It's bad. He's alone and needs help. He needs me.

Cancer. Death. Fear. Time.

Powerful words that seem to not hit Unc in the slightest. I want this memory—of Unc strong and resolute, dismissive of the seriousness of his reality. *Click.* Not with my camera, but with my mind this time. I know I won't forget this image.

"Okay, your turn. If we're getting this out in the open, what's the prognosis? What does the doctor say your odds are and how can I help?" I'm a woman on a mission, charging full steam ahead to handle whatever needs attention. This is what I'm here for, and there's no need to refute it any more or hide it in subtle, secretive moves so I don't poke at his pride.

Unc snorts derisively. "Like he knows a damn thing. He says this is what's gonna kill me, but he ain't got a crystal ball. I might get hit by a bus tomorrow, so no sense worrying about what he thinks he knows."

What a bright, uplifting outlook, I think wryly.

"There are no buses in Great Falls," I challenge.

"You know what I mean. I ain't worrying about things I can't change. And school buses," he counters, plenty of sass in his own voice.

I don't bother reminding him that it's summer and school buses aren't running. "But you're doing what the doctor says, right? Following orders?" I already know the answer, but I want to make him say it so he sees that he's doing too much.

And he is—working six days a week for lunch and dinner shifts the way he always has, with just those rare two days he took off, still carrying boxes around like he's a muscled up man of twenty, drinking his craft beer and eating from Ilene's kitchen every night where even the vegetables are cooked in butter and salt. I'm not sure how to fight cancer, but my gut tells me it involves a lifestyle based on less stress, healthy eating, and eight hours of sleep every night. All things Unc is not doing. Hell, things he's probably never done!

"I'm doing what I want, same as always. No reason to fix something that ain't broke. And to be clear, I ain't broke." This time, I lift one brow, mimicking the move he's perfected. "I'm not," he asserts. "I'm old, not done."

I'm glad to hear that he hasn't given up. His fight is strong, going so far as to fight the doctor and whatever weakness his body has succumbed to with the iron will he's always had.

Relief grows inside my heart, even though nothing has really changed.

Unc still has cancer. But now we're talking about it at least, and that is a change for good.

He's still a stubborn old coot. But now I can call him out on being pig-headed and ornery.

"I'm sorry I wasn't honest with you from the get-go, but I wanted to stay, wanted time with you. I still do," I plead. "I'm sorry if I overstepped with the yardwork and office organizing." I look around the room, gesturing to the file cabinet with drawers that actually close cleanly instead of getting stuck on stacks of crooked papers. "I really was trying to help without stepping on your toes."

His boots wiggle on the desk. "These old boots protect my toes just fine, girl. Don't you worry about dancing on them. If anything, I should be the one apologizing to you."

I shake my head, and he does the eyebrow thing, freezing my tongue before I can argue.

He sits up straight, his feet on the floor once again as he leans forward over the desk. "You said your piece, now I'm gonna say mine. You'd best listen up, too, because I'm not doing this whole thing again." He points from himself to me, like this conversation is the very definition of hell to him. Not because it's me, but because words have power and he's speaking out loud about something beyond his control, a scary prospect for anyone, but certainly for a man like Hank Davis.

I nod, zipping my lip and listening.

"One, nobody knows shit and I intend to keep it that way. The gossipy Guses of this town have enough ammunition to keep them busy six days a week and twice on Sunday, and I don't need them gossiping about me, coming in to check on me, and sending over casseroles like I can't cook my own damn dinner."

He says the word 'casserole' with disgust, and a smile tries to bloom, but I press my lips together.

"Two, you're a damn good worker and an even better bartender. I might have some days where I'd like to sit on my keister and catch a fish or two, so if that's what I want to do, I'm gonna, if that's good with you?"

He means the days he's too tired or nauseous to come into work, but if he wants to call it 'fishing', I'll happily oblige.

"Of course. Fishing is important. Relaxing on a boat in the sunshine sounds lovely."

He looks toward the door, and I know he's trying to escape this next part. But he digs down for courage and says what's on his mind. "Third, there might be some days where I'd like you to go fishing with me, just sit on the boat by my side, you know? I promise not to be a grumpy asshole and throw screwdrivers around when you're trying to help me . . . fish. Sorry about that. It was a bad day."

Tears prick at my eyes, hot and burning, but I refuse to let them fall. If he can be this brave, so can I. "I would love to go fishing any time you'd like, Unc."

He dips his chin once. "Thank you, Willow-girl. You've always had the sweetest spirit and you've already brought so much sunshine to my days."

I smile at the kind compliment. Right up until he finishes . . .

"Now get out there and get to work. The lunch crowd ain't gonna wait for you to get ready for them. They want their drinks and want them now."

He's not my kind uncle anymore, down because of a hard situation. Nope, he's back to my steel-cored, iron-willed boss.

I salute, definitely getting the form wrong, but he cracks a smile, nevertheless. "On it, Unc."

I get up, beelining for the door, only to have him stop me.

"One last thing."

I turn around, eyes questioning.

"How'd you know? Who blabbed?"

Oh, shit. There might not be buses in Great Falls, but this is a loaded question, one that's going to shove someone right in harm's way. But I'm not going to lie, not when Unc is finally being honest with me.

"Doc Jones called Mom. Told her you needed somebody and we're the only family you've got left. She thought it'd be too hard on you to see her, so she sent me instead."

"Asshole. Doc, not your mom. Carrie's sweet to care after so long. Doc, on the other hand, I'll rip 'im a new one for nosing around in my business when it ain't none of his concern."

"If he had something going on, you'd take care of him. Or Richard. You three are thick as thieves. The Three Musketeers of Great Falls. He did what he thought was right. And it got me here, so it's not all bad." I think my case is pretty strong that Doc did right by Unc, but who knows if he'll feel the same way?

"Mmm, we'll see. Maybe I'll just lord it over his head a little. Get him to feel sorry for me a bit so I can win a few hands at Sunday's game." His smile is tinged with ornery devilment.

"Well, you two work it out however you need to. I'm going to get to work, if that's okay?"

His eyes refocus on mine, likely leaving the fantasy world where he wipes out Doc Jones's entire piggy bank without telling him that the cat's out of the bag. "Yeah, thanks. And tell your Mom to come visit soon. I'd like to see Carrie before . . ."

His voice trails off, and I let him leave that possibility on the tip of his tongue. No need to speak it into existence. Instead, I nod. "She'd like that. I'll let her know."

* * *

"Willow Parker! You'd best get your boo-tay behind that bar and start slinging drinks like your life depends on it! Or you can act like we've been bought out by *Coyote Ugly* and climb up there to shake your moneymaker so these heathens don't realize how long it's been since they ordered a Coke! I'm in the weeds, girl!"

Olivia's voice carries through the whole room, and everyone stops what they're doing to look at me. They're probably wondering which option I'm going to choose.

Option one, for sure. There's zero doubt about that.

I step behind the bar, already apologizing. "Sorry, I was talking to Unc."

"Yeah, yeah. Less talking, more drink making," she says, waving a hand to rush me.

I look over and there are four tickets. She's nowhere near in the weeds. This woman could run this whole damn place single-handedly if need be. But she does like giving me a hard time.

Glancing at her, I find her forcing a ridiculously fake, sad frown. "I was really hoping you'd get on the bar. *Really* hoping."

I flick the water on my fingers at her and finish the drinks for the second ticket, already catching up. She laughs and runs them out to table eight while I do tickets three and four. In minutes, I'm back to prep work with zero tickets in my queue, and Olivia is waiting for food orders to be ready from Ilene.

"How was your weekend?" she asks, aiming for nonchalant and missing by a country mile.

"Great. Yours?" I smile warmly, as though I haven't clued in to what she's really asking.

She growls. "Ugh, spill it, girl! I have people here for lunch solely because they know that you and Bobby Tannen had your first official date on Monday when we were closed. I didn't tell them Hank gave you Sunday off yet. I'm holding that ace up my sleeve. But you'd best spill it. Enquiring minds want to know. Was he as good as I dream he is?" She pelvic thrusts the air, apparently auditioning for the *Coyote Ugly* option herself.

I blink the vision away, laughing. "Does Hannah know you're dreaming about sleeping with Bobby Tannen? Seems like she might have a problem with that." Truthfully, I don't know. I have yet to meet the elusive Hannah, though Olivia talks about her as though she's right here in the room at all times. Mostly because they spend all day texting each other back and forth when they're not busy at work.

"Hannah says he's dreamy too. We're secure like that. Fantasies are just that—pretend. Just because the thought of some pretty, growly cowboy taking me rough is sexy, doesn't mean I want to actually do it. People have all sorts of images in their head that get them off, but even given the chance, they'd never do it for realsies. That don't mean I don't want to hear every vivid, messy detail."

She props her chin up on her palms, eyes wide and focused on me like I'm about to give a speech on demand.

Welcome to my TED talk. Today's topic will be 'Sex with Bobby Tannen' with helpful illustrated handouts.

Nope, not a chance in hell that's happening. But I trust Olivia's judgement, even if she is a bit crazy, so I give her one detail.

"We said *I love you*." I nearly squeal it, but my excitement has made me breathless and it comes out more like a whisper-scream.

"What?" she yells at full volume again.

Thanks for that, Olivia! Not!

I nod, not willing to repeat the words lest I jinx the whole thing.

"Oh, my God!" She claps right in front of her heart as though it needs more than a racing beat to show her happiness for me. But then her brows jump together. "Wait. Was this mid-boink? That doesn't count."

"Yes, it does," I counter.

Her happiness melts, going sad as she offers a pitying smile. "Oh, honey, that doesn't count. Guys say stuff like that when all their blood is in their dick. It's science."

Any other time, her doubt would make me question myself. No, not any other time . . . any other guy. But I know Bobby meant exactly what he said.

"He meant it. I meant it. For real. And what do you know about dick science?" I whisper 'dick' so customers don't hear me, even though they most certainly heard Olivia.

Olivia leans across the bar, getting in my face and whispering, "You love Bobby? And he loves you? Like dum-dum-dee-dum?" She sings out the notes of the wedding march song.

"I don't know about that last part, but the rest . . . yeah."

I can feel my face flush, my heart pounding as I remember how good it felt to be with Bobby. I picture the look in his eyes as he gritted out his love. I feel his cum on my skin, his gentle and comforting touch as I cried on his chest, and his marks all over my body, claiming me as his.

I have zero doubt, not about Bobby, and not about my own feelings.

Blinking, I come back to the moment at the bar with Olivia, who is fanning her face. "Whoo, child. Wherever you just went, whatever you were thinking about . . . con-grat-u-fuckin-lations. Because that seems like some Grade-A, heart racing, pussy pulsing, *good* stuff. I approve."

She slaps the bar and hops up to make her rounds, but as she scurries off, I can hear her singing under breath . . .

Bobby and Willow fucking by a tree . . .

F-U-C-K Me-E-E.

I think about that for a second. Would I like to have sex with Bobby outside by a tree? I've never done that before. I picture it and decide that like Olivia said, it's sexy to imagine, but I think I'd be so scared we'd get caught that I wouldn't be able to enjoy myself if we tried it for real. Maybe I'm just a behind closed doors sort?

I picture Bobby locking the door, telling me to lie down and spread my legs for him, him climbing over me . . . yeah, I'm a behind closed doors girl for sure because that is sexy as hell.

* * *

"So, do I need to kill him?" Bobby asks me after his Wrangler-covered butt meets a barstool. He kissed me hello first, and I swear, the whole place nearly sighed in unison.

At my look of confusion, he explains, "Hank. He go hard on you from yesterday's escapades?"

Smiling, I shake my head. "No, we actually had a good talk. We're fine now. Better than fine."

Bobby glances down the bar and meets Unc's eyes. He's stayed on his butt all night, sticking to pulling beers and chatting with Richard while I man the rest of the bar. Just like it should be so he doesn't wear himself out. The two men glare, hard eyed and harder willed, but Bobby defers first, in a sign of respect, not weakness. He dips his chin, then Unc does the same.

Just like that, they're solid gold again. Guys are so weird. But I'm glad they're okay with each other now. Even if I can't tell

Bobby about the c-a-n-c-e-r. I'll keep my promise to Unc and not blab that, not even to Bobby, though I know he's trustworthy.

But it's not my secret.

"So, what's the plan for tonight? Dinner, close down, and clean up?" he asks.

"Yep."

I know what he's asking, but I want him to take the lead here.

"Then what, Willow? Tell me what you want."

Shit.

He pushes me, encourages me to be bolder, louder. In the past, I've hated that, people who thought quiet equaled stupid or shy meant weak. But Bobby isn't trying to change me. He's giving me space to walk with him, not behind him, and . . . I like it a lot. It seems safe to do with him, like he won't judge me no matter what I say, and there's no pressure to do or say or feel the right thing because there is no right or wrong. He truly wants to know whatever's in my heart or on my mind.

I search for what I want. Not what I think he wants. So I openly tell him, "And then we go to my house. Can you stay for breakfast?"

He flashes that cocky smirk. "Sweetheart, you know that if my truck is in your driveway in the morning when people get up to drink their first cup of coffee, I might as well stand on your front porch and yell out that we're together, right? We'll be the talk of the town before the sun breaks the horizon line."

I tease at the napkin on top of the stack in front of me, curling it into a roll then releasing it, only to do it again. "So that's a yes?"

Maybe that's the wrong thing. Maybe he doesn't want that?

"Thank fuck. About damn time you catch up to me, woman." And with that, he reaches across the bar, his palm cupping the back of my neck to pull me toward him, and kisses the hell out of me. I don't think anyone is going to need to see his truck in my driveway to know that our date went well and that not only am I officially Bobby Tannen's girl, but he's officially my man.

He kisses me long and hard and with a self-satisfied smirk, sits back on that barstool. I grab my phone out of my pocket and hold it up.

Bobby smiles for me, the panty-melting grin he flashes when

he's on stage holding the audience in his hand. But right now, it's for an audience of one. Me. *Click.*

I hold his hand on the bar, our fingers interwoven together. His are rough and the cuticles cracked—the hands of a man who works every single day of his life. Mine are small, my nails short and bare, adorned with only the silver thumb ring Mom gave me for my sixteenth birthday and the tiny pinky ring that fits to my first knuckle. I frame the shot just the way I want, catching the texture of our skin, the difference in our skin tones, and the way even his grip seems both possessive and tender at the same time. *Click.*

I don't alter the picture in any way, posting it straight to my blog with a caption that simply says, *Love Is Real* with a heart emoji.

This is my version of shouting it from the front porch. I'm yelling loud and proud, virtually jumping up and down as I wave my arms around like a wild woman. This is my happy dance. I just can't dance for shit. Hence, the less than zero chance you'll ever see me pull a *Coyote Ugly*. Bar rule number four is in effect. Indefinitely, perpetually, forever and always.

CHAPTER 16

BOBBY

"Guess you'll have to come to Hank's tonight, ma'am. Sorry, I don't do impromptu private shows," I tell Mrs. Perkinson, holding out her weekly order of jam.

One part of me thinks she orders so frequently as a way to have someone to talk to, even if it's only for a minute on the front porch, because she's a grumpy bitch, something I do not say lightly because Mom raised me to not speak about the elderly that way. But that brings me to my other theory, which is that she orders just so she can bitch at my brothers and me because her own kids don't come by. It's so bad that Brody flat out refuses to deliver to her anymore, leaving me and Brutal to her sharp words.

I guess the third option is that she's addicted to Shay's jam, but even as delicious as it is, that somehow seems less likely when Mrs. Perkinson's mouth starts running.

"I would not step foot in that Devil's den." She harrumphs. "Alcohol, dancing, filthy music, and filthier men. Bless their hearts." Her sneer is judgmental and catty as she places her hand over her heart, which irritates the fuck out of me. We all know that 'bless their hearts' has nothing to do with an actual blessing. It's an insult if ever there were one.

"Sounds like my kind of place, which is why I sing there twice a month. As you're well aware." *Boom* . . . mic drop.

She looks me up and down like I'm a pile of dog shit on her porch. "Well, maybe you need to sing something a little more classic, see if it'll save your soul. You should try *Amazing Grace*," she suggests. "It's a beautiful song."

I grunt and spin on my heel. I actually do a kickass version of that, but I ain't going to sing it. There's no use in arguing with her. It won't do either of us a bit of good, and I have three more deliveries to make before I can see Willow.

The next delivery is to Esme's house, and though I try to be quick about it, she starts asking questions about Willow and me. "Everyone says your first date was this week, but it wasn't, was it? It was when you two came through my drive-through." I don't answer and she keeps going. "I told Julianna that, but she didn't believe me. Said it didn't count because you might've just been friends then, but I saw the way Willow was looking at you and women do not look at friends like that. No siree."

"Gotta go."

Get me the fuck out of here. Hell, I'd rather sing *Amazing Grace* than this.

Esme waves and calls after me, "See you tonight at Hank's. Break a leg! Not literally, of course." She laughs. "It's a theater expression for good luck."

I climb in my truck and gun it down the street.

Thankfully, the next delivery is no big deal, a quick and easy drop off. No muss, no fuss, the way we all prefer it.

The last one, though . . .

Shit. Loretta Landrum. She's been trying to get in my pants since the day I turned eighteen. Literally diving in and trying to unzip them herself.

I never wanted her hands on me before, definitely don't want hers or anyone else's on me now. Only Willow's.

I ring the bell and step back from the door, planning to keep space between me and Loretta. When she opens the door in a too-small bikini, I take another step back.

"Oh! Bobby! So sorry, I was getting ready to lay out in the back yard for some sun when I heard the bell."

"Mmmhmm." She was definitely sitting in the living room, her body barely half-covered, waiting for me to make her scheduled delivery.

"Come on in. I'll get us some lemonade. Maybe you could help me put suntan lotion on my back. It's hard to reach, you know?" Her hips sway, her fingers twirl her hair, and her teeth bite into her bottom lip.

"No. Here's your jam." I'm being crystal-fucking-clear what I'm saying no to, my voice hard and my eyes narrowed. Manners? Hell, I'm not even playing at being rude. I'm letting all my thoughts of revulsion shine like a grimy diamond.

Have some damn pride, Loretta. You've been throwing yourself at me for years at this point, and it's never gonna happen.

Loretta flinches and doesn't move to take the jam I'm holding out, so I set it on the porch and walk away. It takes her a second to recover, but she calls out loud enough for the neighbors to hear, "Bye, Bobby. Thanks for coming over. I'll see you again tonight!"

Muttering under my breath to myself, I climb in the truck. The whole town's gonna be talking about my fucking delivery route today. Brutal can do this shit next week. I'm out.

* * *

THE PARKING LOT at Hank's is so full that I have to park around back. But with a knock on the back door, Daniel lets me in.

"Hey, man! Good to see you," he says, holding out a fist. I bump it and offer a smile before heading into the bar to find my girl.

She's holding court behind the bar, of course. I watch for a second, enjoying the sight of her simply working. She smiles and fills glasses for customers, making small talk along the way.

She gets down toward Hank, who's sitting by the beer taps. That's become his new perch. Willow's handiwork, it seems. He'll do anything for her, the same way I will. Hell, I suspect most people would. She's just someone you want to treat right and do nice things for because she does them for everyone else.

She laughs at something Richard says, her smile wide, and swats at the bar as though she's admonishing him. But it's all in jest. She's comfortable and right at home.

And now that I see her, I am too.

I make my way through the crowd easily, people moving out of my way. A few say hello, but I ignore them, my eyes locked on my target.

"Hey, sweetheart," I drawl, and that pretty smile of hers goes brighter than the sun.

"Bobby! Look at this crowd. All here for you!" Her excitement would be infectious if I gave a shit about any of these people.

Actually, that's not true. Across the bar, a loud voice I recognize calls my name, and I glance over to see my family at the one table that will hold them all.

Willow follows my eyes and explains, "Shay called earlier and asked me to reserve it for them since they were coming to see you perform tonight."

The crowd, I don't care about, but my family coming means something to me.

But first things first. "Come here." The growled order is too quiet for her to hear, but she knows what I want anyway and leans forward to meet me across the bar.

I hold her cheeks in my palms gently and take her mouth the same way. Her tongue slips into my mouth too, and she tastes like sweet tea. She probably has a glass stashed somewhere behind the bar to sip on while she works.

Around us, there's a chorus of 'aww', and Willow blushes prettily when I let her go.

"You two are the cutest and all, but I *really* need some margaritas," Olivia sing-songs, not looking remorseful in the slightest at interrupting our greeting.

Willow smiles sweetly and says, "Say hi to your family for me. I'll stop over there if I can. I have a good feeling about tonight, like there's something in the air." I lift my eyebrow questioningly, and her shrug is almost shy, though she's nearly vibrating with energy and anticipation. "I just know you're gonna be amazing is all. I haven't seen you perform since that first night, and now it's . . . different."

I peck her lips once more, loving that she admits how serious things have become so freely now. "Yeah, it is. I'll make sure to tell everyone to tip my girl."

Her laugh is all mine, and time freezes for a moment as I breathe it in, breathe her in with all her light and positivity, her heart shining through in everything she does. Even a laugh at a stupid joke from me, one I meant sincerely.

I am the luckiest son of a bitch alive because this woman has let me into layers of herself that she protects from most. My hidey-hole grew into a recliner, and now I'm hanging up neon letters on her heart so that I can shine throughout her, exploring and claiming every bit of her soul.

"Margaritas—that's just lime juice and tequila, right?" Olivia deadpans like she's going to slip behind the bar and make them herself.

Willow rolls her eyes, reluctantly leaving me so she can get back to work. I watch for one more second, drinking her in with my eyes. Eventually, I make my way across to my family and sit down in the booth as they make room for me.

Scanning, I see someone's missing. Two someones. "Where're James and Sophie?"

"Babysitting duty with Cooper and Cindy Lou," Brutal answers. "I think Sophie was tired because she had to assist with a foal delivery early this morning. Pretty sure she volun-told James he was doing Kid Patrol while she took a bath and turned in early."

"Good for her." Shay's statement is punctuated with a high-five to Allyson. "Sometimes, we have to declare it a self-care day and follow through."

I have no idea what self-care is. It sounds like girl code for masturbating, and if that's so, I definitely do not want to have that conversation with my sister. That's Luke's responsibility.

Luckily, I don't find out the answer because a woman comes up to the table. I don't know her, or at least I don't think I do. She's got full hair and makeup done, and there's a guy standing a foot or so behind her. She looks at me directly. "Hey, so this is probably weird and all, but could you sign this picture for me? Please?"

"Huh?" I wish I could say I came up with something more insightful, but confusion is all I've got right now. "Picture?" There, that's slightly better.

She holds up a black and white picture of Shay's goat, Trollie, and a Sharpie. "Please?" she repeats.

"Uh, why?" I have no idea what me and Trollie have to do with one another.

She blinks in confusion.

That makes two of us, woman.

"This is you, isn't it?" She uses the cap of the marker to point to the arm holding Trollie. "That's your tattoo." She looks to my bicep where the Roman numerals are lined up in memory of Mom.

Brody recovers first, though the whole table is looking at the woman like she's grown a third eye in the middle of her forehead. "Where'd you get that?" he growls, and the woman jumps.

Her guy takes a small step forward and puts his hand on her lower back protectively. But he's not challenging Brody. No one is stupid enough to do that, not even a random dude in a bar. Give him credit for guts, but Brody would mop the floor with this guy if he had to. "It was on the blog," the woman repeats. "Willow's blog? *A Day in the Life of a Tree*?" She's explaining my girl's work to me like I'm a clueless dumbass. "There was a whole bunch of goat ones, but this one is . . . you." She's losing steam, and certainty, though she's absolutely right. That is me and Trollie. "I just printed it out because I thought it'd be cool to have you sign it."

I take the marker from her, defusing the situation and silently telling Brody to take it down a notch. "Yeah, that's fine. I just didn't see that picture on there so it threw me. No worries. Here." I sign my name—my first autograph!—and hand it back to her.

"Thanks so much!" she gushes, any nerves dissipating into bubbles of joy as she looks from the picture to me. Brody and his growliness are all but forgotten. She turns around to the guy behind her, who smiles congenially at her, but when she looks down at the photo again, he looks to me like 'whatcha gonna do, man?' I chuckle a bit at the poor sap.

"Found it!" Shay squeals. "Oh, my cheesus and crackers, she posted like ten pictures of the goats. Here's Baarbara, and Trollie, and . . . Oh, here's George too." She's scrolling, not showing any of us her phone so we can see too. But I believe her.

"Did you know about this?" Brody asks.

I shrug, not bothered in the least about the pictures. The random asking for an autograph was weird, but kinda cool in a way, now that I think about it. "I told her she could take pictures of me any time she wants, and she asked about that one. I just hadn't seen it. She's really careful about not showing faces and stuff, though. Said it helps people put themselves in the experiences better if there's not an actual person to relate to. That's why it's always bits and pieces and parts, not a whole face or body shot."

Luke snorts. "Body shot."

Shayanne pats his leg, grinning conspiratorially. "Later. Look at this!"

She spins her phone around, showing everyone the picture Willow took of our hands. I did know about this one, but seeing the caption she added does something hot and fiery to my insides. Maybe love is warm and fuzzy for some people, but it makes me want to strut my ass back over there and finally fuck her on the bar.

Love is real. Her words, my thoughts exactly.

Fuck yeah, it is, sweetheart.

Allyson and Katelyn ooh and aah over Shay's phone while the guys smirk at me. Actually, Rix smirks too, but then she leans over and whispers something into Shay's ear, and Shay giggles.

But none of these assholes are any better. I've watched every damn one of these men get wound tighter and tighter around their women's pinky fingers. I've wanted that too but never felt it until now.

We talk for a bit longer, and a couple more people come up to chat, one with me, and one with Luke about a horse for sale. Before long, it's time for me to hit the stage.

As I step out on the small, makeshift stage I helped Hank build, a calm comes over me. Eyes being on me is usually something that irritates me, pricking at my skin like needles as people judge me.

Those poor Tannen boys. Did you hear about their mother? Did you hear about their father?

Bobby, he's the nice one, though that's not saying much because those

201

brothers of his are hellions through and through. And the sister? Well, poor thing never had a chance.

Cross the street and don't look him in the eye, or he'll probably fly off the handle again. Anger management problems, the whole lot of them.

Pity he could never do anything with that God-given talent. Some people just don't get the same opportunities as other folks do.

Here, onstage, none of that matters.

They think they know me because I stand up here and willingly bleed myself dry for their enjoyment. The truth is, I hold the power with every chord. I choose what I share, what stories to tell, and how they see me.

I've perfected several images. A rough cowboy with a heart of gold. The asshole who'll beat the shit out of anyone who gets in his way. A hard-working farmer with a voice filled with gritty honesty. The man everyone wants but no one gets.

There's truly only one person I care about in this crowd tonight, and she's waving at me with her bar towel. I throw her a smile, knowing that she sees all of me and loves what she sees.

Love is real.

I get to work, planning to put on a hell of a show for Willow.

"Hi, everyone. I'm Bobby Tannen."

With a strum of my strings, I play. Old songs, new songs, cover songs, and originals.

I do the schtick to encourage everyone to get a drink and tip their waitress and bartenders well. "Especially the blonde," I add with a wink, and people laugh, the ladies saying *ooh*.

Sometime around my cover of Cody Jinks's *Loud and Heavy*, I look over to find a guy in a blue polo shirt, khaki slacks, and clean boots leaning across the bar. Willow's standing across from him.

He's probably ordering a drink, man. Chill out.

But as I launch into the chorus again, the animal instinct in my gut says that's not the case. Especially when those gray eyes cut to mine and she doesn't smile. I damn near stop the song and use the microphone to tell this asshole to back away from her. But he's not doing anything wrong. I just feel the need to piss on my territory again, even if I have to punch out another tourist to do it.

Instead, I use another weapon.

I look pointedly at Brutal and catch his eye, then look to

Willow. He follows my gaze and immediately gets up to rescue her for me. We're Tannens, and we've been looking out for each other for a long time. Now, we protect what's important to us too, like Rix, Allyson, Cooper, and even the Bennetts.

And now Willow.

I finish the song and let my fingers dance aimlessly over the strings as I watch. Brutal looks back to me and lifts his chin. 'All good, man.'

Willow's eyes are dancing brightly now, and even from here, I can see the laughter in them. She blows me a kiss, and it's the only thing that keeps me in place and singing the next song.

I finish my set and put Betty in her case, slipping her behind the curtain. I take a quick minute to go around back and wipe down because it's hotter than Satan's taint out there tonight with the huge crowd and lights.

Hank's office door opens and Willow struts in like she owns the place. She basically does at this point, I think.

"Thinking of punching someone out again?" she teases.

"Worked last time . . . got you in here alone with me. Oh, and look . . . worked again. Seems pretty successful, if you ask me," I reply dryly.

I put my hands on her hips, hooking my fingers through the beltloops, and pull her in close as I spin her. Her hands go to my chest, but I've got her, sure and steady as I pin her to the door with my body pressed against hers.

Tonight felt like a private concert for one, no matter how many people were in the room. She was all I could see, all I cared about, and she was too far away. I liked it better when we were sitting together on my tailgate, just the two of us and the night as I sang and she took pictures. That felt right. That felt better than any show I've ever done.

It quieted the beast inside me more. Giving my music to her was all I needed to truly be at peace.

I stare at her lips, making us both wait one more second to let the anticipation build. She licks them, getting ready for the kiss she knows is coming.

"Don't you want to know what that guy was asking?"

I shake my head. "Don't care. Just want to kiss you and feel you kissing me back. I want to grab your ass and lift you up so you straddle me. I want your arms and legs wrapped around me so tight it's like you're trying to climb inside my body, and then I want to get inside yours, fuck you all night and have you tell me you love me every time you come."

"Oh." All the wind is gone from her sails, and she sags into my arms, letting me put her where I want her. I bend down and make good on my words, meeting her lips with mine tenderly and letting our passion ignite into the inferno it always becomes. I grip her ass, and she hops up, her bare legs wrapping around my waist and her arms going over my shoulders.

"Yes," I grunt, grinding against her.

There's a loud knock on the other side of the door, and she freezes, eyes going wide. "Oh!" she says quietly. She unlocks her legs and slides down my body until her tennis shoes hit the floor.

"No hanky-panky in my office, young lady. And where'd you put the Jack again?" Hank calls through the wood.

Willow shakes her head and whispers, "He knows where the whiskey is, but I'm pretty sure that means he wants me to come do the cocktails so he can sit down at the taps. That's what I want too. Nearly had to tie him to the chair to keep him there in the first place, so I'd better go."

She steps away, and I stop her by grabbing her wrist. "That the only thing you want?"

Her blushing cheeks are adorable. "No, I want . . . what you said too, but after we go home, 'kay?"

"Promise?" I demand teasingly.

She smiles and repeats after me, "Promise."

I reward her with another kiss, but the throat clearing on the other side of the door says we still have an audience.

When Willow opens the door, Hank is leaning on the opposite wall, arms crossed over his chest.

"Sorry, Unc. I'm on it!" She hurries past him and back out to the floor.

When she's out of earshot, Hank's blue eyes narrow sharply. "Hurt her and I'll end you, Tannen."

He's protecting Willow, something I deeply understand and

respect. "No need. If I hurt her, what you do to me won't be nearly as bad as what I do to myself."

"Hmmph," he grunts, which translates to 'we'll see about that', and I remember that Hank was in the military for a short while. I wonder what he did and what secret skills he might be hiding. He's damn good with a baseball bat, I've witnessed that firsthand, but for all I know, he's a crack shot and has ninja knife skills. And even if he doesn't, I'm a damn big target, which makes me pretty hard to miss.

We walk down the hall together, me slowing my pace to match his.

"Polo shirt guy was asking questions about you. Thought you should know," Hank says with zero expression on his face as we re-enter the main room. I could almost pretend that I imagined it, but I know he actually said that. Unfazed, he walks behind the bar and plops himself back on his perch.

The info is an olive branch from him, a sign of respect after I passed whatever test that was by not cowering in response to his threat of violence.

I huff a small laugh. Violence, I know. Violence, I understand.

I sit back down with my family, who congratulate me on a great show.

"What's the title of that new one you did?" Allyson asks. "Brutal's been humming it nonstop, so I know you've been working on it recently."

"He has?" I'm surprised. Brutal listens to me write all my songs because I find pockets of time here and there to work, usually in the fields when we're taking breaks. And melodies get in my head and I hum them on repeat until they make sense for a song. I hadn't realized that Brutal was picking up the melodies too. He's scary observant, so I knew he was aware of my process, but singing them when I'm not around is a sign that the tune is catchy. And that he cares. Allyson nods, and I tell her, "It's called *Bridge Over my Broken Heart*."

"It's a great one. My favorite of the night for sure."

"Thanks."

I don't tell her, and sure as shit haven't told Brutal, that they're the inspiration for that song. A love that was meant to be but got so epically screwed up. Fate intervened, and in the end, they got their happily ever after the way it should've been.

I take a sip of the Jack someone ordered for me, sighing as the alcohol goes down my throat, soothing the sting of prolonged singing. Putting the glass down, I realize no one is looking at me. Instead, they're looking off to the side of the table.

Another groupie who wants to hop on my dick? Fuck, don't be Loretta. Please don't be Loretta.

The good news . . . it's not Loretta. The bad news . . . it's polo shirt guy.

"Hi, Bobby. I'm Jeremy Marshall of NCR Records. I'd like to talk to you about your career, if that's okay?"

"My what?" I growl.

Wait. Did he say NCR Records? Like music records?

Polo Shirt—I haven't decided if I'm calling him Jeremy yet—takes a chair from a nearby table, spinning it around. He sits backward, straddling it and putting his arms on the chair back.

As he talks, I can't believe what I'm hearing.

I can't wait to tell Willow!

We're celebrating, sweetheart, because your man's going big time. Maybe.

* * *

WILLOW'S EXHAUSTED after a long shift and a late clean-up once she got everyone kicked out well after two. I'm exhausted from farming, Shay's deliveries, and the show, but I'm buzzing inside.

"Tell me again what he said," she orders.

We're sitting in her bathtub, which is way too small for the both of us, but it'd seemed like relaxation we both need. We both deserve some before we fall into bed tonight. I'm still going to take her, I'm never too tired for that, but it's nice to simply sit here in hot, bubbly water with her ass pressed up against my cock and her back lying against my chest. As she breathes, her tits lift and lower out of the bubbles enticingly.

"Huh?" Distracted by her pink nipples, I have no idea what she said.

"What did Mr. Marshall say?" Her butt wiggles, teasing me, but it's just her excitement, not a seduction.

I smile, not believing it myself. "He said he was in town with his wife for a wedding, but he's a talent scout so he likes to get out to the local dives wherever he goes to 'keep a finger on the pulse'."

"Like Hank's," Willow interjects.

"And he liked my voice and wants me to fly out to Nashville for a meet and greet with his team. Do a demo, maybe hit a few places there to do a short set so they get some real-time feedback. Stuff like that." I'm trying to downplay it because I don't want to get my hopes up too high. This is major, more opportunity than I've ever had.

"Oh, my gosh, I can't believe it! That is so awesome. I told you I had a good feeling about tonight, and I was right. I'm so happy for you."

She twists to look back at me, her smile beaming. Even when she kisses me, that smile stays, and I can feel it pressed along my lips. "Your name is going to be in lights, Bobby Tannen. Just like you always dreamed, just like you deserve."

She sounds so sure that I can almost believe it myself.

CHAPTER 17

BOBBY

*T*he sun rises over the horizon outside Willow's bedroom window, painting highlights and shadows on the walls and the curves of her body. She's curled into my side, her head on my chest as my fingertips dance along her skin. Every fiber of my being strains for her, though I know my cock is too spent to go again yet. Though not inside her, I feel connected with her as we lie here, relaxed into one another.

Moment stretched, a tattoo on my soul in the shape of your smile.

"I wish you could come with me," I whisper. The truth is, I'm nervous and could use her at my side to help me stay calm and not fuck this opportunity up. If these Nashville people like me and my music, this could change everything . . . for me, for my family, for Willow and me.

"Me too, but Unc . . ." Her voice tapers off, and she doesn't finish the thought. There's no reason to. I know Hank needs her here more than I need her to go with me. He's had a rough week for some reason. One day, I thought he seemed a bit pale, but he brushed me off grumpily, and he's been bitching about having to do everything himself while simultaneously sitting on his ass and directing everyone else around. It's made for some long shifts and late nights this week.

In fact, we're not up early for my Friday flight to Nashville.

We're still awake from last night's Thursday two-dollar draft crowd. The bar closed at two. I'd helped with cleanup, but we still hadn't gotten out of there until after three, then we'd made love twice, knowing that the weekend was going to be long and lonely.

But possibly the start of something amazing for my music.

"It's fine. I'll fly out there, meet with these folks, do their dog and pony show, and be back on Tuesday. You gonna be okay without me?"

She will be. I'm sure of it. However, I'm not at all sure that I'll be okay without her. I think my weekend is going to be filled with thoughts of 'what's Willow doing right now?' and obsessively refreshing her blog like a fucking creeper. I already told the family to come by Hank's as much as possible to check on her. They gave me shit for it, but they'll do it.

She laughs sweetly. "Me? I'll be working my butt off slinging drinks and answering all sorts of nosy questions about you this weekend. I'm more worried you're going to go out there and be blinded by those big city lights and not come back to me. I've seen how pretty they can be."

Humor is woven through her words, but I can sense a true fear deep inside. I squeeze her tight, laying a kiss to her forehead, and promise, "There is nothing and no one that could ever make me stay away from you. I love you, Willow."

Her cheek lifts against my chest, letting me know she's smiling again. I did that. I make her happy, and I'll do everything in my power to keep on doing that time and time again.

"I love you too," she whispers into my pec right before she returns the kiss, her lips against the skin right over my heart.

Tattoo my heart with your kiss. It's already whispering your name with every beat.

"Come here, sweetheart." I roll to my back, pulling her on top of me. Her knees bend, dipping into the mattress on either side of my hips. "Can you take me again?"

Honestly, I want her sore. Not because I want her to feel pain, but because I want her to remember me with every step she takes while I'm away from her. I want her to feel the void where I belong inside her body, knowing that I'll fill it as soon as I get back.

She bites her lip, nodding as her hips already sway back and forth along my hardening length, spreading her juices over me. My tip teases along her entrance, and I'm fighting every urge to slam into her. I want to feel her with nothing between us for a moment. No condom, no barriers, no walls, just raw and real, allowing me to fully claim her body and mark it with my cum.

Even the thought puts me on the edge in an instant. "Shit. Condom."

"I'm on birth control," she whispers.

My eyes move from where we're so close to joining up to her eyes. Those gray mood rings are glittering, emotions swirling there that I can't name. I don't want to try right now, but later, I'll picture this moment as though it's one of Willow's photographs and try to put labels on everything I see, everything I feel.

"You sure?"

In answer, she lifts her hips and I line up with her pussy. Holding around her hips, I guide her down my shaft in one hard, quick thrust.

"Oh!" Her voice is high, broken at the end as a shiver runs through her body.

"*Fuck.*" I'm surrounded by absolute heaven—tight, wet, hot bliss.

Her nails dig into my chest for purchase, and I arch into them, wanting that sharp bite of her mark on my skin. I use her hips, pushing and pulling her faster and harder.

This is not gentle lovemaking. And though it's rough and primal, it's not fucking, either. This is claiming, me of her and her of me. Though we'll be apart for a few days, she's mine and I'm hers. This trip doesn't change that. Hell, nothing would change that.

"Take it, sweetheart. Take my cock and take my cum. Tell me you want it," I demand.

She gasps at my dirty talk, still shocked every time, but I can feel what it does to her. The filthier I talk, the wetter she gets. She comes near-instantly when I make her say things my sweet girl would never say on her own.

"I want it." She's holding back, and I give her a punishing

stroke. Her head falls back, exposing her neck as her mouth falls open. "I want . . . your cum. God, I want to feel it, Bobby."

I grunt, her words sending me over the edge. My whole body tenses, and an electric jolt shoots from my spine through my cock as I spill inside her. Bare for the first time. The thought of painting her with my cum is powerfully heady and so fucking sexy. But I need her to come too.

Staying inside, I swipe a thumb across her clit, fast and soft like she loves it and tell her, "You feel so good, Willow. Let me feel you come."

She explodes, losing the rhythm, but I keep pounding at her and rubbing her as she comes and comes.

She has never looked so stunning as she does right now—glistening with sweat, hair plastered to her forehead, naked and bare physically and emotionally, sitting astride me, with our combined cum making an utter mess of us both.

Fuck, I love her.

She collapses over me, panting erratically.

"That was . . . that . . . wow." She gives up on sentences, making me smile.

We lie like that for several long minutes, luxuriating in each other's body and presence. Eventually, I slide out of her, and she squeals, rolling off me as if I give a shit about having our combined cum on me.

"I'll get you a towel. Hang on." I climb out of the bed and head to her bathroom. I wet a washcloth and wring it out, but by the time I get back, Willow is snoring softly. Guess this long week is catching up to her.

Probably wore her out, my ego chimes in like a cocky bastard.

I decide to let her sleep while I get cleaned up to head to the airport, but I can't help picking up her phone from the nightstand. I take a close-up of her face, fully relaxed in sleep, then one of her whole body, half-covered by the nest of sheets we left. I send the pictures to myself then leave them for her to find when she does her next blog posting.

Beautiful girl.

My girl.

* * *

AIRPORTS SUCK. Planes suck. Hotels suck. The city sucks. People suck. Everything sucks.

Or maybe I'm just nervous.

That's a distinct possibility.

I've traveled a time or two, but it was for family trips when I was a kid, mostly. Traveling alone to what might be my new destiny is a pressure I hadn't anticipated. And though my shoulders are broad and strong, this responsibility is something Brody usually handles. Not me. I'm the backup to the backup. Brody, Brutal, then me. Hell, Shay fits in there somewhere too, so maybe I'm her backup too.

"Mr. Tannen? Mr. Marshall will see you now," the receptionist says behind a fringe of long, dark lashes, dyed blonde curly hair, and deep red lips. She gestures with one hand toward the hallway and I follow her.

To my destiny.

To my doom.

Both? Fuck if I know.

But at the wooden door, I take a steadying breath. *Whatever it is, you're good, Tannen.*

Know myself, who I am, and where I came from. Take it or leave it.

Great in theory, but I'm really hoping they take it and want me and my music. My dream is so close I can taste it. All I have to do is not fuck this up.

"Bobby!" Jeremy's voice is louder, his presence larger in this room than it had seemed at Hank's last weekend. "Come in. Glad you got out so quickly. Big city treating you okay?"

He's trying to put me at ease, setting the tone for the room, which means he's the alpha dog here. I wasn't sure that was the case, but now, there's no doubt. If there's one thing I can do, it's read a room.

"Thanks. Yeah, checked into the hotel. It's nice. Bed has six pillows." I add that detail to highlight how fancy the hotel is, but the few people in the room smile as though I told a joke.

I scan the room, seeing a round conference table with six people seated at it. They're mostly young, in their twenties and thirties, I'd guess, a mix of guys and girls, each with a folder in front of them. The woman seated closest to me quirks one salon-sculpted, perfectly-shaped brow when she sees me realizing that the folder has my name on it.

I'm not sure what to feel about that. On one hand, that someone took the time to make six folders with my name seems important. But file folders naturally end up in file cabinets, which means there are likely hundreds of folders just like these. Folders of folks who took their shot and flew, and some who fell flat back down to Earth.

"Sit down. Let's talk through everything, Bobby," Jeremy says as he moves to the head of the table. It's round, so there shouldn't be a 'head' position, but there always is. No room full of people is ever on completely even footing, this one included. And pretending that everyone's equal puts you at a disadvantage from the starting line. Best to acknowledge and act accordingly.

Except talking through things doesn't sound like something I'm going to be good at.

I don't want to talk. I want to sing.

But I sit down like I'm told, willing to play along for this opportunity.

Jeremy clicks a few buttons on a remote, and the window shades roll down automatically, followed by a television on the wall turning on. *Showoff*, I think.

"To remind us all what we're starting with, here's why I've invited Bobby here." He clicks *Play*, and I come to life on the screen, singing my opener song at Hank's. It's a cover, and I see a few looks of consideration. The lady closest to me closes her eyes and tilts her head, listening. But I can't tell whether they like it or not.

Jeremy fast forwards. "And here's an original. It is, right?" He's asking me, and I nod silently.

My own song being judged stirs up fire in my belly. It's one thing if they like my voice. There are tons of artists who only sing songs written by other people. It's an entirely different thing for them to like my words, the ones I work so damn hard to find in my head and heart to express what I want to say.

"What's the working title of that one?" a young guy in glasses asks.

"*Her*. It's about my mom," I reply. It's the song I wrote when she was sick, and I dare him to say one bad word about it.

He frowns thoughtfully, tapping his chin. "Good title, catchy but generic. Never tell anyone who it's about." He splays his hands wide through the air in front of him. "We'll say it's for every woman, a ballad to the fairer sex and all they do to rein us wild guys in." He smiles at me like that made a lick of sense. It did not. Especially when I bet the wildest thing he's done in his lifetime is put whole milk in his coffee instead of skim.

Jeremy nods. "I like it. Very of-the-moment with the whole feminist thing being hot."

I blink. "Feminist thing?"

Glasses Guy laughs. "You know. I am woman, hear me roar. Anything you can do, I can do better. Hashtag whatever. That whole thing, you know?"

I feel like these people are talking a different language. "I guess I don't. I know my sister can outshoot and outride me on any horse. I know I can lift twice as much as she can. The best mechanic I know is a woman, and I can grow damn near anything you want in my garden or fields. We just have different skills, that's all."

Glasses Guy freezes. "Oh, my God, Jeremy. What rock did you pull him out from under again? He's an absolute find!"

What did I say? Was it good or bad?

I have no idea.

But they're all smiling, so I'm going with the hope and prayer that I haven't screwed up yet.

Jeremy claps and moves to open his folder. Everyone at the table follows suit, except for me, since I didn't get one.

"Let's review things. We have a few questions, if you don't mind, Bobby?"

I lean back in my chair, hoping it appears casual. "Open book."

And thus begins the interrogation of my life. Chief Gibson should take lessons from these people because those little folders of theirs contain my entire life story, from birth to damn near what

I had for breakfast this morning—an egg sandwich at the airport —and how often I shit—regularly.

I'm not even sure how they got all this information.

"Who are your musical influences?" Glasses Guy asks, pen at the ready to jot them down on a little yellow sticky note.

"Classics and current stuff, but I try to stay true to myself for my music. Hell, even when I sing Johnny Cash, it sounds a little more me than him."

Glasses Guy hums and writes down *Johnny Cash* like that's some ground-breaking, revealing detail of my inner musician. Everyone they've ever seen in country music probably says Johnny, Hank, and Waylon right off the top.

"Let's do a rundown of your current situation," a lady in a blue blouse says. It matches her eyes perfectly.

"Like my living situation?" I shrug, not having any clue why that'd matter to them. "I live on the farm I grew up on, though we sold it to the neighbors a while back when times got tough. I'm a farmer, grow fruits and vegetables that we sell at market and that my sister uses to run her business. I can tell you about growing heirloom tomatoes, watermelons, apples, peaches, pears, green beans, carrots, potatoes . . . just about anything that grows, I've probably done it if it's climate appropriate for Great Falls."

Blue Blouse smiles pityingly and I keep rambling to see if I can find the answer she's looking for.

"My brother, Brody, still lives in our family house too. His woman, Rix—she's the mechanic I was talking about—comes over a lot. My brother, Brutal, married his high school sweetheart, Allyson, a while back. They have a boy, Cooper, who's smart as a whip. My sister, Shayanne, married the guy next door and now she's a Bennett. But we all kinda got adopted by Mama Louise."

Blue Blouse leans forward, and the words stop pouring thoughtlessly when she taps the table with a pink fingernail. "I meant, what's your situation? Married, dating, single?"

Oh, that I can answer easily.

"Willow. She's mine." I can feel the smile stretching my face. "We met recently and I was done for." I almost say 'she's every-thing', but a little angel on my shoulder tells me that's probably not the proper thing to say to a room full of folks dangling your dream over your head.

Another guy pipes in, "It says here you have an arrest record?" He scowls in disdain. "Three times?" His brows climb so high that if he had a hairline, they'd be in it.

I shrug. "Misspent youth. Nothing serious, some trespassing for field parties and bar fights. Chief Gibson, Judge Myson, and I worked it out all right."

He comes back with a harder jab, "When was the last time you punched someone?"

I grit my teeth, not liking where this is going. "A few weeks ago. Tourist got handsy with my woman when she was working at Hank's. Broke his nose. Chief Gibson reminded him that it's not polite, or legal, to lay hands on a woman without consent."

See . . . I got your feminist thing right here, people. Only we call it being a fucking decent human being and not a douchebag shit stain.

Blue Blouse gasps before covering her mouth with her hand.

What the hell? That ain't no big deal. Happens all the time at home. Well, maybe not broken noses, but a punch here and there is how we settle shit in the country.

But I can tell the tide has turned in the room. They think I'm some out of control hillbilly, and while that might be a little too close to the truth, it's not like I'm a total asshole. I only fight when it's the right thing to do. Or to let off steam. Or when one of the guys needs a target.

Jeremy clears his throat, and all attention shifts back to him. He's been watching this whole show silently, leaning back in his chair and taking it all in. "Okay, here's what we're going to do. I've got you a twenty-minute spot at a place we like to run new and prospective artists through. Good crowds, but they'll let you know loud and clear if you're any good. We'll send a car for you at nine tonight, you'll hit the stage at ten as an opener, and be back in your hotel room by eleven with no broken bones. Yours or anyone else's, am I clear?"

He's talking to me like a fucking toddler, but I pull back on the reins of my temper and simply nod.

"Good. If that goes well, we'll send you to the studio tomorrow. Mission will be to record as many quality tracks as possible. Don't let me down, son."

I know a dismissal when I hear it, and I just bombed the hell out of this meeting. Maybe I can salvage it tonight, though. Chattering away ain't never been my strong suit, but if there's one thing I'm good at, it's singing.

Back at the hotel, I drink a whiskey then decide I should probably do something responsible like hot water with lemon if I'm singing for my life tonight. Room service sends that up quickly, and I swallow it like a shot.

I want to talk to Willow, tell her I fucked up, and let her reassure me that it's going to be fine. She'd probably say 'no matter what happens, it's an experience that you'll grow from. Be in it, feel every moment of it, and use it.'

She's right, even when she's not here. She's a part of me, and I feel her even though she's far away.

So I don't call and worry her yet. She has faith in me and I'll prove her right.

Instead, I pull out Betty and play a few chords. Writing a new song for a show in a few hours is a risky fucking move, but I've never been one to play it safe. And since I met Willow, inspiration fills me easily and words come to me more readily, demanding release.

Chasing down my dream so I can give you yours.
The proof of a man is in his woman's eyes.
Storm for me, shine for me, show your soul for me.
And I'll dig down deep to get mine so you can have yours.

After a while, I have that feeling. This is good. I know it is. I did what Willow would've told me to do—lived in this moment, mixing the opportunity, the fear, and the hope into these words. The melody is driving and urgent, giving it a sense of hunger.

I play it five more times through, tweaking and changing little things to perfect it. It's my ode to Willow and our future. Whether I make it tonight or not.

* * *

THE CAR STOPS OUTSIDE A SMALL, dark grey brick building that looks like it's seen better days. The sign above it is painted on and simply says *Bar*. Is that its official name? Not even The Bar? Just . . . Bar.

Inside, I find Jeremy, Glasses Guy, Blue Blouse, and a couple of other people I didn't meet today crowded around a small table. Actually, everyone in here is crowded around small tables meant for maybe two but which currently host upward of six to eight glasses. The chairs are mismatched and scattered in no pattern I can discern, everyone finding a tiny space to fit their ass in.

Jeremy shakes my hand. "Bobby! Good to see you. You ready for this? Tonight's the night your life changes."

He makes it sound like he's got a golden ticket with my name on it and all I have to do is reach out and grab it. But if it were that easy, anyone could do it.

I nod.

A guy dressed in black gestures for me to follow him, and he leads me to a holding area. There are four green folding chairs and a case of water on the floor. Nothing fancy like the hotel, but I wouldn't expect a bar to be fancy, anyway. I sit as directed and wait my turn.

Too soon, or maybe not soon enough, I'm given the stage.

"Hi, everyone. I'm Bobby Tannen."

There's usually a cheer from the crowd at Hank's, but tonight, it's quieter than a January morning covered by snow. I don't let it faze me and go into my set.

I start with *Bridge Over my Broken Heart*, then do *Her* because Mom's song seems like a good luck charm, as though she's here with me for this. I play the song I wrote today, which I'm calling *Dig Down Deep*, and that's when the crowd really falls under my sway. One more original and my time's up.

It was quicker than a blink and an eternity all at once.

I have done everything I possibly can, cut open my soul, used my blood to write these words, and laid everything I am bare on this stage for these people. If they liked it, fine. If they didn't, fuck them.

I touch the brim of my ballcap as I dip my head. "Thanks for listening."

When I stand, the audience does too, clapping madly.

I freeze, standing stock still as it sinks in. They liked it, and a warm buzz starts in my belly, growing bigger and brighter.

Like my future.

Lucky son of a bitch found gold in the twisted tunnels of a working man's mind.

Backstage, Jeremy comes in smiling and pats me on the shoulder. "Good show, son. Really good show."

"Thank you." The 'son' thing drives me crazy, and normally, I'd have already corrected it, but I'm giving allowances for Jeremy because of who he is. I hate that, but it's the truth.

"The car will be here in a few to take you back to the hotel. We'll get insights from the audience later and the tracks from tomorrow. Car will pick you up at noon for that, so get some sleep tonight. We'll meet with you again on Monday to let you know. Take Sunday to enjoy the city. But no misbehaving. I don't think you'd be able to sweet talk your way out a scuffle here like you do at home." His lips lift as he says it, but the smile is forced and doesn't reach his eyes. Not a real joke but a warning couched as one.

I grunt, refusing to honor that with actual words.

In moments, Jeremy is gone back to the table, listening to the next act. I'm dismissed again.

* * *

I'VE NEVER BEEN in a recording studio, so I have nothing to judge this one by, but I think it's top-notch. The sound board is almost the size of a sheet of plywood and has more knobs and levers than a space shuttle. The room where I'm sitting on a stool in front of a microphone is bigger than my bedroom at home.

"Okay, let's try that first one from the top again. On the third chorus, the repeat one, I want you to add a bit more growl to it. Like it's getting ripped out of your chest and you're furious about it. Okay?" Miller says into my headset.

Miller seems pretty cool. He'd introduced himself as the producer this morning, promised me that we were going to make some prime music today, and had gotten right to it. His critiques

219

and insights have been spot-on so far, and I think my songs are already better after only a couple of hours with him.

I sing my way through *Dig Down Deep*, my voice vibrating in my chest as I add the growl he asked for. It hurts, physically hurts, but when he plays it back, I can hear the improvement. The actual pain reads as emotional angst, giving the song that touch of wow that it needed.

"Hell yes!" Miller yells in my ear, and I laugh. He's been cool as a cucumber all day, but he's damn happy with that take. "That's what I'm talking about, man. That's a number-one hit right there. No doubt."

"Your mouth to fate's plans," I reply, hoping he's right.

Today has gone better than I could've dreamed. A real studio, a real producer, my music recorded and primed for radio.

My dream feels even closer.

Grab it with both hands, hold on, giving everything I have. Mom, look what I've done. Are you proud of me now?

* * *

"Good morning, Mr. Tannen. I've been instructed to take you back for a photo check first thing. Mr. Marshall wants the images to discuss during your meeting." The receptionist clicks down the hall, but my longer strides put me even with her.

"Photos? I didn't know anything about pictures," I tell her.

She smiles kindly, and I realize I'm simply a checkmark on her to-do list.

I'm not ready for pictures today, though I'm not exactly the fresh-shaven, styled-hair type. I just need to mentally prepare myself to pose and be paraded around. The ability to let someone else take control isn't really my best feature.

"Wow," Rory, the photographer says with a smile when we come in.

The receptionist smiles and talks to Rory out of the side of her mouth as though I'm not here. "I know."

I ignore their shit, not wanting or needing their attention that way. Only Willow's.

"Let's see what you've got, Bobby."

Rory pulls a stool from somewhere and sits me down by the large window. "Lean forward, elbows on your knees, hands clasped together. Give me a flirty smile."

Click.

That sound is so familiar. Aching and longing rise up in my throat. I want to check Willow's blog and see what she posted today so I can live her day with her. Since I'm not there, it doesn't seem as creepy. And as this point, I don't give a fuck if it is.

"Yes," Rory coaches. "Madder. Show me angry." *Click.* "Okay, now like you want to hate fuck, not kill me." *Click.*

"Are you comfortable doing a few with your shirt off?" Rory asks. "Your call, but I think we could get some good shots if I'm right about what's underneath that T-shirt."

I'm not shy about my body. It serves me well, doing the work I need it to. "That's fine. As long as they're not . . ." I search for the word I want, but Rory jumps in and reassures me without it.

"Tasteful, of course. Nothing pornographic or too vulgar. Fresh out of bear-skin rugs, I'm afraid." He laughs, teasing, and though it takes me a second to follow suit, I do because I've relaxed with him enough now.

I pull my T-shirt over my head and lay it on the table. I stand where he directs me and he takes several more shots. *Click, click, click.*

He looks at his camera, an even bigger one than Willow's, and smiles. "We've got it. Several options, in fact. I'll send them on to Jeremy right now."

I shake Rory's hand, all professional. "Thanks, man."

"Pleasure was all mine. Good luck, Bobby."

I pull my T-shirt back on right before the receptionist comes back to get me. "This way, please. They're ready for you now."

In the conference room, there's no mistaking the vibe. They're eager, smiling, hungry, and excited. That's got to be a good sign.

"Bobby! Come on in and have a seat. So much to go over." Jeremy is more enthusiastic than he was at Hank's, bordering on Loretta territory. But he wants my music, not my dick. Presumably.

I sit down and see that the folders are back, thicker than they were on Friday.

221

"How's your weekend been, Bobby?" Jeremy starts. "Have you enjoyed yourself?"

I don't see why that matters at all, but the truth is, I have. Singing for a new crowd is something I would've never done, but it felt like a test I aced. And the recording studio time was a learning experience I'll never forget. In the span of a few hours, Miller made me a better musician, something I'll always be grateful for. Room service is also something I could get used to real fucking easily. One phone call, and any type of food shows up at the door, and you can eat in bed leaned back on a pillow fort's worth of feathers.

"It's been an experience," I reply. "A great one."

His smile grows, and I get the sensation of being a fish on a hook, but if the boat is a record deal, reel me the fuck in, Bassmaster.

"Good, good. Okay then, let's get to it. Crowd reports?"

Glasses Guy—I should probably learn his name if this does go somewhere—opens his folder and reads from a sheet. "Overall, positive feedback across the board. The audience really liked the voice, the songs, and the appearance. Some slight variance in presentation versus expectations, as we've discussed."

The voice? You mean my voice?

The songs? As in my songs?

The appearance? Like the way I look?

He's talking about me like I'm a loaf of bread on sale at the grocery store, not a real person.

"Demo?" Jeremy inquires.

The television comes to life, and a camera recording from the studio plays. I hadn't even realized they were recording there, other than the audio tracks.

Miller coaches me on the growl, and it plays back the updated version. If I say so myself, it sounds great. Then there's Miller's praise.

One of the guys from Friday night pipes up, "Miller said this was one of the best voices we've sent him in years. And he's coachable. He's all in with the changes we went over."

I'd love to work with Miller more, but what changes?

"What else?"

Blue Blouse, who ironically is wearing another blue shirt today though this one is pale cornflower, raises her hand. "I've got raw images from Rory. These two are my selections." She types on her phone, then points to the screen where two images of me are displayed side by side. In the first, I'm sitting and snarling at the camera. In the second, my shirt is off and the light through the window creates shadows over my chest and jawline.

Not bad, Tannen.

I'm cocky enough to know those pictures look damn good.

Jeremy nods, humming. "So, we're all in agreement on the direction we're going?"

Everyone else smiles and nods back, mimicking the boss man. Except for me. I lean forward, hands folded over one another on the table. "Excuse me, but what the fuck are y'all talking about?" I growl.

Blue Blouse flinches again. I think I scare her. But Jeremy grins as he points at me. "That. That's what we're aiming for."

I glare, still confused.

I think this weekend has gone well. It felt like it did to me. But I do not like feeling like the only stupid idiot in the room not in on the joke. They've got 'directions' and 'changes' they've discussed, and I don't know a damn thing about any of it.

Jeremy's chuckle irritates the fuck out of me this time, getting under my feathers and scratching deep. "Let me explain how this all works, Bobby. I forget sometimes that regular people don't know this side of the industry like we do." He gestures to the people at the table, not including me in his little clique. "Step one, I have to feel that you have something special. That unique thing that makes me want to know more. Step two, basically . . . this weekend. I'm good, but I have people I trust to help me make these decisions. Like Miller and Rory. Step three, if I think you're good enough, moldable enough" —he looks me in the eye— "and lucrative enough, then we make a deal. That's the goal, right? A record deal, your name in lights, crowds chanting your name and singing your songs?"

I get the feeling he's given this speech before, but just because it's practiced doesn't make it any less true. He's right, and he damn well knows it.

That is what I imagined all those years ago.

I take a breath, forcing myself to settle and hear him out. Not because he's right but because he has something I want, and flying off the handle isn't the way to get it.

"Good," he coos, and I grit my teeth at his tone. "As I was saying, I do think you're good enough. Your voice is special, Bobby. One in a million, instantly identifiable with that first note but with that shock of surprise when you push or break."

Shit's getting deep in here. Part of me wants to preen at the praise and part of me wants some waders to keep my boots clean because this is slimier than pig shit.

"Thank you." Mom and Mama Louise would be proud of my manners. Hell, Judge Myson would be too, considering my past.

"As for lucrative, I think you could be. It'll take a team, marketing to radio, planning appearances, vetting endorsements, and choosing songs, but together, I think we could change your life in a major way. What's something you've always wanted? Think big, Bobby. Anything at all . . . cars, boats, house. What is that thing for you that would truly signal success?"

I feel that fishhook wiggling and swim right after it, wanting in that boat.

"Tannen Farm," I answer easily. There's not even a question. That's what I want more than anything, to own our land again. We'll figure something out with the Bennetts because we're pretty integrated now, and dividing it back up would be hard as hell. But we could do it.

"I can make that happen, Bobby."

Jeremy's smile is predatory. He thinks he's the hunter and I'm the prey. Truth be told, I'm hunting him and what he's hoarding . . . that record deal. *My* record deal. It's the means to an end for me. It'll let me buy the farm, support Willow and me, and give me an outlet to quiet this monster inside me the only way I've ever been able to, with singing on stage.

"What's the catch?"

There's always a catch.

"Not a catch, a question. Like I said, one of the things we look for is how moldable you are. Every artist comes in here one thing and leaves another. It's all about image, perception, character.

Some are family guys, and we do everything we can to make sure nothing gets out that might tarnish that image. Some are party hit makers, and they talk about beer and alcohol like water even when they're one hundred percent sober. It's all about creating Bobby Tannen."

My name doesn't sound like my name when he says it like that.

"Okay," I drawl out. "So you want me to write an ode to Jack Daniels?"

Everyone laughs. I don't get the joke.

"Actually, that's not a bad idea," Glasses Guy pipes up. He writes that down on a sticky note and puts it in the folder.

"You don't need me to tell you that you're an attractive man," Jeremy says, pointing at the television screen that still has my pictures up.

"Uh, what?"

"You have a certain look . . . rough, country, an asshole bad boy." The first of those are true, and honestly, the last one is too, to a certain extent, so I don't argue. I'm hoping we're not discussing my arrest record again, though. "That was the biggest feedback we got at the Bar too. When you came out, people were ready for something harder, edgier from you. I think you have that in you, so we want to play that up. Find you some songs that pull that direction, maybe even have you work with some of our proven writers if you'd like to create some. The plan is to really make you seem Bad Ass—that's with a capital B and A." He winks at me like that was funny.

"So, some new songs? I can do that."

That's totally doable. I can channel into some darker experiences—the anger I felt when Mom died, the confusing blend of relief and fury I felt when Dad died, the heartbreak of losing the farm. And they don't have to be about my life. I can write from someone else's point of view to share their experience too.

Pain, sharp and sweet, like whiskey through my veins. Makes me feel alive, only to make me numb.

I can do that.

"Songs, but there's more. We'll need to put together a band. You can have a hand in selecting from a small group of vetted musicians so that the vibe feels right. We're leaning toward something like this for promo shots—"

He looks to Blue Blouse and she clicks on her phone again. The television screen changes. The picture of me without my shirt on comes to the center, but it's been edited. The shadows are enhanced, the contrast bumped up and some sort of dark, splotchy frame overlaid on it. With my thick arms crossed over my bare chest, featuring the tattoo on my bicep prominently, and my eyes near black and piercing, I look like a man who would beat the shit out you and fuck you at the same time. The text across the bottom proclaims, *To Hell and Back*. Underneath that is my name.

"This is a mock-up of the cover album art," Blue Blouse tells me.

"I look like a mean son of a bitch," I growl out, not sure about this. Blue Blouse shrinks a tiny bit.

"Aren't you?" Jeremy asks.

He's got a point. I guess I'm just not used to seeing myself that way. Nobody's taking pictures when my brothers and me are throwing down. But in this room, I'm definitely the anomaly. Hell, maybe my whole family is the anomaly and most people are softer, sweeter, and kinder than we are. Willow certainly is.

But it's not all that I am. I'm the guy who likes to rub a baby goat's soft belly just because it feels good. I'm a guy who lets my nephew sometimes win at cornhole when he's having a bad day. I'm the uncle who airplanes Cindy Lou around the fields, lifting her to touch the fruit she wants to grab.

I tilt my head instead of agreeing with him.

"Last but not least, I think you're well aware that your primary audience is female. I saw a woman asking for your autograph at Hank's. The crowd there was largely female, and the feedback from the Bar is that the women mostly wanted to sleep with you, whether you could sing or not." He laughs, shooting me a good ol' boy grin that I don't return.

"Yeah, I don't really care about any of that. I've got my girl back home. Willow."

I sense the eyes at the table turning to Jeremy and watch his smile melt into a frown.

"About that, we'll need you to lose the girl."

"What?" I hiss.

Anger boils in my gut. My teeth clamp down and my hands fist as I glare across the table. I measure the distance, deciding whether I need to go around the table to punch Jeremy or I have the wingspan to reach him from here.

He holds up his hands, palms toward me in a 'settle down' motion. "Wait. I'm not asking you to break her heart . . . though that would actually be good for your image if you're looking for a way out?" At my silence, he continues. "But a single, sexy bad boy whom all the women want sells albums. And that's my goal. And yours too, right?"

It is. But not at the cost of losing Willow.

Not when I just found her.

"Not that way. I love her. And she has nothing to do with whether I can sing or not."

"Of course she doesn't. But she has everything to do with the image you project, and it's our job to tell you when what you're doing doesn't work. The way Miller helped *Dig Down Deeper* be better and Rory helped you pose to show your best assets. You can see that, right?"

"That's not the same thing and you fucking know it."

Jeremy looks cool as a cucumber while I'm fired up and ready to walk. He purses his lips, hands steepled in front of his chest. "Here's the deal, Bobby. NCR Records is prepared to offer you a very good deal. This is not the sort of deal most new artists receive, but I believe that you have the makings of a true star. I want to help you get there. On stage, your name in lights, people singing along with every word. I want you to buy Tannen Farm for your brothers and sister."

He knows which knife to twist because I feel that one sharply.

"But only you can decide if you want that. You have to be willing to go all in. You sing cover songs. You think those guys didn't do things they didn't want to do? You think they didn't give up one dream to chase a more important one? Hell, I have a kid who gave up a full-ride scholarship to an Ivy League school for a record deal that was a hell of a lot less than what I'm offering you. You're special, Bobby. But this industry will test you every single day to see how much you want it, how far you're willing to go to get it."

No. It's too much to ask.

I'm ashamed to say that there's a tiny seed of doubt, though. This is something I've wanted for so long, since before I got Betty. This has been growing since I was a kid singing along with the songs on the radio. A dream I lost a long time ago when real life took priority and took away any real chance I might've had at making a go of my music. But maybe I didn't lose the chance. Maybe this is it.

Now.

To get on stage and bleed myself for bigger crowds. Surely, that would quiet the thoughts and emotions and broken phrases of lyrics that never leave me alone.

To buy the farm back. I know Brody wants that more than anything. It holds him back in everything he does, even with Rix. He feels like a failure because we lost it when he was in charge of protecting it and us. It wasn't his fault, but no amount of telling him that can make him truly believe it. But this would let me give him his pride back, his square of dirt that he builds his entire self-worth on.

To show Mom, up in heaven, that her boy did make it. That I'm good enough.

Fuck.

"You don't have to decide right now. In fact, I want you to think it over. That shows how serious you take it, how much this means to you and how dedicated you'll be once you've signed on that dotted line you've wanted for so long." Every word out of his mouth is designed to manipulate me, but that doesn't mean he's wrong. It might very well take that.

The question is . . . is the payoff worth the price of admission?

No, it can't be. It won't be.

The refusal is on the tip of my tongue, ready to be spat out with all the venom I feel at his even considering this a reasonable demand. But my mouth stays shut, my teeth ground together.

"Have a lawyer read over the contract and get it back to me. But don't wait too long, Bobby. You've already waited long enough, stayed in that small town long enough. It's your turn. Your time now."

He's playing me like a damned pro, and he's good at it, hitting every chord just right and letting it reverb so I feel the echo of it like a scream across a canyon inside my soul.

CHAPTER 18

WILLOW

"*Y*ou heard from Tannen yet?" Unc asks for the fifth time today. Forgetfulness is not a side effect of his medication or his condition. However, he's as anxious as I am about Bobby's trip to Nashville and wanting news.

Good news.

"No, and quit asking. I'll tell you when I do, just like I said I'd tell Olivia and half the damn town when I hear."

I'm not exaggerating. Last night was busy, even for a Friday night, with everyone coming up to the bar to order their beers instead of letting Olivia wait on them. They'd been using their drinks as cover to oh-so-casually mention Bobby and inquire what I'd heard. Nothing, nothing, nothing, I'd said all night.

I'm expecting tonight to be more of the same, the Saturday night crowd wanting their piece of flesh and the latest gossip.

But the answer's the same. I don't know anything.

I'm not worried. Bobby said he had no idea what Jeremy's plans were for this meet and greet, so he didn't know when, or if, he'd get a minute to call or text. But he assured me he'd be thinking of me the whole time.

"Well, *excuse* me for giving a shit about the boy. You just make sure that when he gets that first Country Music Award, he mentions his start at Hank's, the best honkytonk in Great Falls, y'hear?" Unc grins, but he's dead serious.

"Come on, we've got orders piling up. Hit the taps and call out my mixers."

He takes the cue that we need to focus. Or actually, that I need to focus on anything but Bobby for a few minutes. I'm a big ball of jangly nerves, bouncing around like jingle bells inside a maraca.

Please let this go well for him. If anyone deserves a dream coming true, it's Bobby.

"Two Jack and Cokes and a Long Island Iced Tea—don't mouth about how gross they are again—and a Girly Beer, table four. Three Girly Beers, table five." One corner of Unc's mouth tilts up in devilment as he looks across the room. "You feeling lucky tonight? Want to make bets on which of my pitchers of Coors Light are going home with your Girly Beers?"

I glance over, seeing three women out for a night on the town at a table next to three guys who are already calling dibs. I've seen it a thousand times, but I've also seen this go the other way.

"I'll take that bet. My call is that the guys buy at least two rounds before they realize none of them are getting lucky tonight. The ladies are looking for a buzz and a spin around the floor, nothing else."

Unc holds out his hand and we shake on it. Standard bet rules apply, loser pulls closing duty. Not that it matters, I'll clean up either way, but fun stuff like this makes the time pass by quicker and adds some fun to the night. And it's the much needed distraction I was hoping for, which Unc full-well knows.

An hour later, we still don't know who's won the bet. The guys are sitting with the ladies now, paired off evenly, which Unc thinks bodes well for him. But they've done two rounds and at least one spin around the floor. Until someone makes a move for the door, we're at a stalemate.

A blonde comes up to the bar, all smiles. "Amaretto sour."

"You want to start a tab?" I ask, already putting a glass on the bar.

"No thanks. You heard from Bobby yet?"

I sigh and look at her again. She looks familiar. I've definitely seen her in here before, but I don't know her name. "About what?"

I've decided that playing dumb is more entertaining than giving nosy people informational fodder. Keeps things interesting, Unc told me, and so far, he has been right about that.

"The music deal, of course," she snips. Her eyes widen, "Oh, unless you two aren't dating anymore. Bless your heart, did he already ditch you for the big city?"

Instead of sorrow, her tone is one of evil glee. And loud enough so that people four stools down can hear her. She's good at playing the rumor mill.

"Loretta, take your drink and sit down. Everybody in here knows that you've thrown yourself at Bobby Tannen's feet more times than Ilene's made biscuits and that he's turned you down every single time. So don't be starting trouble where there ain't none to be had, 'specially when you ain't ready to finish it. Because I am."

"Hmmph," Loretta snorts as she hair flips away with her drink.

"What was that all about?" I ask.

Unc sighs. "Just what I said. You got a man that a lot of people like, and a lot of people don't. Both for no good damn reason I can see. And some people are sad sacks who want everyone to be as miserable as they are. Loretta's all right. She just never had nobody tell her no, about anything, if you know what I'm saying, so it sticks in her craw a bit."

I glance over at Loretta. She's pretty, at least on the outside. Not so sure about her insides, though. They seem a bit sketchy.

"Not a thing to worry about with that one, girl. Or anyone else. That Tannen boy ain't never followed no one around the way he does you." He nods like that's that and goes back to pulling beers.

A little while later, the door creaks open and a group of women I do know come in. Shayanne, Sophie, Katelyn, Rix, and Allyson all walk directly to the bar and me.

"Hey, Willow!" Shayanne yells. "Round of Girly Beers, please!"

"Sure thing. Where you gonna sit? I'll have Olivia bring them over."

Rix points to a stool. "We're sitting right here with you. Brody's orders, Bobby's too."

The other girls laugh like she said something ridiculous. I don't know what it was until Katelyn manages to huff out around her giggles, "Brody's orders? As if you take orders from anyone, much less Brody."

Rix's grin says Katelyn might be on to something. "Well, I take his ideas into consideration, at least." She shrugs, and I get the feeling nobody tells Rix what to do. Ever.

I set the beers onto cocktail napkins in front of each woman. "What was the part about Bobby's orders?"

Shayanne jumps in. "Oh, he told us to check in on you since he was gonna be gone. Pretty sure he wanted to make sure you didn't make a run for it while he was distracted. You're lucky he didn't tie you up and just leave enough water and sandwiches on the nightstand to last till Monday."

"That is oddly specific and concerning that you've considered kidnapping enough to have a meal plan for it." I couldn't explain it if I tried, but her outrageousness makes her more endearing somehow. She says crazy things, but they come out more amusing than terrifying.

She frowns, feigning sadness. "Lessons learned the hard way. I always forget to feed and water the hostages."

Unc appears at my shoulder. "Sophie, where the hell is Doc tonight? You leave him high and dry at the clinic?"

Sophie bites back defensively, "You know I didn't. When I left, he was petting a new kitten and watching Andy Griffin reruns." Her voice softens. "We had a mama cat birth four today. They were feeding okay, but Doc said he'd probably sleep over to make sure they didn't need to be bottle fed."

"Aw hell, you know he'll be there every night for a week then. Never seen a man like cats as much as he does."

Rix snorts first, then Shayanne, then the rest of us catch what Unc just alluded to accidentally. Unc grins big when he realizes why we're laughing. "You ladies, and I use the term loosely, need to straighten up."

We try. We make a truly valiant effort for about two seconds before we all bust out again.

God, I needed that. Silly giggles about a stupid, accidental joke. I feel like my whole body is bathed in champagne, bubbly and warm.

Unc rolls his eyes, fighting his own laughter to appear sternly authoritarian. "Actually, I got another plan. Shayanne, you go get that table right there," he orders her, pointing across the bar to a round booth that just opened up.

She doesn't question it, zig zagging her way over to flash a thumbs-up.

He dips his head in recognition then sticks two fingers in his mouth. The whistle is loud and unexpected, quieting the bar in an instant as all eyes turn to him.

"Y'all know my niece, Willow. She's been in here putting up with your shit for a while now, without so much as a fuss."

What is he doing? I hate being the center of attention and this little speech of his has everyone in the room, and that's a lot of people, looking from him to me. A few tip the necks of their bottles at me and several smile.

"More importantly, she puts up with my shit. So here's what's going to happen. I'm pulling beers and Willow's got one batch of Girly Beer left for tonight. That's all that's on the drink menu. So if you want mixed drinks, go home and make 'em yourself because she's taking the night off to hang out with her friends."

Mouth agape, I blink. Finally finding words, I mouth at him, "What?"

Unc smiles wider. "Take the night off, girl. You deserve it. Hell, take Olivia with you. She deserves it even more than you. Poor thing's been putting up with my grumpy ass since the dawn of time."

"I ain't that old, old man!" Olivia calls out, but I see her coming toward the bar and taking her apron off. "And neither are you." Kinder and quieter, she asks, "You sure, Hank?"

"Hell yeah, I'm sure. I used to run this place by myself and I can damn sure do it for a couple of hours." Louder, to the crowd, he says, "In case you didn't notice, your waitress is off duty and I don't do that shit. If you want something to eat or drink, then you'd best get up and come to the bar and order it yourself, capiche?"

Heads nod, and from over by the pool table, a guy calls out sarcastically, "Yes sir, Hank." His laughter can be heard across the bar and his buddies high-five him.

"Keep it up, Chuckles, and I'll cut you off," Unc threatens.

The table of guys sobers and eye their almost empty pitcher. I'm pretty sure they'll be ordering another one any minute in case Unc decides not to serve them any more tonight.

"Glad we understand each other, gentlemen. As you were."

Unc walks back to his perch, limping slightly, but he covers it by making it seem like he's checking the stock along the bar. Lemons, limes, napkins, ice . . .

They're all good, Unc. You know I got you covered.

Somehow, I find myself sitting at a table with all the Tannen and Bennett women, a frozen Girly Beer in front of me, Olivia at my side and apparently off work for the evening.

Still in shock, I ask Olivia, "Has he ever done anything like this?"

"Hell no. It's like Ebenezer Scrooge woke up and understood the meaning of Christmas or something. But I'm not going to argue. Actually, what I'm going to do is shoot this beer, sneak out the back door, and go over to Hannah's shop and surprise her. If I'm off tonight—no offense to you ladies—but I'd rather spend the evening with my lady."

She's challenging them too, the way she did me at first. But the whole group smiles, Shayanne encouraging her to 'go getcha some.'

Rix tells Olivia, "If Hank says anything, you're in the bathroom. If he questions it, we'll say you got your period. Shuts men up every time."

She's an absolute evil genius and I love it.

Olivia shows her appreciation by swallowing her beer in one long gulp, waving goodbye, and skirting around the dance floor to disappear into the kitchen.

"You think she's okay to drive?" I ask, suddenly realizing that though it was only one beer, she downed it quickly so it'll hit her all at once.

Shayanne laughs. "One, she's no lightweight. Two, Hannah's shop is down the street so she's probably walking over. And three, the way she opened up her throat and poured that beer down, that woman would probably give one mean blowjob."

I blink in shock. So does everyone else. Silently.

"What? I'm just saying," Shayanne replies with a shrug. "You know how long it took me to not choke? Maybe I can ask her how she learned to do that?" She looks off toward the kitchen, and Sophie lays a staying hand on her arm. "Right, not now. Probably not the best time. But later . . ." She trails off.

"Breathe through your nose," Katelyn offers quietly, and all our heads swivel her way. She shrugs, but it starts another tidal wave of laughter.

"I cannot believe you just said that!" Allyson's eyes are wide with shock.

Katelyn's returning smile is coy and innocent.

"What about you?" Shayanne whirls on me, eyes boring into my soul.

I can feel the blood rush out of my face and know I must be as pale as a ghost. "Uh, what about me?"

She is not asking if I choke, surely not. Right? Because that is not a conversation I'm having with Bobby's family. Scratch that, it's not a conversation I'm having with anyone, period. Privacy is a good thing, and as someone who picks and chooses what parts of my life I share, I recognize that more than most.

Shay realizes the direction of my thoughts and waves her hands spastically. 'No, no, not like that. I mean 'what about you?' like 'tell us about you.' I wouldn't go straight for sex life questions. I save that stuff for meeting five, at least. Unless you're feeling like there's something you want to share with the class?" She swirls her straw in her glass, one brow raised in question.

Every pair of eyes around the table weighs on me.

"No, uh . . . nope. I'm fine," I stammer out.

"Don't scare her," Sophie whispers out of the side of her mouth to Shayanne. "We're supposed to make her want to stay, not run for the hills from the crazy hillbillies." To me, Sophie says, "I swear you get used to it. I'm a city girl too. Used to be all designer clothes, mani-pedis, and nightclubs every weekend.

Now, 'fancy' means it hasn't had cow shit or placenta on it, James painting my toes, and Hank's." She looks around the bar, sounding wistful. "Came here for a summer internship with Doc and never left. One day, when he retires—which he never will—I'll take over the whole practice. I can't imagine being anywhere else."

"That's mostly because of James, though," Katelyn says.

"How'd you two meet? Not to gossip, but I heard he used to be a professional bull rider?" I ask. The grapevine works well around here, and I guess I don't mind it so much when it's not about me. At dinner, they'd obviously been deeply in love, with each other and their little girl, but I didn't exactly get everyone's life story.

Sophie's smile is wide and her eyes grow bright at the memory. "I delivered a colt at the ranch. He yelled at me and called me a bitch, and I hated him on sight and put him in his place. So your basic love at first sight story."

All the girls smile a little.

Katelyn holds a hand up. "Mark and I were friends. Poor guy didn't even know the meaning of the word. Literally."

Shayanne pipes up, grinning. "Threw myself at Luke."

I have no problem believing that. Shay is a see it, want it, get it sort.

Allyson adds, "Bruce and I were high school sweethearts. We broke up for a long time, but we got back to where we were supposed to be all along." That sounds like a story if I've ever heard one.

"Fuck buddies who caught feelings," Rix says on a sigh.

Last but not least, I say, "Saw each other from across a crowded room."

Rix doesn't leave it at that, though. "But you made him work hard for it. Good job, Willow." She holds up a hand, and I high-five her, feeling like part of the group.

Actually, I don't know that I've ever felt accepted like this. A whole group of women who, from the outside looking in, don't seem to have all that much in common. Loud and brash, soft-spoken and sweet, sharp and witty—all so many different facets, but somehow, they've blended together into a family. I'm barely on the edge of their group, but their warm welcome is like nothing I've ever experienced. I was always the quiet, shy weirdo on the outskirts of what was going on, the one nobody noticed, the oddball. But these women don't care that I'm weird, or quiet, or sometimes still a bit awkward.

Come to think of it, nobody in Great Falls has made me feel like an outsider. I'm sure some of that has to do with my relation to Unc, but even beyond that, they wave when I drive down Main Street, they greet me by name at the coffee shop, and they comment on the photos on my blog. I think the largest demographic of my new followers is the people of Great Falls. They've accepted me as one of their own.

My eyes burn hot with unshed tears, happy ones. But I blink them away and join back in on the conversation where the girls are talking about . . . stinky guys?

"I'm telling you, make a whole line marketed toward men. Make it smell like wood campfires, pine trees, leather, and diesel. Do one of your pun things with a goat logo saying, *Don't smell like goat ass.* I'd buy a Christmas basket for every guy I know." Rix leans back in the booth, and I see the toe of her black boot peek out where she's got her feet propped up on the bench across from her.

She's the picture of the cool, don't fuck with me attitude. I'd love to take a picture, but my camera is at home. My brain still takes the frame. *Click.*

"Good idea, bad execution," Katelyn corrects. "If you do a male line, don't do anything crass. If it's classy, I could use them as part of my bride and groom kits at the resort."

The light over the table shines on her blonde hair and big, blue eyes giving her an All-American, Barbie doll look. *Click.*

I look around the table again. Each woman is so different and so beautiful in her own way.

"Uh, guys . . ."

My mouth opens before my brain can stop it, and everyone's attention is on me. I almost say 'never mind' and forget about the stupid idea I just had. But somewhere inside, a tiny spark of 'what if' grows brighter.

"Can I ask you a crazy question?"

Shay snorts. "Considering we started the night by discussing blowjobs, I think we've made it quite clear that we're up for anything. Whatcha wanna know? I can't exactly offer everything I know about Bobby, but if you were to ask, I could maybe . . . blink once for yes and twice for no?" Her smile says she thinks that's brilliant.

"No, I . . . uh . . . this is going to sound weird, but . . ." I don't know why this is hard for me to ask. I've done it before, but not with people who mattered this much.

"Spit it out," Katelyn says, pointing a sharp finger at Shay that tells her 'not now' like she could read her mind.

"Can I photograph y'all? Not for the blog, but just because. Like portraits. It's not my primary work, but I think it could be something really special."

There's a half-beat of silence where I think it's the stupidest idea ever before they explode.

"Yes!"

"When?"

"Now!"

"Let's go."

"Where?"

I don't even know who's asking what, but somehow, I answer, "My place? We could go now and get some cool moonlight shots. And the cabin is cute, especially the kitchen. It's cheery and vintage."

Before I'm even done talking, they're getting up, gathering their things, and shoving me toward the door. I manage to squirm my way over to Unc first.

"Thank you so much for tonight. I think I needed this, needed them." It's the truth, and though hard to admit, I hope he can see that needing others isn't such a bad thing. It's not a weakness, it's simply human nature. I kiss him on his sandpapery, scratchy cheek, and he smiles.

"Go have some fun, Willow. I love you, girl."

"I love you too," I tell him. But I turn back once more before I leave. "At two, you get out of here. I'll be in early to do tonight's cleaning and tomorrow's prep. Sit down, pull beers, and don't overdo it."

"Nah, I got it. Pretty sure I lost that bet anyway, so it's my duty, fair and square."

"Nope. The blue T-shirt Coors Light and the green tank top Girly Beer might not have made it out the door, but they made it down the hall to the bathroom," I admit with a grin. "You won."

His laughter is deep in his belly and so fierce, it makes his eyes water. "*Shit*. I don't know how I missed that. All right then, add a deep clean to the bathrooms to your opening list in the morning."

"Men's room. They never go to the women's for a hookup."

* * *

IT HAD STARTED out so well. Simple and sweet, even.

We'd pulled up to my little house en masse, my little Subaru and a few trucks. Katelyn, the wedding pro, did everyone's makeup and hair while we played around with various poses and setups.

I took individual photos of each woman, both planned images and candids of us talking, laughing, and having fun.

Rix sitting on the kitchen table, one boot on the chair and one folded up. She looked stunningly bad ass, glaring into the camera as she complained that she didn't know how to do this. When she saw herself, she'd laughed and I'd captured that expression too. The dichotomy of her hard and soft edges is beautiful.

Sophie had been the opposite, an easy model full of poses and expressions. "I used to pose for paparazzi in my city life *Before James*, and even now, when we go to the World Finals, the press will follow him. I've gotta be able to pull out my A-game when needed." Her shots had been gorgeous, her dark hair curled and her eyes sultry.

Allyson had been more comfortable with over the shoulder looks rather than facing boldly head-on into the camera, and the pose had highlighted the sculptural qualities of her shoulder blades in her strappy tank top and the shape of her eyes as she stared into the camera at an angle.

Shayanne had plopped herself on the couch, ultimately upside down with her crossed feet in the air and a wide, open-mouthed laugh that showed her youthful exuberance.

Katelyn had surprised me the most. She seems sweet, maybe a little softer like me, but when she'd found her comfort zone, she'd gone right into it. Her smile had been seductive and foretold of secret depths to her, giving layers to the photos beyond her beauty.

I'd even let them take a few of me, a true rarity. Photographers rarely flip around to the other side of the camera, I find. Or I don't, at least not in a way that exposes the real me. Bits and pieces can convey one thing, but with a frame full of my entire being, there's nowhere to hide.

And that's when things went crazy.

Or crazier.

To be fair, that might've been helped along by the box of wine in the fridge, along with my entire stash of bark-thin chocolate.

Somehow, my idea of a fun photoshoot to capture tonight in print has turned into something much . . . sexier.

"It's fine. Not like we haven't seen each other in swimsuits at the pond," Shayanne argues. Oddly enough, she's making sense, and I can see everyone else considering her idea of boudoir shots for the guys. "I'll go first."

"Of course you will," Rix says sarcastically.

"No nakedness, right? I mean, I haven't seen you all in swim-suits, and I'm not really looking for my neighbors to start telling folks I'm doing porn shoots over here. I'll lose my rental." I laugh, but I'm dead serious.

"Definitely not," Shay agrees, nodding vigorously. "Y'all don't have to if you don't want to, but I've got a famous photographer here willing to take expert photos of me and a half-decent buzz going on that makes this seem like a good idea. I'm taking advan-tage. YOLO!"

With that battle cry ringing in all of our ears, she kicks off her boots and shoves down her jeans to reveal pink cotton panties with horses on them. She promptly swallows another guzzle of wine too, so I think she's not as brave as she'd have us believe. Several of the women follow suit, me included—with the wine, not the stripping.

"Hang on, I want my boots on for this." While she pulls them back on, she asks the room, "Anybody got a hat?"

Sophie runs out to her truck and gets a straw hat, plopping it on the back of Shayanne's head. "Yass, girl, you got this."

"Damn straight."

And she does.

Shay stands with her feet wide and her thumbs in the waistband of her panties as though there are invisible beltloops, and she rocks it.

"Let me see," she screams after several minutes, a few different poses, and about twenty sexy shots.

We crowd around the tiny screen on the back of my camera. The general consensus is that Shay looks hot, and that seems to give the other girls the push they need.

Rix ends up on the kitchen counter this time. Slouching in just a tank top and boy shorts, I already know this picture will need to be in black and white.

"Hey, Rix, here. You need this," Sophie says. She hands Rix an ice cube and waves around her chest.

Rix laughs, dips the ice cube into her shirt, and in seconds, her basic black tank is covering some diamond-hard headlights.

"Better," I agree and start clicking away again.

Allyson wraps up in a sheer curtain she finds in the linen closet and lies down in the grass outside. We're quick and quiet for her shots, making use of the full moon on her skin, which gives her an ethereal, angelic glow.

Sophie goes classic, leaning over the bathroom counter in her black lace bra. Katelyn added heavy cat-eye eyeliner to her lids and pinned up her hair, letting a few tendrils escape. In her reflection, she slicks red lipstick on her open, pouty lips. It's very 50s pinup, especially with the dated tile of the bathroom.

"I'm doing a bubble bath shot," Katelyn says. She draws a hot bath, filling it up with half a bottle of bubbles, and we step out to give her privacy until she's under the cover of the white foam. "Ready!"

The bathroom is too small for anyone besides the two of us, but the girls stand in the tight hallway, encouraging her with much laughter and cheering.

"Bubble, bubble, you're in trouble," a giggly voice whispers to Katelyn from behind me. I smile but keep shooting.

Katelyn has her legs stretched up the wall, and the bubbles slide down their length from her crossed ankles. Her breasts are covered, but the illusion of skin through the tiny holes of air pockets is sexy in a subtle way.

"Got it," I say.

"Your turn," Shayanne says.

"Oh, no. That's okay," I argue. "The other pictures were already a hard enough sell to my nerves. Sexy shots are way out of my comfort zone."

"Join the club," Rix says dryly.

She's right. This is one of those weird, wild experiences I'm never going to get the chance to have again, like Mom says. I need to let loose and live a little. I don't have to do anything crazy, nothing uncomfortable, but pushing myself creatively means stepping out of the box sometimes. These women have done that tonight, letting me take their photos. It's only fair that I do the same.

Once the decision is made in my mind, my heart gets on board and starts racing. Fear, excitement, nerves, and giddiness war in equal measure.

"Okay. What should I do?"

Help. I need some guidance here. Maybe a divine intervention? Well, probably not that, considering I'm taking sexy photos.

Actually . . .

"Wait, I have an idea. But I'm gonna need some help and a moment alone."

Three, two, one . . .

"What?"

"Oh, my cheesus and crackers, what are you going to do?"

"Uh . . ."

I can't hold the straight face any longer and laugh, my chosen words having their intended effect on the women.

"Not . . . that. Whatever you're thinking. I want to do a full silhouette shot, but it means I need to get the lighting just right or it won't be silhouette, it'll be naked-naked. And I'm not doing that."

Mission ready, Rix says, "Tell us what to do."

We get the lighting just right in my bedroom, do a few test

shots with the camera on a tripod, and once I'm happy with the setup, I nod.

"Get it, girl."

I swallow and close the door behind them. Though they're on the other side of the thin wood, they don't desert me, still talking me through it.

"Think sexy thoughts," Katelyn coaches.

I strip down, tossing my work clothes in the hamper, then climb into the middle of the bed where we tested the light. "Breathe. In, two, three, out, two, three," I whisper.

I close my eyes, hit the remote button for the camera, and the timer light flashes. Right before it takes the shot, I open my eyes and stare at the ceiling so the camera captures my profile. I do it a few more times, praying each time that it's working.

Worst case scenario, I can delete them. Best case, I'll have some hot images to remember a fun, crazy night with my new friends.

This is definitely one of those experiences Mom is always telling me I need to have. But this one is just mine. Not the blog's, not for my followers. But for me to pull out of my memory bank when I'm old and gray and smile at the wild child I was, if only for one second.

When I feel like I've got the shot, I pull fresh clothes on and open the door. Excited eyes meet mine. "That was terrifying," I gush. "I'm so glad I did it."

Suddenly, we're all hugging, bonded through some strange thread of friendship forged under unusual circumstances.

"Finally," Shayanne huffs. "I'm a hugger, but Bobby put the fear of Baarbara in me if I didn't let you hug me first."

"It's okay, I'm a hugger too. Everybody needs hugs, and every day needs hugs."

Shayanne smiles, and I can tell she likes Mom's theory.

"Not to break this up, but . . . I gotta go," Katelyn suddenly says, holding up her phone.

I can see the screen where she sent a close-up of her cleavage, just an extreme close-up of the line between her breasts. Out of context of this evening, you might not even know what it is. Beneath the picture is a reply that simply says, *Home. Now.*

Everyone laughs, but Katelyn is nearly bolting for the door as she shoves her makeup into her purse. "Anybody riding home with me had better get in the truck. Mark's waiting on me."

"It's fine. Hurry home like a good wifey," Shayanne teases her, her laughter growing at Katelyn's whirlwind exit. To me, she rolls her eyes. "You get used to them."

Confused, I ask, "What do you mean?"

The grins tell me there's a lot more to this story. "Well, some folks think Mark is bossy. And that's true for sure, but it's definitely something she enjoys. She sent that picture on purpose because she knows how to push his buttons *just* right."

"Oh." I have no response, my brain blank. After a second . . . "Oh!"

The women laugh, and shortly thereafter, we wrap up the evening.

"I'll go through the images and send them to you. Tonight was . . . fun."

It's the lamest description, but it's all I can come up with because I truly had a good time tonight with them. I felt accepted, welcomed, a part of something bigger than myself.

And it did keep me distracted for the evening from the one thing I thought I'd be thinking about nonstop . . . how Bobby's meeting is going.

I consider sending him a text, maybe a sexy selfie like Katelyn did, and even go so far as to pick up my phone. But instead of opening the camera, I open my photo files and find that the last two shots are of me sleeping blissfully. Bobby must've taken these, I realize with a smile. I look . . . happy, worn out from our lovemaking, and smiling even in sleep.

I flip through my last several shots, finding several of Bobby— him on stage, him driving his truck and singing with the radio, him against a backdrop of green trees.

After a few minutes, I do open my camera and take a close-up, off-centered shot of my smile.

Click.

I post it to my blog with a caption that reads, *Happy. I found home.*

I fall asleep before the first heart or comment comes in.

CHAPTER 19

WILLOW

"He's going to be here any minute. Get that table set, boys." Mama Louise's instructions are nothing to argue with, and Mark and Luke hustle a little faster around the table with the glasses and silverware.

"The sign's crooked on the right. Cooper?" I'm not sure how she expects the little boy to fix the sign that's hanging three feet above his head, but like the rest of the guys, he's on it. He pushes a stool over, climbs up, and makes the needed adjustments.

"Better?" he asks, looking for approval.

Mama Louise looks over her shoulder. "Perfect. Good job problem solving." I see her smile as she returns to her cooking.

She's amazing, in charge of everything and everyone without breaking a sweat. She's sweet and kind, warm and welcoming, but I get the sense that she'd beat you at your own game if you tried to pull one over on her.

"What can I do to help?" I ask, having finished my assigned job of slathering butter on the biscuit tops and sliding them into the pre-heated oven.

Mama Louise scans the room, looking for something, and gives me a new job. "Stand over here by me and help me with this chicken. This bowl is the egg wash."

I listen to her intently, not wanting to get a single thing wrong.

After several minutes, I realize that everyone else is watching her closely too.

The guys are hiding small smiles and the girls aren't bothering, smiling widely as they continue setting serving platters on the table. Sophie and Katelyn look on the verge of happy tears.

They must really love Mama Louise's fried chicken.

Shayanne calls out, "Say cheese!" and before I can react, she takes several pictures of Mama Louise and me, floury hands and all. "Perfect!" Coming closer and proving she knows me better than I'd think, she gets right up on our hands and takes a close-up shot too. "And one for the blog. Caption, bwak-kwak-kwak. I'm delicious."

"Uh, that's my phone. How'd you unlock it?"

She looks at the phone in her hand like she has no idea how it got there before giving me a smirk. "I got skills, girl." She shrugs it off, and I don't bother asking again because she won't tell me, anyway.

"Do those skills involve finishing up the lemon meringue pie?" Mama Louise muses.

Chastised, Shayanne sets my phone on the counter and grabs a lemon out of a bowl. Zesting for her life, she assures everyone, "Yes, they do."

Mama Louise and I finish frying the chicken and washing up as we hear a truck outside.

"Hit the lights," Cooper yells.

In the dark, Mama Louise holds my hand in hers. Her skin is rough and slightly wrinkled from her years in the sun, but her palm is soft against mine. I can hear her whispering under her breath, "Please, please, please . . . let that boy get this. He's worked for it, and everyone deserves to hear his gift." I think she's praying, not talking to me.

This moment is huge—the moment Bobby's whole life changes, his dream comes true, and his family doesn't have to worry anymore.

I'm thrilled for him, excited to witness this moment in his evolution. The instant he becomes *The* Bobby Tannen, something he's worked for and wanted for so long.

I have a mental image of him standing on a huge stage, bright lights aimed up at him, and screens framing him with super-sized versions of that roughly gorgeous face. I try to insert myself into the image, standing in the wings, waiting for Bobby to look my way. But the picture won't come into focus no matter how hard I try. He's there, crystal-clear and sharp, eyes turned to the audience with his arms spread wide. And my place blurs more and more, people bustling around me and through me as though I don't exist.

It hits me that no matter how much he says he loves me, this might also be the moment he'll leave me behind.

I try not to cry. After all, I understand. I want good things for him, and this opportunity is everything.

But there's still a sliver of me that doesn't want to be invisible again. For the first time ever, I like being visible . . . to these people, to this town, and most of all, to Bobby. That doesn't have to change, though. I can still be me—Willow Parker, photographer, blogger, bartender, and niece. Louder and prouder, back straight and eyes unblinking, I can keep going as this new and improved version of myself.

Bobby Tannen's girl, a label that once sent a jolt of shocked offense through me, suddenly seems like the one I'll miss the most when I lose it. There's no way I'll be his girl once he hits the road, filling stadiums with screaming women, and becomes insta-famous.

In the dark, I squeeze Mama Louise's supportive hand back, steeling myself. I can't let tonight be about me. I'll celebrate with Bobby and his family, feigning blissful unawareness of the impending train coming down the tracks to run me over. I'll pretend that a girl like me—the quiet, awkward outsider who's forgettable—really can get it all. The career, the guy, the family, the friends.

The front door opens and swings shut. Bobby's deep voice calls out, "I know you're in here. I could smell the chicken from the front porch."

Cooper flips the light on and we all yell in unison, "Congratulations!"

"Surprise!"

Oops, guess Sophie and James didn't get the memo on what

we were supposed to say because they're looking around in shock. Cindy Lou decides it's a perfect time to let out a wail of displeasure at the loud ruckus.

Bobby smiles, though. "Thanks, everyone. You didn't have to do all this for me."

Mama Louise lets go of my hand and rushes him. She reaches up to his neck and he bends down to hug her. "Oh, hush, you know good and well that we're as excited as can be for you."

When she steps back, his smile looks a little frayed and his dark eyes are tortured. Unbidden, my feet step forward. I need to ease the furrow line between his brows, smooth it out with a gentle caress. He needs to know that it's okay to celebrate his good fortune, that I understand what this means to him. And to us.

I can see the moment he realizes I'm here. His expression goes stormy and he covers the few feet between us in three strides. He scoops me into his arms, hugging me tightly. "Willow. Fuck, sweetheart. I missed you." He holds me like he's already lost me, like he wants to absorb me into him and take some small part with him.

I wrap my arms around his neck, breathing him in and feeling his solidness against me. I memorize him, knowing this will be the last moment where it all seems okay. This will be the memory I pull out at night when my heart is breaking from seeing another headline claiming country sensation Bobby Tannen is dating some country pop star.

"Language," Mama Louise whispers, but it seems to be out of habit.

"I missed you too," I murmur against his skin, pursing my lips to lay a small kiss there too. An invisible mark only I'll know is forever there.

"Tell us all about it while we eat. I'm starving," Brody orders. "While you've been out gallivanting, we've been doing actual labor, you know." He's giving his brother shit. It's how they say 'I love you' in their own gruff way. Bobby has told me how much Brody went through to keep their family together, so having one on the verge of leaving the flock must be hard, even if it's a sign that they're all doing well.

"Yeah, okay. But first, there's something I need to say."

Bobby grinds his teeth together, the muscle in his jaw working overtime. Tension works its way through his body in an instant as he stands tall. Even his hands fist at his sides. He looks as though he's going to battle, warring with invisible forces that only he can see.

"This weekend was . . . well, I'll tell you all about it, but you need to know . . . I didn't get the contract."

Three, two, one. Silent shock lasts an entire three seconds while we wait for him to shout 'gotcha' or laugh at the joke. When he doesn't, the reactions are slow to come as the truth sinks in.

"What?" Mama Louise breathes.

"Those fucking idiots!" Brody snaps. And for once, Mama Louise doesn't correct his language.

"They don't know what they're missing," Shayanne snarls, instantly riled up in her brother's defense.

I touch Bobby's arm and he looks down at me. "I'm so sorry, Bobby."

His nod is stiff, then he hugs me again, even tighter than the first one. I rub my hand along the muscles of his back soothingly. "So sorry," I murmur again.

He sniffs once, and as if nothing happened, he straightens both his face and his back. "Like I said, I'll tell you about the weekend. It was good." He shrugs. "Just didn't work out."

"Let's sit down so we can eat while it's still hot," Mama Louise instructs.

Bobby ducks under the *Congratulations* sign Cooper spent all afternoon making, taking the time to point at it and give the kid a fist bump of appreciation, but no other mention is made of its now-inappropriate message.

We move to the long table on the back porch. The light strands dangling from the rafters look festive, as though this is the party we thought we were going to have.

"Mama, think I'm gonna need a beer with dinner tonight. Anyone else?" Mark says gruffly.

Hands lift around the table, and Mark and Katelyn hand out drinks. Beer to some, wine coolers to others, and a bottle of root beer to Cooper.

Everyone passes serving platters around the table, and Bobby tells Mama Louise, "Thanks for dinner. Making all my favorites is a real nice touch." His plate is piled with fried chicken, fried okra, green beans made with bacon, thick macaroni and cheese with bread crumb topping, and a buttered biscuit.

Mama Louise nods, macaroni-filled fork in her hand as she tells him, "Best get on with it."

Bobby shovels two bites in first, delaying the inevitable. I want to kiss him so he doesn't have to tell this story. I don't want him to relive the pain of his dream not coming true, especially when we thought it was such a sure thing.

As we eat, he tells us about the trip.

"The first meeting was weird. Big ol' fancy office and a whole group talking about me like I was a loaf of bread on sale." His laugh is forced, but we pretend not to notice. "The show, though, was awesome. I sang several songs, including a new one I wrote this weekend."

His eyes turn to me. I could fall into their depths, swim in the darkness there, and not even miss the sun and moon if I were surrounded by him. *Click.*

"You'll have to play the new one at Hank's," Brutal says. "Hank says he's got the stage all warmed up for you this Saturday."

"Good to know I've still got a place I can sell out." There's no snark in the comment. It mostly sounds sad, resigned that the life he had before is what he's returning to. He was happy then, but it's hard to have a dream served up on a silver platter only to have it snatched away. I'm sure it makes your life seem less-than in the aftermath comparison.

Bobby continues as if giving a book report, dry and flat. "I recorded a bunch of songs with Miller, a producer. They sounded great. And I did a photo shoot with Rory. He said I was a natural, and I told him I'd had some recent practice modeling." Bobby's wink my way is the onstage one, fake and practiced.

"Then I met with the team again. They talked about feedback and perceptions, and to make a long story short, it wasn't a good fit. I wasn't a good fit with what they're looking for, so there's no deal."

Even though I knew that's how this story ended, his words are a knife to my gut. I can't believe it. What more could they have possibly wanted? Bobby is amazing on stage, a talented singer and songwriter, and gorgeous to boot. There's no way they could find anyone better than him.

I'm not the only one stuck on disbelief, with several other heads shaking around the table.

"How about here? What's been going on?" Bobby is blatantly changing the subject, obviously done with the previous one.

"We did a photo shoot with Willow!" Shayanne blurts.

I freeze, jaw dropping because I think she's talking about the boudoir shots, and that's not a conversation I want to have now, or ever. Especially in front of Mama Louise.

Shayanne glares at me pointedly.

Oh! The other pictures. The perfectly reasonable portrait ones.

"Yeah, they ambushed me at Hank's and Unc actually gave me the evening off." I tell him about Unc yelling at the whole bar, making the customers wait on themselves so he didn't have to move, and how Olivia had bolted to see Hannah before we went to my house for the photo shoot.

I leave out any and all mention of the second round of photos.

After dinner, we take our lemon meringue pie out into the yard. James starts a fire in the firepit and Cooper mouths about beating everyone at cornhole. We eat and watch, Bobby making no move to play in tonight's tournament or engage in the friendly teasing the rest of the guys dish out. I stay at his side, hoping my presence is a comfort, easing the pain of disappointment.

Earlier than usual, Bobby takes my hand. "I'm beat, guys. Think we'll turn in."

As we walk around the house, he pauses and calls back, "Thanks for tonight. It means a lot to know you've all got my back, no matter what." He swallows thickly as if that was hard to say.

The truck ride across the field to the Tannen house is quiet. Bobby seems lost in his thoughts, and I'm supporting him silently, letting him lead the conversation wherever he needs it to go. Or not go.

In the house, he guides me to the upstairs bathroom and starts to strip. Taking the cue, I do too, and by the time I'm nude, he's got the water hot and the bathroom steamy. He holds the curtain back for me to step inside first.

The water is scalding along my back, but I don't move to change it. Instead, I pull him to me, sharing the small space beneath the spray with him. My hands dance over his skin, soaping away the weekend, the disappointment, the shards of his dream, letting it wash down the drain with the suds.

"It's okay. It was an experience. One you'll never forget," I whisper into the steam between us.

His head hangs, water running in rivulets down his face from his hair. There are even water droplets caught in his dark lashes, but he doesn't blink them away. "I know. I just thought . . . maybe this time, I could be . . ."

He can't find the words, but I feel like I know what he means.

"Shh, it's okay." I reach my thumb up to his lips, swiping away any criticism of himself he was going to voice. "You're amazing, you're home, and you're happy here. Farming, family, singing, and writing songs."

I pause, knowing that earlier tonight, I was selfishly and greedily wanting him to stay, wishing he wouldn't leave me for something better on the road. But now that it's really happening, all I feel is sad for him. I would give anything to make his dream come true.

"Me. I'm right here with you, Bobby. And I love you."

He growls harshly, "I love you too."

And though his words are gruff and his movements sure as he spins me and pins my back to the shower wall, his thrusts are gentle as he enters me. I'm ready for him. I'm always ready for him.

He drives into me in waves, slow and rolling. I lift my leg around his hip, making more room for him, begging him to go deeper. I want him everywhere—inside my entire body the way he's in my entire heart.

We come quickly, having missed each other in the few days apart. As he comes, his eyes stay wide open, locked on me as he grunts my name over and over. "Willow . . . Willow . . . Willow."

We fall into his bed, naked and still damp. I run my fingers through the hair on his chest, petting him to sleep and enjoying the way his fingertips dance along my back in a different pattern. I wonder if it's the new song he wrote and can't wait to hear it. And though our arms and legs are tangled up in each other, our hearts are even more entangled as we fall asleep. *Click.*

Long after Bobby's breathing slows into sleep, I stay awake. I feel like I've run an emotional marathon tonight, from self-pity to sadness to joyful hope to sorrow. But we can be okay, I vow. Somehow, I'll make this okay for him, not getting the deal and staying here with me and his family. I'll love him through the disappointment and bring smiles to every single day I get with him. He deserves that. He deserves everything.

CHAPTER 20

BOBBY

"Goddamn it, pay attention or you're gonna take out a whole fucking tree!" Brutal bellows, his voice echoing through the row. The row I'm not remotely close to hitting with the Gator.

I spin around, doing a doughnut before aiming the vehicle toward the far side of the plot we're checking. So far, it's looked great. No bugs, good growth, and better than average production.

All of which should put me in a good mood. But I've been feeling strangled by my own skin these last few days.

I've worked, same as always. I've gone into town to have dinner with Willow, same as always. I've slept at her house, same as always. We've made love, same as always. And I've left early to get home to start my day all over again, same as always.

It's exactly what I want, so I should be as happy as a pig in slop.

But there's something gnawing at me, making me prickly and even more of an asshole than usual. Brutal can feel it, and I know Willow can feel it.

She's been so sweet, comforting me through the 'loss' of my dream by telling me how amazing I am, that Jeremy will regret not signing me, and that another opportunity will come along. I feel like shit taking her kindness when it's based on a lie, but I can't tell her the truth.

The sour-tongued truth is, I'd do anything for you.

"Shit! Pull over," Brutal orders. He's pointing at a particular tree with one hand and hanging on to the dash with the other as I squeal to a stop. Well, the Gator would've squealed if I wasn't on moist grass. But the irrigation keeps everything watered, so it's more of a power slide that sends us forward in our seats before popping us back.

Brutal's huff is one of annoyance, a sound that might as well be the soundtrack to my life given how many times I've heard it. He hops out and plucks a pear from the tree he indicated.

"I forgot Mama Louise asked for one of these. Run it up to her, will ya? I'll check this row and the next till you get back." He puts the green pear in the cup holder on the dash, knowing full well it won't stay there with the way I normally drive this thing.

"Sure thing. Back in a few," I say, spinning out again to head toward the house.

I swear I hear Brutal yell out, "Take your time, asshole."

The Gator races across the land, bumping and catching a tiny amount of air as I fly over the acres. The wind blows away my swirling thoughts for a brief moment of respite, the speed making me feel like I'm racing toward something and away from it all at once.

At the main Bennett house, I park out front and bound up the porch, pear in hand. I don't knock, we've been told not to bother, and barge right on in to find Mama Louise.

"Mama Louise?" I yell.

Her head pops around the doorway to the kitchen. "What's wrong?"

I can see why she'd think that. We're busy, working sunup to sundown, and she doesn't see much of us mid-day. She's busy too with her own list of chores that keep this place running smoothly. Honestly, her job is probably harder than any of ours. I don't know how she does it.

"Nothing. Sorry, didn't mean to scare ya. Brutal said you asked for a pear sample from the back acre. You thinking of doing something with 'em?"

Her brows furrow together, turning the lines on her forehead into grooves. In confusion, she repeats after me, "A pear?"

Comprehension dawns on her face, then mine.

"You didn't want a pear, did you?" I growl.

Her grin is full of unreleased laughter. "No, can't say that I did. But I'm guessing you've been a bit of grump and Brutal thought a few minutes away from you would be nice."

She's as blunt as a battering ram, and I can't help but argue. "I'm not that bad."

One of her brows quirks and her lips purse. That's all the rebuttal she needs. "Follow me."

She crooks a finger, and I follow her into the kitchen, where she's grabbing two glasses out of the cabinet.

"Is this the part where you ply me with your special sweet tea to make me spill my guts about what's got me in a mood?" I know I'm being rude, but I can't find it in me to tone it down, not even for Mama Louise.

She grabs a blue pitcher from the refrigerator and fills the glasses, setting one in front of me. "No, it's not even two o'clock in the afternoon and my special sweet tea is for evening drinking only."

"It's so bad, you can only do it in the dark?"

She swats my shoulder, but not angrily. "Filthy boy. Drink that water. You need it after the morning in the field, and if Brutal needs to be clear of you for a few minutes, you're not sitting around like a bump on a log. You can help me work."

I grunt but swallow down the cool, refreshing water.

"Good. Follow me," she orders again, and like a good dog, I do.

Outside, her garden is thick and lush. She's definitely got a green thumb, gifted with getting things to grow tall and hardy. Like her sons. Like us Tannens, even though we were full-grown when she pulled us out of our too-small pots and replanted us in richer soil.

"We're weeding the garden and harvesting anything that looks ready." All business and no mushy stuff, we get to it.

It's quiet as we work, and I find myself humming. After a bit,

Mama Louise hums along with me, picking up the melody from *Dig Down Deeper*.

"That one new?" she asks.

She's broaching the subject carefully, casually, as if I won't catch on to our conversational topic if she doesn't spell it out for me in bold, exclamation marked statements like Shayanne is prone to do.

"Yep." That's all she's getting from me, today or any other day.

"It's pretty."

I wait for the questions that don't come—what's wrong? Why are you grumpy? Wanna talk about Nashville?

The answers—Nothing. Same as always. No.

But we're silent. I dig into the earth, feeling its cool graininess in my hands. Mama Louise lets me avoid her unasked questions for a long while.

Finally, she's had enough and stops, resting her dirty hand on her face to shield her eyes from the sun.

"If you've gotten so grumpy that Brutal is ditching you, we should probably figure out what we're doing tomorrow too. You thinking we should can some bourbon carrots or weed the yard? Both gotta get done, so I'll let you choose."

"I can't. Brutal and I have another row to check."

"Then you'd better get yourself in a better mood, mister. Pull that weed," she directs, pointing at a big one I missed with my distracted mind elsewhere.

I yank on it hard, taking out my frustrations on the weed that's grown where it shouldn't be. A lot like me. I've grown tall and hardy here in Great Falls, and it's a great . . . garden. But what if I'm meant for another, bigger garden of my own? Like Nashville.

The weed gives way suddenly, and I go sprawling on my ass in the dirt. Knees bent, I rest my arms on them and let my head fall.

"They offered me the record deal," I whisper. I shouldn't confess to this. It'll ruin everything, but I can't stop it from affecting me and that's ruining me too.

Mama Louise doesn't so much as slow down with her weed

pulling. "Of course they did. The question is . . . why did you say they didn't?"

I blink in confusion. "Wait, you knew I got an offer?"

She stops, her eyes boring into me. She's always had kind eyes, blue and fringed with dark blonde lashes, but now, those eyes are looking at me as if I'm dumber than the tomato plants.

"Of course they'd want you. Your songs are amazing, poetry like nothing I've ever heard. You've got the voice of an angel" —I snort in disbelief, but she steamrolls over me— "mixed with the grit of the devil. It's beautiful, Bobby. A gift."

I let her compliments sink in. Most folks, I simply brush their praise off. But not hers. Mama Louise's means something to me.

"Thanks." That's as far as I get for a long while as I search for the words to explain what happened. Mama Louise doesn't rush me, as if she knows this is difficult for me.

Finally, the story comes.

I tell her how intimidating the office was, with a whole room full of people judging me. I tell her about the crowd at the Bar and how I won them over, which felt amazing. She smiles at that, nodding like 'I told you so.' I tell her about working with Miller and Rory, deeper stories than I told at the dinner table.

"Miller made me feel like I could really do something. I mean, I know I can sing. And I write all the time. But it was like with the tiniest push, it was all on a higher level. One I didn't know I was capable of. What if there's more that I'm capable of?" I wonder aloud, not meaning to say that last part.

"I'm sure there is. You can discover it yourself, though. Or book some time with this Miller fellow yourself if you want to. I'm sure he does private appointments. Everyone does for the right price. It only matters if it's worth it to you."

I mull that over for a second.

"They had conditions for the contract offer," I tell Mama Louise.

She frowns. "What sort of conditions?"

This is the harder part, the confession about what I've done.

"Jeremy said I needed a band, and that was fine by me. Then he started talking about my image. They wanted to turn me into some sort of bad boy manwhore."

"Man-what?" Mama Louise repeats, just shy of a shriek.

I nod, not willing to repeat the word in front of her. She might've not corrected my language once, but she'll damn well do it if I say whore again. "Exactly what you're thinking. They wanted me to be single . . . to break up with Willow."

"And you said no." Her voice is flat, not belying what she thinks about that, good or bad.

"I tried. Jeremy told me to think real hard before I answered either way. I told him no on Wednesday. It's the right thing to do."

"Well, I'll say that I don't know a thing about music, other than what I like to listen to on the radio. But I reckon those people do, so they might be right about the way to make the most of your voice. The question is . . . do you care what they say? Right or wrong, contract or not, what do you want, Bobby?"

I can't answer that. I should be able to. It should be the easiest answer in the world—the contract that so many people, me included, dream of for so long. But on the other hand, I've never known love like this, and I've been searching my whole life. Some people search even longer than I have. And I won't give that up lightly.

"You're choosing Willow over the deal." It's not a question, it's a statement.

"Yeah." I am. She's everything, way more important than this deal. And I'll still have music, just not the big stadiums and bright lights. I can sing at Hank's, and it'll be enough. It always has been.

"You sure?" Mama Louise is giving me an out, telling me it's okay to choose either way, but my decision has already been made. Now, it's just time to live my happily ever after with it.

"I am."

"Good," she says with a smile. She seems . . . pleased? But that can't be right. "You deserve to get what you want, Bobby. Lord knows, you kids have been through enough, and you deserve to have something go your way for a change. I really and truly thought it was going to be this deal, but . . ." She sighs, looking up toward the sky for a moment as if there are answers to be found in the cloudless sky. "If your dream changes, if it looks different than it did when you were eighteen and didn't have a clue about how hard life can be and what's really important, that's okay. And getting what you want now over what you wanted then is still a good thing. I'm happy for you."

I'm looking down, letting her words wash over me and soothe the hurt, all of them—losing Mom, losing my innocence, losing Dad, not when he died but before that when he truly checked out on us, and even losing this opportunity.

I feel her grubby finger on my chin, forcing me to lift up and meet her eyes. "I'm proud of you, Bobby."

Fuck. I didn't know I needed to hear that, especially about this. Choosing Willow was easy, automatic, and I know she's what I truly want. But that doesn't mean not choosing the deal doesn't hurt like a motherfucker.

"Thank you," I grit out.

She nods, like that's that. "Get that one too, will you?" She points to another weed.

And this time, when I pull at it and it refuses to come loose, I wonder if maybe, instead of my being stuck in Great Falls, this weed could be Willow putting down roots here with me?

The weed gives way, but there's another one right next to it so I keep going, clearing Mama Louise's garden long after she goes inside and leaves me to my thoughts.

Root into me, stay by my side. We'll grow together, two as one.

CHAPTER 21

WILLOW

"*Y*ou okay?" I ask Unc during the lull between lunch and what is going to be a crazy Saturday night.

His complexion is looking a bit pasty, his eyes a bit sunken and purple. And that's after he took a break to 'check the books' earlier.

"Have you eaten anything today? Ilene would be happy to make you some eggs and toast." The suggestion makes him turn an altogether unattractive shade of green and shake his head.

"Nah. Just feel like a bug that got zapped by one of those contraptions you put on the back porch. *Zzzzzt.*" He vibrates like a jolt of electricity is going through him. His smile at his own joke is weak, lasting for only a brief flash.

"Take off tonight then. Olivia and I can handle things, especially since you did the same for us last weekend." I'm hoping the reminder of his kindness will let him accept mine.

No such luck.

He lifts one white brow. "I'm fine. Gonna be a busy one tonight, and I won't leave you girls that way."

We could do it without him. It'd be tough, because he's right about the crowd we're expecting since it's Bobby's first show since the Nashville trip. But I'm going to spend most of the night with my eyes on Unc, making sure he's okay.

"Okay." I might as well give in because I'm not going to win against his pride. But I'll do what I can. "What do you need, then? I'll do the prep stuff, but can I at least get you a beer?"

Even when his stomach is turning circles on him, he can always manage to get a beer down. I don't wait for his answer, grabbing one of his favorite craft beers, popping the top, and setting it in front of him.

"Oh, Doc Jones called a bit ago. Said to holler at him when you get a minute. You might want to do that now before we get slammed."

He sighs as if that's a big job, but he climbs from his stool and heads back to his office. Quickly, I text Doc.

Me: Talk to Unc for a bit about something. He needs to rest in the office and is being stubborn.

Doc: On it. Good girl.

While I have a minute, I ask Ilene for a biscuit with a honey drizzle. "For Hank? He need something else to eat with it? I can make him a burger, or a bowl of soup? Or he's taken a liking to my scrambled eggs lately." Her generosity is innate, her willingness to mother Unc straight out of her experience as a mother and grandmother herself. And she doesn't even know about the cancer. She just takes care of people.

Overcome, I hug her quickly. Without hesitation, she hugs me back. "You're the best, Ilene. I think just the biscuit for now."

"Sure thing, sweetie. If you think you can get him to eat something else, let me know. He's getting too skinny for my taste." I'm pretty sure everyone is too skinny for her taste. She shows her love with food, every bite made with her heart and soul.

I smile, quietly stepping into the office and setting the biscuit on the desk in front of Unc. He glares at me, but he's got the phone pressed to his ear, listening to who I presume is Doc. Hopefully, he'll mindlessly take a few bites and get something good in his belly.

Back behind the bar, I do all my normal prep. I'm all set. Looking across the floor, Olivia seems ready too.

And just in time. The dinner rush begins and we're flooded with customers.

I pull tickets one after another, filling drink orders for Oliva.

Unc is still in his office, hopefully dozing on the booth bench after finishing the biscuit.

"Hey," a deep voice says behind me as arms wrap around my waist. I feel a hot kiss press to my neck.

"You're a brave man. The last guy who laid hands on me without permission got his nose broken by my big, strong, sexy boyfriend. He's a little possessive." I can hear the smile in my voice.

"I don't need permission. You're already mine, sweetheart," he growls against my ear.

"I am." The agreement is easy because it's true. I also give him the words he loves to hear in answer to his possessive claims over me, "And you're mine. Though your fans are getting a bit rabid waiting for you to hit the stage tonight."

I spin in his arms, needing to see him.

He's been off the last few days. He's still come in for dinner and gone home with me. But the urgency in his touch, the way he murmurs my name, and the punishing way he's made love to me, as though he can't get deep enough inside my body, are different. It feels like he's marking me again and again, holding me tighter and tighter, which would be amazing if I didn't feel a sense of sadness beneath the layers of his smiles.

He's grieving the loss of the contract. He probably will for days and weeks to come. On some level, tonight might feel like a step backward even though people are clamoring for him to sing, already creating a buzzing energy in the bar.

"I only care about one fan, and she's in my arms," he murmurs into the breath of space between us.

"I love you," I reply. He's wanted to hear it again and again, the chorus to our moments together.

One of his hands moves to cup my cheek, the other gripping my ass tightly. He kisses me like he can't get enough of me, and I let him take what he needs, anything he wants to stay steady and strong.

"I love you too," he whispers against my lips. I take his breath into my lungs, wanting him to be only mine for a second longer.

It's not meant to be, though.

"Bobby!" a voice calls out from across the room. "Woohoo! Welcome back, man!"

"Your fans await," I tell him. "And my customers are getting thirsty."

* * *

THERE'S no way Unc could sleep, or even doze, through the noise of this crowd. The pool table balls crack, people cheer and talk, and the jukebox is playing nonstop.

He comes out, offers me a nod, and perches on his stool. He must've stopped by the kitchen on his way down the hall because Ilene comes out a few minutes later with a plate filled, and I do mean filled, with scrambled eggs and buttered toast.

He looks better, maybe not bright-eyed and bushy-tailed, but open-eyed and upright, at least. And eating.

I keep manning the bar, letting him finish as much of the breakfast-for-dinner meal as he can. When I step down to his end to get a few drafts, he pats my hand with his. That's his version of saying thanks. I don't need him to, but it feels good to know that he appreciates my help.

Since our talk, when we both came clean, he's been better about accepting that I'm here for him. I won't go so far as to say he's happy about my doing things for him, but I think he's letting me if that's what it takes to keep me here.

In the long run, I think fixing what's left of our family is important to us both.

He finishes, wiping at his mouth with the back of his hand, and sets the empty plate in the sink. At least I know he got that down, and as long as it stays that way, the protein will be good for him.

He washes his hands and tells me, "Okay, Willow-girl, I've got the beers. You've got the mixers."

I nod and keep at it.

What seems like minutes later, I hear a few strummed chords vibrate through the room and look up, already smiling.

Bobby is onstage, his hair mussed like he's been running his fingers through it. He slips a guitar pick between his teeth, the flash of white almost smile-like, but he scrubs his palm over his stubble without joy. Taking the pick out, he strums again.

"Hey, everyone. I'm Bobby Tannen," he says, giving his usual bare-boned intro. After a moment, he adds, "Some of you know I went to Nashville last weekend. It was . . . big." The crowd laughs, leaning forward to get any crumbs of information they can direct from the source. "Afraid you're not getting rid of me that easily, though."

That's all he says about not getting the deal we all thought he would. It takes people a second to realize what he means, and I can see the surprise dawn on their faces. A murmur of disbelief goes through the crowd, but it's covered by Bobby starting his first song.

I freeze, letting the grit and gravel of his voice wash over me. His pain threads through every note, adding a break to the end of a line he holds out too long. As his voice cries, my heart does too.

He's amazing, truly gifted. I have no idea what NCR Records could be thinking or what more they could possibly want. Bobby is everything music should be about—heart, soul, rhythm, and connecting people through lyrics that stick in your mind and resonate in your spirit.

The crowd sways with the music, under his spell the same way I am.

He finishes with a vibrating chord, shaking Betty to pull more from her, and everyone goes wild, clapping and cheering, and even a loud whistle from Unc, fill the room.

"Screw them, Bobby!"

"They don't know what they're missing!"

"I love you!"

People call out encouragement, supporting him the only way they know how—loudly and vehemently. Bobby might feel like his family has a bad reputation, but when push comes to shove with outsiders, Great Falls has the Tannens' backs. There's no doubt about that.

"Thanks," Bobby says, and I swear he looks surprised at the positive response. "This next one, I wrote it for someone special."

His eyes lift from the crowd and meet mine across the room.

For all the crowd, there might as well be only me and him here. I swear I can see the future in the way he looks at me. I smile, stopping what I'm doing to listen. I want to hear this, don't want to miss a single note or word because I've seen how hard he works to get them just right.

> *Chasing down my dream so I can give you yours.*
> *The proof of a man is in his woman's eyes.*
> *Storm for me, shine for me, show your soul for me.*
> *And I'll dig down deep to get mine so you can have yours.*

Before he's made it through the first chorus, I'm crying. Happy tears and sad tears, or some combination of the two. He wrote this thinking he would get that deal and we'd start a new life together, not leave me behind. The proof of that is obvious in this song.

His heart is in every line, his dream in every chord.

And though it might not have ended up quite the way we thought that trip would, that future can still be ours. All I need is for us to be together. That's enough. It's more than enough.

He's all I need.

I pull my phone out, taking a picture of him onstage, singing this song to me for the first time. *Click.*

Everyone else claps as the song ends, but Bobby's heated look across the space is all for me. *Click.*

"All right, folks. Enough sappy shit," Bobby says, flashing a cocky grin. "This is a honkytonk, not a Celine Dion concert. You know what time it is . . . get a drink, raise it up, and don't forget to tip your waitress and bartenders."

There's a resounding rush for beers before Bobby rolls off into a few cover songs to get the crowd riled up. They sing along, the whole crowd swaying with their hands in the air, giving the bar a sense of community.

This is Bobby Tannen's party. We're just the lucky attendees to this shindig. And for a moment, he seems more like himself, the rough and tough cowboy with a golden heart who sets my whole body on fire when he says filthy things in my ear while filling me. That's who's onstage right now.

I sing along with him under my breath as I make drinks,

keeping up with the tickets and checking on Unc as I make my way up and down the bar. It seems like he's doing better now, pulling beers and talking to Richard, who showed up a bit ago.

I see a new shirt at the far side of the bar and make my way over. "What can I get you?" I ask the guy's back.

He answers over his shoulder, watching Bobby onstage. "Johnnie Walker Black, neat."

I pour his drink and set it on a napkin. "Tab?"

"No." He reaches for his wallet, pulls out a twenty, and lays it down.

I'm mentally calculating his change when he says, "Keep it."

"Thanks." I drop the bill in my apron, ready to move on to my next customer, but he finally turns around. I recognize him instantly.

"Jeremy? I mean, Mr. Marshall?"

I only saw him the one time, when he was asking questions about Bobby, but I don't think I'll ever forget the man who offered Bobby a shot at his dream before he snatched it away.

"You must be *The* Willow?" There's a sneer in the way he says my name that I don't understand.

"Well, I'm Willow. I don't know about *The* Willow." I have no idea what he's talking about or why he's looking at me like I'm some weird anomaly. It makes me feel the way I used to as an awkward kid. To him, I'm an outsider, easily dismissed.

Jeremy laughs as though I said something funny, and I frown.

"Well, Bobby would disagree with you there. He thinks you're something really special." It should be a compliment, but it certainly sounds like an insult.

"What?" I blink in confusion. "We seem to be having two different conversations here." An idea springs to life, fully formed in my mind, and excitement rushes through my entire body. "Oh, my God, did you change your mind? Are you here to offer Bobby a deal after all?"

I lean forward, praying he says yes. Bobby will be so happy!

I know I thought he might leave me if he made it big, but I can't care about that anymore. I can't be that selfish, not even this one time. After seeing his disappointment at not getting the deal, all I want is for him to get his dream.

And I've felt his love, know the depth and intensity of it. We can make this work. I know we can. He can have the deal and I can have him. I'm sure of it. Any doubts I had left floated away as he sang those lyrics tonight, proclaiming loud and clear that he wanted that deal for us. Not just himself.

Jeremy's brows jump up his impossibly unlined forehead. "Offer a deal? Change my mind?" He's silent for a moment, looking at me then over his shoulder to Bobby.

"I hear hundreds of singers every year, you know? I hit every dive bar, club, and county fair concert in towns all over the country. I watch YouTube videos and shitty TikToks of people who can't sing their ABCs with decent pitch. I have never seen anyone like that guy up there." He tilts his head toward the stage.

"Then why didn't—"

He cuts me off. "I didn't tell him this, but I offered him a better deal than any artist who's sat at my table, knowing he would be worth it in the long run. Told him we'd get a band to back him up, give him an image that'd let him have the sort of fun kids like him dream of. All he had to do was ditch the girl. You."

"Me?" I stammer, not understanding.

Jeremy looks me up and down again. "I don't get it. You don't seem all that special. But shit, you have some magic hold on him, don't you?"

It's starting to click together—Bobby's grumpy mood, his passionate lovemaking, his telling me how much he loves me over and over. He was doing it to reassure himself that he'd made the right choice.

They offered him a record deal, but he chose me over his dream. His dream!

And he hid it from everyone, especially me.

"You offered him a deal," I summarize.

"I damn near laid out a silver platter for him," Jeremy bites out. "And he just walked away." He waves a hand, obviously still in shock that anyone would do that.

This is what Bobby has dreamed of since he was a kid. It's what his family needs. It's what he desperately wants. Before he went to Nashville, he told me how it seemed like something impossibly good might actually happen for him for once.

Sure, he loves me . . . now. But what if he starts to resent me, hate that he gave this up for . . . me? Some nothing-special girl who showed up at a bar a couple of months ago. He can't give up everything for me.

Time shouldn't matter. You can know someone your whole life and barely scratch the surface of who they are or meet someone and know them bone deep in a matter of seconds. I believe soulmates can be like that. But can we be soulmates if it means him losing everything he's worked for his whole life? I'm just not worth that.

I swallow the bile that's trying to rise up as my heart shatters into a million pieces. I know what I have to do. It'll kill me. It'll hurt Bobby. But the sacrifice of my own happiness is worth his. When he said he didn't get the deal, I thought I would do anything to change that. In this moment, I know that's absolutely the truth. Anything.

"Is that deal still on the table? Would you still sign him to NCR Records?"

"Fuck yes. That's why I came here tonight, to talk some sense into him."

I shake my head. "Don't. Let me talk to him. Please."

Jeremy looks at me, sees the tears in the corners of my eyes, then back to Bobby, who's singing his closing song.

"Don't fuck this up for him. He's special—better and bigger than you and me and this whole podunk town." He looks around the bar, and I can tell he doesn't see the blood, sweat, and tears that go into keeping this place open. He doesn't see the history inside these walls or feel the love they hold. He certainly doesn't understand this town or how the people here are welcoming and supportive, even their gossip mostly coming from a place of love because they care about one another.

But he sees what Bobby could be, and that's all I need him to recognize.

With that, he swallows the Johnnie Walker in one gulp, gives me a hard glare, and strides straight for the door.

My eyes are drawn to the stage, to Bobby. He's listening to someone in the audience intently. He nods, smiling, and begins one more song. An encore request.

He sings *Dig Down Deeper* once more.

It hits differently this time, seeming like a prediction.

I'll dig down deep, Bobby, so you can get yours.

CHAPTER 22

BOBBY

"*D*id Ilene make you dinner?" Something's wrong with Willow, and food is always a good guess with any woman. I learned that from Mom and Shayanne early on.

She hums in answer, though it's a complete non-answer. She's here physically, but her mind is somewhere else, her eyes unseeing and her smile nonexistent.

"Hey," I say, grabbing her around the waist and pulling her body to mine, aligning us so that I can get her full attention. "What's wrong?"

She ducks her chin, avoiding my eyes. Oh, we're not playing this game again, sweetheart. I chased you once, and if I have to chase you again to find out what's going on in that pretty little brain of yours, I will.

Tell me all your secret thoughts, I'll protect them from harm. Let me into your private moments, I'll share the solitude with you.

I lift her chin with one hand, whispering, "What's wrong, sweetheart? Did someone do something? Need me to crack a skull for you?" I'm joking—well, sort of. If someone did something to scare or piss off my girl, I will handle it and deal with any consequences that might come. But I was watching all night, barely able to take my eyes off her across the room, too far away for me to touch with my fingertips but hoping my words would reach her heart. But I didn't see anything amiss, so I expect to get one of her soft smiles in return for the joke.

One doesn't come.

She blinks behind her frames, only looking at me for a brief second as if the sight of me pains her.

"Wait . . . did someone say something about me?" Considering my reputation and the lengths some people go to get a piece of me, I wouldn't be surprised if someone was banging on the grapevine a bit. "If so, it's lies. Whatever it is. I love you, only you."

Her nod is of agreement but not resolution. She brushes her bangs back and sighs, "Can we go home? I'm fine, just tired."

Rule number one of women—when in doubt, feed them. Rule number two—'I'm fine' means they are most definitely, one hundred percent, not fine. But I don't argue. If she doesn't want to tell me what it is so I can fix it, I can at least comfort her through it so she knows I have her back.

I pull her to my chest, holding her head against my heart, which is racing too fast with the need to punch something, some- one, whoever made my girl sad. Since I can't do that, I grip her waist a little tighter and lay soft kisses to the top of her head.

"It's okay. Whatever it is, it's okay. I got you."

The slightest jerk of her muscles is all the warning I get before she pulls away. I can see words on the tip of her tongue, dancing in those mood-ring eyes that are wilder than a thunderstorm right now. Whatever she's thinking, I've changed my mind. I don't want to hear it. Not now, not ever. Because I can see that this is not about a handsy tourist. Something's wrong. And I like our little bubble of blissful happiness where all I need is her kiss, her touch, her heart, and everything is okay.

"Yeah, let's go. We can be at your place in five, in a bubble bath in ten." I take her hand in mine, pulling her toward the door. I throw Hank a nod of goodbye. In the truck, Willow lays her head back on the headrest, looking at the starry sky through the passenger window. "Can we . . . go to your place instead?" She rolls her head my way. Though the question seems easy, the plea is in her eyes.

"Yeah. Sure."

The ride through town is quiet, and the silence once we hit the country roads makes me want to scream. The deafening emptiness fills my gut with dread. Whatever it is, I don't want her to say it. This dark void is better than whatever it is. I'm sure of it.

Inside, we tiptoe upstairs so we don't disturb Brody and Rix. I can hear my brother's soft snores from the top of the stairs, and he'll be up in a few hours to start the new day's work.

I pull off my shirt, dropping it to the bedroom floor. I unbutton my pants, but before I toe my boots off, I realize that Willow is frozen. She hasn't moved from the doorway, and if she could make herself smaller, I think she would.

I sink to the edge of the bed, running my hands through my hair, gripping the strands hard in punishment. For what? I have no idea. With a breath for strength, I rest my elbows on my knees and look up at her.

"Tell me, Willow."

She flinches at my harsh tone, but I'm too on edge to be gentle with her right now. I feel like she's walking on eggshells for me, but I'm not capable of that the way she is. I'm more of a boot-stomping, destroy shit type.

"You can't do this." It's a cried plea, but I still don't know what she's talking about.

I narrow my eyes, worried. "Do what, exactly?"

She twists her hands, and I want to hold them in mine, stop her nervous fidgeting. Stop her mouth from whatever poison it's filled with because even the smallest dose already burns with destructive force, ruining me.

"You were amazing tonight. When I see you on that stage, you light up with this . . . joy. I can feel, the whole audience can feel, you letting us into your soul through the lyrics you write, the notes you sing, the chords you play. It's beautiful. And after, it's like your mind is peaceful, resting from the release. Almost like . . . sex."

"Thank you?"

As difficult as words are for me, I can understand exactly what she's saying. I feel that transformation with every performance—the progress from my skin feeling too tight to feeling at home inside myself. Like the show is a purging of all my emotions and a cleansing that allows the sunshine to wash through me.

But as sweet as the words are, they don't sound like the lead-up to anything good.

"You need to go back to Nashville. Talk to Jeremy Marshall, talk to other agents, and play bars there. Whatever it takes. You need to chase that dream and not let anything hold you back. Not your family, not your responsibilities, not . . . me."

My jaw falls open. "What are you talking about?"

"You can do it. Bobby, you deserve that deal. If anyone deserves their dream coming true, it's you."

I have a moment of panic. She knows. How could she know? The only person I told is Mama Louise, and I know she wouldn't have spilled. That woman's mouth is a steel trap.

"I didn't get the contract. I told you that," I growl, mad that she's making me lie to her again. The lie is bitter, stinging my tongue, singeing my soul. I wish I'd never told it, but I couldn't figure out another way to explain it to my family and Willow.

Pain flashes in her eyes and tears instantly flow down her cheeks.

Anger, hot and bright, washes through me. I'm mad at myself, furious at Jeremy for his stupid conditions, and hurt that Willow is digging into the wound I'm trying to let scab over.

My voice is too loud, but I can't hold it down. "Are you disappointed in me? Ashamed that I didn't get the contract and am just a farmer who sings a little?" I'm used to arguing with my brothers, with Shayanne, who will rear right back up at me. Willow does not.

Even smaller, she shakes her head. "No." Her voice weak and shaky. "Of course not. You're—"

Reason fights its way through my blood roaring in my head when I see her reaction. She doesn't need to be handled with kid gloves and is tougher than she thinks she is, but not now. Not like this.

Be easy with her, Bobby. For fuck's sake, be a little gentle.

I stand up, stepping toward her to take her arms in my hands. She needs to hear this and hear it loud and clear. Bending down so that I'm eye to eye with her, I spit out, "I love you. I want you. I want to be here, with you."

I hope it's enough. It's all I have, all I can offer—my heart.

"I'm leaving," she whispers.

"What?" I shout.

She licks her lips, eyes tortured. "I'm going home, back to the city."

"You can't! What the fuck, Willow? Why?" Louder and louder, barked demands for answers pour forth. "Did Hank do something? Did he tell you to leave?"

I push back from her, needing to see her, read her mind. Something, anything that will tell me what the fuck is going on.

"Son of a bitch!" I scream. The pain of losing her is already rushing through my blood, superheating it to a boil. The fear of life without her is dark and heavy, its thick tentacles pulling me under. I instinctively resort to what I know, how I've always handled emotions that feel too big for my body to handle. I spin, throwing a punch at the wall. The sheetrock shatters beneath my fist.

"Ahh!" Willow screams.

I'm on the verge of an apology. I didn't mean to scare her. I'm just frustrated and terrified and confused.

But the door blasts open, hitting the wall behind the frame.

"What the hell is going on in here?" Brody bellows, Rix right behind him in the hallway.

"We're fine," I tell Brody. "Get out. This is between me and Willow."

"The hell it is. Not when she looks terrified and there's a hole in the wall the size of your fist. What's going on?"

He's stepping between Willow and me like he's protecting her from me.

From me!

I would never hurt her. She's the one ripping my heart out of my body with her bare hands.

I move toward her, eyes glaring at Brody then softening when they meet Willow's. I can't help it. Even when she's killing me, I love her.

"Why? Why are you doing this? Willow, I love you." I have no shame, will beg on my knees for her if that's what it takes.

If I can hold her in my arms, kiss her soft lips once more, she'll understand and stay. I don't know what else to say, but I can convince her if I can just touch her. She'll feel how right we are. She'll feel that bone-deep connection we had from the instant I laid eyes on her.

"Willow." I reach for her, and Brody lays a hand on my chest, stopping me.

"Bobby," he growls in warning.

"Get off me," I yell at him. Like so many times before, one second, we're standing there as brothers, and the next, we're fighting.

Brody pushes me off him, but I come back madder. This hurts, everything hurts, and I need to make someone else feel this to get it out of my veins. It's the only way.

I punch Brody in the gut, and he grunts. His arm goes around my neck, not choking me but trying to control me. I spin in his grip, getting free. He's ready, though, having taught me that move himself. Before I can even stand upright, his fist lands in my gut in a return shot.

Willow screams in horror. "No! Don't fight! I'm . . . I'm leaving."

I whirl on her, forgetting Brody in an instant. "No! Stay. Please."

Her tears break me, the shake of her head guts me, but the single step back she takes when I move closer is my undoing. "Bobby," she whispers.

"Willow?"

Over her shoulder, she asks Rix, "Can you take me home?"

"No, I'll do it. We can talk this out. Please."

Rix shoots me a glare, but it melts. If she were capable of tears, I think she'd be crying now too. Fuck knows, I am. "I'll take you, Willow. I've got her, Bobby."

Willow follows Rix down the stairs woodenly. It's not until I hear the roar of Rix's car that it hits me. Willow's leaving. She's actually doing it.

I run for the stairs, busting through the front door to stop her. I don't know how, but I'll come up with something. There has to be some way to make her stay.

But all I see are the red glow of taillights as Rix turns onto the street.

"No!" I shout into the night.

Brody is right at my side, just in time to catch me before I sink to the dirt in the front yard. "What the fuck just happened? Bobby?"

I mutter, "What am I going to do?" The truth hits me so hard, I feel the world spin.

I gave up everything for her! Everything.

"Fuck it, I'm out of here."

"What?" Brody says, but I'm already gone. Running for my truck, I hop inside and grab the spare key from the visor.

The trucks growls to life, and I spin out, leaving Brody in a cloud of dust behind me. I think I hear him call my name, but I don't stop, don't explain.

I'll fill him in later.

Willow thinks I should go to Nashville and try to get a contract? Fuck that. I already have one. One I gave up for her. But if she doesn't want me, I'm going to take it. Guess Jeremy's getting his way, after all.

Fuck.

CHAPTER 23

WILLOW

"*E*ff-why-I, do not, under any circumstances, go wandering by table twelve. They're here solely to gawk and stare," Olivia snaps loudly, fully intending for table twelve to hear her. Her ponytail swishes through the air as she throws a 'dare you to say something' look their way.

"At what?" I ask, getting her drinks—three diet colas with a cherry juice splash, one club soda with lime.

I've kept my head down all day so that no one will see how red and puffy my eyes are. They're the most obvious consequence for spending last night bawling in my bathtub. I'd planned on soaking, letting the heat take away some of the pain of heartache, but I didn't make it that far. I'd climbed right on in, still dressed in my work clothes, and curled up to cry for hours. At least the toilet paper had been close by so I could blow my nose. It's red and irritated now too.

But with my head down, my heart heavy, and my mind elsewhere, I have no idea what's happening around me. I'm going through the motions robotically—read order, get glass, pour drink, set it out for Olivia.

I do look up at Olivia's words, though. Her eyes are popped wide open, her jaw dropped to catch flies. I glance at table twelve. I see four women dressed in their Sunday best, probably fresh from church and here for a late lunch. My lips stretch in a smile automatically, even though I don't feel like smiling at all. The women flash back small smiles of pity before their heads nearly knock together as they whisper.

About me.

"You, obviously," she confirms.

"How do they even know?" I whisper, not bothering to pretend there's nothing to know. There's no use.

Olivia leans in close. "Willow, you could've won at Hank's poker game last night with how straight your face was after Bobby's show. That was already fuel on the fire of 'is Willow okay?' and 'what did that Tannen boy do now?'" She waves her hand in front of her face, staring vacantly. "And if that wasn't enough to raise some concerns, Bobby's truck was seen flying through town around three in the morning, not headed toward your house or his, and he was alone."

My stomach rolls. Did he already leave? So easily? And who was out at three in the morning to see him go?

Tears threaten again, hotly stinging my lids, and I sniffle.

"Oh, shit. Shit!" Olivia hisses. "Go to the back. Check the spreadsheets or whatever. Go, go, girl. Never let 'em see ya sweat or cry."

She's so nice, giving me an excuse the way she does Unc when he needs a rest. Any reason to hide out for a little bit and pull myself together.

"Thanks," I manage to whisper. I wish I were strong enough to walk with my head held high, not caring about the nosy Nellies here to wallow in my misery. But I'm not. I virtually run for the office.

I shut the door before the waterworks come, pooling in my glasses. I yank them off angrily, dropping them to the desk as my face floods with fresh tears.

He's gone.

All it took was me giving him a nudge, and he left. That affirms how much he wants that life.

I did the right thing.

I know I did.

It hurts right now, but in the long run, Bobby will have his deal and his dreams of filling stadiums, fans singing his music, and living like a country superstar, and it will be well worth this pain. That happiness—his happiness—will make this pain seem insignificant. I hope.

I've got today's shift to get through. After that, I can spend the entirety of Monday breaking down and no one will be the wiser. I promise myself a full twenty-four hours of tears, ice cream scooped straight out of the pint with bark-thin chocolate as a makeshift spoon, and an actual hot bath. For now, I swallow down my loss, wipe my face, and steel my nerves.

Hours later, I'm doing okay, mostly passable as a ghost thanks to Olivia's help.

She's running interference for me, shooting daggers at customers if they aim for the bar and shooing them to tables so they can't pester me with questions. She does let Richard sit down in his usual spot, but thank goodness, he doesn't say a single word about my red eyes or hanging head. In fact, I think he might be planted there as a buffer for anyone who gets past Olivia.

"Keep 'em coming, Willow. Draft and water back, please."

I nod, getting his usual.

Still, I can feel the town's eyes, hear their whispered questions, taste their hunger for gossip. I want to hide, be invisible again.

Maybe going back to the city is a good idea?

I'd said that last night as a push to get Bobby to go to Nashville, not actually intending on doing it. But there, I get lost amid the sheer volume of people. Nobody knows me, my name, or my business. I can be outside everything, photographing it as an observer without getting involved. Without getting hurt.

The door creaks open, but I don't look up. I haven't all day.

"I'll sit wherever I damn well please, Olivia, and I'd suggest that you don't get in my way," I hear a deep voice bark.

At that, my head lifts. Brody?

No, it's all of them. The gang's all here, literally. Minus Cooper, Cindy Lou, and Mama Louise, who's probably pulling grandma duty.

Olivia shrugs, mouthing 'sorry' as she lets them pass. I guess even her skills have some boundaries. I don't blame her. Brody's scary on a good day. Right now, he looks like he could pluck someone's head from their shoulders with his bare hands. Brutal would probably toss it around like a football. Which might be a bit amusing if I wasn't sure it was my head they want to roll.

Anyone else I could've handled. Not well, but I could've managed. The Tannen-Bennett gang is another matter entirely.

I go ahead and pull a pitcher of draft beer and a stack of glasses, setting them down in front of Brody. His eyes are dark, burning with fury and accusations, and his jaw is clenched to bite back whatever venom he wants to pour over me.

Ever the angel, Katelyn pours the beers, spreading them out on the napkins I lay down. The Tannens glare at me, Shayanne included. The Bennett guys are doing the stoic-faced looks, backing Brody, Brutal, and Shayanne.

"What the hell, Willow?" Shayanne yells.

My shoulders climb up an inch and my head drops an inch down. "I'm sorry. So sorry."

The truth is, I'm not sorry. Not really. It hurts, I hate it, and I wish it hadn't been the only way, but I don't regret what I did. It's for Bobby's own good. One day, they'll all see that and understand.

But I can't explain that. I won't tell them about Jeremy's visit, about how Bobby lied to us all.

I know that deep down, they love Bobby and are doing what they feel is right to protect him. I wish they could see that I'm on their side.

I love him. I'm protecting him too.

"Is it true? Did he really leave last night?"

I'm as bad as the gossipy lunch ladies from earlier, but I have to know. Did he go to Nashville that easily?

Brody snorts. "Fuck yeah, he did. Climbed in his truck with his pants undone and no shirt on—good thing we've all got extras stashed—and peeled out of the driveway in a cloud of dust. Thought he was chasing you down, but he texted this morning. Said he was almost there and would be in touch."

I sigh in relief. He's okay. He's in Nashville or almost is. He'll probably have a record deal signed with NCR by the end of the day. His dream will come true in no time.

"Thank you for telling me," I say quietly.

"Won't be telling you shit anymore. That's for damn sure." Brody's eyes narrow. "Though that won't be a problem since you're leaving town too."

I guess he heard that part last night.

"Yeah. I don't know how soon, but . . ." I stammer, trying to find a way to explain something I hadn't even really considered doing. I don't want to go home.

I am home!

Even without Bobby, this town, and these people, this life has become my home. One I never thought I'd have, one I certainly didn't expect to find here that first day as I drove in. But fate knew better, putting me right where I belong.

Great Falls. Home. Just missing the one person who makes it warm and filled with love.

"Yeah," I finish lamely.

Brody picks up his beer, chugs it, and lays a twenty on the table. "We'd better get home before Mama Louise gets dinner on the table. Bye, Willow."

It sounds like a last goodbye.

The rest of them follow suit, giving me sad smiles or small waves before following Brody. Except Shayanne.

She leans over the bar, arms reaching for me. I flinch, absolutely certain she's going to choke me or hit me or something painful. I'm right . . . she hugs me tightly, hissing in my ear, "I am so fucking mad at you. Don't be a stranger, girl."

Then they're gone.

Richard lifts an eyebrow my way, having not interfered in any of that. Some bar security he is! I give him the smallest hint of a smile, letting him know I'm okay.

Around dinner rush time, Unc shows up and claims a table for the Sunday night poker game. Doc Jones is close behind with a jar full of coins in his arms, and the three of them get down to business. It looks like it's a Texas Hold 'Em night.

Olivia keeps everything running for the rest of the evening. I guess I help, but I don't really remember any of it.

* * *

THE KNOCK on my door is loud, so loud it wakes me up from a dead sleep. Bleary-eyed, I make my way to the door, swinging it open grumpily. "What?"

"Rise and shine, girl. The day's half over." Unc sounds entirely too chipper and way too awake, considering it's not even noon.

"What are you doing here?" That's what I mean to say, but it comes out jumbled and broken from my scratchy throat.

"Thought you might want to talk about what happened. Even brought bribes." He holds up a white bag that I know holds Darla's doughnuts and a cup of coffee that I can smell from here. Strong caffeine and sugar overload . . . party of one.

I grab for the goodies, giving Unc my back and assuming he'll follow me into the kitchen. He does, closing the door behind himself.

I grab a plate and open the bag. "You didn't want a bear claw?"

He shakes his head. "Nah, I ate a couple of doughnut holes. That was more than enough for me." He pats his flat belly. "But I had some oatmeal this morning, Mom."

The small joke does lift my lips. He knows I'm always keeping track of him to make sure he's eating and drinking enough every day and doesn't look too tired or seem too pale.

"You wanna talk about it?"

Straight to the core, no tip-toeing around for Unc. No way, that's not his style.

"I can't."

No one can know why I did what I did, what I gave up so that Bobby can have his dream come true. That's between me and the jagged shards of my heart.

Unc grunts, looking disappointed. I bet he thought the doughnut and coffee treatment would get me to spill my guts. In any other situation, it probably would.

"Fine. Keep your business to yourself. Of anyone, I can damn sure understand that." Somehow, he has managed to keep his cancer diagnosis out of the grapevine. As far as I know, the only people who know are him, Doc Jones, Mom, and me.

"Thanks."

"Wanna know what I've learned?" He doesn't wait for me to

answer but keeps right on rolling. "When it gets bad and you want to lay down and die, because at least then you wouldn't be in pain, you need a distraction. Like how they get women in labor to do all that huffing and puffing." He demonstrates, filling his cheeks and making a hee-hoo-hee-hoo breathy sound. "Don't know if it does anything special for the baby, but it gives the mama something to do. Distraction." He nods like he's made some groundbreaking discovery. "So, you wanna go fishing with me?"

"Fishing?"

Why in the world would he think fishing would distract me? The idea of sitting still on a boat in the middle of the lake, being quiet so I don't disturb the fish, sounds like the exact opposite of what I need. Out there, I won't have anything to do but listen to my screaming heart.

"Yeah . . . fishing," he repeats with new emphasis. I realize what he's actually asking and murmur my recognition. Quietly, though no one's here but us, he says, "I've got a checkup in an hour. Come with me."

All the stuff with Bobby and my broken spirit freezes. Unc needs me. He needs me so much that he's asking outright for me to go with him. I can thaw out my mess later, cry some more, and remind myself why I did it. But right now, Unc's appointment is the distraction I need. And I'm the help he needs.

I shove the rest of the pink doughnut with sprinkles into my mouth, mumbling around it, "Give me five and I'm ready."

* * *

I EXPECTED to sit in a patient room with Unc since he called this a check-up. But we're in the doctor's small office, seated in two chairs with our knees nearly bumping against the front of the desk. The artwork on the walls draws my attention, as usual. It's bland, boring, and abstract. Its primary purpose is to be unoffensive, forgettable, a simple space filler. Mom would hate it. I do too. Its emptiness reminds me of my own, devoid of meaning.

That's not true, Willow. Don't be so dramatic. I'm not meaningless, I'm just Bobby-less.

Same difference, it feels like.

Unc reaches over and takes my hand. His palm is soft, but the remnants of calluses remain from his years of hard work. The skin feels paper thin, his bony knuckles prominent. I grip him tightly, needing to believe that he's okay and that we have time. I'm thankful that I'm here.

The door opens and a white-coated man walks in. He's younger than I'd expected for some reason, probably in his early forties at most, with perfectly combed hair, reading glasses on the tip of his nose, and kind eyes. He must both love and hate his job as an oncologist, being the bearer of both prayed-for good news and life-ending news.

He's got a poker face that could match Unc's, not clueing me in about today's appointment.

He sits down in the leather executive chair behind the desk, flipping through the papers in the folder he holds. "How're you feeling, Hank?"

Unc shrugs. "Guess that depends on what you tell me, Doc."

The doctor smiles at the gruff answer. "Fair enough. Let's go over your numbers . . ."

He launches into a spiel of numbers and acronyms that don't mean anything to me. He might as well be speaking another language. Well, I guess he is. He's speaking Doctor-ese, or Cancer-ese, or something else that only some people understand.

Unc nods along, seeming to get it.

"I'm sorry," I interrupt, "but I have no idea what any of that means. Can you spell it out for those of us without M.D.s?"

The doctor smiles serenely, looking from me to Unc, who gives a grunt of permission. "Of course. You must be Willow?" I nod, surprised he knows that. He's too far out from Great Falls to be part of the gossip chain, so Unc must've mentioned me. "What it boils down to is . . . it's working. Hank's cancer is responding to the meds, so his blood levels look better than they have since he first came to me. The latest scan shows improvement too."

I sigh in relief. "So he's okay?"

The doctor's head tilts in a way that reminds me of a curious dog. "Well, not yet. But he's well down the road there, and I think the worst of it is past us." To Unc, he says, "Stay the course. Keep taking your meds, rest when you need to, eat nutrient-dense food that stays down, and keep your appointments. We'll do a full-panel blood check again in two weeks, but call me in the meantime if anything changes. If you go more than twenty-four hours without keeping food down, feel like something's off, or have any questions or concerns, I'm only a phone call away, anytime, day or night."

Unc chuckles. "I'll hold you to that, Doc. You know the hours I keep."

They laugh like that's a long-running joke between the two of them, and Unc stands to shake the doctor's hand. "You sure I can't talk you into coming by for a hand or two?"

The doctor laughs even harder, shaking his head. "No way. I didn't forget that you're a card shark. I like my money where it belongs, in my wallet, not yours. Nice to meet you, Willow. You two can head up to the front when you're ready."

And with that, the doctor leaves us alone. Unc sinks back down to the chair.

"Well, I'll be damned," he mutters, a vacant look in his eyes.

I smile, taking his hand again. "That's good news." Maybe he didn't hear that? Or it hasn't sunk in yet?

"It's better news than I imagined. I've been feeling better, a little bit, mind you, but I thought maybe it was the calm before the storm. You know how people get a surge of energy sometimes right before they die, like God knows they need to handle their shit so it's not stacked on someone else's shoulders? But maybe I'm just . . . feeling better." His voice gets softer, losing the gruff edge it usually has. "I'm better."

Tears spring forth again, and this time, they're happy tears. Why our eyes leak for every emotion on the spectrum—happy, sad, mad, surprised—I'll never know, but the overwhelming joy runs down my face into my smile.

"You're better," I parrot.

Unc looks to me, his eyes suddenly bloodshot and blinking rapidly. He's fighting his tears, too stubborn to let them flow.

"I couldn't have done this without you. You know that, right?" he says.

"I did what family does, Unc," I tell him with as much

emotion as I can risk right now. "I'm happy to help, just glad it made a difference."

"Picking up from their life and moving to a town where they don't know a soul, other than a grumpy old man, is not something people do," Unc corrects me. "But you did. I want you to know how much I appreciate it, Willow-girl. It means a lot to me, and I'm damn glad you took it upon yourself to fix what I broke so long ago." He pats my hand, and I know how hard it is for him to say those words.

He's a hard man, much like his brother, but Unc is different. He's willing to be soft when he needs to. I don't know if he was always that way or if it's a newfound clarity found in his looming mortality. But he'll speak his heart when it's needed. I can appreciate that because I do it all the time, and I know how vulnerable it makes you feel. So I give him the out he needs to back away from the dangerous territory he's dancing around, "Well, Doc Jones should probably get some of that thanks. I wouldn't have known you needed me if he hadn't called Mom."

Unc grins devilishly. "You haven't told him that I know that, have you?"

"*No?*" I drawl out slowly.

"Good. Haven't gotten my pound of flesh outta him yet," Unc says, laughing. I'm reasonably certain he means it, though, and I wonder how much he's taken from Doc's coin jar. Card shark, indeed.

I swat at his shoulder, truly smiling for the first time in a couple of days. "You're awful!"

His shrug says he won't argue with that. "Look, Willow . . . I might be better, and I hope to get even better than this." He gestures to his baggy jeans, white T-shirt with a Ford logo on it, and his old boots. He doesn't mean his clothes, though. He means what's inside him, the battle he's still fighting on a cellular level.

"But I'm getting old—don't tell anyone I admitted that or I'll have your hide." He glares for a split second before his expression softens again. "Having you here has been nice, knowing that I could leave the bar in good hands if I needed the day off or wanted to go fishing. Like, actually fishing." He suddenly beams brightly. "I tell you I caught a ten-pound trout last week?"

"No. Is that good? Big? Small? I have no idea."

He shakes his head mournfully. "See, that's what I mean. I need to take you fishing, show you how it's done. I've skimped on my duties as your uncle and not taught you things I'm supposed to." He pauses, swallowing thickly. "I guess what I'm asking is . . . will you stay? Here in Great Falls? At the bar? With me?"

I blink, knowing what that question cost him. The man who wants to stand alone, independent to a fault and grumpy beyond reason. But he wants me to stay and help.

I nod but then shake my head. "I don't . . . did you hear about . . . ?"

Unc's lips press into a thin line, making the lines that foretell of his years of smoking stand out. "I know something happened with you and Bobby, and I'm damn sorry. That pretty little heart of yours doesn't deserve to hurt, ever. But even though that didn't go the way any of us thought it was going to, would you still move out here? I don't trust the bar to anyone but you." He smiles, lightening the moment. "Well, Olivia, maybe. But don't you tell her I said that, either. Besides, you're family, so you get dibs."

"I don't know. It's all so fast, and right now, it's . . . hard to imagine being here without him."

"I can understand that. I love you, Willow-girl. No matter where you are, you'll always have a place to come home to. I just hope it's six days a week, lunch to close, with the occasional day off for fishing or whatever it is you young'uns call it these days." He does the air-quote thing with his fingers, not bending them in the slightest, which makes me smile.

"I love you too, Unc. Let me think about it, okay?"

* * *

AFTER UNC DROPS ME OFF, I can't keep still. He's right. What I needed was a distraction, and he has definitely offered a big one to keep my mind occupied.

Can I officially move to Great Falls forever?

What would that look like after my short-term lease is up? I'm sure I could renew it and stay, though I'd definitely take over the rent from Mom since this time, it'd be my choice to stay.

Can I afford that? Between my wages at Hank's and my blog profits, I definitely can and then some.

My blog. I'd been so nervous that the new surroundings would go over like a lead balloon. Who wants to see a picture of the same mountain day after day? But my following has increased with every picture of that mountain, Shayanne's goats, Darla's doughnuts, sunrise and sunset, and what my life in Great Falls is like. Every little detail seems to intrigue people. City life can be beautiful, no doubt about that, but country life has a different ease about it that calls to people's wanderlust, making them wish for an opportunity like the one I've got. And my hits, comments, and likes reflect that.

But it's not all sunshine and rainbows, as much as I'd like to wish it were.

If I stay, there will be no Bobby. The Tannens and Bennetts, people whom I'd felt comfortable with, something I so rarely feel, are furious with me.

And I'm the biggest subject of the local grapevine, either the one who ran Bobby off or who was left in his wake, depending on which version of gossip you choose to believe.

I'll miss Mom and Dad, and Oakley too. They're all back in the city.

It's a big decision, one with both pain and joy no matter which way I land.

City or country?

The home I knew, or the home I've found?

Mindlessly, I find myself flipping through my photo files. A picture of Main Street with the sun setting—beautiful. A shot with the city nightlife vibrant and energetic—stunning. Unc's wrinkled face smiling back at me—my heart squeezes. An old shot of Mom and Dad, taken years before Oakley and I were born—love in their eyes and innocent dreams in their future.

The next click of the mouse takes me to the pictures I took on that first day at the farm. Bobby holding Trollie, the picture I'd cropped in close for the blog so that I didn't share Bobby with the world. He was mine, if only for a little while. Soon, he'll belong to them all. Brody and Brutal messing around with Cooper in the light of the fire between cornhole games. Mark and Katelyn, heads bent close together, whispering something only they could hear. Mama Louise watching over the whole scene like the queen of her country castle.

And on and on. I'd taken dozens of photos that day and night.

Then, I find the photo shoot with the girls. Smiles, laughter, sisterhood in every shot.

Instantly, I know one thing I have to do, even if I don't have all the answers just yet.

I spend the next couple of hours editing the photos of the Tannens and Bennetts. I print them on the huge printer I brought with me from the city, back when I'd figured some podunk town wouldn't have decent professional photography printing options. This machine was something I couldn't leave behind in my old life, and now I'm glad it's here in my time of desperate need because I'd been right about the printing here. Only the drugstore has a machine that can do same-day printing. Otherwise, it's all online and wait for shipping. And I can't wait, not even a single day.

I print each shot, perfect and pristine, real and raw. Laying them in gift boxes, I separate them with tissue paper so they're protected on their journey. One bigger box for Mama Louise, and smaller boxes for each woman with her private pictures. I find a shirt I don't wear anymore and cut it to shreds, using it as a makeshift bow around the stack of boxes.

Thirty minutes later, before I can second guess myself again, I'm pulling up to the Bennett house. It's late afternoon, well before dinner time, so I shouldn't have to see the Tannens or Bennetts. Except for the one I'm here to see.

I step on the porch and knock with the toe of my tennis shoe, my arms too full to ring the bell properly.

Through the screen door, I see Mama Louise's head pop around the corner from the kitchen. "Willow?" She hurries toward the door. "I wondered who in the world was knocking on my door and not waltzing on in like everyone always does. Come on in, dear."

Her smile is welcoming, as if she doesn't know that everything has changed. But she must know. This family is too close to keep secrets. The whole town is too close for secrets.

"Hi. Sorry to stop by unannounced, but I wanted to . . ." I clear my throat, not sure what I was going to say. Finally, I shove the boxes her way. "Here."

Her brow furrows, and she wipes her hands on her jeans. "What's this?"

"They're for you, for all of you. Well, except the ones that are for each girl. Those are private."

"Oh," Mama Louise says, smiling as if she knows exactly what's in those pictures. Actually, she might. The girls might've told her about our boudoir shoot too. Or maybe she just knows, the way she knows everything—like she plucks it out of your brain without your saying a single word.

"Can I open them now?" she asks, eyeing the ribbon like a kid on Christmas morning.

I shake my head vehemently. "No, please. I can't . . . I don't want to . . . Just . . . wait, okay?" I stammer, unable to explain that while I was editing, I could look at them with an objective eye, not letting my heart get too involved. But seeing them here, in this house, through Mama Louise's eyes, is something I don't think I'm strong enough to handle right now.

"Sure, dear. Of course. Sit down and let me get you some watermelon fresca. It's Shay's recipe, sells out every time she makes a batch."

You can't say no to Mama Louise. Or at least I can't. So I find myself sinking into a chair at the small kitchen table as she grabs two glasses and fills them with pink liquid from a jug in the refrigerator.

She sits down beside me and takes a healthy drink, sighing loudly, "Ahh, that's good stuff. Been out in the barn this morning helping Luke muck out stalls, so this hits the spot."

Small talk. Bless this amazing woman, she's letting me hide the way I want to.

"I'm sure he appreciated the help."

"Stubborn men always do, even though they're not good at telling you so." For some reason, I get the feeling she's talking about Unc more than about Luke. "Though Luke isn't my most stubborn boy, by far."

I smile, trying to decide which Bennett man she's talking about. Or Tannen, I guess. She doesn't seem to differentiate. They're all her kids to care for, even if they're six-foot-plus tall, wide as a doorway men who can handle themselves just fine. They're still her boys.

"Love them all, each and every one, I do," she murmurs around another sip. I get the feeling she's dancing me the direction she wants to go, taking this conversation to a destination she wants regardless of whether I want to discuss it or not.

I hum in agreement, not fighting her resolve. Get this over with, Mama Louise. Yell at me, tell me how disappointed you are, whatever it is . . . rip the Band-Aid off so I can leave and lick my fresh wounds again.

"You know the funny thing about love?"

I don't respond, thinking there's not a single thing funny about love right now. It's the highest high and the lowest low, all wrapped up in one big shredded T-shirt bow.

"People think it's something you feel, an emotion. A noun. Like you love football or your husband or pepperoni pizza."

How does she know I love pepperoni pizza? Oh, she's not talking about me, specifically. Or is she? She does know everything.

When I don't respond, she speaks again. "It's not. Or at least, it's not only that. Love is something you do. A verb. It's in every action, reaction. My husband, John, worked this land every single day to make a life for us. That was love—every head of cattle he bought and sold, every fence he fixed, every bead of sweat he earned through his dedication was a love note to me, to our boys. In return, every meal I made, every load of his dirty clothes I washed, and every sunrise I saw after hours of being up to get the day started was my love note to him. There were other ways we loved each other too. But make no mistake, the day in, day out of love was in the action, the verb of doing something for each other, to take care of one another. We were in this thing called life together. I still write those notes to him, making meals for our family, taking care of his land and cattle, watering that damn tree out front because I can't bear to ever see it wither and don't trust the rain enough to take care of it the way I will."

Mama Louise's blue eyes are bright with unshed tears as she glances toward the front of the house. There is a tree out front, but I didn't realize it had any special meaning for her. I even took a picture of its branches filled with green leaves with pockets of blue sky peeking through. It's in that box on the table. It'd seemed like a pretty shot, and if I'd posted it to my blog, I would've added something witty about a seed growing tall and mighty. Now, I'm glad I didn't. I'm glad that shot is just for Mama Louise and that it'll mean something to her.

"It sounds like John was a great man, a great husband," I say tentatively. I still feel like we're dancing, but I can't see the trail she's leading me down.

"He was. Full of love, full of kindness, full of heart. A lot like you, Willow. I don't need to know the details of what happened. That's between you and Bobby. But know that sometimes love, the verb, I mean, is hard to do, but you do it anyway."

Does she think Bobby broke up with me and I'm supposed to love him anyway?

Does she know I sent him off to Nashville, and she's telling me she understands why I did it?

I don't know.

Hell, maybe this is her way of getting gossip straight from the source, though I don't think she's the type at all.

The oven timer dings, breaking the moment. "Oh, that's dinner. Can you stay?" she asks.

"No. Actually, I'd better be going." I don't want to be here when everyone comes in to eat after a long day. "Tell everyone I hope they like them," I say, lifting my head toward the boxes.

She sets the casserole dish on the stovetop and comes over to hug me, oven mitts and all. "You take care of yourself, Willow. You're so good at taking care of everyone else, don't forget to take care of you too." She eyes me, daring me to disobey. Somehow, I think she'll know if I don't follow her order.

"I will. Bye, Mama Louise."

I'm out the door and halfway to town before the tears come again. I'll miss her and that whole family.

I stop by Unc's house, noting that the flower beds look pretty good. I wonder if Unc was feeling well enough to get out here and weed them? Or maybe Bobby stopped by one day without mentioning it?

I knock on the door and Unc answers quickly. He's moving pretty well, not even limping today as he leads me into the living room.

"I can only stay a second, but I wanted to let you know . . ."

CHAPTER 24

BOBBY

"I'm here to see Jeremy Marshall," I tell the receptionist.

"Do you have an appointment?" Her tone is snippy, like I'm beneath her.

"No. Tell him Bobby Tannen is here, please."

My name doesn't mean shit, especially here. And after last week's phone call where I told a shocked Jeremy that I was turning down his offer, he might not want to see me at all. But I hope he does.

I drove all night into this morning to get here. I slept for a few hours in a truck stop parking lot and dug a fresh shirt out of the backseat of my truck. By fresh, I mean clean, not unwrinkled. Despite the receptionist's lingering glances, I know I look like hell. I feel even worse.

Not exactly how I thought signing a contract was going to go, but here I am.

The receptionist hangs up the phone. "He'll be with you in a moment." Almost as soon as the words leave her lips, the door opens.

"Bobby! Good to see you, man! You reconsider our offer?"

He's excited, eager, even hungry. I can feel it in his handshake, see it in his eyes.

"I am reconsidering," I give him. I'm still not sure how I got here.

"Excellent." His smile beams, blindingly white and straight. "Let's sit down and go over things. Right this way." He throws a hand out, leading me through the doorway. I can feel the receptionist's eyes on my ass as I walk through. I glance back and catch her red-handed, but instead of looking caught, she smiles coyly and lifts one brow.

A growl tries to rattle in my chest. I don't want her to look at me like that. I only want Willow's eyes on me that way.

She owns me—body, mind, heart, and soul. Whether she wants me or not.

Jeremy invites me to sit in his office, not the conference room this time. He opens a small silver door on a credenza, a hidden mini-fridge, and hands me a cold water. "Looks like you've had a long day already," he says, still smiling that too-bright smile.

"Drove in last night. Slept in my truck," I explain, wiping a palm over my shirt to smooth the creases. It doesn't work, it just leaves a trail of condensation along my belly. I look at my hand, not realizing that it was even damp from the bottle of water, and wipe it on my jeans-covered thigh.

"Oh, no. We'll get you a hotel for tonight. No worries about that, man. What else do you need?"

"Nothing," I grunt. "I'm pretty low-maintenance. I'll grab a few T-shirts from Walmart later. That'll get me through."

His lips quiver, though he's fighting it. He's laughing at me.

"What?" I growl.

"Nothing," he says, letting loose that chuckle that makes me feel like a damned fool. "You're just not what I'm used to. Most guys come out here and expect to be wined and dined like they're special when they're not. You actually are special, and you don't give a shit about the bells and whistles. It's refreshing."

"Okay." I don't know what to say to that. I am who I am, what I am, a farmer who can sing a bit and write songs, which wasn't good enough for him in the first place.

"So, the contract?" Jeremy opens a drawer in his desk, flipping through folders just like I thought he'd have. Each one contains someone's dream, and he keeps them filed away like paper airplanes that'll never fly, never feel the rush of air, never come crashing back down to Earth painfully crunched and broken.

Dramatic much, asshole?

He finds the one with my name on it, pulling it out. "Here we go. Are you ready to sign? NCR Records is ready to be your new home, Bobby. I think we can make some beautiful music together."

Cheese spillage, aisle three. How many people has he said that to? How many of them actually bought it?

I stare at the contact, the black dots of the words marching around like ants on the white paper. Signing it feels so final, like the end of something instead of the beginning. Putting my John Hancock on that page is the nail in the coffin for me and Willow, an acknowledgement that it's over, and the end of Bobby Tannen, farmer. Once I sign, I'll be Bobby Tannen, country singer.

It's what I've always wanted, what I've dreamed of. So why does it feel so empty?

Jeremy holds out a pen that I don't take. "Can I read it over again? You told me to have a lawyer look at it, and I'm afraid to say I never did. Once you said that stuff about Willow, I never thought I'd be sitting here. So, I should probably do some due diligence so we both know what we're getting into."

A look of disappointment flashes through Jeremy's eyes, so quick it's gone in an instant. He leans forward, elbows on his desk. "Sure, good thinking. I like that you're not just another pretty face."

I have never been called pretty. Handsome, attractive, fuckable . . . sure. Pretty? No.

"Let's do this. We'll get you a room so you can rest and get cleaned up. I'll send a car by and we'll hit the Bar again tonight. You can listen to other folks, or I can arrange for you to sing if you'd like? You have any new songs? I can set you up with Miller again. I know you liked working with him."

I agree woodenly, the contrast to his excitement obvious. It should be the other way around. He's the pro who should be no-big-deal about another contract, and I'm the newbie who should be jumping for joy at his dream coming true. But I don't have it in me.

* * *

I WATCH a kid play guitar like a demon has possessed his fingers on the stage at the Bar. His voice is good, but his playing is like nothing I've ever seen before. Kid can't be more than nineteen, blond and sweet-looking, but you can tell the music infects him like it does me. He's exciting to watch.

"He's good," I murmur to myself. Jeremy hears me loud and clear.

"You like him? We could see if he's interested in a guitarist position for your band. I don't usually pull guys who want to be solo acts, but his vocals would be a good contrast to yours. I'll get his name and see if he has representation yet."

All that because I said the kid's good.

After that, I keep my mouth shut.

I don't get on stage at the Bar that night. The demon in my gut is screaming loudly, wanting the outlet desperately, but I'm afraid I'll slit myself open too wide and let everything I'm feeling leak out. Vulnerable is one thing, completely and utterly defenseless quite another.

* * *

MILLER IS ALREADY BOOKED, so I have the whole day to myself. Jeremy tried to fill the time with sightseeing tours, as if a trip to the Country Music Hall of Fame is going to keep me in town. He even mentioned getting me a personal tour guide if I wanted. I felt like that was a roundabout way of asking if I needed any company.

I angrily turned him down outright, telling him I'd take the day to write and have something new for Miller tomorrow.

That had appeased him, both that I'm feeling creative and that I'm not leaving town.

Hours later, I'm stuck. This song had poured forth initially, angry, fresh lines of pain, but it needs resolution and I don't have one. Not for the song, not for myself.

I look around the hotel room. That first trip out here, it'd seemed fancy—a sign that I was on my way, that I was going to make it big.

Now, it seems so temporary. Like everything else.

Nothing about this contract deal, this dream feels the way I thought it would. It's not as awesome as I thought it'd be. It doesn't feel exciting and happy. It feels . . .

Meaningless without Willow.

Fuck, I even miss my asshole brothers and the Bennetts. I miss nightly cornhole tournaments and Shayanne's pot roast putting us on edge to figure out what she's up to this time.

I look at the room service menu, searching for pot roast for even a small taste of home. But there's nothing that unsophisticated on the list of dinner options. It's all filet mignon and haricots verts. A quick Google search tells me that's steak and green beans, so why don't they just say so? Even room service isn't all it's cracked up to be.

I let the boredom distract me, staring out the window at the lights for a while and watching some stupid television show where I don't even know what's happening.

I send Brutal a text.

Me: Hey asshole. You check the east pasture?

Brotherly talk for I miss you, are you okay doing your work and mine? It takes a long fifteen minutes for him to respond.

Brutal: Yep. East and did two rows on the southern end too.

Translation, I'm fine. You do what you need to because I've got you covered.

Me: Good work.

I love you.

Brutal: Head in the game, man.

I love you too.

I take his words and his meaning to heart. I have work to do and need to stay focused. This isn't a done deal, for me or Jeremy. At any moment, he could decide that wining and dining me isn't worth his time if I'm not signing that dotted line. So I'd better make sure he still wants me and all that I bring to the table.

I sit on the couch, pulling the coffee table over and re-reading the lyrics I've written so far. I pick up the pen, painfully ripping my soul open to let it pour onto the page.

* * *

Gave you everything, I was yours.
Took your heart because you were mine.
Standing in the tatters that you left behind,
I still love you.

"HOLY SHIT, BOBBY. THAT'S . . . WOW!" Miller breathes out with a wide smile.

The song is slow, plucked chords resonating around notes held until my voice breaks. Until I break.

Miller looks at Jeremy, who's standing over him like a hawk. "We'll do another take to be sure, but I think we got it in one."

Jeremy laughs, jabbing the intercom button. "Goddamn, kid. I guess what they say is true . . . a broken heart is the best inspiration! You're going to be a big hit. You're the real deal, Bobby."

"Play it back again. Let me hear it," he tells Miller. I join them in the booth. The speakers are better in here.

The playback starts, and I hear myself, every note full of pain and heartbreak. Jeremy shakes his head. "Damn, that's good. I can't believe she actually did it. She didn't seem strong enough, figured she'd be hanging on your coattails as long as she could."

He laughs like he said something funny.

"What?"

I have no idea what Jeremy is talking about, but a stone has settled in my stomach. Something's wrong, my instincts yell.

"The girl . . . what was her name? Willa? Winnie? The blonde with glasses." He makes circles with his fingers, laying them over his eyes like glasses.

"Willow?" I growl. "When did you talk to her?"

Jeremy must sense the danger zone he's stumbled into because he stammers, his smile fading quickly. "Uh, that first night I heard you play. She was behind the bar, and I asked her who you were."

That rings false, even though I know that happened. There's more, I can feel it in his need to back away from this conversation.

"And then?"

Jeremy finds his balls, tucked up somewhere in those khaki pants. "Well, you couldn't very well expect me to let a talent like yours go without a fight. I came back out there to track your ungrateful ass down. The girl—"

"Willow," I correct.

He rolls his eyes dismissively, "Fine . . . Willow didn't seem to know about your turning the deal down. She seemed to think I didn't offer you one. I told her what you'd done and she said she'd take care of it for you. I didn't figure she had it in her. Girl like that, and a guy like you, she had to know it was only a matter of time for you to realize you could do better." He scoffs like that's an obvious conclusion when it's anything but. He even smiles like we're good ol' boy buddies and he's not the asshole who fucked up my life.

Red slashes across my vision and my fist flies through the air before I even intentionally make a fist.

Pop!

Jeremy's jaw makes a loud sound as the punch lands. It's a good thing those teeth are all cemented in or I would've knocked one or two out.

I grab his shirt, twisting it in my fist and lifting him up.

"You manipulative son of a bitch. You had no right! I made my choice and you fucked it up." I'm yelling in Jeremy's face, which has gone pale, spitting out the pain he caused, raging with the sharp loss again as though it's new and fresh, not days old.

Miller touches my arm. "Let's all calm down here. Take a breath, man." He's using some soothing, chanting voice I haven't heard from him before. He must have experience talking down crazed musicians because shockingly, it works.

All the puzzle pieces click together in an instant.

The most important of which is . . .

She's mine and I fucking lost her.

Fuck. Fuck. Fuck.

I drop Jeremy to the floor, running toward the door. I don't stop by the hotel, don't need any of that shit. I need to get home.

Now.

Hang on, Willow. I'm coming for you, sweetheart. And we've got some shit to get straight right the fuck now.

Number one, you're mine.

Number two, I'm yours.

Number three, nothing else matters.

CHAPTER 25

BOBBY

I drive all night, fueled by endless energy drinks and total terror. I can only imagine what Jeremy must've said to her. That's what was wrong, why she pulled away from me and told me to go to Nashville. She knew I'd turned Jeremy down for her, and for some damn reason, she thought sending me away and running back to the city was what needed to happen.

His cocky predator's grin, enjoying breaking her heart, flashes in my head. Her face falling in hurt shock. I create scenarios again and again of how that conversation might've gone and get angrier with each replay.

How did I miss this?

Because while Jeremy fucking Marshall deserved that punch, the person who should be getting his ass kicked is me. I was the one who fucked it up by not being honest with her. I ruined it. I didn't protect her.

Instead, she protected me. From myself.

Fuck that.

I'm going home, gonna grab her by that sweet little ass, kiss the fuck out of her, and show her what love is. For the rest of our lives, if she'll let me.

Don't give up on me. Surrender to us. Nothing else matters outside the world we create.

I finally make it back to Great Falls and Hank's late on Thursday afternoon, my hand still aching from punching Jeremy. I've driven straight through and feel like hell, but I couldn't stop, wouldn't stop until I made it to Willow. The gravel in the lot crunches under my boots as I stride toward the door, my heart frozen in my chest.

"Willow!" I yell over the door's creak.

Inside, my eyes adjust from the sunlight, and I see a few faces looking at me in shock from the sudden and loud entrance. The customers don't matter to me, and I run for the bar, looking for her.

She's not there.

Hank calmly and casually sets his Louisville Slugger on the bar, a quiet threat. "You've got a lotta nerve showing your face in here. Think you're some big-shot deal now? Come to rub our faces in your record deal while I've been here cleaning up the mess you left behind you on your way to Nashville?" The slow drawl is not a sign that he's calm and casual. It's designed to give every barbed word accurate aim for maximum destruction. He succeeds, and my heart bleeds out into my chest, making it tight enough to choke me.

The mess I made? I would've never left if she hadn't left me!

Fury boils up. He's standing between me and Willow and I can't allow that. I don't want to hit Hank, so I do something more difficult than relaxing my clenched hands. I search for words. "She told me to go! Said she was going back home to the city! I didn't know Jeremy had told her fuck-knows-what about the deal."

He eyes me, cool as a cucumber for a long second where he holds my fate in his hands.

"Fuck!" I roar but immediately deflate, all my fight draining away until I'm nothing but an empty shell. "I didn't know. I turned it down for her. I love her."

Hank releases his grip on the bat and rests his hands on the bar. He doesn't even have a bandage on the cut from the screwdriver anymore. It's healed over. I don't think this gash in my heart will ever heal, though. It's too deep, too wide.

"All that girl ever did was love and support you," he tells me, blue eyes narrowed as he studies me like he doesn't get what she sees in me. "You ever see her do one single thing for herself? No," he scoffs, "that ain't who Willow is. She's got the prettiest, kindest, most giving heart I've ever seen. She's a damn angel, and you . . ." He gives up on that description, just growling at me instead. I've never felt like less of a man, less worthy of even breathing the same oxygen as Willow than I do right now.

"I know! I don't deserve her, but fuck, I want her. I love her," I repeat uselessly, sagging to the closest barstool.

Every eye in the place is watching me fall apart. I don't give a shit. They're gonna see way worse if I don't get her back. This is the beginning of my end.

Ironically, I feel like the one person I never understood. My dad. He was ugly, mean, raging at the world, and empty inside after Mom died. Now I understand all too well because I could burn everything down, myself included, and it would be a relief to stop this sharp, never-ending pain. The only cure is her or death. And if she's not an option . . .

I slam my fist to the bar. The thunderous sound echoes through the room, which has gone utterly still and quiet.

Hank hollers to the people, waving a hand dismissively. "Go on about your business and leave us to ours." Their heads drop back to their plates, but you can be damn sure they're still peeking up to watch the show.

Quieter, just between us, he confides slowly, "She left her whole life behind to come here and *take care* of my grumpy, grudge-holding ass because that's who she is."

He looks at me pointedly, and moments fall into place in my cloudy mind. I realize what he's saying by not saying it. Just as quietly, I ask, "You okay?"

He dips his chin. "Getting there. But this ain't about me, it's about you. Willow told you to go, did that for you, you dumbass. She shoved a knife in her own gut, broke her heart and yours, so that you could have the dream she knew you wanted. Because that's what she does . . . everything for everybody else. She dips into her own soul and scoops it out so everything around her is damn near glittery with her shine."

I nod morosely. "I know." He makes a snorting sound of disbelief, and I find the balls to look him in the eye and repeat stronger, "I know."

"I thought maybe, just maybe, you'd be the one person who would see what she does and take care of her for a change. Lord knows, I haven't had the energy to. I'm as bad as you are—take, take, take. At least I had a respectable reason."

The judgement is clear. I've lost Hank's respect. But I'll earn it back the same way I'll earn Willow back. By doing whatever it takes.

"Where is she?" I beg.

"Gone," he sighs. "Went home to her parents."

"Tell me where. Please."

* * *

Following the directions my phone calls out, I turn through street after street. It's not as big as Nashville, but there's so much of everything. The sights, sounds, and smells are overwhelming.

How could she have left this when I know what it all means to her? This is the foundation of her work and what she's always known.

On the other hand, how could she have left Great Falls? It's beautiful in its own quiet way. I know she sees that because it's reflected in her photography. Oh, yeah, I've been creeping on her blog like an addict looking for a fix. I damn near jacked off to a picture of her ankles the other day because I could imagine my hands working their way up from those bony bits to the lush, firm muscles of her legs and the heaven between them. But I'd forced myself to keep scrolling, needing more and more of her, wanting to know where she'd been that day, what she'd done, and who she might've seen. And the way she captures my hometown is truly special.

How could she leave that? And Hank? It sounds like he still needs her.

Most of all, I fucking need her!

"You have arrived at your destination," the phone drones. I pull into the driveway of the single-story house in the middle of a suburban street. This is definitely Willow's house.

All the other ones are white, beige, bland and nondescript to the point of being interchangeable. This house is blue with pale yellow shutters, a standout in sea of blah, just like Willow. The yard is pristine, a lush green lawn and flower beds with layers of shrubbery and flowers. That must be her dad's doing. And the house numbers are modern, skinny metal but inlaid in a mosaic tile backing. Her mom's artistic touch?

As soon as I can throw the truck in park, I'm out and running for the front door. She's here, I know she is because her little Subaru is parked in the drive too.

I bang on the door too hard, unable to hold myself back when she's so close I can almost sense her. "Willow!" I holler through the wood door, wishing it had a glass window so I could press my nose to it and see inside. I need to see her now.

The door swings open, and I get a quick glimpse of an older version of Willow with longer hair, but then I see her . . . my Willow. She's standing in the living room, a mere six feet away. It's too far by a mile.

I lose all control, and any words I thought I was going to say float away like dandelions in the wind. I rush her, grabbing her in my arms. A sound of surprise squeaks out of her, but I don't give her time to say no, covering her mouth with mine.

I steal her breath, wanting it as my own. I take her lips, wanting their brand. I claim her mouth, wanting to kiss only her for the rest of my life.

Completely forgetting where we are and not giving a shit about who else is here, I spin her and push her up against the nearest empty wall. I cup her cheeks in my palms, holding her steady so I can mold her mouth to mine.

I'm proving to myself that she's real and promising her that she's still mine and I'm still hers. Nothing will change that. Not even Jeremy-Fucking-Marshall or any record deal.

"Willow," I murmur against her lips, a plea for her mercy.

Behind us, a small laugh sounds out. "So you must be Bobby?"

I don't move to shake her mom's hand, though I know it's rude. I can't take my eyes from Willow, can't not touch her, though I do drop my hands to her waist, feeding my fingers through the beltloops of her shorts so I can brush along her soft skin. "Yes, ma'am," I answer, my eyes searching Willow's face for some sign of what she's feeling.

Those mood-ring eyes are storming, swirling, seeking something in mine. Whatever it is, it's hers. I'll give her any damn thing she wants unless it's to leave again. I can't give her that. I refuse to.

"I'm Carrie, Willow's mom. I can see what you like about him," Carrie says. I can hear a smile in her voice, so hopefully, I haven't scared her too much by bursting into her house and grabbing her daughter.

Not that I give a fuck as long as Willow doesn't mind.

"Nice to meet you," I reply, still not looking away from Willow. "You left me. You left Hank. You left Great Falls."

She blinks behind her lenses, and I'm acutely aware of her palms resting on my chest. I take a breath, holding it so my chest presses into her touch. I want more of it, need it desperately because it's the only thing keeping my feet grounded right here. If she wasn't touching me, I'd have to gather her in my arms and cover her with my body. But the slightest touch from her, one she chooses to give me, is a powerful drug I want more of. "Well, yeah, I had to come home to get my stuff." Her brows dance up and then down in confusion. "I'm going back."

She makes it sound like that's obvious, but it's not to me.

"I'm moving there so I can help Unc more. He wants to slow down, go fishing with Doc and Richard more often, and kinda slow-step toward eventual retirement. I want to help and spend time with him."

"You're going back?" Out of everything she said, that's what sticks. And I need to be crystal-fucking-clear that's the case so I don't have to keep her locked up in my room on the farm like one of those true crime late-night shows she watches. Because that thought has already occurred to me too. I never claimed to be right in the head, just that I love her.

"Yes?" she answers. "Is that okay?"

"Fuck yeah, it is," I huff out, happiness letting my heart start to beat again. She's coming back to Great Falls. "I'm going back too, and you're coming with me." She just said that, but I need her to hear that there's no other option, no other way.

"I don't want to hold you back. I know what this deal means to you. Do what you need to. I'll be in Great Falls when your big tour bus rolls through town."

She's trying to joke, and I think she actually believes I could do that—go on the road and come through town every once in a while for a visit. That's not remotely possible. I want her by my side every day, in my arms every night. I want to hear what goes through her mind, see what photos she takes, and taste her kiss every chance I get. That won't happen if we're apart, not even for a single day.

"I don't want it without you. I love you, Willow. Every day, every way, always. Fuck knows, I'm a complete mess without you, but I want to see every sunrise and sunset with you, give you bubble baths and doughnuts, and play music while you take pictures until your finger is numb." Words are falling off my tongue, pouring out of my heart, coming easily for once. Thank God, because this is when they matter most. I hope they're enough to make her see what we could have, what I'll give her, if she'll only give me another chance at owning her heart.

"The deal? Your music?" she argues, still not getting it.

"That *was* my dream, but I know what's truly important. You. You're everything, and without you, nothing else fucking matters." I can't stand it. I pull her into me, hugging her tightly. I wish I could climb inside her to make her feel what I feel. Then she'd never doubt that all I want is her. She's all I dream of now. Her cheek pressed to my chest, I run my fingers through her short hair, brushing it behind her ear the way she does. I lay a kiss to the top of her head, whispering, "I can't believe I let you do that. I'm such a fucking idiot for believing for one second that you would leave me because I know you feel this too. You've felt it from the beginning, just like me. I'm sorry I didn't chase you down. I just—"

My words falter, and all I can do is squeeze her, a tidal wave of relief at having her in my arms again washing through me. Her arms go around my waist, hugging me back, and a knot in my gut releases as hope blooms.

Quietly, she says, "I don't want you to regret this later. Regret me. What if you never get another chance like the one Jeremy is giving you? What if you only sing at Hank's for the rest of your life? You're too good for that."

"I could never regret you, sweetheart. I only wish I'd found you sooner so I could've loved you longer. You're amazing and special, and I don't care if the only place I ever play is my tailgate and the only audience I ever have is you and our kids. That's enough for me. You're enough for me. Hell, you're more than enough," I say with a small chuckle. This woman is way too good for me, but I'll do my damnedest to make sure I'm worth her.

"Oh, my God, Willow. If you don't kiss that man, I'm going to," Carrie says, laughing through sniffly tears.

Willow looks over to her mom. I still can't. My eyes are only for Willow until she says yes. Until she says she's mine.

"Tell me, sweetheart."

"I love you, Bobby."

I can see her licking her lips in preparation and feel her lifting to her toes. I try to be patient and let her kiss me this time, but at the last second, I can't wait anymore and I meet her halfway.

Though our lips move against one another the way they have dozens of times before, something is different about this kiss. This kiss is a promise of a shared future, of the two of us against the world, of nothing ever coming between us again.

"I love you too." I murmur the words against her lips, unwilling to stop kissing her but needing to tell her again and again.

After a minute, or hell, maybe it's several, Carrie clears her throat. "Not to break up the lovefest, but obviously, you're welcome to stay for dinner, Bobby. And we don't leave for Great Falls until tomorrow, so I'll get the guest room fixed up for you."

Carrie brushes past us, humming a tune that catches my ear. *You Are My Sunshine*, one of my mom's favorites. It feels like a sign that she's here too and approves of what I'm doing. More likely, it's just a common, popular song, but I prefer to think it's Mom.

"Guest room?" I ask Willow, giving her a cocky grin.

She gives me back one of those soft smiles, and I almost gasp at how beautiful it is. I'm going to spend my whole life making her give me those, saving each and every one like shiny treasures in my pocket. Proof of a woman well-loved and a life well-lived.

"Mom is surprisingly old-fashioned about that." Willow shrugs.

"But not the mauling I just laid down on her daughter in her front room?" I growl out on a laugh.

Willow's eyes go wide, the gray popping behind her lenses. "Oh, my God, she saw all of that!" She buries her face in her hands, but not before I see the blush on her cheeks.

I tilt her chin back up with a light touch of my finger. "I don't give a shit, sweetheart. I'll tell your Mom, your Dad, Hank, the whole damn town how I feel about you. You want me to spray paint it on a water tower or something? I'll do it. Write a song? Done. Name it, because I'm proud to say you're mine."

Her blush has turned heated and she meets my eyes boldly now. "And you're mine."

"Fuck yeah, I am."

* * *

DINNER IS . . . weirdly quiet. I mean, compared to one of our family dinners, most folks' meals probably are.

Carrie and Wayne sit at the head and foot of the table, Oakley and his wife, Madison, on one side, and Willow and me on the other. For six people, the conversation is easy and shockingly, everyone takes turns speaking. Like I said, weirdly quiet when only one person talks at a time instead of us Tannens and Bennetts chattering over each other like impatient toddlers.

They ask me the standard questions, and though I've never been serious enough with anyone to do the 'meet the family' routine, I think I ace them, mostly because I love Willow so they're generously forgiving of my lack of slick, practiced answers.

Wayne asks a lot of questions about the soil composition of the farm, and I tell him how we prep for different crops in different fields, rotating them to keep the soil nutrient-dense. "I'd like to see that, maybe run a few tests if you don't mind?"

I shrug, worried more about keeping my fork moving because

I'm so hungry. "I'll have to check with Mama Louise. It's her land now, but I don't think she'd mind." If Mama Louise says no, I'll promise to weed her entire garden for a year to get a yes because I need to make nice with Willow's dad.

He gives me a nod, looking ready to go right now, and I think I'm on his good side.

Carrie tells Willow about a new exhibit that begins at her gallery, and they talk about composition, lines, and the 'transformative power of space'. I have a moment of panic, not understanding anything they're talking about, but when I look at Wayne, Oakley, and Madison, they seem as lost as I am but are still paying close attention.

They're all passionate people with their own interests, but they find it in their hearts to support each other, listen to one another, and love their individual obsessions because they're family. I can see where Willow gets her kind heart. It was cultivated right here with these people.

"Oh, can I show Bobby your gallery collection in the hallway?" Carrie asks Willow.

Willow smiles, hopping up from the table. "Yeah! Actually, I'm going to go get my yearbook too, show him where it all really started."

"Can I see the doughnut-baby picture too?" I ask, and Willow laughs loud and bright at the memory of our first conversation. Our happiest moments, my getting Betty and her photographing a lady's doughnut baby for her first photography paycheck.

It feels like I met you yesterday. It feels like I've known you forever.

Carrie smiles, getting up from the table. "Let me help you find that yearbook. I can't remember what shelf I put it on."

They head down the hallway but don't go too far, and I overhear Carrie quietly tell Willow, "I'm so proud of you. You went out there for Hank, fixed that, and made a whole new life for yourself. It suits you. I can see how much you've grown while you've been in Great Falls, and I think that man in there has something to do with it. You're bigger, bolder somehow. You always were, but it was like you put a lampshade on your brightness. But now, you're shining bright, sharing that heart you've always had."

Willow clears her throat, and though I can't see her, I know she's got one of her soft smiles gracing her lips.

Carrie might be seeing that change now for the first time, but I've known Willow was sweet, kind, and also strong all along. She's had to be to put up with Hank. Fine, and me too.

Wayne asks another question about pesticide residues, and I let Willow take her time finding the pictures to show me. I'm good here, with her people, especially knowing that we leave tomorrow to go home. Together.

CHAPTER 26

WILLOW

"*You* ready?"

Mom and I are standing beneath the glowing light of the sign outside Hank's. I can't believe that it's only been a few short months since I stood here that first time, nervous about what I'd find inside. Now, I'm ready to get in there and check on Hank, say hi to Olivia, Ilene, and Daniel, and get back behind the bar.

I've missed this place, these people, this feeling of home.

Mom grips my hand, her voice a little strained. "He knows I'm coming, right?"

She's nervous, having spent twenty minutes picking an outfit, as if Hank will notice or care at all, and her hand is a bit shaky in mine. I'm surprised, having only seen Mom confident, no matter the room she's walking into.

I squeeze her hand reassuringly as I remind her, "Yes, he knows. You talked to Unc yesterday. He told you to come at lunch today."

"Right, yeah," she says with a mindless nod that confirms she's still uncertain.

The door creaks and we step inside. Before my eyes even adjust, I hear a loud call, "Willow! Carrie! Ooh, if you two aren't a sight for sore eyes. Get over here and hug my neck."

Unc is making his way around the bar, moving quickly despite his limp and looking well. Mom meets him in the middle, and they wrap their arms around each other, swaying away years of hurt and pride.

Tears prick at my eyes. This is why we should've done this a long time ago.

"I'm so sorry," Mom blubbers through tears of her own.

"Hush with that shit. The fault rests on my shoulders. They ain't as strong as they used to be, but I can carry this responsibility. I should've fixed it after Harold died so I didn't miss out on you and your family." Unc's blue eyes meet mine around Mom's head and he shoots me a wink. "You did good with 'em, Carrie. Especially that one over there."

Mom beams proudly as she looks back at me. "I did, didn't I?" To Unc, she says, "How about if we leave the past in the past? No need to even give it another minute of our time. We can start fresh and move forward from this moment right here."

"That sounds nice," Unc agrees, but then he holds up a bony finger. "With one exception. I wanna hear what you've been up to. I've got a lot of catching up to do. There's a lot I've missed." He chokes out, "Too much."

Mom reaches up and grabs him into a hug again, and I hear her whisper, "I'd like that."

Unc leads her off toward a table in the corner, but he calls out over his shoulder, "You'd better get to work, Willow-girl. Prep ain't gonna do itself, and the dinner crowd will be here before you know it."

I can't help but laugh at his roundabout way of saying 'welcome back, glad you're here' that sounds a whole lot like 'you've been falling down on the job'.

"Love you too, old man."

He snorts, but I catch the brightness of his grin as he pulls a chair out for Mom to sit down so they can catch up. I head behind the bar and grab one of his craft beers, popping the top, and pour Mom a glass of red wine. I take them over, promising to grab them some food too.

"Tell Ilene I'll take my usual," Unc requests. "And get Carrie a special." I dip my chin in acknowledgement, and Unc tells Mom,

"Ilene made chili today. It's the best you'll ever have, but my belly can't always handle it."

The casual way he alludes to the cancer is a definite change. I'm sure it's only with the two of us since we already know about his diagnosis, but still, it's a good sign that he's being so open.

In the kitchen, Ilene screeches, "Oh, my goodness gracious, Willow! You're back!" Ilene can't hug me with a chili-covered spoon in her hand, but she kisses the air beside my cheek in greeting. "Thank the heavens because that stubborn old guy out there needs you. Don't let him tell you any differently."

"Actually, he told me to get to work and then promptly sat down with my mom, so I don't think he'd argue with you."

We lock eyes, silent for a split second, and then crack up. "Oh, he'd argue, all right. Thinks he can do anything a man forty years his junior can do." She drops the spoon back into the pot on the stove, stirring slowly as though that makes her next question seem casual. "Speaking of younger men . . . you bring back a particular one with you?"

Gossip from the source, the town pastime.

"*Maybe,*" I drawl out around a grin.

"*Yes!*" Chili goes splattering as she throws her arms high in celebration. "You two are the cutest. Glad you got yourselves worked out."

She gets back to work with her huge pots of chili simmering on the stove, which reminds me, "Oh, Unc said he wanted his usual and a bowl of chili for my mom."

Ilene hums as she pulls down a bowl, and I excuse myself back out to the bar to let her work. Almost immediately, I'm attacked by Olivia.

"Willow!" she shouts, running for me. She has no problem hugging me, her arms wrapping around me so tightly she almost picks me up.

"Olivia!" I parrot her excited tone, laughing and trying to squeeze her back.

She sets me down, pulling back to ask, "When did you get back? Are you already working? Where's Bobby? Did you take him back? Holy shit, you should've seen him come barreling in here demanding that Hank tell him where you were. It was the hottest thing I've ever seen."

She fans her face, and I swat her shoulder, ignoring all the other questions to answer the most important one. "Down, girl, he's all mine."

It feels good to claim him again because he is mine, and nothing or no one is going to change that.

"Yeah, he is."

"Quit yer chitter-chatter and get to work, you two," Unc says, sounding grumpy. But when I look over, he's smiling, his happiness obvious on his lined face and in his bright blue eyes.

* * *

"LET'S GO!" a loud voice calls out over by the pool table.

"Pull yourself together," Unc hollers back, "or I'll cut you off before the party even gets started, Willie."

The young guy, who has a permed mullet—yeah, both hairstyles on one blonde head—isn't the least bit chastised, flashing Unc two thumbs up and a big, open-mouthed grin.

My lips lift ever so slightly, fighting a laugh, because Willie's not even drinking. It's straight Coke in his glass, no Jack. He's just excited because Bobby is playing tonight. He's calling it his 'return tour', and while I'd been nervous that it was a coping mechanism at losing the deal *again*, he seems entirely okay with being home.

Surprisingly, we haven't heard a peep from Jeremy Marshall, either. I worried that Bobby would hear from his lawyer. Bobby said he didn't give a shit and would be glad to step in a room again with him to finish the job, but it's been total radio silence.

The door opens and a whole party's worth of people comes in —all the Tannens and Bennetts.

"Mama Louise!" I exclaim. "I don't think I've ever seen you in here."

That might be true, but she hops up on a stool like she's a regular. "Oh, I get by every now and again, but I had to see Bobby's return tour. Cooper's at a friend's house for the night, and Sophie got a babysitter for Cindy Lou."

Bobby dares to come behind the bar, one of the few people Unc allows that privilege, and for one reason only. He catches me around the waist, his arms vice-tight at my middle and his body pressed to my back. His lips lay a soft kiss to my neck as he inhales me. I probably smell like sweat, beer, and lemons, but he doesn't seem to mind. His stubble scratches at my cheek, but I turn into it, loving the feel of him against me.

"Hey, sweetheart," he growls, peppering more kisses along my jaw.

I turn in his arms to kiss him back. It's quick but meaningful. I don't think I'll ever take for granted the ability to kiss this man anytime I want to, especially since I'm the only woman who can do so.

"Hey yourself." I smile and watch his eyes wander over my lips as though my smile makes him happy. "Your fans are ready for you again."

"I only care about one fan. You ready for me?" His voice has gone deep, dark, and gritty, instantly turning me to mush.

"Always," I whisper.

He groans, and neither of us are talking about his show anymore.

"We got the table!" Shayanne yells in celebration, as if she's surprised at the 'reserved' sign on their booth.

"Go and sit down, relax for a bit. I'll bring a round over." Though he places one more groan-accompanied kiss to my lips first, Bobby does follow the rest of his family to the booth.

Before I can pull a pitcher, Mark is at the bar. He grunts at me as a way to catch my attention, and I lift my brows in question.

"Thank you for the picture of Katelyn," he grits out, sounding like it pains him to have proper manners.

"Of course! Happy to do it."

"Just to be clear, no one ever sees that picture. Burn the negative." The order is clipped, allowing for no argument.

Except . . .

"Uhm, that's not really a thing. It's a digital file," I explain.

"Then burn the computer. The whole fucking thing." He seems to think that's completely reasonable, and I can't help but giggle at his all-consuming love of Katelyn, though I keep it inside, which makes my shoulders bounce. The girls were right. You get used to them, and it's cute after a while.

"How about this? I'll delete it, and the print you have will be the only one in existence."

He thinks it over, then grunts, appeased. Grabbing a stack of glasses, he helps me deliver the beer to their table.

Katelyn stands up, Mark sits down in the seat she just vacated, and then he pulls her into his lap. See? Cute.

This time, they're not the only ones being extra touchy-feely, though. We've gotten so busy, and there are so many of them, that the girls are all perched on their guys' laps as everyone talks.

I set the drinks down, pop another kiss to Bobby's cheek, and get back to work before I put Olivia in the weeds.

Impossibly, we get even busier. I'm prepping Girly Beers, Unc is pulling drafts, and Olivia is running them around as fast as her legs will carry her.

But I pause for a preferred customer. "What can I getcha, Sophie?"

"Four Girly Beers and a water with lime."

"Mama Louise keeping it light tonight?" I ask, assuming the drink distribution.

Sophie blinks, staring at me and not saying anything for a long second. "Uh . . . No, we told her she had to try the Girly Beer."

"Okay." I don't get the importance until the weight of her silence makes me pause. "You drinking water?"

She still doesn't answer, but her smile is answer enough.

"Congratulations," I whisper.

"Shh," she orders, and I lock my lips, promising her that I won't say a word.

She holds the handles of the beer mugs, dancing her way across the floor to take them back to their table. Curiously, I wonder which one of them will come up next to tell me something private. Perks of being a bartender . . . I know what's on everyone's mind and heart.

Like now.

Everyone is ready for Bobby, though it doesn't take a brain trust to figure that out because the crowd has moved from doing walk-bys to chanting his name and telling him, "Come on, man. Get up there."

Before the crowd gets too carried away, Bobby takes the stage. The hoots and hollers get louder and louder, and his smile gets wider and brighter.

Instead of his usual introduction, he goes off-script. "Thanks everyone. I know you thought I might have something to tell you tonight." The crowd quiets, hungry for news. "Well, it looks like you're stuck with me. Assholes out in Nashville—"

"Language!" Mama Louise shouts, and everyone laughs.

Bobby looks to the ceiling as though praying for patience. "Sorry, Mama Louise. I meant, the *people* in Nashville weren't what I thought they'd be, and most importantly, Willow's here. And wherever she goes, I go." His shrug is easy, as if that's the most obvious thing in the whole wide world. His eyes lift from the crowd to meet mine across the room. "Love you, sweetheart!"

"Love you, too!" I yell loudly.

"Aww," several female voices sound out.

It's a sweet moment until a deeper, masculine voice shouts, "Fuck those city boys! Stay here with us, Bobby!"

Hats wave around, hands lift beers in the air, and a general sense of laughter washes over the crowd, though I see a few raised brows. I'm betting those are the tourists from the resort.

Amazingly, not too long ago, I was a tourist, a short-timer planning to stay for a few months. Now, I'm one of the locals. This town is my home. That man on stage is my home. He said he'll go wherever I go, but the opposite is true too. I'd follow him to the ends of the Earth and enjoy every step of the journey at his side.

He sings all my favorites, both his own and covers. His gravelly voice hits me soul-deep, and I fall a little more in love each time I hear him. I dance my way around behind the bar, singing along quietly with him as I fill orders.

"This is a new one I wrote recently. One of those Nashville *people* told me that a broken heart can be the best inspiration. I hate to admit this—you have no idea how much I *hate* to, though some of you might've seen the fallout of that—but he might've been right. Though it's a theory I'm not willing to test again." I can see the pain he went through written in the lines of his frown. "Anyway, may you never feel this way."

> *Gave you everything, I was yours.*
> *Took your heart because you were mine.*
> *Standing in the tatters that you left behind,*
> *I still love you.*

Each word is laced with tortured heartbreak, slicing through me and bringing tears to my eyes. "Oh, Bobby," I say softly, clutching my bar towel to my chest.

He finishes the song on a long, mournful note that holds the entire audience in rapture. And then there's a quiet heartbeat before the crowd claps and cheers.

Bobby flashes that cocky grin. "Don't y'all go thinking I've gone soft. The next one I'm working on is called *Willow, Get Your Ass Over Here and Love Me.*" He laughs, and the audience laughs along with him. Mama Louise doesn't even try to correct his language this time. And I shake my head, knowing that here, there, or anywhere . . . I love him.

I have no problem holding my head high this time as I cross the room. Nope, I walk right up to that stage, catch his eye, and crook a finger at him. He winks at the audience, but when he turns to me, he's my Bobby, sweet and emotional, bossy and possessive, sexy and dirty-mouthed. When he bends down, I wrap my arms around his neck and kiss him like he's my air, right there in front of the whole audience.

"Woohoo, getcha sum!" a shout goes up from the crowd.

"I love you," he whispers against my mouth, just for me to hear.

"Love you too."

I might do a little happy dance back across the floor to the bar, and I definitely sing along louder as Bobby goes into his next song.

* * *

I'M IN THE KITCHEN, waiting for the coffee maker to do its job on Sunday afternoon, when a sight out the window catches my eye. A cloud of dust is visible coming down the driveway, billowing out behind a silver sedan.

"Hey, Bobby, you expecting someone?" I holler up the stairs. "There's a car outside."

I hear a scrambling thud and then several more as he crosses the room above me. He bounds down the stairs and peeks out the window in the front living room. "Who the fuck is that?" he mutters.

The car pulls to a stop and a guy gets out. He's young, early thirties, maybe, with brown hair peeking out under his straw cowboy hat. He's got on Wrangler jeans and boots that look like they've seen a few miles.

"Stay here," Bobby tells me, opening the door to go outside and greet the stranger.

"You here about a horse, looking for Luke?" Bobby questions. It's not a typical greeting, but it's a fair assumption. "He's next door at the Bennetts'. Back out the gate and go left to the next one."

He's clearly telling the guy to get the hell out of here.

Never one to leave Bobby alone, I sneak my way out the door and to his side just in time to hear the visitor say, "Actually, I'm here to see you, Bobby."

Instantly on alert, Bobby pushes me behind him protectively and crosses his arms over his chest. Tension shoots through him as though he's ready to throw down at any perceived provocation. Maybe I shouldn't have come out here because he's only this quick-tempered when he thinks I'm in danger.

"Leave."

The guy doesn't move toward the car but holds a hand out to shake. "I'm Stephen Wheatley from Outlaw Records. I saw you in Nashville at the Bar and liked what I heard. It sucks when someone as good as you are is already signed with another agency. But word travels fast, and I hear you're not represented by NCR?"

He's talking fast, getting his spiel out as quickly as possible, likely having heard of Bobby and Jeremy's last 'conversation' if he's heard as much as he says he has.

"Get off my property." Bobby's not leaving any room for misunderstanding.

Just as I thought, Mr. Wheatley adds, "Also heard you put Jeremy Marshall in his place, made him piss his pants." He seems amused by that, which takes him up a notch in my estimation, but not Bobby's, apparently.

"Three, two, one . . . Brutal!" Bobby yells and then gives a loud whistle. "Fair warning, that ain't my dog, it's my brother. You should go before he gets here."

Mr. Wheatley chuckles, an easy smile on his lips. "You're going to sic your brother on me?"

"No, he's coming to help me load your body in the truck after I kill you for trespassing," Bobby deadpans.

"I'm here to offer you a deal. Not one like Marshall's. A real deal . . . for the real you." Mr. Wheatley has a fire lit under his ass now, stepping a little closer to his car and talking quickly.

I swear a growl is rumbling in Bobby's chest.

"Wait," I say to both men. To Bobby, I appeal, "Hear him out. It couldn't hurt."

"Yeah, hear me out," Mr. Wheatley agrees with me.

"I could make it hurt," Bobby threatens.

I don't want a record deal for Bobby if it means all that stuff Jeremy was trying to pull. The manipulations he was almost successful with nearly ruined everything. But that doesn't mean that Bobby should give up on his dream entirely. We're home, and we're happy, but it truly doesn't cost anything but a few minutes to hear this guy out. Best case scenario, it's worth considering. Worst case, we're five minutes later with getting our coffee.

Holding his hands up in a placating gesture, Mr. Wheatley pleads his case. "I like who you are, where you come from, and what you represent. A real cowboy, a working man, a family man. I don't want to change you into some poster boy for bad boy country. I want you to write what you want, sing what you want, be authentically you. That's what I liked at the Bar and at Hank's last night."

"Look, I'll leave this here. I'm staying at the resort until Tuesday. Come see me if you'd like to talk. If I don't hear from you, you'll never see me again. Good luck to you, Bobby. You've got a real gift."

Mr. Wheatley bends down, setting some paperwork in the dirt driveway. He picks up a nearby rock, adding it to the top of the stack so it doesn't blow away. He doesn't seem to care that his pristine white papers are smeared with dust and grime now. Somehow, that already seems like a better sign than Jeremy Marshall's slick approach.

True to his word, he gets in his car and pulls away without so much as a wave.

Bobby turns for the front door, not even picking the papers up, but as he disappears into the house, I grab them. He should at least check them out. Just because his dream blew up last time, doesn't mean it has to be that way this time. What if there's still a chance for him to have his dream and for us to still be together?

CHAPTER 27

WILLOW

"You sure about this?" Bobby asks me. His hand is in mine, his eyes locked on me as if we're the only two people at the table. Actually, with the intense way he's scanning me, it's more like we're the only two people in the room.

I nod, biting my lip to keep the smile from beaming too broadly. He's going to get his dream, after all. And I don't have to lose him for him to get it.

"We can stay right here, work the farm and Hank's, play music and take pictures, and live a good life. I can give you a good life, Willow. Full of love and happy days, with the occasional fist fight with my brothers or a Bennett." His lips quirk. "Just keeping it real."

I cup his cheek, the stubble scratching my palm as he tilts into my touch. "We could do that. And it would be a wonderful life. But you have this gift and a fire in your belly. I know you need to see if this could go somewhere. I'm good with that. Let's do it together, you and me. There will be time enough to come home and work the farm and Hank's. And I can take pictures anywhere."

We've talked this through several times already. I had picked that contract up out of the dirt, set it right on the kitchen table, and started reading while Bobby had made our cups of coffee. The deal was good, better than good. It's an amazing offer.

Bobby had still said no, justifying it by claiming that Brutal needs him and Unc needs me. I didn't tell Unc's secret. It'd seemed needless considering he's on the road back to health, but I had shared that Unc might not need me quite as desperately in the coming days other than prime fishing days with Doc. I'd smiled in relief that I meant actually fishing and not *fishing*.

"Fuck, you're amazing," Bobby growls as if it's still just the two of us. He kisses my palm, searches my eyes once more, and then holds my hand tightly as he tells Mr. Wheatley, "Okay, run it down again. Every detail."

* * *

Dinner that night is different. There's no special meal with Bobby's favorites, there's no sign in the doorway, and we don't turn off the lights and shout 'congratulations'. It's low-key, more like Bobby and his family. Down to Earth, hard-working cowboys and their women.

Like me.

Somehow, I do fit right in with this motley group of people. I've spent so much time alone, introverted and keeping to the perimeter, an observer to any action. I get lost in the shadows, both literally and figuratively, sticking to my photography as a way to keep the camera between me and others. But here? Around this dinner table with these people, I'm simply one of them.

We can talk about cattle and crops, the resort, legal cases, school, rodeo, animals, town gossip, cars, drag racing, and so much more. And everyone listens and cares, regardless of interests.

But tonight, the floor is all Bobby's.

"I did it. Signed right on that dotted line. Well, it was a solid line, but I signed it!" His smile is almost blinding, his dark eyes alight with joy, and his tone still one of disbelief. "I got a record deal."

"Oh, my cheesus and crackers!"

"Woohoo!"

"Bobby Tannen!"

"What the fuck, man?"

That one was Brody, and he gets an instant, sharp look and reminder from Mama Louise. "Language."

"Pretty sure it's justified in this case, Mama Louise," Brody argues back.

She doesn't agree, but she lets him off the hook with a lift of her brow.

"Tell us all about it!" Shayanne screams, her hands beneath her chin like a kid on Christmas morning.

Bobby goes through every detail of the deal with Outlaw Records. Mr. Wheatley was telling the truth. They really do want Bobby just as he is. The contract allows him to have full control over his music, his songwriting, his albums, his concerts, and his merchandise. They get a much larger percentage of the profits for the first two years, but then the contract allows for renegotiation. Even the percentages had seemed fair when Mr. Wheatley explained what they were going to invest in Bobby's career—producers, advertising, musicians, and radio play. Those were all things Bobby has no idea how to do, so letting Outlaw do the hard work and sticking to the music he loves had seemed like an equitable split.

"You sure it's not another slicker-than-snot deal like Marshall's?" Brutal asks quietly.

Bobby looks at Allyson, who's sitting between Brutal and Cooper.

"Yeah, I'm sure. I had someone with a fair amount of legal knowledge look over the contract first." Bobby's grin says loudly and clearly, 'I hear your concerns, man, and I'm good'. They do have an odd shorthand, gruff and sometimes violent but filled with love all the same.

Brutal looks at Allyson, his brows lifted high on his forehead. "You couldn't have told me that?"

She shakes her head, pleasantly smug to get one over on the big man. "Attorney-client privilege. Well, paralegal-client privilege, but Bobby came in to see Rick and me. You know those meetings are confidential." Her shrug says it's no big deal, but

Bobby told me she was overjoyed for him and he wasn't sure she'd be able to keep her mouth shut for long.

Good thing she didn't have to because Bobby signed today and he's spilling the good news to everyone mere hours later.

"Okay, then," Brutal gives his blessing.

"Congratulations. Always knew you had it in you." Bobby has looked up to Brody for years as his big brother and as a man to strive to be, so the compliment from him is heavy with importance. "Glad you're getting the chance to let it out," Brody jokes, his permission given.

"Like a fart," Cooper whispers, but it's not quiet enough and everyone cracks up.

"Cooper!" Allyson scolds him, but she's fighting a smile too.

Shayanne recovers first. "I'd like it included in that contract that I get front-row seats to every show, a signed copy of every album, and the whole line of Bobby Tannen T-shirts. My boobs will be your billboard!" She blinks. "Wait, that's not what I meant. Well, kinda, but you know what I'm saying." She shakes her head like she's trying to get that image out of her mind.

We all laugh again, and somehow, despite this life-changing news, we end up talking about the goats again. Apparently, Trollie has learned a new trick and it's the cutest thing.

"If he sees you've got food, he'll run laps around your legs, faster and faster like it's the Daytona 500, until you fall on your butt. Then he gobbles up all the treats before you've even checked to see if your tailbone is in one piece. Awful monster!" Shay describes him like 'monster' means the cutest thing ever.

We finish dinner, and Rix and Brody clear the table, taking dishes to the sink. Mama Louise leans my way. "Come here, dear. I want to show you something."

I get up, letting go of Bobby's hand under the table, curious about what she could possibly want me to see.

In the front room, I freeze when I see them.

My pictures. All of the ones I printed are precisely and perfectly hung on the wall in a large arrangement. Mama Louise has added some older pictures of the boys when they were little, a black and white wedding picture of her and John, and there are even some old shots of the Bennetts and Tannens from decades ago. I think my favorite is one of both families, the kids all sprawled out in the grass and dirt with Mama Louise, John, Martha, and Paul looking over them with big smiles on their faces. I didn't even know they were friendly back then, but the closeness is clear in the shot.

"Oh my gosh, it's beautiful!" I whisper, tears popping to my eyes.

"They are," Mama Louise agrees with me. "I love my life, but you captured my family in a way I don't think anyone else could have. Because you're part of it. Just one thing's missing."

I look to her in confusion.

Her smile is sweet, but her tone leaves no room for arguing. "I need that picture of you and me making fried chicken. Got a spot for it right here." She pats an empty space on the wall. "Gotta have the whole family up here."

A crash sounds out from the kitchen and she clucks her tongue. "How they can manage a whole herd of cattle, gently break a horse, and plant and harvest acres of land . . . but not load the dishwasher without breaking something? I'll simply never understand it."

Mama Louise darts around the corner, calling out, "You break it, you buy me a new one."

Allyson, Katelyn, Sophie, and I giggle quietly. They followed Mama Louise and me into the front room to see the pictures too.

"These are so good," Katelyn sighs. "If you ever want to do wedding photography, let me know. To be clear, I highly suggest you *don't* because brides are . . ." She rolls her eyes, and I wonder if she's working with a bridezilla these days. She plasters her professional work smile back on her face and continues. "Most are lovely and would be appreciative of work like this if you want it."

"Thanks," I tell her. "That's not really my thing, though. The blog's going well and is supporting me, so I'm good. Thank you, though."

She nods, and Allyson leans over to whisper, "Thank you for the *other* pictures too. We had to hang ours in our walk-in closet. Cooper knows not to go in there because that's where I hide the birthday and Christmas presents, so he'll never see me naked except for a sheer curtain, lying in the grass like a goddess." She smiles, obviously pleased with how her picture turned out.

"Uh, Allyson?" Sophie interrupts, her brows dropped together, "that's probably the first place he goes then. No kid can resist peeking at presents."

"Oh, he wouldn't . . ." Allyson stops at the looks on our faces because Sophie is right. "Shit," she spits out and then beelines around the corner toward Brutal.

We giggle, shaking our heads.

"Guess I'm glad Cindy Lou doesn't care about her mom in a bra yet."

Katelyn snorts. "Ours is over the tub in our bathroom. No worries about anyone seeing it. Mark wouldn't let anyone in there, anyway. Even if they needed to pee, he'd send 'em outside, not into our room."

"What about Shay and Rix?" I muse aloud, curious.

"Shay's is probably up in the barn for everyone and God to see. Or maybe in Luke's office?" Sophie suggests.

"Hmm, I'm betting Rix's is hanging in Brody's bedroom. She would definitely not want it where any of the guys who work at her shop could catch a glimpse. She works too hard for them to forget she's female and a better mechanic than they are."

"What about yours?" Sophie asks.

I can feel my cheeks blush, the heat burning high and bright. "I, uh . . . I hung it in my bedroom. Bobby . . . liked it." That's putting it mildly. When he saw the dark silhouette of my curves kneeling on my bed, he'd gently traced the lines, his breath coming faster and faster with every inch. Then he'd flashed me a heated grin and asked me to sign it for him. Artist, model, and his. I'd done it with a giggly laugh, having never imagined that anyone would appreciate my photography the way he does.

I look at the wall of photos again. Somehow, that crazy night had turned out some beautiful work.

Of course, it's not hard when the subject I'm photographing is beautiful inside and out, like this family.

"I'm feeling like it's a Special Sweet Tea night," Mama Louise says from the kitchen.

"Oh, God, don't make a rookie mistake," Sophie warns me.

LAUREN LANDISH

"It's stronger than it seems. Pretty sure that's how I got Cindy Lou." Her grin says she doesn't mind that at all.

I think I'll take it easy on whatever this magical concoction is, though. Maybe have some water like Sophie does, though she claims it's because she's gonna have to drive drunk James home.

* * *

THAT NIGHT, after a long shower to wash the day away, Bobby pulls the covers back for me to climb into his bed. It's late, and work will start dark and early for him, but he seems on edge as I snuggle into his side.

My head rests on his chest, and his fingers dance along my shoulder in those patterns that have come to bring me joy, a sign that he's thinking, singing, playing in his mind.

"Tell me, Bobby." I give his words back to him, hoping they work as well for me as they do for him.

I feel his chest vibrate as a small laugh rumbles through him. Then he squeezes me tightly, pulling me on top of him. Our eyes meet, his dark to my gray, and one of his thick fingers gently brushes my hair behind my ear.

"Nothing is going to change, right?" he asks softly.

I'm surprised by the scared, uncertain sound of his voice. I press a tiny kiss to the tip of his nose. "Nothing has to change unless we want it to. This is a big opportunity, but you decide what to do with it."

His nod is a vow. "I promise nothing will change. You and me forever, Willow. I love you."

"I love you too."

I can feel the moment stretch, meaning woven through it. We're on the verge of a cliff, about to jump off into open air. We're holding hands, jumping together, but that's a small comfort to the natural fear of both falling and flying.

But for now, we've got both feet on steady ground, the foundation of us sure and firm.

"You're going to be a big star, Bobby Tannen. But for now, you're still mine. All mine," I whisper.

"That won't ever change." His tone is serious, but I want to

332

ease his worries, not let him fall deeper into them. I pull my glasses off, dropping them to the nightstand, and he takes the hint, changing tones. "What are you going to do with me if I'm all yours?" He's baiting me, teasing himself as he lifts his hips beneath me.

I can feel his hardness pressed to my center, and I move up and down, letting the ridge of him massage my clit and down toward my opening. "Mmm." I moan at how good he feels there, wanting more. But first . . .

I throw the blankets off, moving down Bobby's body, pressing kiss after kiss to each inch of warm skin I discover—his sharp jaw, the muscles of his pecs, his sternum, his ribs as he gasps and his belly goes tight. My nails score down his thighs as I get lower.

"Willow?" he groans from above me.

I look up his body, smiling sweetly and then sticking my tongue out to lick a slow circle around the crown of his dick.

"Mmm." The sound he makes is low in his chest as his hips unconsciously thrust up for more. One of his hands cups my head, and he traces my lip with his other thumb. "Tell me."

"I want to taste you," I whisper so quietly I'm not sure he can even hear me, but he does. Of course he does.

"Do it, sweetheart."

I take him into my mouth, feeling his hardness slide over my tongue an inch at a time. More and more, I swallow him down. Breathing through my nose—thanks, Katelyn—I let him slip into my throat. I move up and down his length over and over.

His breath goes jagged, and he folds his arms behind his head, using the pillow to prop himself up. I open my eyes, meeting his, and his grin is pure, wicked desire as he watches me take him into my mouth.

Again and again, I consume him, am consumed by him. He gets closer and closer to the edge of ecstasy, losing control and moving with me, encouraging me faster, deeper, harder. His hands move, one threading back into my hair to control my head and the other holding the base of his shaft as he fucks my mouth. I moan at the sensation of being under his control. Mostly, I cry out at being his, the only one who can bring him this pleasure.

"Now." The grunted warning comes a split second before he

does, his release hot and salty. I gulp him down, wanting every drop. He shudders, tapping his head against my tongue with a satisfied smirk.

"Come here." His hands reach under my arms, pulling me up to him. He kisses me fully, not caring that I just swallowed him down.

After one deep, thorough kiss, he keeps pulling and pushing, arranging me the way he wants me. I end up on my knees, straddling his face as he reclines on his pillow. Gripping my hips, he stares at my center. "I want you to ride my face, fuck my mouth with this sweet pussy until you come on me. I wanna drown in you."

I don't know what to say to that, but I do as he says and move my hips over him. His tongue laps at me, tasting my skin and juices hungrily. He focuses on my clit, one of his thick fingers filling me in time with the circles his tongue makes. I cry out, quickly on the edge myself. "Bobby!"

He grunts, taking his finger away and holding me tight to his mouth as I come. My hips buck over and over, searching for the release only he can bring me.

Before I've even finished coming, I'm flying through the air to land face down on the bed. Bobby's hands grip my hips, pulling them back so that my cheek is pressed to the pillow and my ass is lifted back toward him. Panting for breath, I manage to gasp as he shoves inside me.

"*Yes,*" he hisses as my body gives way to his welcome invasion.

I bounce against him, his hips slamming into my ass with every thrust. It's rough and powerful, but his words are sweet. "You and me, Willow. Nothing will ever change. You and I are going to tackle the world. Tell me, sweetheart."

"You and me, Bobby. I love you."

He grunts out a sound that I think is 'I love you too', and then he takes me harder and faster. The bed slams against the wall, and I'm thankful that Brody and Rix aren't here tonight, not that I would stop Bobby even if they were in the hallway listening in. I can't. I want this too much.

We're making promises with our bodies, writing vows with

our hearts. He's getting his dream come true, and I'll chase it with him because I've already got mine.

Bobby. Unc being okay and our family reconnected. My photography work. Home. Friends. So many things I didn't even know I was missing. But now that I have them, I can't imagine life without them.

We come at the same time, jumping off the cliff into the free fall of the future to fly together.

CHAPTER 28

BOBBY

"*H*oly fuck." I stare at the piece of paper in my hands in disbelief. "I've never seen that many zeroes. I don't know what to say."

Head down, elbows on my knees, I run a finger over the numbers and then the words, trying to feel them. The paper is smooth beneath my touch, but I can feel the importance of what this means.

Willow drops to her knees on the floor next to me, looking over my arm. "You earned it. Every penny. You heard what Stephen said."

I did hear him when he called earlier this week. I just didn't exactly *believe* him.

Promise me the big time, and I'll be the fool for trusting you.

I signed that contract with Outlaw Records three months ago, and my life has changed since then in so many ways. And it somehow stayed the same in others. It's an odd twist of fate.

On one hand, almost immediately after signing, I'd gone back to Nashville with Willow by my side. We'd had a week of fun—making music, taking pictures, and making love in lots of places that we'll never, ever tell anyone.

Willow had sat by Miller's side while we recorded every song I've ever written. Stephen said that would give us lots of options for the album and to release to radio. We'd chosen *Dig Down Deeper* as my first single, and it'd been an instant hit.

The first time I heard it on the radio, I'd pulled over, yanked the door open, and danced with Willow on the side of Main Street. My voice coming through the radio had been a surreal experience.

I've had another single make the top ten list since then, and yesterday, I gave my first radio interview from the kitchen table. Weird doesn't begin to describe that. The DJ had laughed when I said I had to go because my brother was waiting on me to harvest a batch of pumpkins. I'd been serious, trying to talk about my music while Brutal glared at me from the doorway, occasionally glancing at his watch and then out the window at the height of the sun in the sky.

"Holy fuck," I say again. When Stephen had told me what my share of the profits were, I'd laughed aloud, thinking he was shitting me. But here it is, in black and white.

"You sure about this? We could take this and go anywhere, do anything." Dream talk of 'what would I do if I won the lottery' has become seriously fucking real with this piece of paper in my hands.

She turns my chin so that I meet her eyes and gives me a small smile. "Why would we go anywhere else, do anything else? This is home, yours and mine."

Her mood-ring eyes swirl with happy light, and that she understands what this place means, not just to me but to my entire family, is nothing short of amazing. I don't know what I did to deserve this woman, but I pray I can keep on doing it every day.

I bury myself in her arms, in her heart. In our future.

"Okay, let's do this."

* * *

THE DINNER TABLE is loud and boisterous, as usual. Cooper is telling a story about the school's fall festival, and Brutal keeps jumping in to add details from the several times he's heard the story before. Cindy Lou is screeching, "Mama, more!" no matter how fast Sophie loads her plate with tiny, cut-up bits of carrots. James and Mark are fighting over the best cuts of pot roast, and I've got my woman's hand in mine, smiling as I take it all in.

Once, I thought we were going to truly falter, losing everything. But somehow, I ended up with more than I'd ever thought I would. Mostly, these people, but also . . .

I clear my throat. "I've got something I'd like to discuss."

There's an instant and abrupt stop of conversation. "You want to *discuss* something? Like, with actual words?" Brutal's giving me shit, but this is too important to play into his hand. For now. Later, I'll get him back.

"Shut up and listen," I tell him. He glares back, and I'm pretty sure there'll be a tussle in our future. Fuck, I love that guy.

I turn my attention to Mama Louise and take a steadying breath. I can't believe this is happening. So many tears, so much fighting, so much lost, and so much found, and it all culminates in this moment.

"When things went bad after Dad, you saved us, truly saved us, and I don't think there's any way we could ever thank you for that."

Mama Louise interrupts, "No thanks needed, Bobby. You know that. I'm doing right by your mom. She was a good friend of mine for a long time, and I think Martha would be real proud of how you've all turned out." She looks around the table, meeting my eyes, then Brutal's, Brody's, and Shayanne's.

"I think she would be too, but at least some of that is your doing," I assure her. "We were at a crossroads, but now, we're at another one."

I can sense confusion around the table, but Mama Louise smiles as if she knows exactly where I'm going. She probably does. She always knows everything.

"Things are going well with the music stuff. Real good, actually." I clench my teeth, not believing that I'm about to say this, even though I've studied it from every angle. "You have the deed to the farm. I have money now. I want to make a large down payment and start making monthly payments to you so that we can buy Tannen Farm back. We need to own it again."

Three, two, one . . .

"What? No." Brody's response is exactly what I expected.

"Hear me out," I demand, but his head is shaking vehemently, already having made up his mind.

Mama Louise looks to Mark, but I'm too busy dealing with Brody to decipher their silent conversation.

"I'm supposed to take care of us," Brody argues, thumping his chest.

"You've been taking care of us my whole adult life, literally since I was a grumpy-ass eighteen-year-old kid pouting at the unfairness of life. God knows, you put up with enough of my shit. But I'm grown now, Brody, and in case you haven't noticed, we're a team. We each pull our weight, take care of each other, and this is something I can do for us. For the Tannens."

We don't beg or plead. This is two bulls ramming heads against each other, immovable forces battling for dominance. Mama Louise doesn't even bother correcting my language, letting us work this out between ourselves.

"No, absolutely not. No." He's not going to budge, but I've got an ace up my sleeve. He doesn't want me to do this, but he wants to own our farm again more. I just have to make him admit that.

"That name on the fence used to mean something. It was ours. Tannen Farm, remember? It can be that way again—our land, our property, our farm . . . if you let me do this for us."

Family roots, deeper than dirt, run into my soul and grow toward the sun.

"Maybe if you explain what you're thinking," Mama Louise says gently.

I swallow, feeling like I'm stepping onstage for the first time— those nerves, the questions of whether I'm good enough, and the excitement that I could make something happen. "We'd make a down payment now and work out monthly payments, like I said. You'd essentially be the mortgage company, Mama Louise. And when we've paid off the loan, it'll be ours again, free and clear."

"That sounds good," Mama Louise agrees easily.

Mark isn't such an easy sell, following Brody's refusal but for a different reason.

"Land aside, how're we supposed to figure out the rest of the ranch? We didn't just buy your acres. We bought the whole operation—animals, crops, and equipment. They're all Bennett assets now."

I shrug heavily. "I'm not sure, but I figure between all of us, we can work it out. A co-op, working together? Or we can buy cattle back for a price per head? Ranching and farming have been going well so far, so maybe there's a way to keep things how they are, sharing the profits and the work. We'll still be family, all of us. I don't want that to change. We'll just have our own land, our own legacy back, but a shared future between the Tannens and Bennetts."

I don't have all the details worked out. That is Brody's area of expertise, and I trust him to work with Mark to figure it out, and Allyson can do whatever legal contract work we need. But first, they have to agree to let me buy the farm back.

Mama Louise sets her fork down and interlaces her fingers. "Sounds good to me if it's okay with the boys." She looks at James, who nods, Luke, who holds his hands out, and Mark, who grunts but looks at Brody.

The ball's in his court.

"It's yours, Brody," I tell my brother, sharing business I know he'd rather keep private, but if I don't lay everything out now, we'll all pay the price of his stubborn pride. "I know you need it. But it's ours."

Rix lays her hand over Brody's. I don't know what conversations they've had about our family and our farm, but she seems to know how much this means and how difficult it is for him to agree. I need to give him a way to save face, a reason to say yes. Lighter, I joke, "Besides, I'm gonna need a place to come home to after my concert tours. Roughing it in one of those fancy RV buses with my name on the outside is gonna be hard. Actually, I might just buy one and park it where your truck is now."

He chuckles, rolling his eyes to the ceiling. "You're such a shit. Had to rub my nose in that, didn't you?"

To her credit, Mama Louise still doesn't interrupt to correct his language, though I think she's literally biting her tongue not to do so. I'm sure she can sense that we're on the verge of something major.

"I could probably get you tickets next to Shay's if you want? Probably not free, but at a discount, at least."

Brody throws a solid punch at my shoulder, and I rub at the bright spot of pain. For a moment, I think he's going to agree that easily. But he sobers and shakes his head. "Bobby—"

Willow interrupts his sad tone, musing aloud, "Sometimes, you love by doing things for people. I get that, believe me, I do." Her eyes pin Brody. "You get that. Maybe we do things differently, but you take care of them." She doesn't have to explain who she means. We all know what Brody has done for us, how much he's given up to handle everything when Dad went off the rails. And they all understand why Willow did what she did too. "But I've learned that doing things for others sometimes means letting them do stuff for you."

Brody looks at Shayanne, who's smiling wide enough to see nearly every tooth in her head. Then Brutal, who grunts.

Finally, we're eye to eye.

"It'll be rough out here without you, but I reckon we can make it work while you're on the road in that fancy tour bus with people chanting your name. Can't say I understand it." He scratches at his lip with his thumb. "But I can't fault people for their poor taste if it's buying the family farm, now can I?" The sarcasm runs deep through every syllable. If he's back to giving me shit, that means we're going to be okay.

And it means that he's agreeing.

"To be clear, I don't care whose name is on which acre or what tag is on each cow's ear. I'll expect you all to dinner at six thirty every night like usual, and polite manners require a phone call if you're skipping out. Understood?" Mama Louise's tone allows for zero disagreement, not that any of us would.

"Yes, ma'am," we all say. We might be big, strong, rough country guys, but we know where our bread is buttered and who does the buttering, so we won't ever piss Mama Louise off by *not* showing up at her dinner table.

With that decree, Mama Louise picks her fork back up and gets back to eating. Following her lead, we do the same.

CHAPTER 29

WILLOW

I scrub at the bar so hard the wax sealant is in jeopardy. But I can't stop. I have to get everything spotless, spic and span, and cleaned to within an inch of its life. It's a coping mechanism, I know it is, but that doesn't change the urge to do it.

"Put that towel down, girl. The bar's as clean as it's gonna get," Unc snaps from his perch by Richard and Doc Jones. They're drinking and talking as they watch the game on the television above the bar.

Sighing, I follow orders and drop the towel into the bin of dirties. Not able to truly stop, I pick up the whole bin and scoot my way to the back to start a quick wash load.

Behind the bar again, I fidget with my hands for all of two seconds before giving in and pulling out a bag of lemons to cut.

I feel a dark presence next to me and then a wrinkled hand covers the knife, forcing me to freeze or chop my own finger. It's a harder decision than you'd think. "Willow, sit down and be still. You're making me dizzy with all your scurrying around like a squirrel. Here, there, everywhere at once." Unc wiggles the fingers of his free hand around, mimicking the routes I've been taking all day.

He's being silly, but he's right.

"Tell me what's got you all aflutter." He leans his butt against the counter beside me, crossing his arms and his ankles as if he's got all the time in the world. But we don't.

I sigh, studying the lemon in front of me as if I've never seen one before. Each string, seed, and drop of juice is suddenly immensely interesting. "You sure you can do this without me for a bit?" I hoarsely voice the concern that's been keeping me up nights.

His bushy white brow lifts as he side-eyes me, showing his displeasure at even being asked such an insulting question. "Girl, I've been doing this alone longer than you've been alive. I'll be fine for a few weeks. Don'tcha worry about me a bit."

I've learned a thing or two during my time at his side, and I mimic him, lifting one brow but adding a strong dose of glare to my look. "One, reminding me how old you are isn't helping matters. Two, it's going to be a lot longer than a few weeks. More like three months, at least." The reality of that hits me squarely in my gut and I shrink. "Maybe I'll just stay. That'll be better, anyway. Yeah, I'll stay here and help."

Those brows drop down low over his blue eyes now, turning his wrinkles into deep grooves. "You will do nothing of the sort. I'll kick your hiney out before I let you do that. You're getting on that bus and getting outta dodge, and that's final."

If only it were that easy.

I'm supposed to get on the tour bus with Bobby for his first tour in three days, but ever since we decided to do that, my belly will not stop churning. I'm not nervous about being with Bobby. I'm excited about that part, but leaving Unc terrifies me. What if something happens while I'm gone?

I can't help myself. I throw my arms around his neck, hugging him tightly and likely getting lemon juice all over his shirt.

"Whoa—" He startles but then hugs me back just as tightly. Patting my back, he soothes my fears, whispering in my ear so that no one else hears, "I'm okay, Willow-girl. You heard the doc. I'm officially in remission, all better."

I lean back from him, whispering too. "But what if it comes back and I'm who-knows-where, doing who-knows-what? You're no spring chicken, Unc, and anything could happen."

His reassuring smile turns upside down, the scowl an admonishment. "Don't need you calling me old. These bones have a few more miles in them, so don't you go cutting them short. I'm more worried about you out there." He lifts his chin toward the door like there are monsters lurking right outside, lying in wait for me.

"I'll be fine. You know Bobby won't let anything happen to me." That's an understatement. Bobby has gone above and beyond to make sure this tour will suit the both of us, hitting major markets to do concerts and radio interviews while giving me interesting and beautiful things to photograph for my *Day in the Life of a Tree* blog.

The biggest factor we've discussed is that I need complete and total anonymity. An odd request, it seemed, but Mr. Wheatley had readily agreed. I think he would've agreed to get Bobby a rainbow unicorn if it got him on the road to support this album, but luckily, my request hadn't been quite that difficult to grant. Staying anonymous is key for my blog's success and something I've worked hard to maintain, and I don't want my connection to Bobby to affect that. I won't use him that way or risk my own career. Especially when it's going so well, my number of followers continuing to climb steadily, my hearts and comments growing exponentially, and my kickback profits increasing. The money is nice, giving me a personal comfort level, but the comments from people who tell me they've started documenting their own lives and finding something special about the mundane day-to-day are what really satisfy me.

Unc took it a step further, well aware that quite a few people in Great Falls know about my online career. He'd used the town grapevine to tell everybody in town that if they said a word about me or my blog, they'd no longer be welcome at Hank's. I'd laughed when he told me that, thinking it didn't seem like a very serious threat, but I'd been filled in right quick that if Unc made someone unwelcome, the rest of town would follow suit. So any blabber-mouth would no longer get Ilene's chili, a beer anywhere in town, Darla's doughnuts, a coffee, or gas from the single station in town. I'd been shocked that they'd go that far for . . . *me*. But Unc had simply shrugged and said 'that's what we do in Great Falls, look out for each other.'

"Huh, well then it sounds like we're both gonna be fine."

Unc's decree is final, a sign to the universe that he won't have it any other way. Surprisingly, it does settle the butterflies in my belly.

I look past Unc, down the bar to see Doc Jones and Richard. They lift their beers my way, signaling that they've got Unc. I know for a fact that Doc Jones will call me if he feels it's warranted. He's done it before. And he's got both Mom's number and mine. Plus, Mom is coming back for another visit next month.

Mom is making up for lost time with Unc, much the same way I have. Not by working the bar but by visiting and talking on the phone. I'm not sure about what—that's between them—but whatever happened with Grandpa seems to be water under the bridge.

But I haven't answered fast enough for Unc, and he bends down, getting in my face. "You're getting on that bus, capiche? But you've still got one more shift scheduled so you'd best get to it. No lollygagging about. Don't make me fire you on your last day."

I roll my eyes at his exaggeration but can't help pressing a quick kiss to his scruffy cheek. "On it, Unc."

This time, when I start cutting the lemon, it's with a clearer mind and heart. I'm doing this . . . going on the road with Bobby because Unc is okay. Well, he's still a grumpy, stubborn old man, but he's as healthy as a horse and that's what counts.

Who would've thought this is how my life would turn out that day I drove into Great Falls, yelling at the mountain for judging me? Maybe I just hadn't realized that it was welcoming me home.

* * *

"HEY, EVERYONE. I'M BOBBY TANNEN."

The no-big-deal greeting is almost comical at this point because everyone knows who Bobby is. Literally *everyone*.

He's had two more number-one songs since he got that first big check, and one of his hits plays on country radio every hour of the day. His three-month concert tour is completely sold out, and there's a whole new group of people clamoring to get a piece of him.

But he's taking it all in stride as long as I'm by his side. That's what's important to us both.

He strums the strings of Betty, looking thoughtful. "For a long time, I fought doing this. I would play in the fields, and Brutal was the only one subjected to my shitty songs."

The audience laughs, and Bobby smirks, holding them in the palm of his hand even as Brutal shouts from the reserved family table, "Off-key every time until I taught him how to carry a tune in a bucket."

Ignoring the dig, Bobby continues. "Eventually, I found my balls, and Hank over there gave me a chance."

"Cocky shithead wouldn't take no for an answer," Unc yells over the din, keeping Bobby grounded and not letting his head get too big.

"Not like you paid me for those first gigs, anyway," Bobby retorts.

The crowd looks behind them, waiting for Unc's comeback, but he throws a dismissive hand in the air, giving Bobby the win.

"So I started singing up here," Bobby continues, "and it healed something broken in me. You helped me do that." It's a heavy confession, meaningfully exposing Bobby's soft underbelly, something he rarely does, even to me. "Now they want me to go around and sing for more folks. And I'm excited to do it, ain't gonna lie about that. But it won't ever be the same as singing right here at home. So, thank you . . . for listening, for singing with me, for making me well enough to do this for my family." He throws a meaningful look to the Tannens and Bennetts in the corner. "For myself."

Unexpected silence settles over the crowd, and then applause bursts out.

"Give 'em hell, Bobby!"

"Sing your heart out!"

"Bobby! Bobby! Bobby!"

That one turns into a chant, booted feet stomping to the beat. I think Bobby is getting his first real taste of what this concert tour might be like because his dark eyes go wide in surprise, and under the bright light, I can see a blush to his cheeks.

"Thank you." One last sincere phrase, and then he shakes his head, back to his gruff attitude. "Let's sing some shit."

And he does. He sings all his number-one songs, does a few favorite covers, and then sings a few songs off his just-released album. It's the first time he's played some of these in public, but the crowd sings along as though they've heard them dozens of times before.

I think Bobby's surprised at that, though he shouldn't be. He wrote them on a trip to Nashville in January, and they haven't even hit radio play yet. Miller had been happy to work with Bobby again, regardless of what record company he was signed with, and they'd made some beautiful music together.

The crowd sings along, swaying and holding their hands in the air, completely under Bobby's spell. I can understand that. I still pour Olivia's drinks and wait on the customers around the bar, but I'm slower than Shay's peach molasses because my attention is continually drawn to the stage. To Bobby. To my man.

I hum along too, mouthing the words that hit my heart sharply. Knowing they came from his mind, his heart, his soul, and how hard he has to work to get them just right makes each phrase and chord that much more poignant.

I pull my phone out, taking a few shots of him onstage. This last moment before things change, before he belongs to the world and not only Great Falls and me. *Click.*

My eyes are drawn to the screen, and I touch Bobby's face there, ready to get out of here so that it's the two of us. I need it to be just us one last time, his body pressed to mine, pinning us together as he fills me, making us one.

The music changes into a chord progression I haven't heard, and a throat clears heavily. I look up to find Bobby plucking at the strings. His jaw is tight, his shoulders broad, tension woven through his entire body.

What's wrong?

I scan the front row, looking for someone out of line, but I see nothing amiss. Next, I look along the bar, knowing that if he saw a tourist doing something inappropriate too close to me, he'd go into protective mode.

But all seems well.

I'm still searching when he starts to speak, "A few months ago . . ." He shakes his head, quietly asking himself, "How has it only been a few months? Seems like a lifetime. My life." Swallowing, he looks back to the audience. "Anyway, a few months ago, I stood right here, singing *Friends in Low Places*, and my whole life changed. Not by Garth Brooks, not even by you fuckers drunk-singing along with me. But by the woman I saw across the room."

I freeze, towel stuck in a glass and mouth hanging wide open.

What is he doing? What is he saying?

"I saw her, literally across a crowded room, and knew she was everything. She was . . . *is* mine." Bobby's eyes lift from the crowd, finding mine easily though I'm in the shadows of the bar and he's in the stage lights. He's always aware of me. I have no doubt that he could find me anywhere, even blindfolded. It's like his soul recognizes mine. "Willow, sweetheart . . . can you come here?"

I stutter—my feet, not my mouth, though I think I'm making a nonsensical noise too. "Uhm . . ."

Unc grabs my arm, shoving me out from behind the bar. When did he get so strong?

Olivia takes over, escorting me toward the stage, toward Bobby. Her words are jumbled and fast. "Remember what I said the first night you and Bobby met?" I have no idea what she's talking about and can't search my memory banks when Bobby's looking at me like I can't get to him fast enough.

As I pass the Tannen-Bennett table, they're all grinning. Even the guys, which is scary as hell because they only do that when someone's about to get beaten up.

Olivia gives me a push I don't need, and I find myself at Bobby's feet, looking up at him larger than life on the stage. Casually resting a hand on Betty, he looks down at me as though we're the only two people in the room. Heat and desire light his eyes, filthy promises are in his smirk, and hunger pings between us in a chemical reaction I can feel throughout my entire body.

Is he thinking this is very similar to when I suck him? Because that's what's running through my dirty mind when I look up at him like this.

"Mmm, close. But not close enough." I think he's reading my mind for a moment, but then Bobby leans Betty against a stool to free his hands. He squats down, and there's a moment where I feel like a fan whose wildest dreams are coming true. But truthfully, they already have. His hands grab under my arms, and he pulls me onstage with him, situating me on the stool as he picks Betty back up.

"I wrote a song, which might not seem all that special. But this is the most important one I've ever written, sweetheart. I only plan on singing it once."

Bobby gives me a pointed look, and his meaning hits me with a thud, a sharp arrow right into the depths of my heart. My mouth drops open and my hands slap over my lips. Behind my glasses, I can feel that my eyes are as wide as saucers.

"You ready?"

Yes.

No.

Oh, my God, maybe.

My head nods like a bobblehead.

And then Bobby sings. The crowd is gone and the room might as well be empty because he only has eyes for me and I am pinned in his gaze, lost in his words. His honeyed whiskey voice flows over me, the grit and gravel pricking my skin, letting the sweetness burrow into my soul.

> *Was an empty shell of a man,*
> *Waiting on you to find me.*
> *But when I found you,*
> *I found everything.*
> *All my days and nights belong to you,*
> *There will never be enough.*
> *Your heart belongs to me,*
> *It will always be mine.*
> *Sweet kindness from your soul,*
> *I don't deserve.*
> *But I'll get down on my knees*
> *To worship you.*

Bobby drops to his knee with his last lyric, pushing Betty behind his back to free his hands. He takes mine, the rough calluses on his fingers tracing over my skin like he can't believe I'm real and his. A shuddering sigh works its way through his body, his chest rising and falling raggedly.

"I'm not good with words, Willow. But you know my heart because it's yours. You know my soul. It's where I keep you safe and loved. And I'm deep inside you too—body, mind, and soul. You're mine. And I'm yours. You know what I want—forever." It's not a question, but I know exactly what he's asking of me.

Tears are pooling in my glasses, blurring my vision, but I can see Bobby. I can always see him, can feel him, deeply in love with me. Me, Willow Parker, outside, behind-the-scenes, quiet and forgettable. But he sees me, all of me, and loves me, has given me a home, and wants to spend forever with me.

I can't find words, which is usually the problem he thinks he has, but I nod.

"Tell me, Willow." The command goes through me in a jolt, making me hot and giving me strength.

"Yes," I shout, louder than I meant to, but the joy is so bright that it demands release.

Distantly, I hear the crowd cheering, but I don't care. All I feel are Bobby's arms wrapping around me tightly, his lips pressed to mine as he claims me proudly. I kiss him back, marking him as mine too. He hugs me again, lifting my feet off the stage and growling in my ear, "I love you. And I need to be inside you, right the fuck now."

I blush, hoping he hears my agreement to both of those statements when I say, "I love you, too."

He doesn't finish the set. I don't finish my shift. Hoots and cheers sound up around us, but none of it matters but the man by my side. Well, figuratively by my side, because he's got me scooped up in his arms, striding briskly for the door as the crowd parts for us.

I hear him call out, "Brutal, take Betty home." Then we're outside, the mild spring coolness of the night instantly surrounding us. You'd think it'd quiet the fire in my core, but the flames still lick along my skin from Bobby's hands where they grip me and through my body.

I need him too.

"Get in the truck. Now." His voice has gone even deeper than usual, already entering the bossy, gritty way he commands me when he loses all sense of gentleness and takes me rough and hard.

I would've thought I'd want sweet and tender after that proposal, but he knows me too well by this point. He knows I need him to mark me all over, order me to say filthy things that make me blush as I force them past my vocal cords, and take me like I'm his. Because I am.

* * *

THE BUS IS HUGE, so big it won't even fit through the main gate at Tannen Farm. It's blocking the street outside instead, with Chief Gibson standing out there to direct traffic. Except there's no traffic. He's just here to see Bobby off like a looky-loo.

"All right, fuckers. I'm out of here."

Bobby's using grunts and grumpiness to hide his nerves and fear. It's understandable considering the other guys are doing the same thing. Luckily, the women have emotions enough for us all.

We're a blubbering, snotty, crying mess as we hug and make promises of daily phone calls and texts.

"I'll send you a soap basket every month and overnight cobbler every week," Shayanne vows. Then I'm locked in her arms. "Oh, my cheesus and crackers, I'm going to miss you!"

"Shay, let her go," Luke says, gathering her in his arms comfortingly.

Bobby holds a hand out to Brutal, whose arms are crossed, his face in a deep scowl. Brutal knocks Bobby's hand away to wrap his arms around his shoulders. Bobby startles, likely thinking Brutal's taking an easy shot—that's their way, after all—but he recovers and slaps his back a bit too hard. They push off each other, both looking surprised at the emotion coursing through them. "Don't fuck up the planting or you'll kill the whole year's profits."

Brutal snorts. "I do it all by myself every year. This year, I just won't have to give you busy work to keep you out of my way."

Bobby punches Brutal's shoulder, more of a love tap than

anything. Brutal's brows jump together, and he swats at the empty air around him. "Y'all gettin' eat up by mosquitoes? I swear one just took a nibble out of my arm. Must be 'cuz I'm so sweet."

Brody steps between them, sensing the tussle that'll hide their emotions. "Stop the lovefest, you two. You're giving me cavities with all the sugar." In a fatherly move, he lays heavy hands on Bobby's shoulders and meets his eyes. "You be careful out there. Don't let them take advantage of you or change you. If I see one picture of you with sparkly shit on your ass, I will pull up to that concert venue and remind you of exactly who you are."

"Won't be necessary. I'm a Tannen. I'd rather die than have a rhinestone ass."

They laugh, somehow bonding through the weirdness of the conversation and situation. Brody hugs Bobby too, and though it's quiet, I hear Brody say, "Glad you're getting outta here, man. You deserve it. You always did."

When they break apart, I step forward. "Tannens, get together."

They look at me, instantly standing side by side—three men, so alike but so different, all standing shoulder to shoulder, matching mean mugs on their faces, and Shayanne, looking like a dirty tomboy princess beside them with a big smile. *Click.*

"And Bennetts." They step up, filling in around Bobby. Arms go around each other, making the group look like a big dog pile of rough cowboys and a mix of women. *Click.*

Mama Louise approaches me. "Get in there with them. Let me take one of the next generation." Her blue eyes are bright with unshed tears, and I wonder what she thought her future would hold when she was younger and if it looked anything like this motley group.

I lift the camera strap over my head, handing the delicate machine to her. "Press the button halfway and it'll focus, then the rest of the way and it'll take the picture. Hold it down and it'll take several shots in a row so we get everyone's eyes open."

She nods but whispers, "Take care of each other, okay? Let his strengths balance your weaknesses and yours his. *Love* him—not the noun, the verb—and he'll love you too."

I hug her, knowing that she loves each of us—her whole family.

I join Bobby, and he tucks me into his side, pressing a kiss to my temple. "Are we doing this?" he whispers.

I look up at him, sure. "Dream come true."

Click.

EPILOGUE

BOBBY

"*Hey*, Dallas. I'm Bobby Tannen," I rumble into the microphone. The crowd instantly screams, chanting my name. It's wildly, crazily insane, and I will never get used to it. I still think that I'm going to walk out every time and people are going to ask 'who's this guy?' and boo me off the stage.

Tonight is my last show of the tour. My first tour.

It's been all I dreamed of and then some. This is what I hoped it would be. Stephen Wheatley has done right by me at every turn —arranging sessions with Miller when I have songs ready, helping me pick a great group of musicians to back me up every night, and managing the tour so that I never have to worry about a thing.

I couldn't have done any of this without him, or the guys playing with me, or most of all, Willow. She's been by my side the whole way.

Even when the three months we planned turned into six.

We'd talked it out, called her Mom and Hank, talked to Brody and Brutal, and decided to do it. Hank had sworn up and down that he was fine, and he even hired another bartender, which made Willow jealous but also less guilty about being gone. Brody and Brutal promised that the farm was doing well. They had to hire on a helper full-time, and I'd bristled at being

354

replaced too, but I'd understood. Brutal had bitched about having to teach the guy how to plant and harvest and said he didn't know shit from manure, but I think that was mostly to make me feel better.

Still, even with everyone singing along with me, I'm ready to go home. Both Willow and I are.

The last note of the last song fades into the night. "Thank you everyone!"

It's done. The tour is over, officially.

The guys invite me to party with them—nothing too hardcore, we keep it pretty chill—but I turn them down. I'm exhausted and need to fall into my girl and nothing else.

We did it. We actually fucking did it. Together.

On the tour bus, I jump in the shower to wash the sweat of the stage off. Willow curls up on the couch, sipping tea and flipping through pictures on her computer, waiting for me. It's our nightly routine these days, but tomorrow will be a totally different thing. I can't wait and have already made my requests for fried chicken, fried okra, green beans, macaroni and cheese, and honey biscuits with Mama Louise.

Wearing only boxer briefs, I flop to the couch next to Willow. Her soft smile fills that Willow-shaped spot inside me, making me complete.

Golden shining gray eyes, I fall into your sway, knowing you will save me every time.

I run my fingers through her hair, brushing it behind her ear so I can see her profile.

She tilts the laptop my way, smiling. "What do you think of these?"

She clicks through several pictures she took from the wings of the stage. She's already started processing them, changing some of them to black and white and cropping others. I'm front and center of every shot. I shrug, knowing it'll be what she wants in the end. "Anything you want. That's your area of expertise, sweetheart."

It is. She's been taking pictures of our entire tour, compiling them into a Tour One book with stories and excerpts from me and the band. I'd laughed when she told me the book's name, so sure that there'd be a tour two. Funny thing is, she's right. Stephen's already making plans, but not for at least a year.

I miss having my hands in the dirt, working by Brutal's side, and having dinner around Mama Louise's table every night. Plus, we're not bringing a newborn on the road and Willow is due in a few short months.

Yeah, she's having my baby. Another Tannen generation of a badass boy or maybe a sweet girl. We won't find out until the baby is here. Willow wants it that way as a bit of a surprise, and I couldn't possibly deny her anything. What Willow wants, she gets. I'll move hell and high water to make it so, no matter the request. But this had been an easy one.

She clicks through the pictures again, humming to herself. Does she even know she's humming one of my songs? I look back to the screen to see what's got her so enthralled, a zing going through me when I see that it's me. She keeps working hard, and I try to wait patiently, though it's difficult when I want to be the focus of her attention. The real me, not the me on the laptop.

But she's dedicated, spending time every day prepping for the book and posting to her blog.

The tour book will be published under a pseudonym because Willow has been exceedingly careful to keep her identity as my wife and her blog persona very separate. She'll go out in whatever city we're in—explore museums, visit street vendors, and see the sights. She always comes back excited, telling me about the architecture, the gardens, the colors, and the life as she shows me each shot. I'd love to go with her, but I'm a bit too recognizable now, so I live vicariously through her. I don't have any interest in museums, anyway, but I am interested in her and making sure that she has every reason to smile that soft smile every single day.

I think she's right that people prefer the anonymity of the blog, though, finding themselves in some aspect of the pictures she takes. Whatever it is, it's working well for her because her number of followers keeps rising higher and higher.

"Ooh!" She startles and grabs her phone. Zooming in on my boots on the floor, she takes several shots. *Click.*

Those boots have seen a lot of miles, Tannen Farm dirt,

Bennett Ranch cow shit, and roads all over the nation. And now they'll see home again.

"I've already got a heart and a comment," she murmurs a second later.

"What'd you caption for my dirty old boots?" I ask, snuggling into her side. I'm done with pictures and singing, ready to fall into bed with her.

"*Love my rough country man.* With a diamond ring and a heart emoji," she says smugly, knowing I'll like that.

"I love you too. Let's go to bed and then go home."

I place my large palm over her belly, but I need to feel the satin of her skin. I push her shirt up over the growing bump, and she wiggles, trying to silently argue against letting me see the few pink marks that recently appeared there. I still her with a gentle kiss to each one.

"You're beautiful, always. You do everything for everyone, and now, you're doing the most amazing thing anyone's ever done for me, carrying my baby."

As if the baby hears my voice, I feel a small bump against my hand. I gasp, grinning at the feeling. When I look up at Willow, she's holding her phone low in front of her.

Click.

I growl, shoving the phone down and climbing up her body. I hold myself up on my arms, keeping my weight off her, but I need to kiss her to celebrate. I need to feel her . . . under me, around me, owning me, and letting me claim her.

The kiss is sweet, our lips smacking as we smile against one another. But as always, it turns heated quickly.

"Fuck, sweetheart, flip over. Let me inside."

She moves, following my order. Kneeling with her arms on the back of the couch, I stand behind her, glad the bus won't move for a few hours while the crew breaks down the stage equipment. I run my hands down her back, and she arches for me, her bucking hips telling me how much she wants my cock.

"Tell me, Willow. You ready for me?"

"Always," she gasps.

"What do you want?"

"Fill me." She knows that's not enough, not by a mile. I

squeeze her hips, denting the supple flesh there, and she groans. "Fuck me."

Shit. I lose control when she says anything slightly filthy, and she knows it, uses that knowledge to push me to the edge of sanity. I know what she wants too.

"I'm gonna fuck you, Willow, fill this sweet pussy with my cock, rub that little clit, and make you come for me. Over and over. I'll decide when you're done coming because this pussy is mine. You are mine."

The words meant to drive her wild affect us both. When I push into her, she's slick and her body gives for me easily. "*Yes*," she groans.

I grunt in bliss. "How do you feel like heaven every time?" I murmur, lost in the sensation of her pussy gripping me tightly.

Though I mean to fuck her hard and fast, I can't do it right now. I need her slow and tender. My Willow, my girl, the mother of our child.

I don't know how I got so lucky. I'm just a rough country asshole, but this sweet woman saw something in me worth taking a chance on, and I'm so thankful. Every day, I show her how much I love her. I might not have the words, but I show her every way I can.

Chasing down my dream so I can give you yours.
The proof of a man is in his woman's eyes.
Storm for me, shine for me, show your soul for me.
And I'll dig down deep to get mine so you can have yours.

Thank you for reading! I hope you enjoyed the conclusion to the Tannen Boys and the great cast of characters in this world! It's sad to say goodbye, they will forever have a place in my heart… and hopefully in yours!

EXCERPT: DIRTY TALK

KATRINA

"*C*heckmate, bitch," I exclaim as I do a victory dance that's comprised of fist pumps and ass wiggles in my chair while my best friend Elise laughs at me. I turn in my seat and start doing a little half-stepping Rockettes dance. "Can-can, I just kicked some can-can, I so am the wo-man, and I rule this place!"

Elise does a little finger dance herself, cheering along with me.

"You go, girl. Winner, winner, chicken dinner. Now let's eat!"

I laugh with her, joyful in celebrating my new promotion at work, regardless of the dirty looks the snooty ladies at the next table are shooting our way.

I get their looks. I mean, we are in the best restaurant in the city. While East Robinsville isn't New York or Miami, we're more of a Northeastern suburb of . . . well, everything in between. This just isn't the sort of restaurant where five-foot-two-inch women in work clothes go shaking their ass while chanting something akin to a high school cheer.

But right now, I give exactly zero fucks.

"Damn right, we can eat! I'm the youngest person in the company to ever be promoted to Senior Developer and the first woman at that level. Glass ceiling? Boom, busting through! Boys' club? Infiltrated."

I mime like I'm sneaking in, shoulders hunched and hands

pressed tightly in front of me before splaying my arms wide with a huge grin.

"Before they know it, I'm gonna have that boys' club watching chick flicks and the whole damn office is going to be painted pink!"

Elise snorts, shaking her head again. "I still don't have a fucking clue what you actually do, but even I understand the words *promotion* and *raise*. So huge congrats, honey."

She's right, no one really understands when I talk about my job. My brain has a tendency to talk in streams of binary zeroes and ones that make perfect sense to me, but not so much to the average person. When I was in high school, I even dreamed in Java.

And even I don't really understand what my promotion means. Senior Developer? Other than the fact that I get updated business cards with my fancy new title next week, I'm not sure what's changed. I'm still doing my own coding and my own work, just with a slightly higher pay grade. And when I say slightly, I mean barely a bump after taxes. Just enough for a bonus cocktail at a swanky club on Friday maybe. *Maybe* more at year end, they'd said. Ah, well, I'm excited anyway. It's a first step and an acknowledgement of my work.

The part people do get is when my company turns my strings of code into apps that go viral. After my last app went number one, they were forced to give me a promotion or risk losing my skills to another development company. They might not understand the zeroes and ones, but everyone can grasp dollars and cents, and that's what my apps bring in.

I might be young at only twenty-six, and female, as evidenced by my long honey-blonde hair and curvy figure, but as much as I don't fit the stereotypical profile of a computer nerd, they had to respect that my brain creates things that no one else does.

I think it's my female point of view that really helps. While a chunk of the other people in the programming field fit the stereotype of being slightly repressed geeks who are more comfortable watching animated 'girlfriends' than talking to an actual woman, I'm different. I understand that merely slapping a pink font on things or adding sparkly shit and giving more preloaded shopping options doesn't make technology more 'female-friendly.'

It's insulting, honestly. But it gives me an edge in that I know how to actually create apps that women like and want to use. Not just women, either, based on sales. I'm getting a lot of men downloading my apps too, especially men who aren't into tech-geeking out every damn thing they own.

And so I celebrate with Elise, holding up our glasses of wine and clinking them together in a toast. Elise sips her wine and nods in appreciation, making me glad we went with the waiter's recommendation.

"So you're killing it on the job front. What else is going on? How are things with you and Kevin?"

Elise has been my best friend since we met at a college recruiting event. She's all knockout looks and sass, and I'm short, nervous, and shy in professional situations, but we clicked. She knows I've been through the wringer with some previous boyfriends, and even though Kevin is fine—well-mannered, ambitious, and treats me right—she just doesn't care for him for some reason. So my joyful buzz is instantly dulled, knowing that she doesn't like Kevin.

"He's fine," I reply, knowing it's not a great answer, but I also know she's going to roast me anyway. "He's been working a lot of hours so I haven't even seen him in a few days, but he texts me every morning and night. We're supposed to go out for dinner this weekend to celebrate."

Elise sighs, giving me that look that makes her normally very cute face look sort of like a sarcastic basset hound.

"I'm glad, I guess. Not to beat a dead horse," —*too late*— "but you really can do better. Kevin is just so . . . meh. There's no spark, no fire between you two. It's like you're friends who fuck."

I duck my chin, not wanting her to read on my face the woeful lack of fucking that has been happening, but I'm too transparent.

"Wait . . . you two *do* fuck, right?" Elise asks, flabbergasted. "I figured that was why you were staying with him. I was sure he must be great in the sack or you'd have dumped his boring ass a long time ago."

I bite my lip, not wanting to get into this with her . . . again.

But one of Elise's greatest strengths is also one of her most annoying traits as well. She's like a dog with a bone and isn't going to let this go.

"Look, he's fine," I finally reply, trying to figure out how much I need to feed Elise before she gives me a measure of peace. "He's handsome, treats me well, and when we have sex, it's good . . . I guess. I don't believe in some Prince Charming who is going to sweep me off my feet to a castle where we'll have romantic candlelit dinners, brilliant conversation, and bed-breaking sexcapades. I just want someone to share the good and bad times with, some companionship."

Elise holds back as long as she can before she explodes, her snort and guffaw of derision getting even more looks in our direction.

"Then get a fucking Golden Retriever and a rabbit. The buzzing kind that uses rechargeable batteries."

One of the ladies at the next table huffs, seemingly aghast at Elise's outburst, and they stand to move toward the bar on the other side of the restaurant, far away from us.

"Well, if this is the sort of trash that passes for dinner conversation," the older one says as she sticks her nose far enough into the air I wonder if it's going to be clipped by the ceiling fans, "no wonder the country's going to hell under these Millennials!"

She storms off before Elise or I can respond, but the second lady pauses slightly and talks out of the side of her mouth. "Sweetie, you do deserve more than *fine*."

With a wink, she scurries off after her friend, leaving behind a grinning Elise. "See? Even snooty old biddies know that you deserve more than *meh*."

"I know. We've had this conversation on more than one occasion, so can we drop it?" I plead between clenched teeth before calming slightly. "I want to celebrate and catch up, not argue about my love life."

Always needing the last word, Elise drops her voice, muttering under her breath. "What love life?"

"That's low."

Elise holds her hands up, and I know I've at least gotten a temporary reprieve. "Okay then, if we're sticking to work, I got a new scoop that I'm running with. I'm writing a piece about a certain famous someone who got caught sending dick pics to a social media princess. Don't ask me who because I can't divulge that yet. But it'll be all there in black and white by next week's column."

Elise is an investigative journalist, a rather fantastic one whose talents are largely being wasted on celebrity news gossip for the tabloid paper she writes for. I can't even call it a paper, really. With the downfall of actual print news, most of her stuff ends up in cyberspace, where it's digested, Tweeted, hashtagged, and churned out for the two-minute attention span types to gloat over for a moment before they move on to . . . well, whatever the next sound bite happens to be.

Every once in awhile, she'll get to do something much more newsworthy, but mostly it's fact-checking and ass-covering before the paper publishes stories celebrities would rather see disappear. I know what burns her ass even more is when she has to cover the stories where some downward-trending celebrity manufactures a scandal just to get some social media buzz going before their latest attempt at rejuvenating a career that peaked about five years ago.

This one at least sounds halfway interesting, and frankly, better than my love life, so I laugh. "Why would he send a dick pic to someone on social media? Wouldn't he assume she'd post it? What a dumbass!"

"No, it's usually close-ups and they're posted anonymously," Elise says with a snort. "Of course, she knows because she sees the user name on their direct message, but she cuts it out so that it's posted to her page as an anonymous flash of flesh. Look."

She pulls out her phone, clicking around to open an app, one I didn't design but damn sure wish I had. It's got one hell of a sweet interface, and Elise is using it to organize her web pages better than anything the normal apps have. It takes Elise only a moment to find the page she wants.

"See?" she says, showing me her phone. "People send her messages with dick pics, tit pics, whatever. If she deems them sexy enough, she posts them with little blurbs and people can comment. She also does Q-and-As with followers, shows faceless pics of herself, and gives little shows sometimes. Kinda like porn but more 'real people' instead of silicone-stuffed, pump-sucked, fake moan scenes."

She scrolls through, showing me one image after another of body part close-ups. Some of them . . . well damn, I gotta say that while they might not be professionals or anything, it's a hell of a lot hotter than anything I'm getting right now.

"Wow. That's uhh . . . quite something. I don't get it, but I guess lots of folks are into it. Wait."

She stops scrolling at my near-shout, smirking. "What? See something you like?"

My mouth feels dry and my voice papery. "Go back up a couple."

She scrolls back up and I read the blurb above a collage of pics. *Little titty fuck with my new boy toy today. Look at my hungry tits and his thick cock. After this, things got a little deeper, if you know what I mean. Sorry, no pics of that, but I'll just say that he was insatiable and I definitely had a very good morning. ;)*

The pictures show a close-up of her full cleavage, a guy's dick from above, and then a few pictures of him stroking in and out of her pressed-together breasts. I'm not afraid to say the girl's got a nice rack that would probably have most of my co-workers drooling and the blood rushing from their brains to their dicks, but that's not what's causing my stomach to drop through the floor.

I know that dick.

It's the same, thick with a little curve to the right, and I can even see a sort of donut-shaped mole high on the man's thigh, right above the shaved area above the base of his cock.

Yes, that mole seals it.

That's Kevin.

His cock with another woman, fucking her for social media, thinking I'd probably never even know. He has barely touched me lately, but he's willing to do it almost publicly with some social media slut?

I realize Elise is staring at me, her previous good-natured look long gone to be replaced by an expression of concern. "Kat, are you okay? You look pale."

I point at her phone, trying my best to keep my voice level. "That post? The one right there?"

"Oh, Titty Fuck Girl?" Elise asks. "She's on here at least once a month with a new set of pics. Apparently, she loves her rack. I still think they're fake. Why?"

"She's talking about Kevin. That's him."

She gasps, turning the phone to look closer. "Holy shit, honey. Are you sure?"

I nod, tears already pooling in my eyes. "I'm sure."

She puts her phone down on the table and comes around the table to hug me. "Shit. Shit. Shit. I am so sorry. I told you that douchebag doesn't deserve someone like you. You're too fucking good for him."

I sniffle, nodding, but deep inside, I know that this is always how it goes. Every single boyfriend I've ever had ended up cheating on me. I've tried playing hard to get. I've tried being the good little go-along girlfriend. I've even tried being myself, which seems to be somewhere in between, once I figured out who I actually was.

It's even worse in bed, where I've tried being vanilla, being aggressive, and being submissive. And again, being myself, somewhere in the middle, when I figured out what I enjoyed from the experimentation.

But honestly, I've never been satisfied. No matter what, I just can't seem to find that 'sweet spot' that makes me happy and fulfilled in a relationship. And while I've tried everything, depending on the guy, it never works out. The boyfriends I've had, while few in number considering I can count them on one hand, all eventually cheated, saying that they just wanted something different. Something that's *not* me.

Apparently, Kevin's no different. My mood shifts wildly from self-pity to anger to finally, a numb acceptance.

"What a fucking jerk. I hope he likes being a boy toy for a social media slut, because he's damn sure not my boyfriend anymore."

"That's the spirit," Elise says, refilling my wine glass. "Now, how about you and I finish off this bottle, get another, and by the time you're done, you'll have forgotten all about that loser while we take a cab back to your place?"

"Maybe I will just get a dog, and I sure as hell already have a buzzing rabbit. Several of them, in fact," I mutter. "You know what? They're better than he ever was by a damn country mile."

"Rabbits . . . they just keep going and going and going," Elise jokes, trying to keep me in good spirits. She twirls her hands in the air like the famous commercial bunny and signals for another bottle of wine.

She's right. Fuck Kevin.

DERRICK

My black leather office chair creaks, an annoying little trend it's developed over the past six months that's the primary reason I don't use it in the studio. Admittedly, that's probably for the better because if I had a chair this comfortable in the studio, I'd be too relaxed to really be on point for my shows.

Still, it's helpful to have something nice like this office since it's a hell of a big step up from the days when my office was also the station's break room.

"All right, hit me. What's on the agenda for today's show?"

My co-star, Susannah, checks her papers, making little check-marks as she goes through each item.

She's an incessant checkmarker, and I have no idea how the fuck she can read her sheets by the end of the day.

"The overall theme for today is cheaters, and I've got several emails pulled for that so we can stay on track. We'll field calls, of course, and some will be on topic and some off, like always. I'll try and screen them as best I can, and we should be all set."

I nod, trying to mentally prep myself for another three-hour stint behind the mic, offering music, advice, hope, and sometimes a swift kick in the pants to our listeners. Two years ago, I never would've believed that I'd be known as the 'Love Whisperer' on a radio talk segment called the same thing. Part Howard Stern, part Dr. Phil, part DJ Love Below, I've found a niche that's just . . . unique.

I started out many years ago as a jock, playing football on my high school team with dreams of college ball. A seemingly short derailment after an injury led me to do sports reporting for my high school's news and I fell in love.

After that, my scholarships to play football never came, but it didn't bother me as much as I thought it would. I decided to chase after a sports broadcast degree instead, marrying my passion for football and my love of reporting.

I spent four years after graduation doing daily sports talks from three to six as the afternoon drive-home DJ. It wasn't a big station, just one of the half-dozen stations that existed as an alternative for people who didn't want to listen to corporate pop, hip-hop, or country. It was there I received that fateful call.

Looking back, it's kind of crazy, but a guy had called in bitching and moaning about his wife not understanding his need to follow all these wild superstitions to help his team win.

"I'm telling you D, I went to church and asked God himself. I said, if you can bless the Bandits with a win, I'll show myself true and wear those ugly ass socks my pastor gave me for Christmas the year before and never wash them again. You know what happened?"

Of course, everyone could figure out what happened. Still, I respectfully told him that I didn't think his unwashed socks were doing a damn thing for his beloved team on the basketball court, but if he didn't put those fuckers in the washing machine, they were sure going to land him in divorce court.

He sighed and eventually gave in when I told him to wash the socks, thank his wife for putting up with his shit, and full-out romance her to bed and do his damndest to make up for his selfish ways.

And that was that. A new show and a new me were born. After a few marketing tweaks, I've been the so-called 'Love Whisperer' for almost a year now, helping people who ask for advice to get the happily ever after they want.

Ironically, I'm single. Funny how that works out, but all the good advice I try to give stems from my parents who were happily married for over forty years before my mom passed. I won't settle for less than the real thing, and I try to advise my listeners to do the same.

And then there's the sex aspect of my job.

Talking about relationships obviously involves discussing sex with people, as that's one of the major areas that cause problems for folks. At first, talking about all the crazy shit people want to do even made me blush a little, but eventually, it's just gotten to be second nature.

Want to talk about how to get your wife to massage your prostate? Can do. Want to talk about how your girlfriend wants you to wear Underoos and call her Mommy? Can do. Want to talk about your husband never washing the dishes, and how you can get him to help? I can do that too.

All-in-one, real relationships at your service. Live from six to nine, five days a week, or available for download on various podcast sites and clip shows on the weekends. Hell of a lot for a guy who figured *making it* would involve becoming the voice of some college football team.

So I want to do a good job. And that means working well with Susannah, who is the control-freak yin to my laissez-faire yang.

"Thanks. I know this week's topics from our show planning meeting, but I spaced on tonight's focus."

Susannah nods, unflappable. "No problem. Do you want to scan the emails or just do your thing?"

I smile at her. She already knows the answer. "Same as always, spontaneous. You know that even though I was a Boy Scout, being prepared for this doesn't do us any favors. I sound robotic when I read ahead. First read, real reactions work better and give the listeners knee-jerk common sense."

She shrugs, scribbling on her papers. "I know, just checking."

It's probably one of the reasons we work so well together, our totally different approaches to the show. Joining me from day one, she's the one who keeps our show running behind the scenes and keeps me on track on-air, serving as both producer and co-host. Luckily, her almost anal-retentive penchant for prep totally doesn't come across on the air, where she's the playful, comedic counter to my gruff, tell-it-like-it-is style.

"Then let's rock," I tell her. "Got your drinks ready?"

Susannah nods as we head toward the studio. Settling into my broadcast chair, a much less comfortable but totally silent one, I survey my normal spread of one water, one coffee, and one green tea, one for every hour we're gonna be on the air. With the top of the hour news breaks and spaced out music jams, I've gotten used to using the exactly four minute and thirty second breaks to run next door and drain my bladder if I need to.

Everything ready, we smile and settle in for another show. "Gooooood evening! It's your favorite 'Love Whisperer,' Derrick King here with my lovely assistant, Miss Susannah Jameson. We're ready for an evening of love, sex, betrayal, and lust, if you're willing to share. Our focus tonight is on cheaters and cheating. Are you being cheated on? Maybe *you* are the cheater? Call in and we'll talk."

The red glow from the holding calls is instant, but I traditionally go to an email first so that I can roll right in.

"While Susannah is grabbing our first caller, I'll start with an email. Here's one from P. 'Dear Love Whisperer,' it says, 'my husband travels extensively for work, leaving me home and so lonely. I don't know if he's cheating while he's gone, but I always wonder. I've started to develop feelings for my personal trainer, and I think I'm falling in love with him. What should I do?' "

I *tsk-tsk* into the microphone, making my displeasure clear. "Well, P, first things first. Your marriage is your priority because you made a vow. For better or worse, remember? It's simple. Talk to your husband. Maybe he's cheating, maybe he isn't. Maybe he's working his ass off so his bored wife can even *have* a trainer and you're looking for excuses to justify your own bad behavior. But talking to him is your first step. You need to explain your feelings and that you need him more than perhaps you need the money. Second, you need to get a life beyond your husband and trainer. I get the sense you need some attention and your trainer is giving it to you, so you think you're in love with him. Newsflash—he's being paid to give you attention. By your husband, it sounds like. That's not a healthy foundation for a relationship even if he is your soulmate, which I doubt."

I sigh and lower my voice a little. I don't want to cut this woman's guts out. I want to help her. "P, let's be honest. A good trainer is going to be personable. They're in a sales profession. They're not going to make it in the industry without either being the best in the world at what they do or having a good personality. And a lot of them have good bodies. Their bodies are their business cards. So it's natural to feel some attraction to your trainer. But that doesn't mean he's going to stick by you. Here's a challenge—tell your trainer you can't pay him for the next three months and see how available he is to just give you his time."

Susannah snickers and hits her mic button. "That's why I do group yoga classes. Only thing that happens there is sweaty tantric orgies. Ohmm . . . my . . ." Her initial yoga-esque ohm dissolves into a pleasure-induced moan that she fakes exceedingly well.

I roll my eyes, knowing that she does nothing of the sort. "To the point, though, fire your trainer because of your weakness and tell him why. He's a pro. He needs to know that his services were not the reason you're leaving. Next, get a hobby that fulfills you beyond a man and talk to your husband."

I click a button and a sound effect of a cheering audience plays through my headset. It goes on like this for a while, call after call, email after email of helping people.

Well, I hope I'm helping them. They seem to think I am, and I'm certainly giving it my best shot. In between, I mix in music and a hodgepodge of stuff that fits the daily themes. Tonight I've got some Taylor Swift, a little Carrie Underwood, some old-school TLC. I even, as a joke, worked in Bobby Brown at Susannah's insistence.

Coming back from that last one, I see Susannah gesture from her mini-booth and give the airspace over to her, letting her introduce the next caller.

"Okay, Susannah's giving me the big foam finger, so what've we got?"

"You wish I had a big finger for you," Susannah teases like she always does on air—it's part of our act. "The next caller would like to discuss some rather incriminating photos she's come across. Apparently, Mr. Right was Mr. Everybody?"

I click the button, taking the call live on-air. "This is the 'Love Whisperer', who am I speaking with?"

The caller stutters, obviously nervous, and in my mind I know I have to treat this one gently. Some of the callers just want to laugh, maybe have their fifteen seconds of fame or get their pound of proverbial flesh by exposing their partner's misdeeds. But there are also callers like this, who I suspect really needs help.

"This is Katrina . . . Kat."

Whoa, a first name. And from the sound of it, a real one. She's not making a thing up. I need to lighten the mood a little, or else she's gonna clam up and freak out on me.

"Hello, Kitty Kat. What seems to be the problem today?"

I hear her sigh, and it touches me for some reason. "Well . . . I can't believe I actually got through, first of all. I worked up the nerve to dial the numbers but didn't expect an answer. I'm just . . . I don't even know what I am. I'm just a little lost and in need of some advice, I guess." She huffs out a humorless laugh.

I can hear the pain in her voice, mixed with nerves. "Advice? That I can do. That's what I'm here for, in fact. What's going on, Kat?"

"It's my boyfriend, or my soon-to-be ex-boyfriend, I guess. I found out today that he slept with someone else." She sounds like she's found a bit of steel as she speaks this time, and it makes her previous vulnerability all the more touching.

"Ouch," I say, truly wincing at the fresh wound. A day of cheat call? I'm sure the advertisers are rubbing their hands in glee, but I'm feeling for this girl. "I'm so sorry. I know that hurts and it's wrong no matter what. I heard something about compromising pics. Please tell me he didn't send you pics of him screwing someone else?"

She laughs but it's not in humor. "No, I guess that would've been worse, but he had sex with someone kind of Internet famous and she posted faceless pics of them together. But I recognized his . . . uhm . . . his . . ."

Let's just get the schlong out in the open, why don't we? "You recognized his penis? Is that the word you're looking for?"

"Yeah, I guess so," Kat says, her voice cutting through the gap created by the phone line. "He has a mole, so I know it's him."

There's something about her voice, all sweet and breathy that stirs me inside like I rarely have happen. It's not just her tone, either. She's in pain, but she's mad as fuck too, and I want to help her, protect her. She seems innocent, and something deep inside me wants to make her a little bit dirty.

"Okay, first, repeat after me. Penis, dick, cock." I wait, unsure if she'll do it but holding my breath in the hopes that she will.

"Uh, what?"

I feel a small smile come to my lips, and it's my turn to be a little playful. "Penis, dick, cock. Trust me, this is important for you. You can do it, Kitty Kat."

I hear her intake of breath, but she does what I demanded, more clearly than the shyness I expected. "Penis, dick, cock."

"Good girl," I growl into the mic, and through the window connecting our booths, I can see Susannah giving me a raised eyebrow. "Now say . . . I recognized his cock fucking her."

I say a silent prayer of thanks that my radio show is on satellite. I can say whatever I want and the FCC doesn't care.

I can tell Kat is with me now, and her voice is stronger, still sexy as fuck but without the lost kitten loneliness to it.

"I recognized his cock fucking her tits."

My own cock twitches a little, and I lean in, smirking. "Ah, so the plot thickens. So Kat, how does it feel to say that?"

She sighs, pulling me back a little. "The words don't bother me. I'm just not used to being on the radio. But saying that about my boyfriend pisses me off. I can't believe he'd do that."

"So, what do you think you should do about it?" I ask, leaning back in my chair and pulling my mic toward me. "Is this a 'talk it through and our relationship will be stronger on the other side of this' type situation, or is this a 'hit the road, motherfucker, and take Miss Slippy-Grippy Tits with you?' Do you want my opinion or do you already know?"

"You're right," Kat says, chuckling and sounding stronger again. "I already know I'm done. He's been a wham-bam-doesn't-even-say thank you, ma'am guy all along, and I've been hanging on because I didn't think I deserved better. But I don't deserve this. I'm better off alone."

Whoa, now, only half right there, Kat with the sexy voice. "You don't deserve this. You should have someone who treats you so well you never question their love, their commitment to you. Everyone deserves that. Hey, Kitty Kat? One more thing. Can you say 'cock' for me one more time? Just for . . . entertainment."

I'm pushing the line here, both for her and for the show, but I ask her to do it anyway because I want, no need, to hear her say it.

She laughs, her voice lighter even as I know the serious conversation had to hurt. "Of course, Love Whisperer. Anything for you. You ready? Cock." She draws the word out, the k a bit harsher, and I can hear the sass, almost an invitation, as she speaks.

"Ooh, thanks so much, Kitty Kat. Hold on the line just a second." My cock is now fully hard in my pants, and I'm not sure if my upcoming bathroom break is going to be to piss or to take care of that.

I click some buttons, sending the show to a song, Shaggy's *It Wasn't Me* coming over the airwaves to keep the cheating theme rolling. "Susannah?"

"Yeah?"

"Handle the next call or so after the commercial break," I tell her. "Pick something . . . funny after that one."

"Gotcha," Susannah says, and I'm glad she's able to handle things like that. It's part of our system too that when I get a call that needs more than on-air can handle, she fills the gap. Usually with less serious questions or listener stories that always make for great laughs.

Checking my board, I click the line back, glad that Susannah can't hear me now. "Kat? You still there?"

"Yes?" she says, and I feel another little thrill go down my cock just at her word. God, this woman's got a sexy voice, soft and sweet with a little undercurrent of sassiness . . . or maybe I really, really need to get laid.

"Hey, it's Derrick. I just wanted to say thanks for being such a good sport with all of that."

"No problem," she says as I make a picture in my head of her. I can't fill in the details, but I definitely want to. "Thanks for helping me realize I need to walk away. I already knew it, but some inspiration never hurts."

"I really would like to hear the rest of the story if you don't mind calling me back. I want to hear how he grovels when he finds out what he's lost. Would you call me?"

I don't know what I'm doing. This is so not like me. I never talk to the callers after they're on air unless I think they're going to hurt themselves or others, and I certainly never invite them to call back. But something about her voice calls to me like a siren. I just hope she's not pulling me into the rocky shore to crash.

"You mean the show?" Kat asks, uncertain and confused. "Like . . . I dunno, like a guest or something?"

"Well, probably not, to be honest," I reply, crossing my fingers even as my cock says I need to take this risk. "We'll be done with the cheating theme tonight and it probably won't come back up for a couple of weeks. I meant . . . call me. I want to make sure you're okay afterward and standing strong."

"Okay."

Before she can take it back, I rattle off my personal cell number to her, half of my brain telling me this is brilliant and the other half saying it's the stupidest thing I've ever done. I might not have the FCC looking over my shoulder, but the satellite network is and my advertisers for damn sure are. Still . . .

"Got it?"

"I've got it," Kat says. "I'll get back to you after I break up with Kevin. It's been a weird night and I guess it's going to get even weirder. Guess I gotta go tell Kevin his dick busted him on the internet and he can get fucked elsewhere . . . permanently. I can do this."

"Damn right, you can," I tell her. "You can do this, Kitty Kat. Remember, you deserve better. I'll be waiting for your report."

Kat laughs and we hang up. I don't know what just happened but my body feels light, bubbly inside as I take a big breath to get ready for the next segment of tonight's show.

Read the full book here or just search Dirty Talk by Lauren Landish on Amazon!

ABOUT THE AUTHOR

Standalones
The Dare | | My Big Fat Fake Wedding | | Filthy Riches | |
Scorpio
Bennett Boys Ranch:
Buck Wild | | Riding Hard | | Racing Hearts
The Tannen Boys:
Rough Love | | Rough Edge | | Rough Country
Dirty Fairy Tales:
Beauty and the Billionaire | | Not So Prince Charming | |
Happily Never After
Get Dirty:
Dirty Talk | | Dirty Laundry | | Dirty Deeds | | Dirty Secrets
Irresistible Bachelors:
Anaconda | | Mr. Fiance | | Heartstopper
Stud Muffin | | Mr. Fixit | | Matchmaker
Motorhead | | Baby Daddy | | Untamed